Tears swam in Daisy's eyes. She tried to blink them away. Eddie never had the chance to know about his son. Never had the chance to hold little Eddie in his arms. Roy Kemp had seen to that. Daisy didn't even know where Eddie's body was. Only that he was dead. She wiped her eyes with the back of her hand. Determination swept over her once more.

While she'd been in Greece awaiting the birth of her child she'd planned her revenge against Roy Kemp. She'd waited until her baby was old enough to be left with her Greek friend Maria and, although it cut her to the heart to leave him behind, she knew he would be safer in Kos than with her in Gosport. Not one hair of her child's head would be harmed by that London thug, she'd make sure of that.

BROKEN BODIES
JUNE HAMPSON

An Orion paperback

First published in Great Britain in 2007
by Orion
This paperback edition published in 2008
by Orion Books Ltd
Orion House, 5 Upper Saint Martin's Lane
London, WC2H 9EA

An Hachette Livre UK company

A CIP catalogue record for this book is
available from the British Library.

Typeset by Deltatype Ltd, Birkenhead, Merseyside

Printed and bound in Germany
by GGP Media GmbH, Pößneck

The Orion Publishing Group's policy is to use papers that
are natural, renewable and recyclable products and
made from wood grown in sustainable forests. The logging
and manufacturing processes are expected to conform to
the environmental regulations of the country of origin.

With love to Karen and to Peter who have made it possible for Aurora, Charlie, George and Phoebe to enrich my life.

I am indebted to Jane Wood, my editor and
Juliet Burton, my agent. Gratitude to everyone
at Orion – a very kind 'family' who
look after me. You know who you are, thank you.

'Wherefore hast thou despised the commandment of
the Lord, to do evil in His sight?
Thou hast taken His wife to be thy wife.'

Samuel 12.7

PROLOGUE

'Tell me what you want me to do to you.'

'You're doing great,' he said.

He ran his hand over her smooth stomach and let his fingers play in her damp curls before he flashed her his little-boy grin. His eyes lingered a while on the satin blouse pulled up over her heavy tits, then he bent his lips to her dark nipples. Cheap perfume mingled with the musky scent of her skin. She moved, impatiently unbuckling his belt, and he raised his arse so she could ease down his jeans. His boxer shorts came next, releasing his erect cock. She smoothed her hand over the length of it and, despite the confined space of the car, wriggled down and took him in her mouth. Every muscle in his body seized up, suspended as her tongue probed. When he could hold back no longer he drove himself into her warm mouth.

When it was over she lifted her head, her eyes glittering in the moonlight. She smoothed her blouse down over her breasts as he wrestled himself back into a sitting position and adjusted his clothes. Again he smiled.

Then he grabbed her with his right hand and squeezed her neck hard until she was squirming and choking. He smelled the acrid stench of piss combining with her sudden fear. He let her go, only to raise his fist again and punch her with a quick right hook to the jaw. She slumped against the leather upholstery with a peculiar gurgling sound until dark blood ran from her mouth and his hands slipped back around her neck to finish the job ...

In the beech forest the clearing was quite still until some small scampering creature broke the silence. Satisfied there was no human presence, the man climbed back into the driver's side of the car and examined the seat where the girl had sat, gratified that no trace of her remained except the keepsake he had taken which now resided in his inside pocket. Even her cheap plastic handbag lay locked in the car's dark boot with its owner.

'Fuckin' slag,' he muttered, and turned the key in the ignition. Soon the lights of the city beckoned and he was driving down familiar back streets where the traffic was minimal. He was humming and tapping his fingers on the steering wheel. The miniature black leather boxing gloves hanging above the rear view mirror were swinging gently when he pulled up outside the double metal gates of the breaker's yard. He got out, leaving the engine running while he unlocked the gates and pushed them wide open. He drove the car in, past the wooden office with the weight ramp in front, past the parked silver-grey Mercedes, and towards the rear of the yard where four cars, two of them undrivable wrecks, awaited Jock's attention tomorrow with the crusher. Parking his car next to the others, he unhooked his good luck charm from the rear view mirror, pocketed it with the keys and walked to the office.

Once inside he switched on the light and scribbled a note for Jock, careful to make the writing large and legible. Jock's eyes and hearing weren't what they used to be, and the man knew he valued his job at the breaker's yard.

He glanced in the oval wall mirror and ran his fingers through his wavy dark hair, pulling a few strands back over his forehead exactly the way he liked it. He stared at his reflection: the broken nose that only made his boyish looks more rugged, the finely arched eyebrows and the grey-green eyes that oozed sincerity. He smiled at the small dimple in his chin that women liked to touch, then he carefully adjusted his coat collar, pulling it up at the back. Satisfied with his looks and himself, he took the keys to the Mercedes from his inside pocket and turned off the light.

There had been no need for him to enter the car's registration number and particulars in the ledger. The vehicle he'd returned had already been detailed to be mashed first thing in the morning. In a matter of hours the car – and the girl – would be a neat metal square.

CHAPTER 1

'Lovely veg. C'mon missus, two marrows for the price of one. Can't be fairer than that, can I? Eat one today an' save the other for tomarrow!'

Daisy Lane laughed but shook her head at the cheeky stallholder's spiel.

'No thanks, mate,' said her friend Vera, winking at the man.

It wasn't fruit and veg Daisy was looking for but a second-hand book stall. Gosport market was crowded with bargain hunters and stallholders willing to give a bargain – at a good profit. Everything has its price, Daisy thought. Blaring out from the Black Cat cafe was 'Can't Buy Me Love' sung by the Beatles.

'Too right money don't buy love, eh, Vera? What d'you think of the Fab Four?'

'Dunno, Dais. If I was a few years younger maybe I could give you a better answer but I certainly wouldn't kick that dishy John Lennon out of me bleedin' bed, that's for sure.'

Daisy linked arms with the small woman at her side whose dark hair framed her strikingly attractive, heart-shaped face. Vera's eyes, fringed with false eyelashes, lit up as she turned her head and smiled.

'It's good to 'ave you 'ome again. I ain't 'alf missed yer.' The Californian Poppy perfume that was Vera's trademark teased Daisy's senses. This was her best friend.

'I couldn't come back before, you know that. But I was bloody glad to see you when you came to Kos. The villagers thought you was lovely.'

'I 'ad to come to Greece to be with you, didn't I? Couldn't let you 'ave Eddie's baby on yer own.' Daisy broke away from Vera, sidestepping as a very large, determined woman staggering beneath the weight of two overflowing carrier bags barged between them. 'Mind out, missus,' called Vera. 'You could 'ave bleedin' said, 'scuse me!' Then to Daisy in a softer voice, 'Everything all right back there?'

Daisy nodded and warmth flooded her body. Her sensible self told her that little Eddie would be fine with Maria and Aristo, her good friends. They both spoke excellent English and their Taverna Asfendiou had a telephone so Daisy could keep in constant touch. And she certainly wouldn't have left her child unless she knew for certain he would be looked after and loved by them just as much as they cared for their own happy brood. Her worrying self had wanted to get right back on the plane and return to Greece immediately she'd landed at Gatwick Airport. She didn't want to be apart from little Eddie any longer than was necessary.

She adored being with her son and living in their white stone house with the blue painted windows. The house that Eddie, the man she had loved with every fibre of her being, had bought for her. Sadness filled her heart. Being back in Gosport made her remember Eddie even more vividly. His smile, his glossy dark hair . . . why, she could almost smell the citrus tang of his cologne . . .

5

'Bloody cold, ain't it, Dais?'

She snapped back to the present.

'Tell you what, Vera, it's a bleedin' sight colder 'ere in Gosport for November than over there. You need your fleecy lined drawers on.'

Daisy's eyes continued searching the colourful stalls lining the High Street. She'd almost forgotten how welcoming the market was. Smells issuing from the wet fish stall reminded her of the sea, the Solent waters that surrounded Gosport and divided it from Portsmouth just a short ferry ride away. Then there was the sharp tang of disinfectant overlaid with cheap perfume coming from the household goods stall, along with a transistor radio playing 'Do Wah Diddy Diddy'. Manfred Mann was a local group and the stallholder had turned the volume up. Everywhere she heard the noise and bustle of people and the flap-flap of colourful cheap clothing swinging from market rails in the light wind.

'Look at the price of this!' Daisy stopped and picked up a can of Johnson's Baby Talcum Powder. 'It's half the cost 'ere to what it is back home.' Daisy's heart constricted and another wave of longing for her son engulfed her.

She thought of his smile, the way he chuckled after his bath when she would wrap his chubby, talcum-powdered body in a warm fluffy towel, leaving a small corner to cover his head and face, then carefully lift up the corner and say, 'Boo!' And his face would break into a huge smile and he'd laugh, and that laughter would warm the very cockles of Daisy's heart. Then she would gaze into his big serious brown eyes, which stayed unblinking as she moved her face closer and closer to his until his eyes went out of focus and became as round as juicy brown currants, and he would giggle anew and grab at her hair.

Vera sniffed loudly and stared at her, almost, Daisy thought, as though she could read Daisy's mind.

'You calling that place 'ome now, Dais? Deserted your real 'ome in Gosport for a Greek island, 'ave yer?'

Daisy turned to Vera. 'You know I 'aven't. But because Eddie got me that little house I feel safe there and imagine, he's there with us.'

Vera made the kind of noise a camel might make as it sneezed, Daisy thought, before she said, 'Fair enough, girl, but there's been a lot going on 'ere just lately an' I might just as well let you catch up on some local news. Remember that poor girl they found dead in the boatyard a couple of years back? The one with the nail through 'er skull?'

Daisy nodded. 'The murder Vinnie Endersby tried to pin on my Eddie?'

Vera stared at her. 'The very same. They only gone an' found another woman in almost the same spot. Poor bitch 'ad needlemarks.'

'Like she was a druggie?'

'No. Well, she was that an' all, but these was like holes in 'er skin. All over her body. An' they found a nail 'ad been driven into one of 'er titties. And she'd been strangled.'

'How come you know all this?' Vera was always a mine of information on what went on around Gosport, thought Daisy. Bit like the *News of the World* but Vera's interpretations were usually spot on.

'Gloria told me. She said it was a new girl from the Forton Road brothel. She'd only been there a few weeks.'

''Ave they got anyone for it?'

'Nah.'

'If you ain't buyin', ladies, move away from me pitch. You're blockin' me goods from the view of me potential customers . . .'

Vera turned to the luckless stallholder.

'Shut your gob, Timmy Jenkins. You ain't 'alf the costermonger your father was. I knew your daddy when . . .' Daisy pulled Vera away so that the rest of her words were lost in the noise of the crowd, but still Vera managed to slip away from Daisy's grasp and yell back at the man. 'And I've changed your stinkin' nappy!' The red feather on Vera's hat wobbled ferociously as, with a last look at Timmy's crimson face, she said triumphantly, '*That* told 'im. 'Is father used to come round to me every Friday night regular as clockwork for a quick one.'

Daisy put her hand up to her mouth to stifle her laughter. 'Vera, you are funny, you know everyone, 'specially the blokes.'

'Well, when you been on the game most of your life you get to see all sorts of people,' replied Vera. 'Certainly these turds round 'ere.' She waved her arm, jangling with jewellery at the wrist, to encompass the crowds.

The bitter scent of chrysanthemums and winter foliage coming from the flower stall ahead couldn't quite smother Vera's perfume, but Daisy was revelling in it, and in being with Vera. The street vendors' cries were music to her ears. There was nothing like this in Kos, she thought. The sky above was a clear, icy blue and both women were dressed for the cold.

Or rather Daisy was, with a black scarf wound warmly around her neck and her black belted wool

8

coat tied firmly at her waist. Vera wore a suit the colour of holly berries, its skirt so tight she could only take small steps on her five-inch heels. The blouse beneath was of black silk and low cut so that the swell of Vera's breasts was on show for all the market to see.

'No wonder you're cold. Why don't you cover up a bit more?'

'I'm like the market traders, Dais. Got to set out me stall.' She glanced down at her neat figure with all its curves in the right places. Vera had the eyes of every man with breath in his body looking at her. 'See what I mean, Dais? You either got it or you ain't. And while I 'ave, I'll make the buggers gag for it!' Vera waved at the bloke on the pot stall.

Daisy yanked on Vera's arm to stop her dawdling and laughingly pulled her further into the crowd. 'When you catch pneumonia don't ask for my help,' she said.

Vera suddenly stood stock still. Daisy looked at her small, pained face. 'What's the matter? You got a face like a bag of spanners.'

'If I was really poorly, you would 'elp me, wouldn't you, Dais?' Daisy realised that beneath the bold exterior her friend was as vulnerable as she was. She took a deep breath.

'Vera, next to my little Eddie, you are the only person in this world I truly care about. I would trust you with my life and my son. And with my last fucking breath I'll keep you as safe as I can.' She looked into Vera's eyes and saw they were swimming with tears. 'Don't you fuckin' start that! I couldn't bear it if I made you cry.' Then, more briskly, 'C'mon, you daft old tart. We got a red-haired bloke to find.'

She grabbed Vera and pushed her ahead through the shoppers.

The stallholders, too, were muffled against the bitter weather. Daisy knew they had arrived at four in the morning to unload iron bars and erect stalls on their pitches. The street lamps and a heavy white frost had been their only light to help them set up in readiness for the day's hard work. Fingerless gloves and layer upon layer of shapeless clothing and endless cups of tea from flasks kept the traders warm as they unloaded boxed goods from vans.

'There he is, Dais!' Vera pointed ahead. 'Yoo, hoo, Bri,' she called. She tottered towards the second-hand book stall. The man finished serving an elderly lady with four popular romance novels, grinned at Vera, and then unexpectedly popped another slim volume into the woman's open shopping bag.

'For good luck, darlin', he said. The old woman smiled up at him.

'God bless you, son,' she replied.

'Hello, Vera.' His eyes quickly moved towards Daisy who had to peer upwards because Bri towered above her. She saw the instant recognition in his sea-green eyes even though they'd met only for a fleeting moment once before. That had been when Bri had lounged against the jukebox eating a bacon sandwich in Bert's Cafe. He had been one of Eddie's henchmen. Daisy's heart thumped against her ribcage.

Eddie, she thought, why did you have to go out that night? If only you'd stayed with me, you'd be safe now.

'Hello, Daisy.' Daisy pulled herself back from her grief. Now Bert's Cafe belonged to her and she was back in Gosport to avenge Eddie's death. She hoped that finding Bri could be the start of a union that would bring about the downfall of Roy Kemp, the gangster who had killed her man. She took Bri's outstretched hand which was firm and warm.

'Hello,' she said. When he let her go she casually glanced at his stall. She wanted to gain the measure of the man before she put her plan to him. He'd worked with Eddie, had liked Eddie – and Eddie had trusted him. Vera had said good things about Bri Deveraux. But Daisy had, after all, met him only once.

Bri had set the tables to make the most of the space within the twenty-foot pitch. The canvas sheet covering his stall was raised and pegged so the punters had an all-round view of the books. *From Russia with Love* by Ian Fleming, books by the up and coming Catherine Cookson, and Nicholas Monsarrat's *The Cruel Sea* were treasures Daisy spotted, and at the back John D. Macdonald's Travis McGee mysteries. Bri knows his stuff, Daisy thought, noticing that if it rained the sheets could be let down quickly to protect the stock. Bri must have sensed Daisy's thoughts for he said:

'Wet books don't sell.'

'How did you know that I was thinking about your stock?'

He laughed and briefly his eyes held hers.

She gazed at the titles, most of them by popular authors, all stacked for easy customer selection and very reasonably priced.

'Lovely selection,' she said.

'Glad you approve.'

Books were her weakness and she knew she could have browsed for ages. But his bookstall wasn't the reason she had searched for him.

Freckles rode the bridge of Bri's nose, and his skin was tanned and weathered from being in the open air. He wore blue jeans and a navy wool donkey jacket around which a dark blue canvas money bag was tied. A polo-neck sweater kept his throat warm and a knitted navy pull-on hat almost hid his vibrant hair. Almost, but not quite. His hair was as red as a fox's brush.

He took the money offered by an elderly man from a leather half moon flip-up purse. Bri slipped the crime novel into a brown paper bag and held it out. The man was struggling with stiff fingers to fasten shut the purse.

'Ta, mate,' Bri said, waiting patiently.

Without warning Daisy and Vera were pushed aside.

'Oi!' shouted Daisy, colliding with Vera who careened into a freestanding wire rack containing more best-sellers. Suddenly Bri was out of his pitch and chasing through the crowded market. Vera, upright on her high heels, again tried to straighten her hat. Its feather had slid sideways across her face.

'Has 'e got 'im?'

'You fucking bet he 'as.'

'The little toe-rag.' This last from the opposite stallholder, a woman dressed more for warmth than fashion with a thick woollen hat pulled well down on her blonde hair which fell to her shoulders.

The frail old man was gripping on to an upright metal pole on the stall. He was shaking but was being comforted by the blonde, who'd left her flower stall and produced a stool for him to sit on. She had also picked up the circular metal book stand.

Out of the commotion further down the market, Bri appeared, firmly clasping a struggling, swearing, stringy-haired blond boy by the scruff of his zipped windcheater.

Bri marched him up to the old man.

'Thanks, Jacky,' said Bri to the flower seller. He gave her a grateful smile as she wrapped the old man's hands around a warm mug of dark brown tea. Daisy saw Jacky colour up.

'God bless you,' said the old man.

Daisy couldn't fail to notice that Jacky had the hots for Bri and he'd have to be thick as a bleeding plank not to know it.

In a calm voice Bri spoke to the wriggling kid, who couldn't have been more than ten years old.

'What you gonna say?'

From the boy's agonised face, Daisy thought Bri might have been squeezing the lad's neck a little too firmly.

'Go on,' Bri insisted. The hesitant reply came quietly.

'Sorry, mister.'

The old man stared at the lad. The boy's sullen gaze dropped from the man and he looked up at Bri.

'Go on,' urged Bri. The lad put his hand in his pocket and the purse emerged. The old feller's eyes lit up.

'That was the last of me pension in there,' he said softly.

Bri squeezed the boy's neck. 'Oww!' came the strangled cry. 'I said sorry! You got cloth ears?' He reluctantly handed the man the purse.

'Say it an' mean it.'

'I'm sorry.' The lad looked into the gutter. Daisy saw the old man smile.

'Thanks, lad,' he said. The boy shifted from one foot to the other then stumbled as, without warning, Bri let him go, giving him a short sharp clip around the ear with his other hand to send him on his way.

'Don't let me catch you around 'ere again or it'll be the police I tell next time.'

The lad scrambled up then disappeared in the crush of shoppers.

'Thanks, son,' said the old man.

Bri smiled at him. 'No worries.' He grinned at Jacky, who shrugged and went back to her own stall to serve a customer.

Vera nudged Daisy's arm.

'Good bloke, eh, Daisy?' Daisy nodded.

The old feller had finished his tea and left, clutching the paper bag containing the book he'd paid for and another, a free gift. Daisy said, 'You shouldn't go giving your stock away even though that was a real nice thing you did for that old bloke.'

'Weren't nothin'. I don't like injustice, that's all.'

''Ave you got any Monica Dickens?' Several punters were now clamouring for attention. Bri had to go to the back of the stall to find some copies of the requested author's books before serving a young woman with a crying baby in a pushchair. She'd picked up a couple of romantic novels.

''E's got a livin' to make,' said Vera, tugging at Daisy's arm and nodding towards Bri. 'Let's come back later.' Bri must have heard for he shouted across at Daisy:

'It's even busier this afternoon. Fancy a drink in

The Black Bear on the corner? Around eight this evening?' Daisy grinned back at him and waved goodbye.

'See you, then.'

CHAPTER 2

Daisy and Vera sauntered on to the relative quiet of North Street. Outside Bert's cafe Daisy paused. She looked up at the top rooms of the neglected red brick building where she, Susie and Vera had lived. And where she'd loved Eddie.

'Empty and cold lookin' as the fuckin' morgue,' said Vera. And momentarily Daisy was transported back to when she'd re-opened the place a few years ago.

Her husband Kenny had been in prison for robbery then and Daisy had tried and succeeded in making a go of the place after the old man who'd owned the cafe died and passed the management to Kenny. She remembered how she'd slogged her guts out working all hours of the day and night to make money for when Kenny's two-year sentence ended so he could have a good business to come home to. Eddie, Kenny's older brother, and Vera, whose home had always been the cafe, were fixtures in her life. Then she'd taken in a young, abused girl, Susie. Together the four of them, along with Vera's beloved cat Kibbles, had become a sort of family. Daisy smiled at the memory.

She remembered the visit to see Kenny in Winchester prison where she'd met Moira, wife of the

South London gangster Roy Kemp. Moira had become her friend and that's how it had all started. High-flying Eddie had wanted to make money. Big money. And he did so by running prostitution, extortion and drugs. That he was poaching on Roy Kemp's manor he either didn't know or didn't care. Eddie was fast becoming a big fish in a small pond. Not that Daisy knew anything about that at the time because she'd made sure Eddie never brought any of his work home to her doorstep. But Daisy, against her will, had fallen deeply in love with Eddie and Eddie had paid the price of his crimes with his life. But not before Kenny had died in prison, murdered by another con who was subjecting him to repeated rape.

Tears swam in Daisy's eyes. She tried to blink them away. Eddie never had the chance to know about his son. Never had the chance to hold little Eddie in his arms. Roy Kemp had seen to that. Daisy didn't even know where Eddie's body was. Only that he was dead. She wiped her eyes with the back of her hand. Determination swept over her once more.

While she'd been in Greece awaiting the birth of her child she'd planned her revenge against Roy Kemp. She'd waited until her baby was old enough to be left with her Greek friend Maria and, although it cut her to the heart to leave him behind, she knew he would be safer in Kos than with her in Gosport. Not one hair of her child's head would be harmed by that London thug, she'd make sure of that.

'You got the keys to the caff, Dais?' Daisy left her trance and stared at Vera's upturned face.

'I have. But it'd 'ave to be a bloody good reason to make me set foot in there again.' Daisy shuddered.

'Don't be daft. It's only an empty building. We 'ad some good times...'

'An' some bloody awful ones. I can't put meself through it yet. There'll be memories of my Eddie clinging to every part of that place.'

'Neither Kenny nor Eddie actually died in the caff...' Vera's voice was soft. 'It ain't the caff's fault, Dais.'

'Ain't it? Bert died there. Moira's baby was snuffed out there. After Eddie's death, I died a death meself there. I don't want the place no more, Vera. I'm selling it. An' I'm getting even with Moira's old man.'

'Daisy, I ain't never seen you like this before.'

'I ain't been shat on so many times before. Roy Kemp's got to pay for Eddie's death.' There. She'd said the words. Given vent to the feelings that were consuming her. 'I loved Eddie. Fucking loved the bones of him...' Vera put her arms about Daisy.

'I knows you did, Ducks. I knows you did. C'mon, Dais, let's get you back to my place.' She cocked her head to one side and gave a sort of half smile. 'I got a surprise back at me flat for you. Should be there about now.'

Daisy shrugged her away. 'It 'ad better be a good surprise.' She dabbed at her eyes with a handkerchief and tried a smile. 'I'm all right, really. This hate 'as festered until it just has to come out. Roy Kemp tricked me. That bastard needs to be taught a lesson.'

'An' you, a mere woman, is goin' to do it?' Vera raised her pencil-thin eyebrows.

'Too fucking right I am. Look, I'm not asking you to get involved if you don't want to. Finding Bri for me was the only thing I needed. And it seemed he wanted to find me an' all. The years of graft you've put in to open that massage parlour on the High Street is all you got to worry about, Vera. But one thing I do ask is, whatever 'appens, will you go on being me mate?'

'Dais, I'll always be your best friend. I reckon you've 'ad long enough to think about this so you knows what you're doin'. We left the bleedin' fifties long behind, girl. It'll soon be nineteen sixty-five. No woman 'as to live in a fuckin' bloke's shadow no more.'

'Too right.'

'You'll stay at my place as long as you like?'

''Course. If you'll let me.' Daisy had spent her first night back in Gosport in Vera's flat, tucked up in the spare bedroom with Kibbles, Vera's beloved cat, purring his fishy breath all over her. And she had revelled in it.

'Well, you ain't got nowhere else to go until this place is sold, 'ave you?'

'You know I ain't short of a bob or two, Vera.'

'But you don't want to broadcast that about, do you?' Vera grabbed at her arm.

Daisy shook her head. It certainly wouldn't do for people to know Eddie Lane had left her well provided for. Money going into the bank from house lettings in Gosport, and another large house in nearby swanky Alverstoke, rented out to a naval couple, provided the money for Pappy, Eddie's senile father, to live in relative luxury in The Cedars, a rest home. There was cash in the bank and Daisy owned outright the small property in Kos.

Remembering Kos, Daisy fancied she could still smell the exotic scents of jasmine, oleander and gardenia which surrounded her house from early spring onwards. It was a simple life there and she couldn't wait to get this business over with so she could return to little Eddie. She was even beginning to speak a few words of the Greek language.

'You're bleeding right. Let the buggers here think I'm so hard up I 'ave to stay with you until I get cash from the sale of the caff. Good thinking, Vera.'

'Stay with me as long as you like.' Daisy put her arms around her friend and gave her a fierce hug.

'I don't want to be in the way of your clients.' She grinned.

'Garn,' Vera said. 'I keeps me favourite punters 'appy the way me girls do, down in the massage parlour. You should know by now, no man ever invades my private livin' quarters. Except one, that is.' Daisy knew she was referring to Kibbles.

'Fucking fleabag.'

'I noticed you didn't push 'im off your bed last night. An' don't forget the separate entrance means you'll not come into contact with the girls, neither. Unless you've a mind to pop in on them for a cuppa.' She fished around in her handbag. ''Ere, take this.' She handed Daisy a key from which hung a wooden cat-shaped fob. 'Just so's you'll feel at 'ome.'

Daisy took the key. The key fob cat was striped grey, black and white. Just like Kibbles.

'C'mon,' said Vera. 'Let's get back an' 'ave a nice cuppa tea. You can see me surprise then.' Before they began walking up the street, Daisy took a last look at the cafe window.

The once white net curtains were now yellowed. Eddie had helped her thread and hang the freshly washed nets on the plastic wires. It seemed an age ago, now. Laughing and joking they'd been that morning.

She sighed out loud. Stop it, Daisy, she warned herself. That part of your life is over. She had a new life now. A score to settle. And hopefully someone with a bit of muscle to help pull it off. She thought about Bri. He'd been a mate to Eddie. Would he be a mate to her?

Opposite the cafe, facing North Cross Street and North Street, was the vacant shop Daisy hoped to buy. She was pleased with the terms she'd negotiated with the agents. It had been a bicycle repair shop with living accommodation above. It wasn't as tall as the cafe, but Daisy knew there would be a fine view of the creek from the side and back windows, and further along, of the pontoon and the ferries which ran every fifteen minutes across the muddy harbour to Portsmouth.

Vera pointed up to the windows above a tobacconist's shop. 'Jacky lives there. You know, 'er what we've just seen in the market. The flower girl.'

'The blonde trollop that fancies Bri?'

'You're in a nice mood,' Vera said. 'I'll ignore you an' go on with what I was tellin' you about me shop, Heavenly Bodies. Did you know I got a fortune teller? She's a nice lady. Bit long in the tooth for bein' on the game now. She's a bit mystical.'

'How do you mean?'

'Tells fortunes by palms, tarot, tea leaves and so on. She's really good. Mind you, since she was born in Gosport an' slept with 'alf the husbands of the women who wants their fortunes told, she's very accurate. My girls is qualified beauticians as well. They only look after the blokes at nights.'

'Only at night?'

'Well, sometimes durin' the day as well.' Vera's eyes twinkled.

'Anyway, Madam ZaZa reckons she makes more money inside my shop than she ever did outside in the cold. You'll like 'er. Per'aps she'll tell your fortune?'

'Per'aps,' said Daisy. 'You must be coinin' it?'

Vera looked pleased with herself.

'Got a feller, too.'

'I'm hearing things,' said Daisy.

'Straight up.' They were walking back through the market now. The Animals were giving full voice to 'The House of the Rising Sun' from Sam's Electrical Stall.

'Mostly durin' the day we cater to women who come in for aromatherapy.'

'Aromawhat? What's that?' Daisy shouted.

'Oiling the body. Massage with natural plant oils. Soothing away the stresses of everyday livin'.'

'Bugger me, you sound like a cinema advert,' Daisy said. 'You mean women pays for this from other women?'

'Oh, yes. But more especially when a good-lookin' bloke does it to 'em. That's what I meant when I said I got a feller.'

'You crafty cow.'

'His name's Robin and he's very much in demand. He's BIG in demand, if you get what I mean? And after a nice massage if they wants any little extras . . .'

'An' this is all above board?'

'All above board. I run a respectable place. I'm Authority Accredited.'

'You can't even spell that,' Daisy laughed.

Vera looked pained but Daisy knew she wouldn't

take it to heart. They could both dish it out and take it back.

'At Heavenly Bodies we're in to all the hippy stuff.'

'Hippy?'

Vera puffed out her cheeks and tried to look important. With the feather on her red hat nodding in the breeze she wasn't doing a very good job.

'People think it's all modern but it ain't. Eighteen seventy-five it all started. Some woman called Madame Blavatsky or something. She reckoned all kinds of goings on from mystical feelings to aromatherapy, crystals, relaxation, alternative healing and such are the answers to spiritual exploration. A sort of new age religion.' Daisy looked at Vera.

'Bugger me, our Vera!'

'Nah, listen, Dais. Most of what she believed come from the East. That we are one with the universe. Even the Beatles 'ave been talking about it. I'm just getting in first like, before some other bugger starts selling the gear. Tell you what,' she went on, 'your Eddie believed in it, though 'e didn't know it.'

'What d'you mean?' Daisy was on the defensive.

'Wasn't his favourite song "Wheel of Fortune" by that Kay Starr? And wasn't he always tellin' you what goes around comes around? An' I 'eard 'im mention the word "karma" more than once. Your Eddie was canny. Didn't 'e try to get out of the bad business to be with you? He knew 'is card was marked, Dais.'

Daisy pondered Vera's words. She was right on all counts. If only Eddie *had* got out of the business sooner . . .

Vera walked quickly towards the fish stall.

'Just gonna get a nice bit of cod for Kibbles' tea,' she called.

'Wait for me.' Daisy caught her up. 'That's what I like about this market. You can get practically anything you've a mind to.' She eyed the fish, the piles of sprats, the glossy grey trout and oily mackerel. Pink shrimps bigger than a man's thumb. All smelling fresh from the sea, set in white enamelled trays and decorated with fresh green bits of parsley.

'What you doin' for Christmas, Dais?'

'Dunno,' she replied. 'I ain't going back until I done what I came for.'

'Not even for . . .'

'If I go back to see little Eddie I won't want to leave again. I only been away from 'im for a day and already my heart feels like it's split in two. No, I want to get this over and done with as soon as possible. I know what I'm doing!' Daisy's voice held a sharp edge to it.

'Hello, Daisy Lane. Buying a nice bit of Dutch eel for your tea?'

Daisy spun round and came face to face with Detective Sergeant Vinnie Endersby, dressed in a dark brown suit under a fawn raincoat. His hat was set jauntily at an angle. He was so close she could smell the soapy freshness of him.

'Fancy seeing you? It's been a while, but then we was always bumpin' into each other in the market, wasn't we? Apart from the few times you called in the caff.' She was struck anew by his odd-coloured eyes of chocolate and amber that only heightened his attractiveness. His curly dark hair helped a lot as well, thought Daisy.

'Per'aps because only the most discerning Gosport people come here. Eddie not shopping with you then?' He was looking at her strangely. He knows something, she thought.

24

'Why are you always so sarky? No. Eddie ain't with me. As you can see, my mate Vera is.' Vinnie tipped his hat to Vera.

'I take it Eddie's not going to make an appearance?'

Daisy stared into his eyes. Please don't let me cry, she prayed, please? Her voice was as steady as she could make it.

'No.'

A frown crossed Vinnie's face. He put his hand on her shoulder. 'You don't have to pretend with me, Daisy Lane.' There was kindness in his tone. 'I don't know everything but I do know one thing, that you're very much on your own. For what it's worth, I'm truly sorry Eddie's gone . . .'

Daisy's emotions suddenly erupted. 'How could you be sorry? You're a fucking copper!'

He broke in with a voice like velvet, squeezing her shoulder gently as if she was a child who'd fallen and grazed her knee and needed consoling. 'Eddie and me went way back. Once upon a time he was my hero, Daisy. As a boy, I worshipped him. He was everything I wanted to be. But life dealt him a bad hand of cards . . .'

'Don't tell me about my Eddie. You know fuck all!' Daisy turned, shrugging away his hand. She couldn't help herself, tears were streaming from her eyes. Then blindly she ran through the market, bumping into people and apologising in her haste to get away from the detective. At the entrance to Bemisters Lane she paused for breath, realising Vera wouldn't know where she'd gone and would be worried. She wiped her eyes with her fingers and then took deep breaths, pretending to look in the window of Bishops, the shoe shop. He knows, she thought. He knows Eddie's dead. But how?

'You gonna see the estate agents to put the caff on the market, Dais?' Vera was breathing heavily, her shoulders rising and falling, but she held on to the piece of wrapped cod like it was gold-dust. 'Take no notice of Vinnie Endersby. He's a good bloke at 'eart, for a copper,' she gasped, taking a very deep breath. 'An' he could be just fishin' because he is a copper. An' next time bloody wait for me,' she chided. 'Nearly give meself an 'eart attack runnin' through the market after you with me titties jiggling about like two jellies on a plate. Good thing I gets enough regular exercise. Well, we goin' into the estate agents?'

'No.' Daisy's eyes widened. 'I already have a buyer for the caff.' Vera's forehead creased.

'Who?'

'Roy Kemp, who else?'

The look on Vera's face was a joy to behold.

'Shut your mouth, you look like you're catching flies,' Daisy said.

'You got the cheek of the devil, you 'ave, to get 'im to buy that place. I bet he don't even know he's gonna do it yet!' Daisy shrugged. She looked about her.

'I could do with a cuppa, Vera. Let's get back to your place. And what's this about a surprise for me?'

CHAPTER 3

Vera waltzed along the pavement and into an alley at the back of the High Street shops. The alley was more like a small roadway, wide enough for vehicles to park and unload goods. Eventually she came to a high black wrought-iron gate beyond which Daisy could see the scrolled metalwork of the stairway leading to Vera's flat above her premises. The front of Heavenly Bodies faced the noisy main road of Gosport High Street but here at the back it was relatively quiet. Sitting on the inside window sill was a huge tabby cat. He blinked at them as they climbed the stairs.

'Yoo, hoo!' cried Vera. 'Look, 'e's waiting for us.' She put her key in the lock and immediately scooped up the weighty animal. Someone was already in Vera's flat. The kitchen door opened and arms were flung around Daisy. It all happened in a blur of red rose fabric, 4711 eau de Cologne and blonde curls.

'Suze!' And then the three of them were talking at once and hugging and kissing each other until Vera said, 'For fuck's sake get in the living room and let me shut this bleedin' back door. All the heat's gettin' out!'

'I just 'ad to come an' see you, Daisy. Is little Eddie with you?' Daisy shook her head. Seeing Susie was a wonderful surprise which, obviously, she and Vera had planned between them.

27

'How long you staying? An' where's Meggie?'

'Only overnight. My darlin' daughter is with 'er proud father an' bein' spoiled bloody rotten by her nan and grandad an' the rest of 'em. Though I shouldn't say it, it's nice to 'ave five minutes to meself. But anytime you're Devon way you pop in and see me and Si, promise? Why ain't little Eddie with you?'

Daisy smiled at Susie, whose sparkling eyes showed her happiness. Susie's baby girl was named for Daisy. Meggy was short for Marguerite, after the tall daisies.

'I don't know what's going to happen, Suze. I didn't want any harm coming to 'im. He's more settled where he is at present. I don't half miss him though. He's grown ever such a lot since you saw him last. He was just a scrap then.'

'It was lovely of you to send me an' Si the money so's we could visit you.' Susie's eyes were shining.

Daisy marvelled at the change in Susie. From the skinny girl, abused by her stepfather, she'd befriended, Susie had got herself together and married Si, the delivery lad who'd worked for The World's Stores in Gosport High Street. Now, within a couple of years, she'd grown into a 'mumsy' woman with confidence oozing out of every pore. 'Married life don't half suit you, Suze.'

'So it should. Si loves me to bits, and we got a nice little rented place in Devon, ain't we? I got me baby – you know she's toddling about now? – thirteen months old, who'd 'ave thought it? And because Si's mum and dad only lives up the road we all go out a lot together. Si's got the gardening bug and is forever growing veg an' stuff so I eats really well.' She patted her ample curves.

Daisy asked, 'You get on all right with his family,

then?' Susie put her hand on Daisy's arm and stared into her eyes.

'You was my family when I was at the caff.' She nodded in the direction of the kitchen where Vera was busily clattering crockery. 'You an' Vera. But Si's mum an' dad an' Si's brothers and sisters treat me like one of their own. You know what my mum was like, pissed out of 'er skull all the time on drugs and drink an' that bastard of a bloke of 'ers crawlin' into me bed? Now every day I wake up with Si beside me and our baby in the cot an' I'm laughin', yes laughin' at me good fortune, Daisy. An' it's all because you took me in . . .'

'Shut up.' Daisy felt a lump rise in her throat. 'I can't be doing with all this. You're a lovely person, Suze, an' you deserved better. Thank God you got it.'

"Ere we are.' Vera swept in and set a tea tray on the coffee table. Daisy took a bourbon biscuit and bit into it. 'Ain't you gonna dip it in yer tea, Dais?'

'What, Vera, and have you bloody laughing at me when the biscuit breaks an' it falls in me bleeding cup?'

Susie kicked off her high heels and curled her legs beneath her, next to Kibbles.

'Push up, miss,' said Vera to Suze. 'You ain't so bleedin' big yet you needs all the sofa.' She squeezed down beside Kibbles and smoothed his mackerel-coloured fur. 'Right, girls, I've poured out the tea. We're all cosy with no-one to disturb us. An' I for one am dyin' to know 'ow you thinks you can get one over a big shot like Roy Kemp?'

'Why didn't you just tell the coppers he hurt Eddie?' Susie stirred the dark brown liquid in her cup.

'For a married woman you can be so thick at times,

our Suze. I'm no grass.' Daisy frowned at Susie's pout. 'Besides, what would they have done? There ain't no body. Can't have no murderer if there ain't no body. An' Roy Kemp has got someone he's giving a back-hander to over in South Street nick . . .'

'Not Vinnie . . .' Susie looked horrified.

'I'd bet my life Vinnie Endersby is as straight as a die.'

'So would I, Vera, so would I,' Daisy said.

'So what are you goin' to do, Daisy?' Susie was staring at her.

Daisy set her cup back on the saucer.

'I'm going to set Roy Kemp up as the boss behind a series of long firm frauds.'

Vera looked at Susie. Both were silent until Susie said, 'What's a long firm when it's at 'ome and how d'you know about such things?' Then she caught Vera's eye again and together they chorused, 'From Eddie.'

Daisy nodded. 'He told me the kings of the long firm frauds are Charlie and Eddie Richardson. Mind you, the Kray brothers are in it up to their necks as well, but separate manors like.'

'But what is it?' Vera was impatient.

'I'm gonna get Roy Kemp to set up fraudulent businesses. He'll need a bank account in 'is own name. He'll go to warehouses all over the place and buy goods, loads of goods which at first he'll pay for. He'll be such a good payer that the warehouse people will be falling over themselves to offer 'im more business and credit. He'll 'ave money coming into the bank in such large amounts that his overdraft won't 'ave no ceiling to it.'

'Sounds like you're doin' 'im a favour.'

'Let 'er finish, Suze.' Vera glared at Susie and Daisy pushed the plate of bourbon biscuits towards her knowing she wouldn't be able to resist.

'Pretty soon, after he's been paying 'is bills, establishing himself as a bloody good payer, he'll then start paying 'is bills at the end of the month after he's got the invoice, like everyone else. The warehouses won't worry about the amounts of gear he's taking away or 'aving delivered to various venues because he's good for the money. Ain't he already proved this? Meanwhile his money is going in an' out of the bank. Big amounts. He's always in the black. Sometimes though, he might have to go into the red to cover his bills. But the bank don't mind. He's good for it, ain't he?'

'I still don't see . . .'

'Sshh!' said Vera.

'Then comes the crunch. He takes all the wholesalers for as much gear as he can. Electrical stuff, washing machines, fridges, kettles. He takes 'em for clothing and fancy goods, small stuff that goes in markets. An' he don't pay 'em. He don't pay no money back neither to the bank what's financed the buying of all this gear. And the sale of the goods leaves Roy Kemp with bloody good pickings. Then he goes off into the sunset.'

Daisy saw Vera and Susie's foreheads pucker.

''Ow can you be sure Roy Kemp would do a thing like this?' Susie asked.

'Ahh, well, *he wouldn't*, but if he had a double . . .' Daisy grinned at the two amazed faces.

Vera spoke first. ''Ang on, won't money be needed to set this up? An' where you gonna get another Roy Kemp?'

Daisy said, 'One thing at a time. And I got money, Vera.'

'How do the wholesalers and banks get over this? Won't they involve the police?' Susie picked up Kibbles and set him on her lap. He looked pained at being moved.

'Yes, eventually. Insurance should cover most of the money and goods involved.'

'But it ain't just the money is it, Dais? If the Krays find out Roy is movin' into their manor, taking business away from them on their side of the river Thames, so to speak, they won't like it.'

'No, they won't, Suze. That's the point. I can't think the Richardsons'll give Roy Kemp their blessing, neither.'

'So Roy could find his greedy ways might be his downfall?'

'Exactly.'

'But the real Roy Kemp wouldn't do that, Daisy. He's too clever to start up long firms on their patches. And why "long firm"?'

'Because it takes a long time to set the firms up, Vera.'

Vera shook her head. 'I don't know . . .'

'There'll only be four people who know I've set Roy Kemp up. Three of us are round this coffee table. You two I trust with my life. The other person will be the man who's going to impersonate Roy Kemp. This man will get half of everything I make off the long firms. He'll make enough money to be on easy street for quite a while. And when the Krays decide they've had enough of Mr Roy Kemp he'll be dealt with in the same way he dealt with my Eddie. I told that bastard I owed him and I'm goin' to fucking pay him back.'

'It's a bleedin' good idea, Dais, but couldn't you just stick a knife in 'is guts or something? Sounds much simpler to me.'

'Vera, that would do me a lot of good, wouldn't it? I'd be bloody hanged like Ruth Ellis and my little Eddie would grow up knowing 'is mother was a murderess.'

'You know Daisy can't even kill a bleedin' spider, Vera. She 'as to set it free in the yard.' Susie picked at her nails. 'This could work, Daisy. But if this ain't really gonna be Roy Kemp but someone else pretending to be 'im, who will it be?'

'Too right,' said Vera. 'Roy Kemp is good-lookin'. He's over six feet tall an' he's got a tan from spending time out in Spain with 'is dopey wife, that Moira. An' he's got gypsy dark hair. Who d'you know fits the bill, Dais?'

'Yes, c'mon,' said Susie. 'Who you gonna ask to impersonate Roy Kemp, who you can trust to keep 'is mouth shut and do a good job? Dick Barton, Special Agent?' She started to laugh and Vera joined in. Daisy waited patiently until their giggling quietened.

'If you've both stopped taking the piss, Bri Deveraux's my man. All I got to do after I've convinced 'im, is to get 'im to dye his gorgeous hair.'

CHAPTER 4

Bri had intended to go to the barbers for a hair cut before he met Daisy that night, but decided against it. After all, wasn't it the thing nowadays for a bloke to let his hair grow? Look at the Beatles and their mop heads. That George hadn't seen a barber for ages, Bri was sure of that. And what about them Rolling Stones? All the young kids were copying their strange hairstyles and clothes but Bri didn't think he'd go as far as that Mick Jagger did with his skintight trousers.

Timewise he was adrift because he'd had a cup of tea and a bit of his favourite seed cake with blonde Jacky after he'd put the stall away and stored his van at the back of her flat in North Cross Street. This had led him to changing a light bulb on the stairs for her, after which he'd fixed her dripping kitchen tap. So now he was rushing against the clock to have a wash and change before meeting Daisy Lane.

Mind you, he thought, it was bloody good of Jacky to let him store his gear and van at the back of her place. She even insisted on doing his washing for him. She had a bit of garden and a rope line with a prop.

He really had to think about getting a flat of his own. Staying at The Black Bear pub had its disadvantages. He couldn't get to sleep until the punters had left the place at half past ten. Sometimes it was after midnight before he slept. When he had to get up at four o'clock in the morning for work, that wasn't funny, though he blessed the fact he didn't have to go through the pub to get to his room at the top of the building. A separate door at the side led up from the street. But if he wanted a pint, he didn't have far to go. He didn't only work the Gosport market but Fareham, Portsmouth and Waterlooville as well, so he needed his kip. What was it Jacky had said? Come and stay at my place? Yeah, he thought. That really would be bed and breakfast, her bed! She was all right though, was Jacky. Comfortable to be around, and easy to talk to. But not the sort of woman he had in mind to settle down with.

He'd always fancied Daisy, ever since he'd seen her in the cafe that time, but Eddie had a prior claim. Now she was back in Gosport – and alone by the look of it. He needed to know where Eddie was, which was the reason he'd asked Vera to get in touch with her. He'd thought Eddie and Daisy were rock solid when they decided to make a go of it together and live in Kos, so why was she here by herself? And why had she been asking after him? Well, he'd find out later, wouldn't he?

Daisy was better looking than ever. She'd filled out a bit and let her hair grow so that it hung round her face in a sort of bob, a bit like that film star Julie Christie. She also had a maturity about her now that suited her.

He was whistling as he walked up the deserted street towards The Black Bear. The council cleaners had made a good job of sweeping the road so the market debris was long gone. It was winter dark but the street lights cut through the blackness showing up the frost on the pavements; he blew on his hands and rubbed them together for warmth. A few of the shop windows were already decorated with tinsel and filled with Christmas stuff, though it wasn't December yet. People liked to shop early. His mum was the one for that, she loved Christmas.

He breathed deeply, his breath white in the cold air. He could smell the sea and a north wind was blowing briskly. Tomorrow would be another cold one. One of these days, he thought, I'm going to have a regular eight 'til five job and throw the fucking alarm clock out the bleedin' window. But what would he do? He'd tried most jobs, even fish farming in Scotland. Trouble was he liked the books. Really loved buying and selling them. He put his key in the side door of The Black Bear and the sound of Louis Armstrong singing 'Hello, Dolly', the fug of fag smoke, and the smell of beer drifting into the passageway swallowed him up.

Within half an hour he was washed and changed and on his way down to the public bar to meet Daisy. Not expecting her to be on time he was pleased to see her sitting in the alcove, waiting.

He nodded then called over to her, 'Want a drink?'

She shook her head and pointed to the half-pint glass in front of her containing what looked like shandy. She was wearing a black belted woollen coat and black high-heeled shoes. She looked good in black, he thought. Eddie had told him once he liked Daisy to wear black. In that tawdry bar, with her blonde hair, she stuck out like a princess in a pig pen. She smiled at him and his stomach did a backflip. He carried his pint over to her table.

'You're on time,' he said, sitting down next to her.

36

'Don't sound so fucking surprised. I have got a clock. You smell nice,' she added.

'Some stuff they was flogging off cheap in the market. Probably fell off the back of a lorry, but who's complaining?'

'Reminds me of pine forests.'

'Ain't many of them round 'ere, Daisy.' He watched as she leaned forward and picked up her glass to take a sip. Her hair fell forward and she pushed it back with her other hand. 'So?' he asked, when she'd returned the glass to the ring-stained table. 'Why were you looking for me?'

'Way I heard it, you wanted to get in touch with me, an' all?'

He smiled. 'I asked first.'

'Okay. I'll get straight to the point. Vera reckons you can be trusted and from what I seen today you seem a good bloke. Did you like Eddie?'

That question caught him unawares and he took his time in answering.

'I worked for Eddie. Both him and Kenny were pretty close to me.' He could see this wasn't quite the answer she expected, so he carried on. 'And before he left with you, he saw me all right.' He stared at her and saw she was trembling. 'There's something I'm not sure about. You said "did" I like Eddie? Past tense. Something's happened, hasn't it? Has he left you?'

'In a manner of speaking.'

'I never thought he'd do that, Daisy.'

Her face had gone grey. He thought she was going to cry and if she did he wouldn't know how to comfort her. He decided to change the subject to one less distressing for her but she beat him to it.

'Thought you'd gone to live up north?' She seemed to have composed herself. Bri took a good pull at his beer.

'I did. Along with my mate, Pat. Up to Scotland, Sutherland, it was. In the fish farming business. I thought we were set for life. A little stone house to live in set in a nice bit of ground. Right near the sea. Mountains to the back of the place. Lovely part of the country. Only things I didn't like were the fucking midges and the rain. You'd get bitten by a single bloody midge, slap it dead and three thousand midges'd come to its fucking funeral. We could see the Orkney Islands from the house. There's a saying up there in the village, If you can see the Orkneys across the sea, it's goin' to rain. If you can't, it's already bloody raining.' Daisy laughed. He decided he liked to hear her laugh and it had eased the tension between them.

'Me and Pat was goin' on all right at first but Pat couldn't stand the solitude. He started drinking again.' Bri felt a lump rise in his throat. It was too early in their relationship for him to spill his guts to her, and no doubt she had secrets which she'd prefer to keep hidden. He swallowed and it took a moment for him to continue. Daisy put a hand on his arm.

'Don't go on if it's too painful,' she said. He looked into her eyes and saw the compassion there.

'Some of it needs to be told,' he replied gruffly. 'Pat ran his fucking truck off the road and killed himself. I carried on for a while, even met a girl, but the goin' got too tough for me and then I fancied a change from all that heather. I wanted to walk down a few dog-shit-filled alleys instead of them mountain passes with deer droppings.'

38

'But that ain't all the truth, is it? I can tell.'

'You're right. But you ain't gettin' no more until you tell me why you came looking for me?' He saw the determined tilt to her chin, her brows creased to a frown.

'Okay.' She took a deep breath.

'Will I be needing another pint?'

'I'll pay,' she said, opening her clutch bag and taking out a ten shilling note. 'What do you want? I need a large brandy and lime, myself.'

But he left her protesting and having to put her money away again for he was already on his way to the bar. The Black Bear was unusually quiet and he was back sitting next to her again in no time at all. He saw her take a good slug of the double brandy, like she needed the confidence the alcohol would give her.

'Eddie's dead.'

Bri set down his glass. His heart was hammering against his chest. Fucking no! He couldn't speak.

Daisy's head was bowed. When she looked up her eyes were glittering as though she was bravely trying not to cry. She asked in a quivering voice, 'Can I trust you?'

'You wouldn't be sitting here if you thought you couldn't.' His words came out too quickly. He could understand why Eddie had fallen for her in a big way. Daisy was a good woman. It was a pity he'd never got to know Kenny and her as well as he'd have liked. His mum would have loved that, an' all ... But Eddie dead?

'How? How did he die?'

'He never left Gosport. He was killed.'

He mustn't show his emotions. Whatever his

feelings, whatever was in his heart he'd be no use to Daisy if he didn't keep himself in check.

'You've heard of Roy Kemp?'

She was watching him, waiting for his answer.

'Roy Kemp, Eddie and Charlie Richardson, the Kray twins – ain't much to choose between them, is there? Hard bastards every one of them.'

'Roy Kemp killed my Eddie. And if you help me set up a business there'll be money in this for you. Big money, Bri.' Now she was brittle and businesslike. 'I can't do it myself because it would give the fucking game away, but now it's payback time for Roy Kemp.' She paused so he could take in the information. 'I promised myself I'd get even with 'im for killing Eddie.'

It didn't surprise him that Eddie had got mixed up with the London mob. He'd been sailing pretty close to the wind with some of the stunts he'd pulled around Gosport.

'Wait a minute, Daisy. You know this gangster? This Roy Kemp?'

She nodded. 'We go back a while.' She didn't elaborate. He didn't dare ask more. He could see if this relationship between them was going to work it had to be built on trust, so he let her continue, 'You'll be able to do what I can't. The likes of Roy Kemp treat most women like they're playthings, to be looked after some of the time, but women mostly without a brain in their heads. But I can use that to my advantage because he'll never guess it was me who planned his downfall. And the best of it is, the plan is fucking foolproof. I can't go down for this. Neither will you, I promise you.'

Bri thought for a moment. Then he picked up a beer

mat and tapped it on the wooden surface of the table. Already he'd made up his mind her offer was too good to turn down; besides, didn't he owe it to himself and Eddie to help her?

'If Eddie was killed before you left for Kos why's it taken you so long to decide Roy Kemp needs to be taught a lesson?' He cast the beer mat aside.

He thought he'd thrown her on that question but she was ready for him.

She leaned across the table and took his hands in hers. A gold bangle glittered at her wrist. He could smell her perfume, warm and subtle.

'I've 'ad stuff to sort out. It wasn't the right time then but now it is. I've 'ad long enough to work this out, Bri. It *will* work.'

She gripped his hands, her knuckles turning white. Then just as suddenly she released him and reached for the remainder of her drink, downing it in one go. After setting her glass on the table she ferreted in her clutch bag and withdrew the ten shilling note.

'Drinks on me, this time.'

'Keep your money,' he said.

'Take it.' Her voice was sharp. 'If we're to work together as equal partners I pay my way.' His instincts told him to do as she wanted even though he didn't agree with women buying drinks for blokes.

After bringing back the drinks he said, 'Right, let's stop fannying about. What do you want of me?'

He saw her body slump with relief. She gave him a big smile. 'I'm selling the caff to Roy Kemp. With the money I'll buy the empty shop opposite. You can have the shop when all this is over. And half the money we're going to make from this scam.' Was he hearing right? His heart did a double take as he listened carefully to her words. 'Vera tells me you're lodging here. If you're willing to carry on for the present eventually you'll have decent living accommodation, the yard at the back of the shop, well most of it, for your van and gear. Open the shop as a bookshop if you like, you won't need to work so many markets then. I know how hard it is travelling about in all weathers trying to make an honest bob an' being on your bleeding feet all day.'

'I suppose you're moving into the flat above the shop?' Daisy nodded.

'Wouldn't it be better if I moved in there with you?' One look at her face told him he'd said the wrong thing. He tried to make amends. 'I didn't mean us live together, sharing...' Words almost failed him. He tried again. 'I meant, I could get out of this pub and be on hand if there was any trouble like...' His words tailed away at her stony look. Then she smiled at him. But that smile was tinged with pain.

'Sorry, but it's too soon for me to go into a bathroom and find a bloke's razor on the shelf. I'm too raw inside to live with anyone, let alone share a flat with another man. I'm sorry Bri. I've set out the terms and if you're not happy...'

He stared at her earnest face. He could understand how she felt. She really had loved Eddie, still loved him.

'All right, all right. Got it all worked out, haven't you? But what 'ave I got to do for this? What if it's not what I want?'

'You 'ave to trust me. I ain't saying nothing until I know you're willing to help. Pretend you're doing one last job for Eddie. You trusted him, so trust me.' He could feel her eyes boring into him, into his soul, his heart, looking for the answer he knew meant so much to her. She pulled at a strand of blonde hair and tucked it behind her ear. He could feel himself melting beneath her gaze.

'I've got money of my own from the sale of the fish farm. I may be a market trader, but I'm not short of a bob or two.' He was making excuses and they both knew it.

She broke in with, 'You're not telling me my proposition ain't tempting?'

'Too fucking right. This is a very generous offer you're making.' But he knew he wouldn't do it just for the money.

'In or out?'

'You better tell me a bit more, Daisy.'

'Sure,' said Daisy. 'But one step at a time. I'll unfold the plan as we go along. It involves long firming. You know what that is?'

'I weren't born yesterday. I know what a long firm is.'

'Okay. Keep your hair on. I need Roy Kemp to think I'm spending all the money from the sale of the caff on the shop an' the venture is leaving me skint. So I'll work in the shop for you. I like books an' I'm sure you can teach me a lot.'

'I'm not killing anyone for you.'

Her brows creased to a frown.

'Have I asked you to?'

She was clever all right, thought Bri. But then, what did he really have to lose? And if she wasn't going to tell him the whole of her plan now, so what? He could look after himself. And look after her an' all, if she wanted.

'All right, Daisy Lane,' he said. 'Me an' you should rub along together all right.'

He saw the relief in her eyes. Then she asked, 'As it's not just for the money, I'd like to know why you've agreed to help me?'

Bri ran his fingers through his hair. 'Together we'll get even with Roy Kemp, Daisy. We'll make a good team.'

'You 'aven't answered my question, Bri. And what d'you mean, *we'll* get even with Roy Kemp for Eddie's death?'

He'd better tell her the truth. He looked her straight in the eyes.

'When you moved away, I was happy for the pair of you but I needed to keep tabs on Eddie.'

'Why?'

'Because, Daisy Lane, my old lady ain't getting any younger an' she needed to make her peace with him.'

'I don't understand . . .'

'Well, you couldn't know, could you? Even they didn't 'ave a clue. Eddie and Kenny? They was me brothers.'

CHAPTER 5

'You asked for it, you got it. You snivelling fucking turd. Tomorrow I want your homework brought in on time. Understand?'

The figure in front of Sammy Wilson nodded his head frantically, eager to please. Despite the tears running down his cheeks there was a happy smile on the man's face beneath the red peaked school cap. He lay naked apart from grey school socks and lace-up boots. He was stretched across two sturdy kitchen stools bolted to the floor, handcuffed to them by his ankles and wrists. His buttocks were a mass of fiery weals.

Sammy threw down the cane. He wore a mortar board and gown beneath which there was nothing else except his hard-on. He moved around to the front of the stools and aimed his penis at the prone figure's mouth.

'Take it, you wanker,' he said. 'You got the stripes and now I get my turn, so swallow every fuckin' drop.'

The Headmaster of St Jude's Junior School, Martin Dowsey, with a string of fancy letters after his name including an OBE, and a penchant for small boys, obligingly opened his mouth.

Much later, Sammy patted the top pocket of his

blazer, the one with the brass buttons and the Cambridge University badge which he had bought quite reasonably in a second-hand shop in Portsmouth. He sighed, the notes felt good. A nice little sideline he had going here, he thought; not so sure what Roy Kemp might think, but he had to find out first, didn't he?

Sammy went over to the chest of drawers, picked up his steel comb and ran it through his hair. It was a woman's comb with a needle-sharp handle but Sammy preferred it to the stupid plastic ones you could buy nowadays. Afterwards he lifted the bottle of Old Spice, shaking it before pouring some into his hands and rubbing them on his face. He breathed in the scent with great satisfaction, before taking a card off a small pile on the top of the chest and glancing at it admiringly.

Public Schoolmaster gives Extra Curriculum: the phone number was printed below. He had distributed these cards in prominent places like public phone boxes and men's toilet cubicles. He put the card back on the pile and began to tidy the room.

Sammy replaced the cane on the wire hanger in the wardrobe beside the other hangers containing belts, thongs and leather whips. A collection of wooden rulers in a shoe bag sat on a shelf. He could be anyone the punter paid for. Sailor, soldier, rich man, poor man, beggarman, thief. He laughed to himself at the absurdity of the old nursery rhyme as he hung the black gown on a padded hanger next to his other dressing-up clothes and replaced the mortar board on the top shelf with his collection of hats.

Sammy wasn't interested in the women prostitutes who also lived here, in the Georgian whorehouse in

Forton Road. But ever since Eddie Lane had moved in on Roy Kemp's territory, Roy paid Sammy fucking good money to make sure no chancer did the like again. Roy knew Sammy wouldn't take no liberties with the girls because he hated every last one of the cunts. Thinking about the slags reminded him he was one down. That dozy cow Marie hadn't been able to handle the pace of the party. Started choking with a prick in her mouth, silly bitch. True, she'd had every orifice filled at the time but you couldn't blame the blokes for wanting to finish what they'd started, especially when they'd paid him good money for the extras. How was he to know she was going to have a bad reaction to the drugs? Talk about dead weight when he'd dumped her down the boatyard.

New blood, that's what he needed, before Roy realised his legitimate takings were down. Still, Roy didn't have to know what had really happened to Marie, did he? Silly bastard always told him to let a new girl take her time in getting used to turning tricks with the punters. Sammy liked to hurry them up with a few drugs. Once a girl had a taste for the bait, she was like a fucking fish what couldn't get off the hook. Maybe he'd take a walk down the railway station or the ferry, see what he could pick up, see if any girls needed a good home. Sammy laughed to himself. Sometimes the wretches even came knocking on the door, asking to be taken in, with a daft dream that they could make money and retire while they still had their bodies, brains and looks intact. Fucking stupid, some of the cunts.

Sammy's speciality was corporal punishment, and he was surprised at how many men, including himself, revelled in it. He never saw a punter on spec. Phone appointments or recommendations only.

Mostly it was a one-to-one jobbie. Him dressing up and beating them any way they wanted and then turn and turn about. With sex afterwards. Sometimes there wasn't any sex. Terry Allen came just to be locked in Sammy's wardrobe. He would sit in there for hours with a large brown paper bag over his head, asking to be let out. Only Sammy knew he didn't really want to come out. Because he had to say a magic word before Sammy would unlock the door.

Then there was Philip who didn't want anything more from Sammy than to decorate his penis. Philip provided the decorations, different ones every time, bits of colourful ribbon, lipsticks to draw with and bead necklaces to hang around it.

Threesomes were requested quite often. It was good getting paid for something so enjoyable, he thought.

Sometimes he had to provide kids. The money for that was phenomenal. But he hated it when it went wrong. Like the last time. He wouldn't think about that now but if Roy Kemp found out about the kids he'd go fuckin' mad. Sammy reckoned as long as Roy knew he was doin' his job well enough he'd close his eyes to Sammy's tricks, but not the kids.

Sammy dreaded the day they'd make sex between consenting males legal. He'd listened to a programme on the radio about it. Nineteen sixty-seven the powers that be reckoned they'd push the bill through. So he had a while yet before his earnings fell. Anyway, he thought, there had been female prostitutes since time immemorial, and even with the pill and free sex going on in these liberated days, prossies would always be around. So maybe the future wouldn't be as bleak as he imagined. Anyway, maybe the Labour government which had just been elected after thirteen years of Tory rule would abolish the bill of consenting male sex. Harold Wilson seemed a straight-up geezer for a new prime minister.

Sammy pulled the mock fur cover over the bed and slipped the handcuffs in the drawer. He washed his hands at the sink in his front bedroom, which he had commandeered when he moved down from London. Rosa had been furious about that as the room had belonged to her. Until he'd smacked her one. Then she'd given in gracefully.

The room looked out over the front garden and the chestnut tree by the side of the path that led to the wooden gate and the main road. Must have been a grand house once upon a time, he thought. Pity there was only the one toilet when there were so many rooms in the place. God, he hated sharing that with the fucking women and their punters. But he kept an eye on them all right. Bitches, every last one of them.

He'd be sorry to leave here. Moving this lot into the town wouldn't be easy. Still, Roy Kemp had been going on about relocating to Bert's Cafe in North Street for ages now. He wanted to gut this place out and put in more rooms and toilet facilities. But nothing had come of it yet.

'This kiddie they found dead? Local?'

Queenie Deveraux had opened her front door and launched straight into her questions. Even though she knew her Bri liked to get inside before she 'started on at him', as he good-naturedly called it.

'Hang on, Mum. Let me get me breath.'

He gets better looking every time I see him, she

thought. And that hair. If it wasn't for the rich redness he'd look just like his father. Thank God he wasn't like him in ways, though. She pushed thoughts of her husband away and concentrated on the strapping hulk of her son in the process of taking off his overcoat.

'Bein' out of doors is doin' you a power of good,' she said. Her walking stick helped her make her way over to the sink where she filled a small kettle and put it on the Baby Belling ready for tea. Bri liked his cup of tea.

He came up behind her and planted his strong arms firmly around her small scraggy body, giving her a kiss on the back of her neck. She'd had a bath that morning, which she could still manage because the baths were all low down with bars to enable her to lift herself in and out. She wasn't even fifty yet but a husband with heavy fists and kicking feet had left Queenie feeling and looking much older. Still, she got on with life, and today she smelled of lavender from the bath salts her Bri had given her as part of her birthday present.

'You smell lovely,' he said. His eyes roved around the limited space of her home. 'Looks nice in here, Mum.'

She'd begged holly from Joe the council gardener, and the red crepe paper swathes she'd cut and twisted herself hung along the backs of her picture frames. She'd even woven a few strands through the iron bars of her bed. Pity she wasn't able to climb up on a chair and set the decorations higher but her days of climbing were over.

As if reading her thoughts, Bri said, 'I'd have hung your decorations for you. You know that. And ain't it a bit early? It's only bloody November.'

'November it might be but you know I likes the colour around me. I wishes it could be Christmas twice a year. And I know you'd put me 'angings up if I asked, son. But I like to be independent.' What she really meant was he worked long hours on the stall and she didn't want to be a burden. She was only too grateful that he came visiting as often as he did. Some of the other residents never had anyone calling on them.

Barclay House was council run and smack bang in the middle of Gosport town. There were nineteen flats upstairs; the twentieth belonged to the warden. And twenty downstairs. Queenie lived downstairs as she found the stairs difficult. It was centrally heated and the other residents were, in the main, friendly. She thanked her lucky stars she was near the shops, the market and the bus terminal and ferry. When her leg wasn't playing up she could get out. Bri was mashing the tea. Any minute now he'd open her fridge door.

'You looking after yourself, Mum?' he'd say. Then he'd examine the food in there.

And that's exactly what he did. Queenie smiled to herself.

'This cheese is a bit mouldy, Mum.' He was holding up half a pound of fluffy cheddar.

'I just cuts it off. It's fine underneath.' She saw him sigh. 'Anyway, now I don't 'ave to cook for you, you bein' so pernickety like, I eats what I likes.'

'Then you won't be wantin' the bag of groceries I just got from The World's Stores?' Queenie waved her stick at him.

'Don't you be givin' me any of yer cheek. You ain't too big for an 'iding.'

As an answer he picked her up and swung her

round in the living room then set her down on her favourite chair and planted a kiss on her head.

'You sit yourself there. I'll bring in the tea.' She heard him whistling as he put away the shopping.

'You're a good boy,' she yelled.

'Not so much of the boy,' he called back. 'I'm six-four in me socks.'

'You'll always be my boy. My first born. The apple of me eye.'

'You don't 'alf talk some twaddle, Mum.' He put a china cup and saucer down beside her on a small round table. There was also a plate with some Garibaldi biscuits because he knew they were her favourites. Then he went back into the kitchen and returned with his mug. It had 'The World's Greatest Son' written on it. 'Right, one question at a time,' he said. He wasn't as relaxed as he usually was and his eyes lacked their habitual sparkle. She wondered if there was something on his mind.

'The lad? Tell me about the poor little lad they found?'

'You don't want to know about this, Mum.' Queenie's eyes strayed to the photographs she had in brass frames by the side of her bed. An incredibly roguish young man with dark hair, standing against a brick wall. He was in shirtsleeves. She could see part of the gleaming handlebars of the Norton motor bike which had been her husband's pride and joy in the early days of their marriage. The black and white snap didn't show the reddish glint in Pappy's hair. You couldn't mistake Eddie's features etched on his father's face though, nor the shape of Bri's firm chin.

'I 'eard the boy'd been interfered with and that they

found 'im in the mud of the creek by Ratsey and Lapthorne's, the sailmakers.'

'You're a glutton for punishment. But I don't know much more meself. Is that all I am, the *News of the World*, to you?' Bri took a swig of his tea. Then he set down his mug which she could see was now only half full and came and knelt on the thin carpet in front of her. She was surprised when he took the biscuit she was eating and set it back on the plate. What was it he wanted to tell her? She looked into his eyes and saw the pain.

'Mum, Eddie's dead.' At first she thought she'd misheard him. But she could see by the look on his face this wasn't so. That's what's been the matter with him, she thought. He's been thinking about the best way to tell me. Poor Bri, having to be the bearer of such awful news.

Then what he'd said hit her.

She couldn't speak. She just sat there holding on to his hands, the clock ticking more loudly than she'd ever noticed before. She couldn't hear anything else except the rhythmic click-clacking of the pendulum clock.

She wouldn't cry. Not now. Not in front of Bri. He might feel he would have to stay longer to calm her. He was like her. He'd have shed his tears in private so no one would know how much he was hurting. Don't show your feelings, her father had told her. Don't give anyone the satisfaction of getting so close they'll have the power to hurt you. And hadn't her father been proved right? Pappy had nearly killed her. Her mind and her body almost destroyed because she'd let her guard slip and shown she'd loved the bastard. An' now her Eddie had gone as well.

'How?' Her voice was clear and calm.

Bri shook his head.

'That bad?'

'Mum, you have to trust me on this one. He got mixed up in some shit.'

Queenie knew what he meant. Only too well. Hadn't she begged Bri to stay close to Eddie? And he'd done as she asked, looked out for him as best he could. But Eddie was a law unto himself.

'Daisy's back in Gosport. I've been thinkin' it's time you met her. You'll see how much she loved him. Enough to make him go straight, only it was too fuckin' late by then. Would you like to meet her?' That stumped Queenie. Daisy had married her youngest son because she was in love with him and after his death had loved her middle son more. Well, she'd soon find out how that sum added up, wouldn't she? But only if she met her, only if Queenie was strong enough to tell the girl why she'd stayed away from Eddie and Kenny, why she'd not been a part of her sons' lives.

'She's nice, Mum. Honest and reliable.'

'Where's she staying? Back at the caff?' Queenie knew the cafe had been empty. She'd wandered round many times looking for signs of life.

'No. She's two minutes away. Vera's place.'

Queenie sniffed. She admired Vera for moulding her own life but would never let the woman know that. 'I don't know.' She took her hand away and ruffled his hair. He looked at her earnestly.

'Don't you think it's time we got everything out in the open? Haven't we been keeping secrets too long?' Bri stood up.

He wasn't a child any longer. Their roles had

somehow been reversed, like he was the parent and she was the child. And God help me, she thought, what he was saying was the truth. Hadn't she come back to Gosport to be near her sons? Even had to hear about their lives and deaths secondhand instead of being a part of their existence. And why? Because she'd deserted them.

Queenie made up her mind. 'If she'll come, go an' get 'er. Get 'er round 'ere quick 'fore I changes me mind.'

'You sort the kettle for more tea. I won't be too long.' He found her stick and put it into her hand.

When he'd gone she made her way to the kitchen, stopping to look in the mirror on the way. She didn't like what she saw.

If it wasn't for the long silver scar running from the right side of her eye to her chin she'd say she was still pretty in a washed-out way. Naturally she looked older than her years but that was the life she'd led. Every sorrow etched in a line. And now Eddie was gone. Queenie blinked her eyes rapidly to disperse the tears. Bri'll be back soon, don't get maudlin, you silly ol' cow, she told herself. You can cry all you like when Bri and Daisy have gone. She filled the kettle, left it ready, and stood in the kitchen doorway for a moment surveying the living room.

It was tidy and fresh and welcoming.

When the boys were small she'd done her best. They'd been clean and cared for. She took her hanky from her cardigan sleeve and rubbed at an imaginary spot on a photograph of Eddie and Kenny taken when they were little. She ran her finger over Kenny's cheery smile. Little blond charmer he'd been. Eddie's hand lay protectively round his brother's shoulder.

Dark, mysterious Eddie. Her silent boy. Brian in his school uniform stared self-consciously back at her from a lone photograph. But that's how it had always been – Bri, set apart from his brothers.

'You've a lot to answer for,' she told the man in the shirtsleeves, her husband. 'A fuckin' lot to answer for.'

CHAPTER 6

It seemed no time at all before Queenie heard footsteps along the corridor. Mustn't ask too many questions, she told herself, don't scare Daisy away. But what if Pappy found out she was meeting Daisy? What if Pappy found out she, Queenie, was back in Gosport after all these years? Would he come after her again? He'd surely kill her this time. But with two of her boys dead, did that matter?

After opening the door she ushered Bri and Daisy inside. Why she's only a little slip of a thing, Queenie thought.

'Pleased to meetcha,' Queenie said, in a voice that didn't sound at all like her own. Daisy's blonde hair framed her face and her large eyes were inquisitive and long lashed. A pretty face, serious, and without make-up. Queenie decided Daisy must have been settled indoors for the night. Should she give her a hug? Or shake her by the hand?

'Hello,' said Daisy taking Queenie's welcoming handshake. 'This is a surprise.' Then she laughed, showing even white teeth. 'It's bloody warm in 'ere. Can I take me coat off?'

Queenie moved aside. She could see there were no airs and graces with this woman. What you saw was what you got. Queenie felt herself begin to relax.

Daisy shrugged herself from her coat to reveal a tight black skirt and black vee-necked jumper. Queenie moved to take the coat from her but Bri stepped in and took it instead, laying it on Queenie's bed along with his own. He motioned Daisy to sit on an armchair near Queenie's chair. He likes this woman, thought Queenie. His eyes locked with hers for a moment. 'I'll sort the tea,' he said gruffly.

Daisy had sat down, but now she was up again and looking closely at a painting hanging on the wall in a simple wooden frame. It was a view of a ferry boat arriving at the pontoon with the sea and skyline of Pompey in the background.

'Nice, that,' said Daisy.

'Bri did it.'

'Really?' Daisy turned and faced her. Queenie could smell her perfume. Classy. Not cheap. Not overpowering either. Bri was right. She looked a good sort.

'Got some others I'll show you later. Sketches. He's very talented. I told 'im he should do some local scenes and frame 'em, put 'em on 'is stall. They'd sell. He don't believe me. You know what blokes are like, think they know best.' Queenie laughed and Daisy laughed too, raising her eyes heavenwards as though agreeing with her.

Bri came back with a tray with clean cups and the teapot, a bottle of milk and a bowl of sugar. The spoon had been wet when it had been put back in the bowl and it was thickly coated with tea-stained sugar. What will she think of me, thought Queenie? Bri set the tray down, then fetched a kitchen chair and sat astride it.

'It's a great painting,' said Daisy. Queenie noted

that Daisy waited until she had lowered herself in her chair before she sat down.

'Thanks,' mumbled Bri. Daisy had embarrassed him with her praise. Ah, bless him, thought Queenie.

'I thought you was dead,' Daisy said.

'There's nothing like coming straight out with it, is there?' Queenie's stomach was churning but she admired the girl's bluntness. 'What did me boys tell you about me?'

Daisy gave a slight cough, raising her hand to her mouth. Then she said, 'When I met Kenny he said you was dead. He believed you was dead.' She sighed. 'Then out of the blue comes a brother an' a mother-in-law I never knew existed. But I'll tell you the truth, Kenny and Eddie both believed you was dead.' She paused. 'I got one thing to ask you though. Where was the both of you when I fucking needed you?'

Bri spoke first.

'Daisy, you don't understand.'

'That's for sure! And what's with this Deveraux business an' all? I thought your maiden name was Smith?'

Queenie, shocked at Daisy's question, gathered her wits about her. 'It's a long story,' she said. 'But first you got to tell me how Eddie died.'

Queenie saw the pain in Daisy's eyes as she leaned forward in her chair and looked her straight in the face. She reached towards Queenie and took her hand.

'Don't you think I'd tell you if I knew the full circumstances?'

The girl was telling the truth and Queenie knew she was going to cry. But I mustn't, she thought. I must not give way to my feelings.

'All I know is Eddie got mixed up in something he

couldn't handle. But I promise you, Queenie, he was trying to go straight when it all went pear shaped. I don't know the ins an' outs and frankly I don't want to. Neither do you. You 'ave to be like me and accept it.'

It was true.

'Kenny died in prison. I read about it in the papers,' Queenie said quickly.

'If I'd known where you was, you'd 'ave been by my side at his cremation.'

'I was living in Portsmouth and Bri was still in Scotland, then.'

'You gonna tell me what all this is about?' asked Daisy. Bri had poured tea. The full cups lay untouched. Daisy took a sip of hers.

'That'll be cold now.'

'It's fine. An' I'm waiting.'

Queenie sighed.

'First of all me real name *was* Smith but I got a right to Deveraux because it was me mother's maiden name. I met Pappy when I was still only a girl but I fell in love with him, and I 'ad a baby. He was a good-looking bugger. Just like Eddie. I couldn't 'elp meself even though I knew he wasn't no good, I still loved the bastard. He got the name Pappy because he was the biggest bastard around with his fists. Nobody crossed him. He was the "daddy" or the Pappy of all the local villains. He couldn't show no softness. When I told 'im about Bri bein' on the way, he hit me an' swore it wasn't his baby. I think 'e was scared of bein' tied down. I was terrified about tellin' me parents, but eventually I 'ad to tell me mum. It was a scandalous crime in them days for a woman – an' I was only sixteen, remember – to 'ave a baby without bein' married. I was packed off to Portsmouth to live with me nan.'

'Did Pappy come after you?'

'Did he hell!'

'What happened then?'

'Me nan, Bri called her Nan as well though she was really 'is great nan, took on Bri and I came back to Gosport. Me mum and dad told everyone I'd been on holiday. I tried to keep away from Pappy but somehow we drifted back together again. But before we got together I 'ad a bit of a thing with Bert – you know – 'im as 'ad the caff before you?' Daisy nodded her head.

'Bert was well set up, even then. Me mum and dad was all for me settling down with Bert. In their eyes because he had property he was respectable. They was frightened I'd go off the rails again, see? Bert knew all about Bri, was even willin' to bring him up as 'is own. I tried to make meself love Bert because, in spite of 'is bad ways when he was young, he was a good man at 'eart. An' for some reason he worshipped the ground I walked on. But we women don't know what's good for us, do we? We always goes for the wrong blokes. Before long I was back with Pappy and in the family way again. Some of his mates 'ad got married and he reckoned we should do the same. I was eighteen, an' I thought me ship had come into harbour at last. Didn't see the rough seas ahead of me.'

'What about Bri?'

'On me wedding night I asked if I could bring Bri back from me nan's. He knocked ten bales of shit out of me and told me I was never to remind 'im that I'd bin with some other bloke, ever again, though I 'adn't. That night he gave me a wedding present.' She raised her hand towards the scar and ran her fingers down the length of it. 'He did this with a Stanley knife. Told me no bugger would go near me again. I spent me wedding night up at Haslar Hospital gettin' stitched up. I told 'em it was an accident, that I fell on the blade. That was the first of me "accidents". When I got home from the hospital Pappy was asleep. I didn't dare wake him up. In the morning he told me if I ever went near that kid again he'd kill me. Your name is Queenie Lane, he said and my mark is on you. No one else is ever going to have you.' The look on Daisy's face was one of wide-eyed horror. Queenie looked at Bri. 'I'm so sorry, son,' she said. There were tears in his eyes and his face was grey.

He got up and took the tray into the kitchen. Queenie heard the sound of the tap running. She knew Bri was hurt and she wanted to go to him and tell him how much she loved him. But he already knew that. Her throat was dry.

'I'm not asking for your sympathy,' she said. 'Just telling you 'ow it was.' Daisy took a handkerchief from her clutch bag and blew her nose.

'It ain't my job to judge one way or another,' she said softly. 'But I admire your guts in pulling no punches in the telling. Why d'you think Pappy wouldn't accept Bri?'

'Guilt,' Queenie said. 'Then 'e couldn't back down an' show 'e 'ad an 'eart. You're a good girl, Daisy, do you want me to carry on?'

Daisy looked towards the kitchen. 'What about Bri?'

'He knows the score. He went into the kitchen to give 'imself a break from 'is feelings. I didn't see Bri for five years. People might say why let a bloke dictate to you like that? Why not leave 'im? Only they don't understand how it is 'aving no money and bein' so cowed down that you 'ave to watch every word you say. Where would I 'ave gone with a kiddie? For that's what I 'ad now. Eddie 'ad arrived. I'd no money, a babe in my arms and no fuckin' strength to say boo to a goose. Leave 'im? He'd 'ave come lookin' for me and I knew it wouldn't be just a cut face I'd get next time.'

'What about the police?'

'Nah. Police weren't interested. A domestic is what they calls it. Oh, a neighbour might send for 'em but the coppers' 'ands was tied. They'd 'ave a word with Pappy and it would be all right while they was there. He'd be all smiles an' make out I was a dozy cow. He'd even 'ave a laugh with 'em an' tell 'em I wasn't right in the 'ead and was always after attention. But when they'd gone I'd get it in the ear again for making so much noise that they was called in the first place!'

'Wasn't there anywhere you could go?'

'Weren't no refuges, then. People accepted that men 'ad a right to chastise their wives. I 'ad to get on with it.'

'What about your nan? Couldn't she bring Bri to see you?'

'No. I wasn't allowed out unless it was to go to the shops. When I got back he'd question me on who I'd spoken to. Pappy was a jealous man. He needed to know every little thing. I wasn't allowed to visit me parents and they wasn't encouraged to come to our place. Then they got themselves killed in a train smash up north. Anyway, I'd 'ave been ashamed for anyone to set foot inside my 'ouse. We'd fuck-all that wasn't broken during Pappy's rages. In them days the man's word was law. Bri, where's that cuppa?' she yelled.

63

'Tell her about Kenny bein' Bert's, Mum.' Bri had come in and was sitting on the hardbacked chair again. His tanned face was strained. He'd shifted the chair around so that his long legs were stretched out in front of him.

'After a specially bad beating I ran out of the house clutching Eddie and went to the caff. I knew Bert would take me in. I'd left Pappy out cold on the bedroom floor. He'd gone to take another swing at me and he fell an' 'it his head on the chamber pot which he'd just pissed in. There was blood and mess all over the floor but I could see he was all right really. Drunks fall about all over the place and don't 'ardly 'urt themselves. I knew when 'e woke up he'd blame me so I skedaddled. He'd already done somethin' to my arm. I couldn't move the bastard and me shoulder 'urt like hell. So there I was running along Clarence Road with a kiddie clutched in one arm and me other one doin' its own thing. Bert opened the street door of the caff and took me in straight away. He took one look at me arm and knew exactly what was wrong. First 'e settled Eddie, then 'e made me lay down on 'is bed after giving me a stiff drink of whisky. He told me it would 'urt but I'd be all right afterwards. Then he got 'old of me poor arm and yanked me shoulder back in its socket. I passed out.'

'I'd have done the same,' said Daisy. 'Passed out, I mean. Then what happened?'

'When I woke up. I was still in Bert's bed and he was sittin' on a chair by the side of me, and 'is eyes were closed like he was dozin'. The bed was all nice and clean smelling. He must have washed me because I 'ad cream stuff on all me cuts and such. But I could move me arms – both of them. It was sore, but nowhere near as bad as when it 'ad been 'anging all funny. He opened his eyes and looked at me like I was an angel come down from 'eaven. I asked where Eddie was but Bert said he was asleep. He'd made up a little bed for 'im on the floor, so he wouldn't roll anywhere and 'urt himself, he said.'

Queenie looked away from Daisy's face and swallowed a few times to hide her feelings. 'I knew he loved me. When he came to bed himself, later, it seemed natural to lay cuddled in with him. He made love to me, gently, so as not to 'urt me. I tried to love him back. But I didn't feel nothing for him, only gratitude. Does that make me a bad person?'

Daisy shook her head.

'Nah,' she said. 'I'd probably have done the self-same thing.'

'In the morning before it was properly light I crept out and went 'ome. Pappy was sitting in the kitchen. He 'adn't cleared up nor nothing. He had 'is 'ead in his 'ands and he was cryin' his eyes out. All he could say was, "You came back, you came back". I told 'im I'd spent the night in an open beach hut along Stokes Bay.'

'He believed you?'

'He believed me. And when I was bathing the blood off his cut head and he was sitting on the chair, he put his arms round me knees and told me how much he loved me. He buried his 'ead in me stomach and cried like a baby. He couldn't 'elp 'imself, he said. Pappy never knew nothin'. If he 'ad he would have killed me. And both the kids. Funny thing, though he was bloody 'ard on the both of them it was Kenny he was always more lenient with. Kenny had my colouring you see. Eddie was like Pappy. It was as if Pappy knew Eddie would be just like him when he grew up. Yet when he wanted, Pappy could be tender and lovin'. I used to think 'e was my black angel. But that wasn't the worst of it.'

'So you stayed?'

'Sort of,' said Queenie. 'I'd thought of leavin' him for years and when I finally did it 'appened quickly.' She looked at Bri. 'I've 'ad enough, now. You take over for a bit.'

Bri cleared his throat, then said, 'It was my passing the eleven plus examination that changed everything. Nan and Great Grandad bought me a brand new uniform for the grammar school. They was that proud of me it was decided I ought to be allowed to see my mother. Mum and Pappy were living at Elson then, in a rented place with a front garden full of brambles and a long path to the front door. As soon as we opened the gate, Mum came rushing out. She put her arms round me and told me she loved me but begged Nan to go. Pappy comes out, staggering down the path and swearing somethin' terrible about her loving me more than the other two and that I wasn't his brat. Eddie and Kenny were cowering in the doorway, their faces all white. Kenny's crying, Eddie's holding on to him. Mum's telling Pappy not to be so daft, when he suddenly pulls a flick knife from his trouser pocket and before you can blink he's cut Mum—'

'It went in clean as a whistle.' Queenie lifted her jumper and vest and let Daisy see the scar. 'There's blood everywhere all over the path. All over me clothes. Me grandad, who wasn't a young man, rugby tackled Pappy. A neighbour manages to separate them and get the knife off Pappy. Everybody's shouting an' I'm on the floor. There's only the scar there now but at the time I thought I was going to breathe me last. This bloke from next door 'ad Pappy pinned to the ground. God knows how 'e managed it but Pappy gets free of 'im and while I was there gaspin' an' bleedin' he jumps on my hip. I heard the bones crack. He stumbles and everyone's cryin' and shoutin' but all I see is Pappy's face and the words "whorin' bitch" coming out his mouth. The police arrive, and an ambulance. I ain't passed out yet so I sees everything.'

'Didn't they charge him?'

'No. An' I didn't want no fuss. He'd bundled the other two kiddies back indoors and I knew then that would be the last I would see of them. If he went inside for 'urting me I thought the authorities would take Eddie and Kenny away and put 'em in care and then neither of us would be able to have 'em. They might take Bri away an' all. And if I tried to fight him legally he'd have 'urt them. So, God help me, I left them two boys with their father and when I got out of 'ospital it was with this.' She showed Daisy her cane. 'I went back to Portsmouth to be with Bri and although 'e's been the light of my life there wasn't a day went past that I didn't think about Eddie and Kenny.'

'I'm making fresh tea,' said Bri. His eyes were wet. Queenie smiled at him. He brushed a hand across his face and went into the kitchen. I've tried to make it up to him, Queenie thought, really tried.

'That's a story and an 'alf. What a decision to have to make. I don't know how I'd 'ave coped.'

'I was stuck, Daisy. Me nan an' grandad was gettin' on. I couldn't get no proper work and it took every penny to feed the four of us. Then Grandad died and it sent me nan round the twist. They'd been together

67

since she was a girl. She couldn't cope without 'im. In fact she wouldn't believe he wasn't there and she talked all day to 'im as though 'e was in the house. She'd leave the house when I wasn't lookin' an' she'd not bother to dress 'erself. And as for tryin' to get me other two kids away from Pappy . . . ' Queenie sighed. 'And so it went on and on. You know, Daisy, I'm better off now than I've ever been in me life before. Or I was, until me boys died. I begged Bri to find Eddie and Kenny. I also made him promise not to let on who he was for fear they'd think I'd made a choice between them. I knew them two boys would never forgive me for running out on them. Pappy had drummed that into their 'eads.'

'The bastard.' Daisy spat the word.

'Not really. He didn't know you 'ave to let the people you love 'ave a bit of freedom. His jealousy was his downfall. He thought it showed his tough side but it was really his insecurity comin' out.'

'Eddie was jealous an' all,' said Daisy. 'I did love him, you know.'

'Bri reckons you still do?'

'Always will.' Queenie saw her mouth shut in a thin line like she might have said more but decided against it.

'And Kenny?'

'Kenny was a funny lad. A happy, funny lad until he went inside.'

'Let's not rake over any more coals, Daisy. It's enough for me to know my boys loved well. And were loved in return.'

'That's a generous thing to say, Queenie.' Daisy got up and went over to pick up the photo of the boys. 'I gave Kenny a good send-off, you know.'

68

'It was all over by the time I read about his prison suicide in the papers,' said Queenie.

Daisy turned and looked at Bri. Queenie saw an unspoken signal pass between them. Just the merest hint, but it was there.

Bri said, 'When Eddie paid me off, I could see he loved you, so I was happy enough to go to Scotland. Kenny would have been all right without the pair of you because he'd have had the caff. You made sure there was a living for him, worked bloody hard, didn't you, Daisy?' Daisy shrugged.

'Bri sent me money from Scotland,' said Queenie. 'Didn't you, son?'

'I also knew you was safe here in Barclay House, Mum.'

'Yet you still been worrying all this time what Pappy would do if he knew you was livin' in the area again?'

'You don't know 'im, Daisy. A meaner bugger never walked the earth.'

'He don't do much walking now, Queenie.'

Queenie looked at Bri, then they both stared hard at Daisy. Whatever did Daisy mean?

'Eddie made provision for Pappy to be well looked after. He's in a home in Alverstoke. Can't hurt a fly, now. Don't even know what day it is, by all accounts.'

Queenie put down her cup. Her hands were shaking so much she was sure she'd spill her tea.

'Is this true?'

'Yes.'

Queenie knew her voice was betraying her. And this time she couldn't stop the tears.

'Eddie's gone. Where's the money comin' from to

look after Pappy? There ain't no council-run 'omes in Alverstoke.'

Daisy looked puzzled. Queenie had to listen hard to catch her reply.

'My account. I promised Eddie I'd look after 'im.'

Queenie knew neither of them would understand her reasons but she asked anyway.

'Daisy, can you take me to see my 'usband?'

CHAPTER 7

Trying to find a parking space for Eddie's MG outside Roy Kemp's terraced house in London was a nightmare. Daisy drove up and down the street becoming angrier by the minute. When a man started up the engine of his car to leave, Daisy mouthed a grateful thank-you at him. The line of large expensive cars parked bonnet to boot told her that at least Roy was home, even if he was having a meet with his gangster mates in his mother's upstairs room.

She wondered how she'd feel coming face to face with Roy Kemp after all this time. The last time they'd met was on a rainy night in Gosport when he had come to the cafe to tell her Eddie had been disposed of, as though he was so much unwanted street rubbish. Which, to Roy Kemp, he was: poaching his business was just not on, he'd said. Bastard, thought Daisy.

After knocking and being spied on through the front door's peephole, Violet, Roy's mother, opened it.

'What a lovely surprise, Daisy. I was thinking about you earlier today and only saying to Roy—'

'Making tea for the boys, Violet?' Daisy broke in. Violet nodded. Her grey bubble cut had been freshly washed at the hairdresser, for Daisy knew she never did it herself. Daisy could smell the aroma of just baked scones coming from the back kitchen. She felt as though she was in a time warp for it seemed nothing had changed in this small house. Violet gave her a hug and Daisy followed her along the hall.

'Moira's not here, my dear. She's still away. Getting better every day, the doctor says.' After her breakdown Moira had gone to hospital in Spain. Daisy wondered whether she had been banished from her husband and mother-in-law's lives indefinitely – an embarrassment. 'Anyway, you come on in, dear. Roy will be ever so pleased to see you, but you haven't called at a very good time. When the meeting's over we got to get ready to go out. We're going along to the Kentucky Club in Mile End Road. It's owned by Reggie and Ronnie, dear, but you must know that. We're having a bit of a party to celebrate Val winning the big fight.'

Daisy realised she must have looked confused for Violet pulled out a chair from beneath the scrubbed whitewood table and said, 'Why don't you sit down, dear? You look all in.'

Daisy asked, 'Will Moira ever be right?'

'We can only hope,' replied Violet with a sigh, and began setting a tray with cups and saucers. This is a repeat performance of my first visit, thought Daisy. Before Moira tried to kill Roy, before she slashed her wrists and aborted Roy's child and hid the baby in the wardrobe above the cafe. Daisy shook herself, she didn't want to go back down that road.

'What fight?'

'Why, Valentine Waite is light-heavyweight champion now, dear. You must have heard of him? It's been in all the papers.' Daisy shook her head. 'But he's a television personality.'

'I 'aven't got no television.' Neither had Vera, thought Daisy, and she certainly wasn't going to tell Violet that she'd been out of the country. Vera had been chuntering on about getting one.

'Haven't you heard of Valentine's? His lovely nightclub in Piccadilly?'

Daisy shook her head. 'You know I don't come up to London much.'

'Tell you what, Daisy, why don't you come with me and Roy tonight? He'd like that, he thinks very highly of you, you know.'

'I can't go to a club, Violet. I'm not dressed for it.' Last time she'd been to a London club, Moira had lent her a frock to wear.

'You look a treat in that black woollen dress. You'd fit in anywhere.' Violet paused and looked at Daisy with her head on one side, like an inquisitive bird. 'I know, I've got the very thing. Won't be a moment. Keep your eye on that kettle.' Within moments she was back with something wrapped in tissue paper. Just then the kettle whistled and Violet thrust the package into Daisy's hands. 'Pin that on your dress, Daisy. I always say you can't beat real diamonds.'

Daisy fumbled with the tissue and a large oval of brilliance set in gold twinkled up at her.

She gasped. 'Fucking 'ell, I can't borrow this, Violet. It must 'ave cost a fortune. What if it gets stolen?'

Violet started to laugh.

'Who's going to dare to steal from Roy? He'd soon sort them out, wouldn't he, dear?' Daisy put her hand to her mouth and also began to laugh. Anyone caught stealing from Roy Kemp would likely get their hands chopped off.

'You're so right. What a daft thing for me to say!'

'Pin it on, Daisy.' Daisy nervously undid the clasp and pinned it high on her left shoulder. She'd never worn anything so expensive in her whole life. Her gold bangle jiggled at her wrist. Eddie had bought it for her in Southampton. The diamond brooch might have cost a hell of a lot more than the bangle but it didn't mean half as much to her as Eddie's gift. Then she looked in the wall mirror and gasped. The brooch made her look and feel most elegant.

Violet asked, 'What do you think?'

'Violet, I think it's a beautiful brooch and I'd be happy to wear it and come with you tonight.'

'It's not the brooch that makes you look good, Daisy. With your hair like that and wearing black, you make the brooch look good. Now let's have a cup of tea and something to eat. Did you come on the train, dear?'

'I drove up. I inherited Eddie's MG and learnt to drive it.'

Though even climbing in the small red car had reminded her so much of Eddie that her heart had hurt. Daisy counted the cups and saucers as they were stacked. Five. So there were five thugs upstairs, were there? She glanced at the pictures of Roy on the windowsill, the photographs of Reggie and Ronnie Kray with their mother, also named Violet.

'You must be hungry after your long drive? This is for you, dear.' Violet was cutting a mouth-watering golden brown scone and putting raspberry jam inside. Daisy watched her spoon a generous dollop of cream on top of the jam.

'Whoa! Only one, please, Violet. I adore your cooking but I'm getting too fat as it is.' Violet's eyes scanned her body.

'Nonsense, dear. You're a mere wafer of a girl. You could be a model with your figure.'

'Thank you. How long they been up there, Violet?' Daisy took a bite of the crumbling delicacy. 'This is smashing.'

'Ah, well. They've not long got going with their business. Haven't even had a cuppa yet. And I've got some lovely seed cake as well.'

Violet was busy with the jam and cream, piling the overflowing scones on to a large flowered plate. Daisy knew from past experience that sooner or later, probably sooner, someone would come down to take the tray upstairs to the meeting room.

'I'll take the tray up.' She knew if she had to sit for hours wondering if Roy was going to agree to her request for him to buy the cafe she'd go daft. But it wasn't wise to get on the wrong side of Roy's mum. Daisy knew he set great store by what his mother thought.

'If you're sure, dear.' Violet put a sugar bowl filled with lumps on the tray along with a pair of silver tongs. Daisy took the tray and went along the hall, up the thickly carpeted stairs and knocked on the door of the conference room.

'Tea up,' she yelled. She heard muffled voices and the sound of chairs scraping on the lino floor. And then the door was opened by Roy. As soon as he saw Daisy his face broke into a huge smile.

'Welcome, stranger,' he said, leaning forward and kissing her on the cheek. Her heart began thumping loudly. She didn't know what it was about him but his gypsy darkness had always disturbed her. Taking the tray he ushered her into the room where four other men sat on chairs around the large table. There was little else in the room, except curtains at the sash window and a huge wardrobe which almost filled one wall.

'This is a pleasant surprise,' Roy said. She smiled at the men in turn. Reggie and Ronnie and a man she'd seen on the films, John someone or other who was always typecast as a villain. There was a really good-looking bloke who got up to reach across the table to shake her hand.

'I've heard a great deal about you, Daisy Lane. You are the Daisy from Gosport, aren't you?'

'I've heard about you an' all, Charlie Richardson,' she said. She extracted her hand and looked at Roy. So it wasn't true that the Richardsons and Krays didn't get on. South and North London might be manors apart but when it came down to business the bosses got together. But Charlie Richardson was too charming for comfort, she thought. He was immaculately and expensively dressed, as were the twins, but he seemed to shine like a jewel amongst glass. She looked at Roy and smiled. 'You don't mind if I steal you for five minutes, do you? I've driven a bleeding long way to see you.'

'No need, Daisy,' he replied. 'We've finished our business. Over and done with in a gnat's wink today.'

'No problem,' agreed the twins in unison. 'We'll still eat your mum's goodies, Roy. There's only one better cook in London and it's our old lady.' Reg reached for a scone. Daisy turned for the door closely followed by Roy.

'Sorry about this,' she said, once they were outside in the hall. 'Hope I wasn't interrupting anything.'

'No, we were just deciding what to do about a certain toe-rag who wants to use the twins' name, paying them £500 a month for that privilege. This toe-rag collects rents, if you know what I mean?' Roy tapped the side of his aquiline nose.

'Extortion?'

'Daisy, *rent collecting* sounds so much better.'

'Sounds a bleeding good deal to me. If they ain't got to do nothing.'

'This certain bloke, this fucking toe-rag owns a seedy dance hall in Wardour Street. He's got mattresses on the fucking floor for just that – fucking. Slags you can rent an' you can buy your drugs of choice as you enter.'

'So?'

'The twins don't want to be associated with that crap, do they? The place'll be closed down soon enough and whose name is gonna be all over the papers? Who's gonna be investigated by the coppers? They're paying enough people in high places backhanders as it is. It just ain't worth the trouble.'

'S'pose not.' Then his words hit home. 'You mean some London coppers can be bought?'

'Daisy, you're precious. Everything's got a price. The system ain't as clean cut as you think. Some coppers cook up the evidence when they want to bang a certain villain up. If he's got the means to bung back a few quid to get off, why shouldn't he? Wouldn't you do that?'

'I suppose I would,' Daisy said. 'I only hope I'm never put in that position, though.'

'That's what the twins have said many times.

They're being fitted up now. That's why they can't afford to take chances.'

'What do you mean?'

'Evidence is being cobbled together on a "demanding with menaces" charge on some club in Soho. They also reckon Ron had a knife.'

'Is it true?'

'Load of bollocks. Anyway we don't need to talk about that lot in there.' He nodded towards the door. 'Why don't you tell me why you've come to see me?'

'It's about the caff. I need to unload it on you quick.'

'Now?' His dark eyes held Daisy's in a way she found disturbing.

'I need money quickly. It's yours for five thousand quid.'

'You don't think you've got a cheek coming into my home and *telling* me what you want?'

'Not when you once promised me a fair price the night you killed my Eddie. No.' Daisy could see he was taken aback for a moment, but she knew that was what he admired about her, the way she wouldn't beat about the bush when she wanted something. He smiled slowly.

'Been abroad, haven't you, Daisy?' Had he been keeping tabs on her? Did he suspect anything?

'Yep, and now I'm skint!' She'd have to play him at his own game and not let him see he'd rattled her cage. 'Not even a new pair of drawers to me name. That's how skint I am. All I have in the world is the bricks and mortar of the caff and I don't want the bloody place.'

Daisy could almost see him thinking as she looked into his slate-coloured eyes.

'I was going to say living abroad has done wonders for you. You are one lovely lady. Especially wearing the brooch I gave my mum for her last birthday. She thinks a lot of you. So do I.'

Is he trying to flirt with me, wondered Daisy. Her stomach did a flip over but she decided to ignore his flattery.

'Violet lent it to me for tonight.' His eyebrows rose. When he didn't say anything, she continued, 'Do you want it or not, Roy? The caff, I mean.' There, she'd chucked the ball into his court but he was entitled to more of an explanation. 'I want to buy the premises over the road in North Street. Turn it into a bookshop. Make an honest living for meself.' She could see she had his interest now. 'I don't want to work for you, minding your business, like you once asked me to do. But I'll be near enough to keep an eye on things in the caff, if you wants.'

'All right.'

Daisy whirled around. This had come from Violet. Unheard, unnoticed, she'd come up the thickly carpeted stairs and was standing behind them.

'Pay her whatever she wants, son. Move in Sammy and the girls from the Forton Road house, like we talked about. It'll be a good investment, that caff's right in the heart of the town. In the meantime Forton Road can be cleaned up and you can do what you want with it. Partition off the rooms and you'll be able to stable more girls. I trust Daisy, son.' Roy pursed his generous lips and considered.

'I ain't got all that cash on me at present, Mum. But about three quarters of it is to hand.'

'Sign a paper saying you'll owe me the rest and I'll deliver the deeds when you hand over the balance,'

Daisy said. 'You get it sorted by a solicitor. After all, so far you've been straight with me, haven't you? I've no reason to think you'll be otherwise about this.' God, forgive me, she thought. Any minute now a thunderbolt is going to come down out of the sky and strike me on the bleeding head for telling lies.

Violet produced a pen and pad from her apron's vast pocket, wrote out a makeshift bill of sale then passed it to Roy. After he'd signed his name with a flourish, she told him to get back in with the boys. Daisy was glad when he closed the door. His presence was disturbing the hell out of her, making her heart beat a tattoo against her ribs. Violet handed Daisy the slip of paper.

'Come with me,' she said, and Daisy followed her downstairs. From underneath the kitchen sink Violet took out endless bottles of detergent, packets of Fairy soap and large packets of OMO washing powder. She started emptying the contents on to a large metal tray. Along with the powder, out rolled bundles of bank-notes. Ten rolls of the notes went into Daisy's hands. Then she began scooping up the clean-smelling powder and returning it to the boxes.

'Can't be too careful, can you, Daisy?' Daisy smiled at her. They were like two conspirators. Violet was repacking the cupboard beneath the sink.

'Do you want me to sign anything now?' Daisy asked.

'We know where you are. That's not necessary.'

'Fine.' She'd got what she'd come for. 'I can put my old life behind me now, Violet. Start again.'

'Want another cup of tea?' Violet was washing her hands at the sink.

'Violet, a cup of tea leads to a scone, leads to

another, leads to a so-called sliver of your seed cake, the sliver being about a quarter of the cake. I'll end up not being able to waddle through your front door tonight. So I hope you won't be offended if I say no.'

Daisy could see she'd pacified Violet because, along with a big kiss on her cheek, Violet hugged her and left the scent of violets clinging to her skin.

'Put that money away safely.'

'I ain't got a bag big enough,' said Daisy, thinking of her clutch bag.

'Then I'll put it in a carrier bag an' leave it in your room.'

'Am I staying the night?'

'Silly girl, how can you go out to a nightclub, come home at all hours, then drive home? You can have the room you was in before. I always think of it as your room.'

'I guess it's settled then.' Daisy thought for a moment, 'Can I phone me mate Vera? I'm staying with her an' she'll worry if I don't let her know where I am.'

''Course you can, dear.'

Daisy had barely finished talking to Vera when the men came down the stairs. Reggie Kray was carrying the tea tray which he left on the kitchen table.

'See you tonight, Daisy,' he said. He was a big bloke and towered over her. 'Come on, Ron, we ain't got all bleedin' day,' he yelled to his twin brother, who was coming down the stairs talking excitedly to the man Daisy had seen in films.

'Keep yer 'air on, our Reg,' he shouted back. Then, 'Thanks, Mrs Kemp. Lovely tea as usual. I'll tell Mum you said 'allo.'

'You do that. And you're very welcome, boys.'

'See you again, Daisy.' Charlie Richardson smiled at her. He's a shrewd man, that one, she thought, very clever indeed. And a bit of all right.

When they'd gone and the women were alone in the kitchen, Roy came in and handed Daisy a pair of black silk monogrammed pyjamas.

'You'll be needing these,' he said with a twinkle in his eye.

'You stay in your own room, you scallywag. Don't go tripping into Daisy's room to see if they fits her properly,' said Violet.

Later, in the shower cubicle, Daisy remembered that this was the very first shower she had ever used. Moira had to leave the water running because Daisy wasn't sure how to adjust the spray. As she rubbed lemon-scented shampoo into her hair and stood beneath the hot jets feeling the water running down her body she thought of all that had happened since then. Especially she thought of Eddie.

'Tonight's not the time for tears,' she told herself. After all, she'd got from Roy Kemp what she'd wanted – to unload the cafe. The next part of her plan could now be put in action. And tonight was a bonus. She was going to a nightclub. Daisy started to sing 'The Sun Ain't Gonna Shine Anymore', a Walker Brothers favourite song of hers. She didn't realise she was singing so loudly until Roy shouted into the bathroom, 'And the fucking moon will have disappeared if you don't get out that bleedin' shower and let someone else get in!'

Five minutes later Daisy was swathed in a towel the size of a sheet and drying her hair with the dryer Violet had thoughtfully left on the bed. Soon her hair hung like a shining cap around her face. Luckily Daisy always kept some make-up in her handbag. She looked at herself in the dressing table mirror.

'That'll do,' she said after she'd applied mascara and lipstick and used her powder compact.

She'd started to feel bad about agreeing to go to the club with Roy and his mother. In a way it was taking needless advantage of them. But what else could she do? She had to keep their friendship – for the time being.

CHAPTER 8

Daisy gasped as she saw the deep red carpets and the mock gilt antique chairs and tables of The Kentucky Club. Twinkling chandeliers and mirrors in gilt frames added to the opulent interior. Barbra Streisand was playing, loudly enough to hear but not so powerful that the record swamped the goings-on in the room. They were shown to a table where already an older man and woman and another younger man were sitting next to Reggie Kray. Reggie got up and extended his hand to her.

'Hello again,' Daisy said.

'This is Charlie, my brother, he's the eldest, and this is my mum and dad.'

'Give us a kiss, love,' said the woman. Daisy bent and kissed her on her cheek. She smelled of some sweet, expensive perfume. 'Call me Violet and my old man is Charlie as well. Sit down, love. Take the load off your feet.' Then she looked at Violet. 'Though she ain't got much of a load 'as she, Vi?'

Violet laughed and said to her, 'How you doin', Vi?' They sat together and began earnestly chatting. Roy looked at Daisy and shrugged.

'Fancy a drink?' Daisy nodded. Roy picked up a bottle and pulled back the wire at its neck. The pop of the champagne cork was like a gunshot. Roy smiled at her and began filling glasses. The men were all wearing dinner jackets.

'There are gaming tables through there.' Roy waved an arm towards a closed door. Daisy didn't say she'd been in a gaming club before in Bournemouth, with Eddie, because she realised now that Eddie had been there creaming off Roy's money. She simply nodded, picked up a menu and gulped at the prices! Thank God she wasn't paying. She drank the champagne quickly only to find her glass immediately refilled by Roy.

She spotted the man walking through the crowded room towards their table, the most attractive man she'd seen in a long time. He was tall, broad-shouldered and well built, but she could see by the way he walked it was toned muscle and not fat. He had dark hair which flopped across his forehead and finely arched brows beneath which his eyes stared at Daisy as though she was a slice of chocolate cake ready to be gobbled up. His nose was slightly off centre. It must have been broken once but this only added maturity to his boyish looks.

'Here he is. The man of the hour. Come and sit down, Val. Yes, opposite Daisy. I think we all know each other, except you haven't met Daisy, have you, Val?'

He shook his head at Reg Kray, and mouthed 'Hello, Daisy,' at her. The back of her neck tingled.

'Let's have a toast to Val. Excellent bit of boxing, me old mucker,' said Reg. The men started to debate good-humouredly about boxing exploits while Daisy swallowed her champagne.

'Where's Ron?' Val asked, looking round the table. 'He'll be here in a minute,' Reg said. 'Bit of business.' He'd hardly finished talking when in swept Ron Kray in a long dark overcoat which he slipped off and passed to one of the girls selling cigars and cigarettes from boxes slung around their necks. They were all dressed alike in long black evening dresses which showed off their figures and didn't leave much to the imagination, thought Daisy. Closely following Ron was a blond-haired young man.

'Does he have to flaunt that Billy?' Violet Kray sniffed.

'Come on, Mum, Billy's a good kid. Be nice to 'im.' Violet sniffed again but she smiled at both of them when they joined the table and introductions began all over again. There was lots of giggling and laughter, lots of animated talk that now drowned out the music. She heard Reggie ask Roy whether he'd like to meet the American actress Judy Garland who was coming to London to sing in concert with her daughter Liza Minelli on the ninth of November. Daisy didn't hear the reply as her food was placed in front of her and she had to try to battle her way through the juiciest and largest steak she'd ever seen. She felt she'd never be able to start eating it let alone finish. She could feel Val's eyes on her. She looked up and into his unfaltering gaze. She waved her hand at the steak in a gesture of helplessness and he laughed. Something deep inside Daisy began to ache. Roy topped up her glass.

Daisy needed to go to the lavatory. She whispered to Roy and then got up, making her apologies to everyone. As she walked across the floor she knew Val was watching her.

Inside the Ladies, which was approached by a long corridor, Daisy leaned her head against the cold wood of the cubicle door. She knew she'd had too much to drink.

She redid her lipstick and fluffed powder over her nose, which had begun to shine in the heat. A quick comb through her hair and she was ready to face the party again, but better to leave the champagne alone from now on, she told herself.

Opening the main exit door of the Ladies she found her way barred by Valentine Waite.

'I'd like to kiss you,' he said, moving very close. Daisy let the door close behind her. She couldn't get past him. She was trapped momentarily by the door and him.

Val's mouth was warm and moist. Surprising herself, Daisy tilted into his kiss as he put his arms around her, pressing her soft flesh into his hard body. A tingling sensation spread through her, hot as hell, and a low moan escaped her. His musky sandalwood scent was all around her. Then his hand snaked down, reaching between her legs, pushing up her woollen dress, his fingers running lightly over her nylons and up past her suspenders to stroke the outside of her damp silk panties. Daisy whimpered as he buried his tongue in her mouth. She froze.

'What the fuck am I doing? I don't even know you!'

She jumped away from him, her heart thumping against her chest and at the same time pushing him away. He started to laugh, the sound deep and mocking, then the door at the end of the corridor opened and two women emerged, talking and giggling. They stared and became silent as they reached Daisy. Val moved once more towards Daisy and rested his hand on her shoulder. He pulled Daisy aside so that the two women could enter. The door closed behind them.

'You've no right,' Daisy hissed.

'Most women like it. And so did you, else you'd never have kissed me back.'

'I'm not most women.'

'No,' he said quietly. Then he raised his hand to his mouth and began to lick his fingers, grinning at her. Daisy's heart was beating fast. No man had ever behaved so familiarly with her on a first meeting like this. She was taken aback at him and herself. What was she thinking of when her beloved Eddie usually filled her every waking thought?

And suddenly she knew why she'd allowed Valentine Waite to get close to her. She was lonely – lonely for a man's arms about her. Don't be silly, she told herself, look at all the people who love you. How can you be lonely with a baby to care for? And with a consuming mission in life to avenge Eddie's death? She sighed. The truth was there, staring her in the face. She *was* lonely, more lonely than she'd ever been in her life, because she'd known great love and it had been snatched away from her.

Then Valentine said softly, 'You go back in to the party first.'

She smoothed down her dress and walked away from him.

The next afternoon on her way home, near Guildford, Daisy stopped her MG in a layby, put her head on the steering wheel and sobbed.

Who am I to think I can put one over on a clever bastard like Roy Kemp? And why did I let a man I hardly know put his hands on me?

The thing was, she'd enjoyed Valentine Waite touching her. She brushed her cheek where his lips had rested. In the confines of the car she felt the heat of embarrassment rush to her face again. Oh, Eddie, she cried, why did you have to leave me?

There was frost in the fields near Winchester and along the country lanes farmers were already advertising fir trees on sale for Christmas. In some backyards and on waste grounds Daisy had spotted bonfires built and awaiting Guy Fawkes night's festivities.

It was almost dark when she arrived in Gosport and Daisy decided to go straight to Vera's flat. She wouldn't think any more about the party or Valentine Waite. She would change her clothes, then look for Bri. The sooner they got the ball rolling on sorting out the shop, the better.

Heavenly Bodies was a good earner. Raking in so-called legitimate money had done wonders for Vera's morale.

'Fuckin' 'ard on me feet, though.' Vera was sitting on the sofa with Kibbles on her lap, a cup of tea on the table beside her and her feet in a bowl of salt water. The room was warm and filled with the scent of Californian Poppy. The sight of Vera and the place was comforting and welcoming. It made Daisy smile. Kibbles opened one eye but decided Daisy was no threat and went back to sleep. His purring eclipsed all other sounds.

'Want to come and look over the shop?' Daisy asked. Vera lifted one dripping, dainty, prune-like foot and began to dry it on a towel. Kibbles took exception to the movement and jumped with a thud on to a nearby armchair where he spent ten circles of his life before he curled up on the same spot he'd landed on.

'Why not? You got the keys?'

''Course. How long your feet been in that water? They're all shrivelled.'

A guilty look stole over Vera's scrubbed face. 'I fell asleep, didn't I? 'Ang on and I'll get meself ready. I don't 'ave to ask if you sold the caff to 'im, do I?' Daisy shook her head, then opened the carrier bag and showed Vera the money.

'Fuckin' 'ell,' she said. 'So the silly sod fell for your tale of woe that you was broke until you sold it?'

Daisy nodded. 'And guess who was at their house?' She wanted to share her adventures with Vera, but not all of them.

'I don't know,' Vera said, drying her other foot. 'Who?'

'Those Kray twins and Charlie Richardson. He's a bit of all right.' Daisy grinned. 'I was going to say to Reg Kray, I hope you get off with that extortion charge that's being slung at you. But I didn't like to. He's getting married and if he goes inside there won't be no happy day for 'im, will there?'

'That's a sneaky charge they're setting up against them two brothers,' said Vera, 'Everyone knows they keeps their manor clean. With the 'elp of their brother an' the rest of The Firm, no kids or women gets hurt on their patch. Mind you, if these are the sort of villains you're now associating with, you'd better be careful, ducky.'

Daisy was surprised Vera knew so much about the goings-on in London, but Vera was nobody's fool.

'I will. Why do you think I'm keeping little Eddie out of it? Why do you think I ain't telling anyone I got Eddie's kiddie?'

'Don't you think you ought to be honest with Bri,

though? And what about 'is mum? She'd be over the moon to find she 'as a grandchild.'

'I know, Vera. Don't think I 'aven't thought carefully about this.'

Vera sniffed. 'It ain't fair, Dais.'

'I'll tell everyone when the time is right. Queenie's a lovely lady but I got an idea she'd be so happy she'd broadcast the news. What if somehow it got to Roy Kemp's ears? When he finds out how I've tricked 'im he might take revenge on me by harming little Eddie . . .'

'Thought you said he can't abide anyone who 'urts kids?'

'Vera, there's always a first time, ain't there? He's already taken the love of me life, what if he takes—'

'Don't think about it, ducks. 'Ere, they said that Nipper Read, the copper, is out to get the Krays.'

Thank God she's changed the subject, thought Daisy, and watched as Vera took a mirror from her voluminous make-up bag and started spreading pan stick all over her face and neck, smoothing it in and blending it with her fingertips. 'You don't need to get dolled up, Vera. It's dark outside an' we're off to see an empty shop, not going to a dance.'

'Stop moanin' at me and take this bowl of water out and ditch it down the sink. It won't take me long to put me face on.' Then she laughed throatily. ''Ere, Dais, me face is in this bag.' She shook her bag and all the make-up inside rattled against the plastic.

'Well, hurry up and get it out. I don't want to be out in the cold all bleeding night.'

'That Nipper Read 'as vowed to clean up the city of London of crime. The twins is 'is main target.'

'That so, Vera? I met their mum and dad and their

brother and that bloke what's in the films and,' she gulped, 'Valentine Waite.'

'What, 'im who's the boxer? He's just won a big fight, didn't he?'

Daisy nodded.

Vera was on to the mascara stage now.

'Pity Roy Kemp is so nice to me now because I bloody hate 'im. Even though I've helped him conceal the truth on more than one occasion.'

It was true he'd sorted out Kenny's killer in prison. But by taking Eddie's life Roy Kemp had destroyed Daisy's future, and taken away the one chance little Eddie ever had of knowing his father. How would he feel if he grew up and discovered it had been within Daisy's power to avenge his father's death and she'd done nothing?

Daisy took advantage of the wait to freshen herself up after her long drive. She changed into a pair of tight black slacks with a black polo-neck jumper and slung a fake ocelot fur coat over the back of the chair to slip on when they finally left the flat. Flat black boots, a quick dab of lippy and a brush through her hair and she was set. Vera was still trowelling on the muck.

Eventually Daisy breathed a sigh of relief as they opened the door on to the High Street.

'Can't you smell the murky water from down the ferry?' said Vera, huddling herself further into her fur coat. She locked the door behind them.

'No, only your Californian Poppy. It shuts out everything else me nose comes into contact with.'

Vera puffed out her cheeks and took on a pained expression, but it was all a show. Daisy knew Vera wouldn't forget she'd once asked her for a dab of her perfume when she'd been going away with Eddie.

Daisy loved the smell that was part of Vera. That and her bloody red hat with the feather in it.

The crunch of frost beneath their feet sounded sharp and clear. Suddenly Vera's feet slid from under her. Daisy clutched at her, steadying the slight figure, glad she had on flat-soled boots and not sheer nylons and four-inch heels like Vera.

'Thank, Dais. Thought I was a goner, there. Gosport's such a lovely little town, ain't it? 'Cause of all the alleys and lanes they built in the days of smugglers an' press gangs, you can cut through anywhere you wants, instead of having to trek round all the roads. That reminds me. Where's your MG?'

'Out the back at your place. I'll soon be needing the space at the lock-up in Seahorse Street for stuff from a warehouse.'

'You'll be needing the yard at the back of the bookshop, as well.'

'Too right. But there'll be enough room for Bri's van.'

Arm in arm they reached the shop on the corner of North Street. Daisy fumbled in her pocket for the key. By the light of the street lamp she unlocked the door and groped for the light switch.

'Lucky I 'ad the electric put on, wasn't it? Much better with a bit of light on the subject.'

'It don't 'alf smell funny in 'ere,' said Vera, kicking away letters and newspapers that had accumulated behind the door.

'Don't you start that again,' Daisy said, remembering how they'd searched every room in the cafe trying to establish the cause of the stench that eventually turned out to be Moira's aborted foetus. 'What you can smell is rubber tubing and old glue from mending punctures. You know this used to be a cycle repair shop. Them smells don't go away overnight. And you got to remember this place 'as been empty a while.'

'S'pose so,' said Vera. ''Ere, it's a big shop, ain't it?'

'Sort of similar layout to the caff, except this ain't so high up. And it's been looked after more.' Vera had gone through to the back.

'Fuckin' 'ell,' said Vera. 'Look at this, Dais?'

Daisy followed Vera to where she was pointing to a butler sink with a wooden drainer. A large bow-fronted fridge and white enamelled gas cooker had been left behind. All in good condition.

'Saves me bloody buying, don't it? Only wants some lino down in 'ere. A few cupboards and a table and couple of chairs and the shop 'as its own kitchen. Pity the toilet's upstairs in the bathroom.'

Daisy knew Vera wasn't listening as she was already halfway up the uncarpeted stairs, her high heels clattering on the wood.

'What's up 'ere?'

Daisy didn't bother to answer, figuring she'd soon find out.

'Ooh! There's two nice bedrooms, a dinky little kitchen and a fair-size living room.' Then Daisy heard her say, 'Fuck!'

'What's the matter?' Daisy was up the stairs and into the bathroom like a shot. Vera was sat on the lid of the toilet rubbing her foot.

'I banged me ankle on the corner of the shower.' She looked up at Daisy and beamed. 'Got a bath and a shower, ain't you? You and Bri'll be able to use the bathroom together.' She gave Daisy a broad wink.

'Why, you mucky-minded woman!'

'Don't say you 'aven't noticed 'ow tasty he is. Even a blind man could see he's a bit of all right.'

'He ain't moving in with me.'

'Didn't think you'd let 'im, duck. That's 'ow it started with Eddie, you and 'im under the same roof. Besides I know you ain't over Eddie yet. Just teasin' you, gal. Can't you take a bit of fun?'

Daisy glared at her.

'I really hope this is going to work, Vera. If it don't I'll be joining Eddie a lot sooner than I reckoned.'

'It'll work, lovey.'

Daisy walked into the room she'd decided would be her bedroom. It had two windows, one looking across at the cafe and to some open ground. The other window showed the winking lights of Portsmouth across the dark expanse of sea near the ferry. A brightly lit squat ferry boat looking like a sliding slug was bringing passengers home to Gosport. Soon it would spew them on the pontoon where they could walk to the lines of buses ready to spread into the furthest reaches of the town. Ships lay at anchor in the dockyard, their lights showing their bulk in the blackness.

'Yes,' said Vera. 'This could be a very nice place.'

'I ain't planning on staying.'

'You'll need to get some insurance if you're plannin' on selling books. Too much paper about means a fire hazard.'

'What are you? Selling bloody insurance now?'

'Daisy, I'm only sayin'. You only got the one way downstairs. Through the shop. Not like my place, I got a fire escape.'

Daisy stared at Vera's earnest face.

'If I want Roy Kemp to think I'm determined to

make a go of this because I need the money, I'd better sort it, do all the right things. No doubt he'll be poking his nose in where it's not wanted.'

'Get what sorted, Daisy?' Daisy tried to spin round at the sound of Bri's voice but found herself trapped by two strong arms.

'Fucking hell! You gave me a fright. Where did you spring from, Bri? I never heard you come upstairs.'

'Quiet as a cat burglar, me.' His eyes were twinkling. He'd come up behind Daisy and put his hands on her waist. Vera had her hand over her mouth to stifle her laughter. 'You left the door open,' he said.

'We was talking about getting some insurance for this place.'

'Good idea, Daisy. Don't want to lose my stock, do I? Sorry about making you jump. I saw you go past when I was in Jacky's having a bite to eat.'

Daisy rounded on him. For some sudden unaccountable reason she was angry.

'That woman is trouble, mark my words . . .'

'Hang on a minute.' Bri's face changed from smiles to anger. 'You're buying my loyalty. Not that I wouldn't give that for free. But you sure as fuckin' hell ain't buying my soul. What I do, where I go and who I do it with is my own fuckin' business. Got it?'

Daisy stepped away from him. Opened her mouth to speak but he cut her off.

'I've seen too much jealousy and domination in my life. You only got to look at my ma for that.' He pointed his finger at Daisy. 'You got problems, you fucking deal with 'em!'

And then he was gone, his footsteps stomping heavily down the stairs. The door slammed behind him.

'That told you, didn't it, Miss Bossy Boots?' Vera's mouth was now pursed like a cat's arse and her eyebrows were raised like two arcs in her skilfully painted face.

Daisy looked at her. 'Don't you dare say another word,' she said.

CHAPTER 9

Now he'd fucked him, the stale sweat coming from the lad offended him. Even the boy's lank blond hair smelled of the countless filthy places his head had lain since the last time he'd had the little arse bandit. Sammy raised himself from the skinny body and looked down at his wet shrivelling cock. He then pulled up his trousers and zipped them and fastened his belt in place. The boy couldn't move and daren't speak and Sammy sensed the lad's fear and pain.

'We 'ave to learn not to steal from the hand that feeds us, don't we?'

Sammy didn't expect a reply. It would have been more than the fuckin' little shit would have dared, to interrupt him when he was just getting started.

'You sell the fuckin' stuff, not put it in your own fuckin' veins and down yer own gullet. Do I make myself clear?'

This time the boy turned his tear-stained face and tried to look back at Sammy. His whole body had started to quiver. It was very white beneath the bruises and grime. So white that the damaged veins were in sharp relief against the papery skin covering his bones. He made a whimpering sound.

'Shut up. I can't stand tears. You ask for everything you get.'

Sammy went over to the wardrobe, opened the door and pulled out a shopping bag. He extracted a small folded paper and threw it at the boy. It fell to the floor but the lad pounced on it. Now there was gratitude on his face. Once upon a time kids wanted money for fireworks, Sammy thought, they'd make guys and beg on street corners for pennies. Now the little bleeders wanted fireworks of a different sort. They still hung around street corners begging, but this time they looked like ragged, hastily put together guys themselves. Still, who was he to complain? He was making money by selling kids the fireworks they wanted, and the bigger the bangs he could provide, the more they came back to buy from him again and again.

'Get dressed and get the fuck out of here,' Sammy said. 'You disgust me.'

Vinnie Endersby stirred the cup of tea. He hated it milkless but there was only the empty bottle in the fridge. Neither could he have any toast because he couldn't face the single stale crust in the enamelled bread bin. When he got to the station in South Street he'd have a brew then. Who said station tea was crap? It was a bloody godsend when it was all there was on offer. Then he remembered it was his day off. He'd either have to go and buy some food or buy a breakfast. Either way it meant a trip into Gosport.

Perhaps he'd go in The Porthole for fish and chips with plenty of well buttered slices of bread and a good strong cuppa? They'd be open about ten, and his mouth watered at the thought. Or maybe The Dive Cafe on the corner of Market Place opposite the bus terminus? Pity Bert's Cafe was no more. His stomach rumbled with the memory of Daisy Lane's fry-ups. Her fried bread was to die for. And now she was back in Gosport.

Eddie had seemed so settled with her, so happy, the poor bugger. Vinnie didn't like to think of Eddie wiped out. He knew what a brutal childhood Eddie had had but that hadn't stopped the bloke looking out for his brother Kenny and for Daisy. Vinnie took a mouthful of tea. Fucking awful without milk.

Fucking awful without his wife, too. He wondered what he missed most, her or the milk.

He got up from the kitchen stool and went into the bathroom, slipping out of his pyjamas as he went. He hated pink paint and pink fittings and pink curtains. He wished now he'd remonstrated more with Clare about the colour scheme. But God knows she'd gone on about changing the bathroom to the colour of her choice until he thought he'd have paid willingly to have it gold-plated if only she'd stop moaning. And all because he'd said he'd liked the plain white decor of it when they'd moved in. It wasn't a bloke's bathroom at all now. Yet here he was, climbing into the shower, standing on the tray and pulling a pink frill about him to stop the water swilling all over the floor.

She'd got in a right strop about his transfer to Gosport. But he'd got his promotion to detective sergeant and she'd liked that. Funny, but now he seemed to have almost lost interest in his work. Even though his job was the only thing that could tempt him out of bed in the mornings.

As the water cascaded over him he rubbed soap into his skin and realised Clare never once said she liked the house. She'd wanted to live in Alverstoke because it was the posh part of Gosport. But he couldn't afford the classier end; Western Way was out of his reach. Out of the reach of most people actually. So he'd put a deposit on this one just outside the village and she'd set about trying to change it.

Clare liked nice things. Once upon a time, Clare had been nice, but not any more. And it was probably in her mind to leave him even before they left London. He'd thought the transfer might save his marriage. How naïve was that? She hadn't gone back to London, though, but to Al Fielding, his so-called mate.

Finding out she was having an affair was bad enough but her shagging his superior? That had made him die inside. Though he reckoned, at first, if he did nothing but waited for the affair to blow itself out, he could pick up the pieces. The waiting had damn near killed him. And it hadn't happened. Clare still didn't want him.

She'd gone to stay with her parents in Liss, a greener and nicer part of Hampshire. There was no question she wouldn't take Jack with her. He couldn't deny she loved the boy. His grandparents would indulge Jack but would that really matter in the grand scheme of things? They had also told Vinnie he'd be welcome any time in their house. Clare said she wanted to be civilised about the split. He wanted to break her neck.

He thought about the cases he'd been working on in London. Prostitutes gone missing – three over the past year – and so far no clues to go on and the cases had gone cold. But not in Vinnie's head. There was something he had been missing about the disappearances. Still, that case was out of his hands now he was back in Gosport, but he'd been presented with two deaths in quick succession here in the town. A tortured woman and a buggered boy. What was the matter with everyone? Couldn't they live in harmony? And everyone knew if a case wasn't solved in the first few weeks when it was hot, it could probably drag on until it went well and truly iceberg cold.

Was it a simple coincidence the young girl had been found in the boatyard in practically the same place as the earlier body had been discovered? Funny, he'd had Eddie pegged for the first girl's death. And he'd been glad when Eddie had been provided with alibis to prove he wasn't there. Only now Eddie was gone an' all. Poor Daisy.

'Damn, damn, damn,' muttered Jacky Price. One glimpse of Daisy Lane and off he runs. Why did I ever ask him if it was snowing yet? If he hadn't got up from my comfiest armchair and looked down into the street he'd never have seen that bloody woman waltzing up the road with that Vera from the knocking shop. Not that she had anything against either Vera or Daisy. Vera worked bloody hard, always had been a grafter, that one, and Daisy was nice enough, but she was a threat. Jacky had seen the hungry look in Bri's eyes when Daisy had first appeared at his market stall.

Nice meal Jacky'd cooked for him, as well. Liver and onions, Bri's favourite. And who knows? After a few beers, she might have got him in bed tonight.

Funny bloke, Bri, she thought. Reliable, yet quiet. Always immersed in his books. Spent all his time reading, even on the fuckin' stall. You'd see him sitting on a tall wooden stool at the back with his nose in the pages. But he was sharp. Oh, yes, eyes in the back of his head, that one. Could spot a potential thief a mile off. Look how he'd seen that kid snatch the old man's purse? And no one took liberties with Bri Deveraux. Not the other stallholders and certainly not the blokes who ran the market. Respect, that's what Bri had, respect.

Jacky didn't have respect for him. Oh, no, she thought, she just wanted to tear his clothes off and squirm all over him. Run her hands all over that lovely firm body and snake her fingers through his hair that reminded her of fire embers. She wouldn't mind betting that after a bit of proper loving he'd open up and she'd get more out of him than the short sentences and one-word replies that were the norm.

She put the dirty dishes in the sink and turned on the tap. She let it run for a moment then thought better of washing up. Yes, she thought, if she could get him to move in with her then perhaps she could give up the flowers and give up the treks down to Forton Road to fuck strangers who phoned Sammy because of her strategically placed 'tart cards' in the local phone boxes.

Sammy'd arranged for her to work four nights a week and all day Sunday, phoning when she had clients. She hated it that he took such a big cut of her money but he let her use the front upstairs bedroom at Chestnut House in Forton Road. He took her calls and didn't let on that Virginia Waters, the blonde who gave golden showers, was really Jacky the flower seller from the market. Sammy didn't mind that she wouldn't work Sunday nights because Monday mornings she had to leave her flat at two in the morning to be at Brighton flower market to buy the choicest blooms and potted plants at the lowest prices. Then she'd be back at Fareham Market to set up her stall by seven o'clock. It was a hard grind. Jacky thanked God she was strong and healthy. And a woman on her own had to survive as best she could.

Sammy was a bastard. For some reason he hated women. Why on earth he was left in charge of the Forton Road brothel she couldn't fathom. Eddie Lane had been a bastard too, but if you kept out of his way it wasn't so bad. He wasn't sadistic like Sammy. She wondered where Eddie was. Hadn't seen his handsome mug about for a long time now. Thought he'd moved on with Daisy Lane. Jacky supposed it was possible he'd moved on again since then. Men like him don't hang about long in one place, she thought, or with one woman.

Jacky was just thinking she might wash up after all when she heard a loud knock at her street door. She went to the window and looked down. Fuckin' 'ell, she thought, Mr Lovely himself! Perhaps he'd come back for his pudding after all!

'Won't be a minute, Bri. Be right down.' As she passed the mirror she gave herself a wicked wink and patted her mop of thick blonde hair back into its springy waves. She then gave a big sigh. It wouldn't do for Bri to know about her other life in Forton Road, would it?

At the door she pulled back the bolt.

'Didn't expect to see you here again,' she said with a grin. 'But you're very welcome.' He looked cross. 'You all right?'

'Why shouldn't I be?' He stepped into the small hall at the bottom of the stairs. Why does this place always smell of stale cabbage, Jacky asked herself. One of these days I'll give it a mop down.

'The kettle's on, or there's a bottle of beer if you'd rather.'

'You're a good sort,' he said making his way up the stairs. She could smell the cold on him. He paused, as though making up his mind whether he should be there or not. Jacky knew it was late, and that they both had an early start in the morning for the market. But this was one chance she wasn't going to waste.

'Go on up, then.' She practically pushed him up the flight of uncarpeted wooden stairs to her flat. She could smell the piney scent of his cologne. That was one of the things she liked about him. He was always well turned out. From his jaunty woollen cap covering his blaze of hair and keeping his head warm to his polished boots. She'd heard you lost ninety percent of your body heat through the top of your head.

'Cold out there, Bri?'

'Yes.' He took off his coat and threw it over the back of a chair. Then he collapsed on to the ancient sofa. She closed the door to the flat and went to the sideboard, took out a bottle of whisky and two tumblers and set them on the small table next to the sofa. She poured a generous measure in one of the glasses and a small drink for herself. She passed the larger drink to Bri.

'Get this down you to warm you up.' She watched him knock it back. It didn't matter that his mind wasn't on her, his surroundings or the whisky. He was here, that's what counted. He turned his hypnotic eyes towards her.

'Want another?' He nodded and seemed to relax as the alcohol hit him. She gave him another large shot. 'I'll leave the bottle handy. I got plenty. Dave from the antiques stall always brings me a few bottles of drink back when he goes over to France for the Sunday markets there.' She didn't add he preferred to be paid in kind for her regular supply of booze.

Jacky watched him raise the glass to his lips and decided she'd do her domesticated bit by washing up. Not that she wanted to but she sensed he wanted to be alone for a while. Besides, he might think she was a good housewife if she took more of an interest in the cleanliness of the flat.

When she returned to the sitting room, he'd taken off his sweater and boots and was lying full length on the sofa. He gave her a lazy grin. She saw the contents of the whisky bottle was well down but she didn't mind that at all.

'Come and sit with me,' he said, and made room for her. No, she didn't mind it at all.

CHAPTER 10

Someone was banging at his head with an icepick and the pain was excruciating. He put his fingers to his temple, surprised there was no metal sticking out his forehead. Bri opened his eyes. Where the fuck was he? He was naked. His stomach churned, he was going to throw up. He clambered across the sleeping woman and his feet found the cold lino. He stumbled towards the door and only just made it to the lavatory.

Bri sat on the tiled floor and rested his head against the toilet seat before feeling strong enough to hold on to it for support, lift himself and pull down on the chain to flush the stinking mess away. Before the water had finished swirling around the none-too-clean bowl, he'd chucked up again.

He washed his face at the sink and dried it on a smelly towel, but acknowledged he felt better. Then he rinsed his mouth out from the tap and drank, gulping the clean water as though his life depended on it.

It was Jacky's flat and Jacky in the bed and it had been Jacky's whisky he'd drunk to get in this state. Fuck it! He examined himself in the mirror, pulling his face this way and that. What had he done? Got fuckin' bladdered because that cow, Daisy, had mouthed off at him.

But why? He sighed. She couldn't really be jealous, could she? She was being over-cautious wasn't she? He reasoned that she didn't know him all that well and she had a lot to lose. A great deal was going on in that clever little head of hers. Stuff that she didn't want him spreading about. Especially not to Jacky. He wouldn't have done that anyway, but Daisy couldn't be sure of that, could she? And what had he done at the first sign of trouble? Come back here, got drunk as a skunk and fucked the brains out of Jacky.

It was cold in the bathroom. He rinsed out the sink and sluiced his face and hands again. God, he could murder a cup of tea. He looked at his watch. Ten past three. If he was back at The Black Bear he'd have been getting up soon anyway. He smeared a smidgen of Jacky's toothpaste on his finger and rubbed it over his teeth. It made him want to throw up again but he managed to hold the bile down.

Jacky groaned and opened one eye when he shook her shoulder.

'Come back in,' she said. He turned his face away from her morning breath. He didn't even fancy her much. She wasn't his sort. She was too fleshy for him, too obvious.

'It's coming up to quarter past three. I gotta go.'

'No.' She sleepily pushed aside the grey sheets and the smell of sex and sweat hit him anew. Her plump legs were winter white.

'You gonna be all right?' She was eyeing his nakedness, his dick hanging shrivelled like it didn't know what all the fuss was about when last night it had been as lively as a tiger. She put out a hand and touched him tenderly.

'Even when you're small you're big, ain't you?' He

felt himself blush but she continued. 'I wish I didn't have a fuckin' business to run. I bet you do, too.'

'Yes.' He hated himself for lying to her but he wanted to get out of the place with as little conversation and fuss as possible, but he'd better remind her. 'You gonna get to Brighton in time?'

'Fuck!' Then she was throwing clothes on, the same ones she'd worn last night. He realised she had no intention of washing herself. He went to the chair where, strangely, his own clothes were neatly folded. She must have done that for him because he never folded his clothes, simply hung them over the back of a chair or slipped his gear on a hanger. He began to dress.

'How come you can you hold your booze so well?' His voice hurt his head.

'I only had one drink. You 'ad the rest.'

That explains the hangover, he thought, but he also knew he shouldn't have taken advantage of her. He knew she liked him but that was no excuse to get in her bed.

'I'm sorry about last night.'

She was fully dressed now, down to her heavy work boots.

'Well, I ain't sorry at all. Why do you think I've been inviting you round for your meals? You've paid me back for 'em now. In fact I've had interest on top.'

She laughed, then she came towards him and flung her arms round his neck.

'I ain't got time to make you tea, but you know where the stuff is.' Then she kissed him full on the mouth. It was a sudden action, and automatically he kissed her back before pulling away, embarrassed. Then she was gone, blue canvas money belt in one hand, her van keys in the other, and shouting back at him. 'Make sure you shut the street door properly on your way out. See you later.'

After the thunder on the stairs that was her leaving came blessed silence.

He finished dressing, then pulled up the bedclothes and straightened the musty-smelling counterpane. In the kitchen he groaned at the mess. She'd washed the pots but bits of dried food still clung to them. She'd not bothered to empty the sink of water and it was scummy and clouded with grease. He pulled out the plug and set about washing up properly. He emptied an overflowing ashtray from the bedroom which must have been under his nose all night while he slept, nearly throwing up again in the process. Then he collected the rubbish from the living room. Old newspapers, empty crisp bags and sweet wrappers lay where Jacky had let them fall. He threw these into a swing-top bin, or tried to, but it was overflowing. So he pulled out the soggy brown paper-bagged mess and rolled the lot in newspaper to take with him when he left and deposit in the market bin on the corner. He'd lost his yearning for a cup of tea but drank three more glasses of water. In the kitchen drawer he found a bottle of aspirin and swallowed three.

The headache was still there, throbbing away. But that wasn't the reason he'd decided to give Fareham Market a miss today even though he'd still be liable for the pitch rent. He looked around the flat and, after returning what little remained of the whisky to the sideboard cupboard and thinking he'd left the place tidy enough for Jacky to get back to, he let himself out, shivering at the early morning cold.

Daisy had been in the shop last night so she had the

keys. She'd be getting a set done for him, so she'd said. If he got hold of some paint he could start redecorating and sorting out the bookshelves like they'd already discussed. With a bit of luck and some help from Daisy they could open before Christmas. It wouldn't be an ideal time to open a second-hand bookshop but not everyone had families to feast with at Christmas and New Year. Past experience on the stall had shown him that for these people their main solace was a good book or three to get them through the lonely season. If he contacted a wholesaler he could see what new titles they had on offer, that's if they had anything left at all. He was thinking about cookery books, factual stuff that sold well as gifts at Christmas. He had an excellent stock of second-hand fiction at present and was due to see a woman he regularly did business with about a collection of crime novels she wanted rid of. Good sellers. He'd make a healthy profit there. He walked down the frosty pavement of North Street feeling better.

First he had to phone the manager at Fareham Market and tell him he wouldn't be in. They'd make double money today by renting his site to a casual.

When the shop was up and running he might even be able to sell a few of his own local sketches and water colours. Headache forgotten, he started whistling. The sky was getting lighter. The birds had woken up and they were giving it their all. It was going to be a cold bugger of a day, but one, he thought, that was full of promise. Later he'd go round to Vera's and find Daisy.

At nine-fifteen Bri pushed open the door of Heavenly Bodies, breathing in the scent of perfume and feeling the warmth hit him after the bitter cold outside. Vera was standing like a small dark Gestapo officer addressing her troops, in her tight black skirt, red top, black stockings and high-heeled black patent shoes. She looked tiny compared to the three girls she was obviously instructing about the day's activities.

The girls were well coiffed, immaculately made up and also wore black stockings and high-heeled black shoes. All three had on white hospital coats, very short and tight and unbuttoned to show acres of well-developed cleavage.

'You four are a sight for sore eyes on a winter's morning,' said Bri. Then he noticed an older woman, wearing a black shawl and a beaded headscarf, sitting inside a small tented contraption. She smiled at him, revealing a gold front tooth, and her skin was pock-marked and the colour of old shoe leather.

'Want to know what's in store for you today, darlin'?'

He shook his head. Bri knew only too well what he was going to do today.

''E's a friend. Leave 'im alone, you silly cow,' said Vera. 'You ain't much of a fortune teller if you can't tell who wants their bleedin' fortune told an' who don't. Better still, go and make a cuppa, I'm parched.' The woman sniffed, hoisted herself up and shuffled towards the back of the shop in her tartan slippers.

To stop himself from laughing Bri said, 'It's cold enough for snow.'

'Won't be a tick, Bri,' said Vera, handing each girl a red Santa hat with a white fur trim and a bell on the point which she took from a Woolworth's paper bag. 'Put these on. Adds a Christmassy feel, don't you think, even if it's only November?'

A plump girl was giving Bri the eye. It didn't escape Vera's notice.

'Not a customer, Kirsty, dear.' She shooed the girls away to the rear of the shop. 'What can I do for you, Bri?' Vera fluttered her eyelashes at him. He saw the left one had come unstuck. He wondered whether he should draw her attention to it but decided against it. It might make her cross, so he looked about him at the spotless premises. A comfortable blue sofa with matching armchairs occupied the waiting area and paler blue walls and a bowl of forced spring daffs contrasted brightly on the polished chrome table.

'Nice premises, Vera.'

'Glad you like my place. You come for a sample of what's on offer at the back? Samantha, Margo or Kirsty especially will make you very glad you came.' She grinned at him. 'Geddit? Or you here for Daisy?'

He laughed. 'You get worse you do. I need to find Daisy. Got a van load of paint, ladders and the offer of a couple of hardworking lads to start on the book-shop. I need the keys.'

'Tryin' to make amends for last night?' He nodded. 'Go through the back of the shop, outside, and up the steps. She's expecting you.'

'How can you say that when I didn't know I was coming 'ere myself?'

'I could say Madam ZaZa told me.' At the sound of her name the woman looked up from the tray she was carefully carrying and winked. 'Only she can't tell the time, let alone the bleedin' future. Nah, you're a bloke, ain't yer? Predictable as shit.' He grinned at her. 'Fuck off,' she said. 'I've got a business to run.'

'What do you want?' Daisy had opened the door to

the flat and was staring at him through about six inches of door space and frame.

'That's a nice welcome, especially when Vera said you were expecting me.'

'I'll swing for her,' she said, opening the door wide. 'You'd better come in. I'm sorry, Bri. I 'ad no right to go mouthing off at you.'

'And I'm sorry I got angry.'

'So now we're back at the beginning. What do you want?' She walked ahead of him into the cosy flat.

'I got a van load of stuff and two strong blokes. You up for a spot of decorating?'

Daisy turned and clapped her hands together, a big smile lighting her face.

'You darling!' She threw her arms around his neck and planted a noisy kiss on his cheek. As she drew back he thought how her smiling face could light up even the greyest, coldest day. 'You want to wait for me? Shall I make you a cuppa?'

'No. I'll get round the shop and make a start.' Suddenly there was a lot he wanted to say to her, but as he didn't know where to start he turned on his heel, embarrassed, and walked out and down the wrought iron stairway.

'Bri,' she called over the balcony. He stopped in mid-flight and looked up. 'You'll be needin' these. Don't return them, they're yours.' Daisy dropped the keys and he caught them. Whistling, and with a light heart he ran over to his white Thames van and climbed aboard.

By the time Daisy arrived at the shop with a flask of tea, bacon butties in greaseproof paper and three bottles of Newcastle brown ale, the work was well under way.

The first thing she'd do was get the gas turned on so they could use the downstairs kitchen. She'd give it a good clean this morning, she thought.

'Did you check for damp?' Daisy asked.

Bri nodded. 'No cracked plaster, no mould, no damp patches, so it's really a job of just getting on with it. You want any alterations doin'?'

'No. I simply want it all clean and the shop made into a proper welcoming place. You'll 'ave your own ideas on that score. And shouldn't you be at Fareham Market today?'

'This is more important.' He cropped the tops off the beer bottles. 'Come upstairs and see.'

Daisy followed him up. 'They're making a good job,' she said. The two men were slapping white distemper on the ceiling of a bedroom. 'Elevenses,' she said. Bri showed them the bottles. They jumped off the stepladders and downed brushes.

'Harry and Carl,' Bri introduced them. They nodded at Daisy who smiled back. 'I got bacon sarnies downstairs,' she said. 'Better eat 'em while they're still hot.'

She went down and within seconds was back handing out breakfast. She saw the bathroom ceiling and the second bedroom had already been painted.

'With you all going like the clappers you needs to be well fed,' she said. 'Don't you worry, none of you, I'll see you all right.'

'And I reckon you two ought to go professional.' Daisy picked up on Bri's teasing and understood. Harry and Carl ran a decorating business.

'You're just in luck we're slow this week,' said the

taller of the two, Harry. He'd already swigged back his beer and was opening a packet of fags. 'Cheers, mate,' he said to Bri as he lit up from a box of Swan Vestas.

''Ope you got some choccie biscuits to go with me bacon sarnie?' laughed Carl.

'What, and have you bloody skiving even more?' Bri joked.

The men finished eating then went downstairs while Daisy was changing in another bedroom, putting on a pair of old jeans and a thick jumper she'd begged from Vera. Upon her return Bri poured her tea from the flask.

'I could only get white paint,' he said. 'Hope you don't think it'll look like a bleedin' winter wonderland when it's finished.'

'I won't. The caff was dark, with horrible paint. Me and Eddie did our best but it was a dreary old place, still is.' She looked across the road at the building where her hopes and dreams had gone bust. 'It'll be nice to have this shop all light and airy.' She dragged herself back from the bleak place that held her memories.

'What are you thinking?' Bri asked. It was almost as though he had tuned in to her thoughts.

Her body stiffened at his words. 'About Eddie.'

'I think about him a lot, too, Dais. I was wrong to keep an eye on him as Mum wanted without telling him who I really was.'

'Makes no difference now. For you it seemed the right thing to do at the time. It wouldn't have made no difference to the way he died.'

Downstairs Carl and Harry were laughing. They were too far away to overhear the conversation.

'Eddie was good at seeing past people. Looking into their hearts. He'd 'ave understood your mum's fear. He always understood Kenny's fears. And despite everything he looked after Pappy to the end and beyond,' Daisy said.

'I believe my father was a bastard to both of them. An' he was no fuckin' father at all to me,' said Bri.

'So how do you feel now, knowing your father lives ten minutes away and is a defenceless old man?'

'He can rot in hell, for all I care.'

Bri set down his flask mug with such force it smacked on the wooden orange box Daisy had used as a makeshift table.

'Good eats, Mrs Lane,' called up Carl.

'I'm Daisy, to you,' she called back.

'Mum's wittering on about going to see Pappy. Can you believe that?'

'Yeah, I can. She loved the bloke and in his own way, he loved her. But he wanted to own her body and soul. Your mum's got unfinished business in her heart. I already knew about Kenny belonging to Bert, Vera told me. But it was nice your mum confiding in me like that.'

'I don't agree with her seein' him.'

'You ain't just a little bit curious?'

''Course I am. Everyone wants to know where their roots lie. Do I look like him, Daisy?'

'I don't know. I ain't set eyes on the bloke. Eddie used to visit regularly but I never knew your father was still alive until just before Eddie was killed.'

'Where is he?'

'I told you, Alverstoke. The Cedars.'

'So you're forking out for a man you've never met?'

'I'm not forking out anything of me own. It's

Eddie's money. Some of Eddie's money goes into this place.'

'You'll not be putting your heart and soul into the shop, then? Like I will?'

'I'll be donating money, and my heart and soul. I can't afford for it to look like I – we – ain't trying to make a go of this. Are we going to 'ave another fuckin' row? If so, I'm out of here.'

'I'm sorry.'

She sighed and softened towards him. 'I got ghosts to make lie down. There's dead people walking about and I got to make 'em go away for their own peace of mind. And mine.'

He didn't speak. Daisy produced a handkerchief from her sleeve and blew her nose.

'I'm sorry,' he said. 'I always seem to be saying "sorry" to you.'

Sudden tears sprang to her eyes. But he didn't reach out and touch her.

'We'll see this through together,' he said at last, softly.

'If you mean it, there's something else you got to do for me,' she said. 'I know you can draw and paint a really lifelike picture. Them boats and the pontoon at the ferry on your mum's wall took a lot of skill.'

'So?'

'Could you forge a signature?'

She could see by his face he thought she was joking. When he realised she wasn't he asked,

'Whose?'

She took a paper from her jeans pocket and passed it to him. It was the receipt Roy had signed at his London house. Bri opened out the folded sheet and whistled.

'Don't see why not. Bit of practice, I'll have it off perfect.'

'So perfect you could write it without thinking about it? I want you to be able to sign for stuff using that signature.'

'That's forgery. I could go down for that.'

'You won't get caught. I told you that an' you got to trust me.' Surely he wasn't going to back out now, she thought. 'I've had long enough to make sure this is a foolproof plan.' She stared hard into his face.

'Mum, if she knew, would say to me go ahead, Bri. She'd want retribution for her son. I don't doubt that Roy Kemp's downfall will benefit a lot of people. Even the coppers might give you a pat on the back, Daisy. Some of 'em anyway. There'll be coppers who'll be poorer from the lack of his handouts.'

'In or out?'

'In, you silly cow.' She grinned at him.

CHAPTER 11

'What the fuck is that?'

'You can see what it is. A leg at each corner and a tail stickin' up showing what looks just like your face. A cat's arse!'

'Is that right?' Vera put out her hand to smooth the heart-shaped grey patch on the cat's head. The animal rose and arched its back, moving from the doughnut position it had taken on the shop counter. 'Aren't you sitting pretty for your Auntie Vera? Where did you come from? What's your name, then?'

'It's a moggie, Vera. Not bloody Supercat. It ain't gonna talk back to you.'

'My Kibbles talks to me.' Vera looked pained.

'Well, that ain't Kibbles, an' any moment now—'

'You little fucker!' Vera jumped back about three feet and surveyed her hand. Two small drops of blood appeared. She raised her hand and sucked it off, leaving in its place bright red lipstick. Daisy laughed.

'As I was saying, Vera, any moment now he'll have you.'

'Nasty little bugger.' Vera and the cat surveyed each other.

'He's had a rough life and don't know much about kindness.'

'Bit like you then, Daisy. Thank God you don't go

about scratching an' biting people. Give us that cup of tea?' Daisy passed her a mug and Vera helped herself to a bourbon biscuit.

'Where did Mr Nasty come from?'

'He's not Mr Nasty but Bertie. I named him after Bert from the caff.'

'Daft you are.' Vera dipped her biscuit in her tea. She took it out and the wet end promptly fell back into the mug. 'Fuck!'

Daisy laughed at her. 'Jacky gave him to me, said he was a peace offerin' after the row with Bri.'

'Why didn't Jacky keep it?'

'She's 'ardly ever indoors, is she? Pets need company. Anyway, a bookshop should 'ave a cat asleep on the counter.'

'How did she know you'd 'ad a bit of a to-do with Bri about her?'

Daisy shrugged and picked up her mug and sipped the tea. 'You 'spose Bri mentioned it?'

'Nah. But it's possible. She's a clever bitch that one. Just as long as 'e don't tell 'er much else. The head that shares the pillow shares the secrets. Milly saw him comin' out of her flat early one mornin'.'

'How early?'

'Early, early.'

'Milly being another of your street friends?'

'All I'm sayin', missy, is, you be bloody careful. She's after Bri.'

'So what?'

Vera said, 'I never really liked 'er or 'er family. She went to the same school as me. St John's. Only I was just leavin' when she started in the infants. She was all golden ringlets and a pretty smile. Her dad interfered with her, got 'er in the family way later. They took the baby away, but something 'appened while the baby was bein' born an' now she can't 'ave no more kiddies.'

'It ain't like you not to like someone just because they 'ad ringlets in their bleeding hair. Anyway, I invited her round. She's coming in now.'

'Cor, fuck me.'

'I'm sure someone'll take you up on that generous offer, Vera.'

The front door bell jangled. 'Hallo, Jacky. Vera was just saying how nice it was you gave me Bertie.'

Daisy saw the two women eye each other warily. Jacky was wearing grubby jeans and a sweater that had seen better days. She had heavy boots on and her hair scraped back into a pony tail. She was dressed more to keep out the cold. Vera believed in cleanliness and glamour.

''Allo,' replied Jacky. 'He looks well, Dais.' She nodded towards the cat. 'Can I 'ave one of them?' Without waiting for a reply she picked up a biscuit and bit off half. Daisy took the cosy off the brown earthenware teapot and poured Jacky a mug of tea. 'Smells clean in 'ere. I like the smell of fresh paint. When you an' Bri openin' this place?'

'Soon as possible, Jacky. The way Bri's been working and getting his two mates to graft all hours, it shouldn't be long now.'

Vera said, 'I remember your mum.' Daisy glared at her.

'Don't talk to me about that fat cow,' snapped Jacky, her face fierce.

'Why?'

'Because, Vera, she never believed me when I told her me dad was fingerin' me.'

Vera and Daisy stared at each other unsure of what to say.

'Didn't you go to the same school as Vera?' Daisy asked tentatively.

'She left as I started. But you was at the same school an' all. Don't you remember?'

Daisy thought hard then shook her head. She'd had her nose in books from the time she could read, which was before she started school, so she didn't play about much with the other kids. Her mum had taught her to read and there'd been no stopping her. Her favourite book had been *Heidi*. She remembered reading until the natural light from her bedroom window faded.

'I was jealous of you. Little shy thing you was. But you 'ad a mum who came to collect you every day. Always waiting outside the school gates she was, to make sure you got 'ome safe. I wasn't safe even when I was at 'ome.'

'Where's your mum now?' Vera chipped in.

'Don't know, don't care. Same filthy 'ouse we lived in before, I expect. If they ain't condemned it and pulled it down.'

'Didn't you marry an old bloke?'

'I never married him. Just lived with him. When he died he left me enough money to start up the stall and put a deposit on me flat. I ain't never bin married.'

Daisy collected the mugs and put them on the tray then went into the kitchen to make fresh tea. She heard Vera say, 'You always going for older blokes is a bit like lookin' for a father figure, ain't it?'

'What are you, Vera? A fucking shrink now?' yelled Daisy.

'I gets to sort out all kinds of problems in my line of work,' came Vera's speedy reply. Daisy heard Jacky laugh. A full-throated sound. It was going to be all right between them now, she thought. There certainly wouldn't be the need for her to do any digging to see if Bri had spilled the beans. Vera would have Jacky telling her life story and more in next to no time without the poor woman realising a thing. Daisy liked Jacky. There was a roughness about her. No airs and graces. Running a market stall was tough for a woman on her own. So what if she had her eye on Bri? Couldn't blame any woman for wanting a piece of him. That hair alone made a woman want to run her fingers through it. Pity she was going to ask him to dye it!

Would he agree?

He'd have to if the plan was going to work. He'd need to look a dead ringer for Roy Kemp and his dark looks. Bri already had the height, and the breadth. Even Bri's tanned skin, caused by being out in all weathers, was like Roy's year-round Spanish tan. But Bri's flaming mop would give the game away in a blink.

Daisy took in the fresh tea and clean mugs. She smiled to herself. Vera and Jacky were getting on just fine. Bertie was asleep on the counter, laid out like he owned the place, his belly rising and falling with his deep breathing. The two men were upstairs tiling the bathroom and they'd had their elevenses. All was right with Daisy's world, she thought.

The sale of the cafe had been speedily completed by Roy's solicitor and the remainder of the money was in the bank. Daisy looked through the window at the cafe opposite.

'The caff's off my 'ands, now,' she announced.

'Good thing,' agreed Vera. 'But you ain't moved far, have you?'

'There ain't no bad memories this side of the street. An' I always fancied a bookshop,' Daisy said.

Jacky asked, 'Sure it ain't Bri you fancies?'

'Don't be daft. He's got the stock and I've got the premises. It's strictly a business venture, I ain't lookin' for nothing else. My Eddie was all I ever wanted.' Too late Daisy realised what she'd said.

'Where is he?'

'Where do you think?' Vera was quick off the mark with a question for a question.

'Knowing him, 'e's ditched you.'

'What you asking for, if you already know?'

Hardly anyone knew that Eddie had been killed by Roy Kemp and she'd like to keep it that way. Daisy smiled to herself. It was about time Roy's dealings in Gosport and Portsmouth came under police scrutiny.

Sammy hated the caff. The girls had been absolute bitches to move down from Forton Road, squabbling and fighting. Even Rosa, who was usually the most sensible of the lot, had given him lip. Why they wanted rooms of their own when they were well used to shagging on the street he didn't know. Well, they couldn't have separate rooms, there wasn't the space. Not when he needed to be private. Still, that's what Roy Kemp paid him for, to keep the fucking bitches in order and take their money. Sammy gave each girl a 'no quibble guarantee'. If a guy fucked them over and knocked them about – don't come quibbling to him. He wasn't a fucking minder or a maid, was he? But he did a nice line for himself in setting up a few 'outsiders'. Women who didn't want to be full time prossies but liked a bit of extra dosh. He'd do the lining up of clients from the women's own advertising and let them use a room. For which, of course, he'd expect a good cut. He didn't think Roy Kemp would object. Anyway, he'd already set two more girls on for Roy. One was raring to go, the other needed to be led into the life gently. That was okay by him and Roy never wanted his slags rushed anyway. And after all there was plenty of money for both him and Roy. Mind you, he didn't want to queer his own pitch. He laughed at his own joke. Queer was right. And a punter was due at three o'clock.

Sammy was dressed for Captain Albert Mooney. He patted his sailor's bell bottoms. Feeling the wool material tight over his buttocks exactly the way Captain Albie liked them, so he could run his hands up and down Sammy's thighs. His cap was perched jauntily on his head. This afternoon he was a lowly able seaman and about to give his client a good seein' to, then turning the tables and allowing the Captain to pull rank, or anythin' else he wanted to pull.

No kid today. The little bleeder hadn't turned up. Fucking good job he wasn't needed for anything more important than selling the schoolkids dope. Sammy knew he'd be along when he wanted some money or some charlie for himself. Sammy looked at himself in the mirror.

'Not bad for your age,' he thought. He smoothed back the skin on his boyish face. 'Bit saggy in places though, darlin', but it don't seem to put the punters off none.' He picked up his steel tail comb and pulled it through his hair.

Going over to the wardrobe he took out his cat o' nine tails and laid it ready on the bed. A dry mop in a pail. And a packet of fig rolls on the dressing table. It was a bit difficult to get hold of weevil-infested hard tack biscuits. The fig rolls were sort of squarish, he reasoned. The hard tack, or fig rolls, were used as a reward. But only if the Captain deserved it and mopped the deck properly.

Sammy heard the buzzer on the street door. Looking out the window and satisfying himself it was his guest he went downstairs to let him in. The buzzer was Sammy's idea. None of the girls except Rosa had a key. If they had to buzz to get in he could keep a check on their punters. No freebies here, he'd decided.

'I'll be down,' he called out of the window to the portly gentleman wearing a long mackintosh and a trilby and clutching a brown carrier bag. The bag contained his regulation hat and the mac concealed his uniform. Games would commence only when the door to Sammy's room was locked on the inside.

'Come on up,' he said to Albert. As usual the Captain's top lip was bathed in sweat. He could see it glistening from here. Albert, for all his weight, took the stairs two at a time.

'My, my. We are eager today, aren't we?'

In a few moments it would be Sammy giving the orders to 'mop the deck', 'kiss my arse', 'suck my cock'. After the whipping would come the mutual gratification, if Albie could hold out that long of course.

Later, Sammy would be standing to attention, saying, 'See you next week, sir. Would you be requiring the services of a cabin boy?'

Then he'd count his money and gloat yet again over how good it was to be paid for a job he liked doing.

*

'You want me to what!' Daisy's gone fuckin' mad, Bri thought. 'Forging Roy Kemp's signature's one thing. I've practised so I've got it off to a "t". In fact I'd defy an expert even to spot the difference. But dye my hair black?' He shook his head in disbelief at Daisy. Then began picking up the books he'd dropped when she'd suggested it. 'You must think I've come up the Solent in a bucket!'

He began slotting the novels alphabetically into place on the shelves, in the order of their genres. Romance, crime, science fiction, westerns, horror. He breathed deeply. Bri loved the smell of books. It didn't matter to him whether they were new or falling to bits. Each book to him was a live thing of beauty and wisdom, each with its own scent, from the damp mustiness of the well-aged and yellowed pages to the crisp tartness of a thin-papered new book. Dyeing his hair indeed!

'It won't work unless you act and look like 'im,' pressed Daisy. 'You have to deposit money in the bleeding bank. The staff need to remember you – and your hair ain't the right fucking colour.'

'I like my hair just the way it is.' He ran his fingers through the chestnut gloss. She gave him her lost puppy look and his heart melted.

'I like it, too. Ever so much. But we could dye it so it would wash out gradually. I don't know what your problem is? You keep your woollen 'at on when you're down the market, don't you? So keep the bloody 'at on in here. Who's going to know the difference? An' it is winter, ain't it?'

Bri saw she had white gloss on her cheek. She was completing the painting round the windows. The shelves were up, the carpet down, the till paid for and the upstairs apartment very nearly livable. Him and Daisy and his two muckers had worked all hours and the result had paid off. And if they could pull in a few Christmas punters, so much the better, especially the ones who left everything until the last minute and needed presents quickly.

'I've always hankered after a shop,' Bri said, his thoughts taking flight in speech.

'Don't change the bleeding subject.'

Daisy came over to him. She laid her hand on his arm. Her eyes met his, hers big, wide and soulful, their lashes covered with black mascara. The transistor radio on the shop counter was playing 'Where Did Our Love Go' by the Supremes. Diana Ross, now she was a bit of all right, he thought. She wouldn't ask anyone to dye their hair for her, surely? Daisy's blonde hair held specks of white paint. She'd tied it back with a chiffon scarf but that hadn't helped, tantalising strands had fallen free. He suddenly wanted to erase the white smudges on her face with his fingers, gently, oh, so gently. But she was out of bounds to him. Not because she'd been in love with Eddie and married to Kenny but because she was special. And she was on a mission. He knew her well enough to know she wouldn't look for affection until that mission was accomplished. He admired her for her strength of feelings. Eddie's light must still be burning strongly, he reasoned. Though why she'd waited so long before coming back to Gosport to avenge Eddie's death was beyond him. Wait a minute though, wasn't there a saying, "Revenge is a dish best served cold"?

Bri could feel the heat generated by her touch. He stared at the slight figure with her appealing eyes.

'I'm used to the barber. I ain't going into one of those posh hairdressers.'

'You don't have to,' she breathed, staring at him as though he was the only man in the world. 'You don't know how happy this makes me.' He wanted to move away and yet he didn't want to move away at all. There was a smile hovering at the corners of her mouth. She was teasing him. She'd known all the time he would do as she asked.

He was beginning to think she could twist him round her little finger any time she wanted. Even her perfume worked for her, earthy and sensual.

'Then tomorrow night I'll do your hair,' she said. His heart fluttered with panic.

'I don't want no cock-ups.'

'See any cock-ups with me own?'

'No,' he said grudgingly. 'Don't you make me look like a pansy.'

'No one'll see your hair, except me an' the people in the bank an' the wholesalers. It's fucking winter, ain't it? I already told you you can keep your hat on the rest of the time. And make sure you pull it well down. The first time I saw you again in the market, I only noticed you by your chestnut mop.'

He sniffed. 'Blokes don't dye their hair. You don't seem to realise what a sacrifice I'm making.'

'I do. And you're doin' it for your brother, for Cal your mate who was also killed by Roy Kemp . . .'

'Okay. Shut up then.'

'No one'll find out your hair's not red anymore unless you goes to bed with 'em. But you could keep your hat on an' all for that . . .'

Bri threw a copy of *The Wind in the Willows* at her. He deliberately missed. She laughed.

Next morning he was up early and thinking there wasn't a lot to show around him for how hard he'd worked. His room at The Black Bear was clean, well-fitted, and the arrangements were that he helped himself to food from either the bar or the kitchen fridge whenever he had a mind to. The fact that he couldn't be around at a decent hour for breakfast or dinner wasn't lost on the landlord.

Bri thought about his stock, it was worth a great deal. Certainly allowed him to spend a bit on his mum. He also had the proceeds from the fish farm in Scotland in the bank, but the money from Daisy's scam wasn't to be sniffed at. Not that he was going into it just for the money.

His mother had her dreams that she could have made her peace with Eddie, that he would have understood the true reasons she had disappeared from his and Kenny's lives. Now that would never happen and she'd go to her grave without either of her estranged sons having known how much she'd loved them. And Roy Kemp was to blame.

Then there was Daisy. One day perhaps she might come to care for him. Or perhaps it would be one of those things that was never meant to be. But whatever happened he was going to give it his best shot and stick by her. He believed he had everything to gain and nothing to lose. In the meantime he had a shop to open up.

He wondered what Daisy was doing this morning? Perhaps at this very moment she was lugging her suitcase down the short distance from Vera's. He'd offered to help because women always seemed to collect such a great deal of stuff. But she'd been adamant.

'I can manage,' she'd said. She was an independent cow was Daisy. He liked that. His mother, Queenie, was strong too. His brow furrowed remembering the argument they'd had the last time he'd popped round.

'I want you to come with me when I visit Pappy.'

'I don't think so, Mum.' He'd been angry she'd even asked him.

'But he is your father.'

'Coming from his loins don't make him a good father.' He'd hurt her, told her the truth which she'd known anyway. The air had cooled between them and he'd left her flat under a cloud of despondency. Oh, he'd go and visit the old bugger, Pappy, eventually. They both knew that. But he'd be doing so for Queenie's sake, not because he was interested in the old man.

He walked along North Street. The bookshop was on one corner and at the other end of the street was The Black Bear, barely a stone's throw away. There was a sharp frost this morning but he'd known colder on the stall. He'd like to give up the markets as soon as possible, but to cut out the stall now would be foolhardy until he knew just how much profit he could make with the shop. Daisy had come up trumps there.

'We're in this together,' she said. 'I'll mind the store. I've had enough practice with serving in the caff. It should prove a pleasant change of pace an' if I get problems I can refer people to you.'

'Problems? Drunks and druggies don't often show up in bookshops. They aren't desperate for a quick fix of Catherine Cookson or Jean Plaidy to see them through the next couple of hours.' She'd laughed at him. He liked it when she laughed. It was like a shaft of light shining down a coal hole. 'You'll soon get the hang of things,' he said. He thought for a moment then took a key out of his pocket. 'I've got a key to this place so it's only fair you have this key to the side door of The Black Bear. My room is directly at the top of the stairs, you can't miss it. I know you don't want me to move in here with you but I'd feel happier knowing you can get hold of me at night if you need to.'

'If you think so.' Daisy took the key. 'You are a nice man, Bri Deveraux. I'll use it if it's absolutely necessary, but anyway I'll have to pull my weight when you go off getting stock for the scam. Just you make sure the stock you buy then ain't bloody books so it gives the fucking game away.' She'd laughed again.

'As if I would,' he'd said.

Bri unlocked the shop door and took a deep breath. It was all so fresh and clean. A telephone stood on the counter and dark blue carpeting ran all through and up the stairs with lino down in the kitchen. His van was outside in the covered yard and there was even room for Daisy's MG. She was going to use the garage in Seahorse Street for some of the scam stock. He kicked the door closed. He'd fix up a bell later so they'd know when customers came in if they'd nipped upstairs to the toilet or the kitchen. He heard soft footfalls on the stairs and looked over to see Daisy coming down dressed in a white belted dressing gown.

'Hope you ain't serving customers in that get-up,' he said.

'Oh, you! I heard the door and thought you'd like a cuppa.'

'Sure would. Thought you was moving in today?'

Her hair was a bird's nest where she'd slept. She looked wholesome, he thought.

'Seemed silly not to walk round with me stuff last night, 'specially as Harry from the second-hand shop had delivered that stuff we chose for the flat. Looks good, don't it?' She waved an arm to encompass the shop.

He saw the satisfaction in her smile. He wanted to give her a hug but felt it might be overstepping the mark. Fragile ties bound their relationship.

She bent beneath the counter and produced two small vials. For a moment he wondered if she had a bottle of wine there to celebrate the shop's opening, but the tiny bottles were much too small for wine or spirits.

'What's that?'

'Hair dye. For tonight.' She passed them to him and he twisted the cap off one and sniffed it.

'Jesus, it smells like ammonia.'

'It's proper stuff. I got it in Hills the Hairdressers opposite Woolworth's in the town. We put one on first, that's the dye, then after a while we rinse it off and give your hair a bleeding good massage with the stuff in the other bottle. Then we wash that off an' all. It's what they use in the salon.'

'How much?'

'No charge.'

'How come?'

'He's a friend of Vera's.'

'Oh, I get the idea.' Bri was always intrigued by Vera's male friends, especially as she had so many and they all seemed to keep a special place for her in their hearts. Most of her friends were highly professional businessmen and pillars of the Gosport community.

'I'm not looking forward to this.'

'I know,' said Daisy. 'An' you're a very brave boy. I'll go and make the tea now, shall I?' She took back the vials and put them in her dressing gown pocket. 'Tell you what, why don't we go down The Dive caff and 'ave a big fry-up to set us up for the day? I ain't got no food in yet. I'll treat you.'

'Really?'

'Yeah, but it won't become a fucking habit!'

He climbed the stairs, liking the ambiance of the place more and more with every step he took. They were going to be all right, him and Daisy.

He found the kitchen, passing her room as he did so. He saw the rumpled bed, the stockings thrown over the back of the chair, the frilly underwear on the end of the bed. His heart was beating fast. It was a hell of a risk they were taking to complete this scam. Would they be able to pull it off without Roy Kemp finding out? If he did, they were both dead meat. One part of him was exhilarated by the idea of the scam but the other wished that Daisy could just accept the past and move on with her life.

CHAPTER 12

Daisy dressed hurriedly, putting on her jeans and a vee necked jumper. She ran a comb through her hair and tied it back before switching on the radio; the Beatles were telling someone she loved them. She hummed along, thinking this group of four lads was really going to make an impact on the pop scene. She liked their cheery music and the lad named John best because he was witty and reminded her of Eddie.

She wondered if Bri had any bad habits. Would any of his mannerisms remind her of Kenny, or worse, Eddie? Working with a man she didn't know might cause problems. It had been different when she was living at the caff and she'd had to contend with bed and breakfasts. Vera was easy to get on with, and Suze had also been easy to live with – probably because they all had their own separate lives and a common interest in the caff.

Then there was Eddie...

When this was over she'd go back to the white-washed house in Greece and pick up the threads of her life once more with his child. In the heat, among the shady olive groves, the colourful and sweet-smelling perfume of jasmine and gardenias, she could be at peace. Don't think about missing little Eddie now, Daisy, she told herself, and don't start thinking about

Eddie, it won't bring him back. She wiped her hand across her eyes.

Bri was setting out cups and saucers and singing along to 'Sixteen Tons' on the radio.

'The old ones are the best,' Daisy said.

They drank tea in virtual silence, yet it was a companionable silence until Bri said, 'We ready for the off then? The thought of that fry-up is making me mouth water. Since we can open the shop ahead of schedule, I wondered whether you'd like to do the dastardly deed this morning. Me hair I mean?'

'Okay,' she said, barely able to contain her excitement.

'I could open the bank account this afternoon then. In my new disguise as a London gangster.'

'You're on.'

Later, in the bathroom, Daisy massaged hair dye into his lovely auburn locks, with her hands in two plastic bags so she wouldn't get them covered in dye. Bri had stripped to his jeans.

'Nice body,' Daisy said. Something deep within her stirred.

'I expect it's all that lifting. If it ain't the market stall it's the heavy boxes of books what keeps me fit.'

Not an ounce of fat anywhere, she thought. His male scent as she rubbed at his head was quite intoxicating. He didn't talk a lot, but then he wasn't a gabby sort of bloke, was he? Daisy could plainly see why Jacky fancied him.

At last it was done.

'Sit on the edge of the bath. I've towelled it dry but I want to brush your hair the way Roy has his. I'll need to trim it a bit. Do you mind?'

'I'll have to not mind,' he said. He sat in silence while unfamiliar strands of dark hair fell on the lino.

'I'm through, now,' she said. She felt sick with nerves. What would he think about the transformation?

'Thank God,' he replied, getting to his feet and turning towards the mirror. 'Fucking hell!'

'It's as near Roy Kemp's style as I can manage.'

He was standing mesmerised. 'I hate it.'

'Don't mince your bleedin' words, do you?'

Daisy reached across and fluffed his dark curls.

'I mean,' he said, twisting around and catching her hand. 'You've done a good job. It looks natural enough. You've even put some dye on me eyebrows. But it's not me.'

Daisy sighed and shook herself free.

'You'd 'ave looked a bit odd with ginger eyebrows. I'll 'ave to leave your lashes.'

'Bloody sure you will! I ain't 'aving that vile-smelling stuff near me eyes. I don't know how you women can bear to be messed about like this—'

Daisy cut him off. 'I'll have to touch up the roots every so often.' His face was a mask of horror. 'Don't be a baby. That don't take long and it won't hurt. An' if we get this long firm business out the way quickly I won't 'ave to do it many times.' While Bri was mulling all this over in his mind Daisy said, 'I was terrified you'd emerge looking like Eddie. But you don't. With the right gear on you'll be a dead ringer for Roy Kemp. It also means you look like a brooding Heathcliff from *Wuthering Heights*, or Mr Darcy from *Pride and Prejudice* – and every woman fancies them.'

He was looking at her strangely. Under his breath she just heard him murmur, 'Pity you don't.'

'I'll clear up. You get used to your new look,' she said quickly.

After wiping down the bathroom and putting the towels in a bucket to soak, Daisy went back into the living room and found Bri sitting at the table. Bertie was on his lap.

'He's not fond of people,' she said.

'He likes me, though.' With a grin Bri picked up the purring bundle and held him to his face. Nose to nose.

'He'll scratch . . .'

'No, he won't, and you'd better get used to the fact that Bertie is a lady.'

'Well I bloody never!' Daisy said. 'Not only do you have a way with women but you know all about cats. You're going to get on fine with Vera. Do you suppose Bertie will mind keeping the same name? He . . . She comes when I call her now.'

'Doubt she'll care. Animals and kiddies, I understand. Women, never. Now shall we get on with the business, Daisy?'

Daisy went into her bedroom and took two large envelopes from the dressing table drawer. She presented them to Bri.

'You know what you have to do?'

'I ask to open an account and I deposit this money.' He opened the larger envelope and emptied the bundles of white five pound notes on to the table. 'You sure about this, Daisy? There's still time to back out.'

'I don't want to fucking back out. That's half the money I got for the caff. In the other envelope are the deeds to the caff and a solicitor's letter showing that you, Roy Kemp, are the new owner of Bert's Cafe.'

'Hang on a minute. Shouldn't Roy Kemp have these in his possession?' He pointed to the deeds. 'I thought contracts had been exchanged.'

'I took a chance. Roy doesn't like his proper London address on his shady dealings. Anything to protect his mum, see? And I was right. All I had to do was pick these up from the caff. It's obvious he picks up his post when he meets that bloke Sammy who's minding the place.'

'How did you get in? And I thought that place gave you the willies?'

'It does.' Daisy went to the china teapot on the windowsill. Glancing out of the window and down to the street, with a sharp intake of breath she registered Jacky going into the cafe. Couldn't have been, she decided. She was seeing things. She shook the teapot and out fell a key along with a couple of buttons and a packet of needles.

'To the street door of the caff.' She held the key up by its piece of string.

'Where did you get that? I thought you handed over the keys?'

'All except this one. The locks weren't changed, but even if they had been, I'd still have got in. I didn't live with Kenny and Eddie all that time and not learn how to pick locks and file down keys. A buzzer's been added to the door but other than that everything is as it was.'

'But what about the bank statements and invoices that'll go to the cafe? If one is forwarded on to Roy?'

'Ain't gonna happen. The postman never changes his delivery times. About seven to seven thirty. No one gets up early in that place – I've watched. Only the bloke in charge over there has a key, along with one woman, Rosa. All the other girls have to press the buzzer to get in. I'll remove any letters to Roy Kemp as they arrive.'

'So all I have to do is get dressed up and go down to the corner bank, open up an account and sign my new name?'

Daisy nodded. 'I bought you a suit. Had to guess the bleeding size so I hope it fits. An' the ring. There's also an overcoat with a velvet collar and a couple of silk shirts. All the stuff Roy likes.'

'Better get them out the wardrobe then.'

This was the anxious moment she had waited for. Would Bri look sufficiently like Roy to get away with it? She slipped into the bedroom and emerged with the new clothes over her arm. In one hand she held a pair of the softest Italian leather shoes. Bri took one look at the expensive gear and whistled.

'I guessed you was the same size as Eddie so I got nines. If they're too big I'll buy some heel grips. It would have been silly not to buy the right kind of clothes. Most of the London crowd have their stuff hand made, suits from Savile Row.' Bri fingered the silk. 'Eddie knew a Portsmouth naval tailor, used to make his clothes for him.' Daisy continued. 'I paid him to come up with this lot. Told him I was buying the stuff as a gift for a bloke, which isn't far off the truth.

'I'd best go and change then.' He took the stuff from Daisy's arms and disappeared back into the bathroom. Daisy went into her bedroom and came out with a small brown paper package. She knocked on the bathroom door and opened it wide enough to put her arm round to give it to Bri.

'Cologne. Roy's is distinctive enough to be remembered.' She heard him unwrapping the paper.

'This didn't fall off the back of a lorry down no fucking market, did it?' He called. Daisy didn't answer.

'Close your eyes, I'm coming out.' Daisy realised her hands were clammy and she had gouged nail marks into her palms as she waited. 'You do realise that eventually we'll get rumbled? That Roy Kemp is going to work things out?'

Daisy opened her eyes. 'Fucking hell!' The likeness to Roy Kemp was amazing. Another gasp left her throat before she managed to say, 'Only his mum and close acquaintances wouldn't be fooled. But if people met you first and thought you was 'im . . . ' He walked around her, then up and down the room, studying her all the while. 'Slow down!' Daisy said. 'He has a lazy walk, determined but easy. Like he owns the place. Someone who says, "Jump!" And the buggers does it without daring to ask how high. And you're right. Eventually we might get rumbled. But by that time, he won't be able to do a fucking thing about it.'

Jacky pressed her finger on the buzzer. She heard the sash window rise and looked up.

'Key coming down,' said Sammy. It landed in the street. Jacky let herself into the cafe, thinking he was bloody lucky there was no drain nearby.

'God this place fuckin' stinks,' said Jacky to herself. At least when Daisy owned the place it was kept clean. The stairs were littered with fag ends and empty cigarette packets. She sidestepped so as not to tread on a discarded syringe. She wondered why Sammy hadn't come down to let her in as he usually did. Busy with one of his own clients, no doubt. She wished she didn't have to come to this place.

But what was the alternative? Take punters back to her flat? Definitely not. One whiff how she made extra money and she'd have no chance of landing Bri.

Yet wasn't she already taking a risk? With the caff opposite the bookshop, sooner or later someone would see her going in or out, but it was a chance she had to take. If she could give up the game she would. But the flower stall always suffered in winter. Blooms were expensive and Gosport punters always wanted something for nothing and wouldn't pay for expensive flowers. She also owed more pitch money than she cared to think about, and money to the wholesalers at the flower market. All her utility bills were stacked up on the mantelpiece, behind the clock, unpaid. And, worst of all, she now owed Sammy big time as well.

He charged extortionate rates of interest, but what choice did she have? Her van had needed a new gearbox and she'd borrowed from Sammy, but without her van on the road, she couldn't do the markets. It was a vicious circle. She'd missed a couple of payments to Sammy and still had the bruises to show for it.

'Sammy? You there?' It would be more than her life was worth to hang on to the key. She knocked on his room door and waited. After a while she heard footsteps and music playing, 'A World Without Love' – Peter and Gordon had it sussed, there wasn't any love in her real world. She told herself to stop being maudlin. There were muffled voices, then the door opened a crack. Just wide enough for her to pass the key through to him.

'Thank you, darlin'. Room at the front upstairs. You got six punters, first one in ten minutes.' The door closed again. It wasn't often he was nice to her. Darling meant he had a client in there. It certainly wasn't her he was trying to impress, the bastard.

Jacky trudged up to the top landing and opened the door.

'Fuckin' 'ell,' she thought. The place was a tip. Not that she minded a bit of mess herself. After all, hadn't she been brought up in a mucky house by a slovenly mother?

'No wonder punters don't stay long,' she said aloud. In the drawer she found a silk coverlet and a couple of fairly clean pillow cases. She remade the bed, casting the heavily soiled linen to the back of the wardrobe and shutting the door on it. Luckily there was kitchen roll and Vaseline on the bedside table. She tried to open the window to let in some air but she could only raise the sash a couple of inches. She sat down on the edge of the bed to wait for her first punter.

An hour and a half later there was a knock at the door.

'You decent?'

'Yes, Sammy. Come in.' She knew he'd have walked in anyway whether she was decent or not. In his hands he held a half bottle of red wine and two glasses.

'This room stinks. You girls are filthy cunts. Still, you do your best, Jacky, better than the others, so have a glass of wine with me before you go.' She sighed. It wasn't any use her saying she really just wanted to leave. She took the glass of wine and knocked it back in one gulp. She handed him back the empty glass. His hand touched hers and she shuddered. He was smiling at her, his gold tooth gleaming. There were beads of sweat on his forehead and his top lip. He looked evil and she preferred it when he didn't pretend to be nice to her.

'Thirsty work, isn't it?' He poured himself a small measure and refilled her glass. 'Drink up.' She did so, frightened to refuse, setting the glass on the bedside table. Then she put out her hand for her share of the money he'd collected.

'I need to go. Can I 'ave what you owe me?' He knocked her hand away.

'Havin' a laugh, ain't you? You owe me.'

Jacky stared at him. The heavy smell of his Brut cologne was every bit as sickening to her as the foetid stuffiness of the room.

'I just done six punters. One was so fuckin' big he tore me and another smacked me about. I want me money . . .'

'An' I want what you owe me.' He was very calm and his voice was soft as silk. Jacky thought of the money she owed everyone and how she'd been depending on the cash from today. She didn't even have a packet of tea or a slice of bread in her place. She was hungry, and her body hurt where she'd been manhandled. It all seemed too much . . .

'You bastard,' she cried, and lunged at him. But he was too quick and sidestepped neatly. His fist was ready and it slammed into her cheekbone. Jacky staggered, then fell.

When she awoke she was sitting in a chair, still in the same stinking room. She was bound by her ankles with duct tape to the bottom rungs of the chair. Her hands were taped together at the wrists. She could hear laughter coming from somewhere in the building and music. The naked bulb from the ceiling showed up the bruises and blood on her thighs. She couldn't cry out. Her mouth was taped and a roll of duct tape lay on the bed.

Her head was thumping and her shoulders burned as though red hot pokers had been slid across them. She realised she was naked apart from her white cotton knickers. Blood seeped through at the crotch. She tried to look closer at the hundreds of tiny gold buttons shining on her arms, upper body and breasts. Around each gold button was a ring of red. Then she saw each gold button was a brass drawing pin embedded in her flesh and the ring of red her own blood. Jacky passed out.

When she came to again it was dark. She heard the chimes of Holy Trinity Church, ten strikes. It was raining. She was lying on the ground and the rain had seeped into her coat. At least she now had a coat around her, but beneath it she was completely naked. How did she get here? She was cold, so very cold. She could smell the wet earth but strangely she felt as though parts of her body were on fire.

She struggled to a sitting position and promptly vomited. Her coat took most of it. She was no longer tied up. Had she been tied up? It was difficult to remember. The wind was whistling eerily in the oak trees surrounding the church. Using a grave's headstone she managed to stand upright, her legs seeming not to belong to her.

Looking towards the ferry Jacky could see the lights of Portsmouth winking through the rain, the orange glow lighting up the darkness. A ferry boat was just leaving the pontoon. She wanted to go home. She tied the belt of her coat, then felt in her pockets. Both were empty, so she couldn't get a bus or taxi. It wasn't far but she didn't think she could make it back to her flat walking.

She staggered unsteadily across the cut grass, weaving through the obelisks and outstretched arms of marble angels. Visions of the drawing pins came back to her and she tore at the front of her coat until she'd exposed her skin. The drawing pins were gone but the darkness of the pinpricks was testimony to the indignity she'd suffered. But who did it? Had it been just Sammy? Surely not. Sammy wouldn't go near a woman if you paid him.

She had a memory of him saying, 'Pay up or next time it'll be worse.' Worse than this? Worse than the torture he'd inflicted? She knew she'd been raped and sodomised. She was bleeding and sore. She had another memory of men laughing, grabbing at her. She carefully made her way, half staggering, half crawling, towards a wooden seat in the ferry gardens.

When the effects of whatever drug he'd given her had fully worn off, she guessed she'd be lucky if she could even move. She had to get home. And soon. Get to bed. Be safe. She winced as she sat down on the wet seat.

She was so deep in her troubled thoughts she didn't see the man until he was standing in front of her.

He was small, with a scruffy flat cap atop his grinning face. She smelled the beer fumes through the rain. He swayed unsteadily.

"'Ow much, darlin'?'

A giggle rose in Jacky's throat. Money in her hand for a shag against the wall in the rain meant she wouldn't have to walk home. She could get a taxi from the rank on the corner.

She told him her price.

'You're cheap, ducky,' was his reply. He helped her to her feet and together they staggered towards the back wall of the ticket booth and its encompassing darkness.

It hurt as he entered her and started to thrust. Jacky realised she'd asked this dirty stranger only for the meagre sum she usually received from Sammy after he'd taken his cut. What a fuckin' mess, she thought.

CHAPTER 13

Bri pulled down the navy-blue knitted cap until it practically covered his entire head and surveyed himself in the bathroom mirror. He looked like an out of work skate, with his blue jeans and navy sweater. He met Daisy coming up the stairs with the till tray in her hands.

'I just closed the shop up. If you're wanting to refill the shelves for tomorrow, I won't put the kettle on yet.' It was a ritual they'd got into, her counting the takings and him restocking shelves before he left to go back to The Black Bear. But they were working well together, he had to admit it.

'It won't take me long. Put it on anyway.'

'You looks like you lost a shilling and found a penny. What's up, Bri?'

'I can't get used to wearing this hat indoors.'

'You only wear it in the shop so the regulars don't know you've 'ad a dye job. You can take it off in a minute, you daft lump. Actually, you looks quite tasty in that get up.' Daisy set the till drawer on the table and pushed a strand of blonde hair back behind one ear. She pulled the chair closer to the table and sat down. She started counting out the money. Bri didn't move.

'I ain't gonna run away with the fucking takings,' she said. He shuffled off down the stairs.

'How have we done?' he asked when he came back. He tugged at his hat and breathed a sigh of relief as he was able to run his fingers through his hair. He stuffed the hat in his back pocket, and looked at the neat piles of coins and notes lined on the table.

'Bloody 'ell. That's more than I usually take on a good day. Should have 'ad you as an attraction on me stall a long time ago, Daisy.'

She sighed. 'Get off with you. This is hard work on me feet. I forgot how bleeding tiring it is standing all day, I can't wait to soak 'em in a bowl of salt water.'

'Go on then. I'll just make a note of what books I should be looking for at Chichester, tomorrow.' There was a Christmas Fayre, always a good venue to pick up books. He saw Daisy open her lips to say something then close her mouth tightly.

'Will you stop worrying?' he said. 'I've got everything in hand. Now we've got a chequebook in Roy Kemp's name I'll go first to the wholesaler's in Portsmouth to buy kitchen wares. Then on to Southsea for bed linens and fancy goods. They won't deliver immediately because they'll wait for the cheques to clear. Come to think of it, I might even pay them in cash,' he said. 'The Christmas Fayre isn't until two in the afternoon so I'll have plenty of time to get back here and change out of that posh suit that makes me look like a fuckin' gangster. An' I'll remember to park the van up the road at the wholesaler's so the managers think I've come in a posh car.' He saw the relief spread over Daisy's face and a smile return to her lips. 'In three or four days the back of this place and the lock-up in Seahorse Street will be full of stock for me to flog on.'

He started humming an old song, 'Wheel of Fortune'.

'Please don't do that!' He stared at Daisy. She was trembling.

'What's up with you?'

'I . . . I don't like that song.'

'It's only a song.'

'Please?'

He shrugged. If she didn't want him humming, so be it. Sometimes women could be funny buggers.

'I'm going to get a bowl of water for me feet.' Daisy waved towards the money and the notebook she'd been totting up figures in. 'You check it, but I reckon we've 'ad a cracking day.'

'Fancy some fish and chips? I could go along to The Porthole?'

'Dutch eel for me,' called Daisy.

Bri watched her walking towards the bathroom in her tight black trousers and black chunky polo-necked sweater. Absentmindedly he started to hum 'Wheel of Fortune' again. Then he remembered the Kay Starr song had been Eddie's favourite tune. If he wasn't whistling it, Eddie was tunelessly singing it. What a thoughtless bastard he'd been for not realising it would upset her.

He picked up Bertie who snuggled into his neck.

'Good girl, ain't you?' He was rewarded with a loud purr and a head nudge. The cat had blossomed. During the day she kept vigil on the counter in the shop but as soon as they closed up she'd come upstairs with Daisy.

Daisy wandered in with a steaming bowl of water

and her trousers rolled up to the knees. She sat down with a contented sigh.

'What do you think about Christmas?' she asked.

'What about it?'

'There you go, answering a question with a question. You're as bad as Vera.'

'Me mum wants to cook, she wants to make it special. An' for you an' Vera to be there as well.'

He was interrupted by fierce banging on the shop door downstairs.

'Stay where you are. I'll see who it is.' He looked down from the window into the street and saw Vera, hopping about like a demented sparrow. 'It's Vera. She looks upset.' He made for the door.

Spilling water and without bothering to wipe her feet Daisy jumped up and ran down the stairs after him. Bri opened the door and Vera fell into his arms.

'You've got to come. Jacky's in a bad way.'

'I'm not her minder,' Bri said. The look that Vera gave him told him he'd said the wrong thing again.

'What's up?' asked Daisy.

'Just come, Dais. Please?' She looked down at Daisy's bare feet.

'I'll get me shoes,' Daisy said.

Within seconds all three were running along the street to the open door next to the tobacconist's shop.

'I warn you. It's not a pretty sight,' Vera said breathlessly.

At first Bri thought it was a bundle of rags on Jacky's unkempt bed. As he drew closer he saw her ashen face and open staring eyes. As Jacky recognised him, he saw those eyes pool with tears.

'Get out of the way, Bri,' snapped Daisy. 'Let the dog see the rabbit.' She pushed him roughly aside and made room for Vera. Vera bent down and touched Jacky's forehead. Bri could smell stale sweat and the metallic stench of blood.

'She's got a fuckin' fever,' announced Vera. 'Get out the way, Bri,' she said. 'Better still, make yourself useful and go back to Daisy's place and get some clean bedding. Sheets, pillowcases, towels. Oh, an' one of her old clean nightdresses. A cotton one, not one of them lacy, nylon things. Bring 'em back, and then fetch some warm water in 'ere and make yourself scarce while me an' Daisy gets on with it. Make us a cuppa, or something.' He looked to Daisy for confirmation and she nodded.

It didn't take him long to get back to the shop and gather all the items he'd been told to get from Daisy's flat. Back at Jacky's, the stuff was snatched out of his hands by Vera. Daisy appeared to be examining a now naked Jacky so he looked away out of politeness. He couldn't fail to see she was in a bad way. Blood and bruises covered her body and face. Poor bitch, he thought, whoever did this to her ought to be strung up. He was surprised he felt so angry about it. When he found out who'd inflicted this on Jacky he'd bloody kill the fuckers.

In the kitchen he started running water in the sink until it reached a decent temperature, then he rinsed out a bowl, filled it and took it back to the bedroom.

'Tea,' snarled Daisy. He almost turned tail. 'On second thoughts I'm sure you've seen a naked woman before.' What he saw nearly made him heave. Jacky was covered in small pus holes all over the upper parts of her body. Her lower regions were badly bruised and cut, especially around her pubic area. Daisy had Jacky stood up and when she turned her in her arms, he saw the marks on her back. They could only have been caused by a whip or something similar, he guessed. Dried blood was crusted over her entire body except where it was oozing and poppy red.

'Fuckin' hell,' he said. 'What cunt did this?'

No one answered him though Vera said quietly to Daisy, 'You think Roy Kemp 'as anything to do with this?' Daisy shook her head.

'I'm willing to bet this is nothing to do with him.'

'Fair enough. Watch 'er, Dais, I'm runnin' down the road to get Henry.'

Daisy nodded at her and said to Bri, 'Jacky won't let us send for an ambulance. Can you hold her up straight while I change this bed?' He nodded, and Daisy transferred Jacky from her own arms to his. 'Don't let her fall, for Christ's sake.'

Jacky sagged against him. Her naked skin was hot and her hair stank of piss. He held her away from the bed as best he could while Daisy spread the clean sheets and changed pillow cases. All the time he was holding Jacky her eyes had neither blinked, nor left his face. It seemed to him she had given up.

Together they gently lifted Jacky and laid her on the bed.

'On her side, I think,' Bri said. It was difficult to decide which part of her body would hurt least when it came in contact with the surface of the bed covers. Footsteps sounded on the stairs and Vera emerged with a small man, balding, grey-eyed and heavy-jawed. He carried a doctor's black bag. Bri thought he could smell whisky on the man's breath.

'Thank God you've not tried to wash her yet,' he said.

'We waited for you.' Daisy showed him the bowl of water and clean cloths.

'Let me get on with it then.' He stared pointedly at Bri. Bri took that to mean he was to disappear. He thought of the dirty kitchen and unwashed pots. Vera followed him out.

'You wash and I'll wipe,' she said. 'They don't need us.'

Bri asked, 'Who's he?' He upended soap powder into the sink and ran hot water and began scrubbing plates.

'Friend of mine. Good bloke. He won't say anything.'

'Does it really matter if he does talk to the police about this? Whoever did that to her wants stringing up.'

'You got a short memory, Bri. Didn't Eddie teach you nothin'? She's been done over. If she says anything, it won't be her injuries what kills 'er. Jacky's not fuckin' stupid. An' I don't really think you wants any coppers nosing around you or Daisy, do you?' He shook his head. His first thought had been for Jacky. Momentarily he'd forgotten about the scam.

'But this can't go unpunished.' He understood the delicate situation Daisy and he were in, but Jacky? Poor, poor bitch. What had she done to deserve this?

'Jacky really don't want no bother. She made me promise.'

'Vera, she don't know what fucking day it is.'

'That's the drugs. She 'ad enough sense to get 'ome, though.'

'How come you found her?'

'I was on my way round to you to say I met your mum in town an' she'd been nattering on about

Christmas. I 'ad to pass Jacky's an' the door was open. That ain't right, I thought. So I came up an' 'ere she was.'

'Lucky you did. And it's a good job you know this doctor then. I trust he'll keep quiet?'

Vera laughed. The sound eased the tension between them.

'He'll be the soul of discretion, if only 'cause he'll be gettin' paid for this in cash.'

'Why?'

'On account he's been struck off.'

Bri knew he was gawping with his mouth open so he closed it and got stuck into the washing-up. As he washed and scrubbed and set the pots on the wooden draining board for Vera to dry and put away he realised this was probably the doctor all the local toms relied on. Thank God for Vera's know-how, he thought.

Afterwards he searched in vain for tea and milk then came to the conclusion there wasn't any.

'I'm off to Daisy's for provisions,' he said.

Later, after cleaning the kitchen and making tea, Vera perched herself on the edge of the table and Bri sat on a stool listening to the muffled sounds coming from the bedroom. Eventually the door opened.

Daisy came through and swilled the bowl of bloody water away. She looked tired. There were dark circles beneath her eyes and deep furrows across her forehead. She was followed into the kitchen by the doctor who was wiping his hands on a bloodied towel.

'Is she going to be all right?' Bri asked him.

'This is Doctor Henry Dillinger,' Vera said to Bri. 'We've known each other for years. If he can't sort 'er out no one can.' The man looked embarrassed. He looked at the dirty towel he was using and turned on the hot tap and began washing his hands with soap. Bri set a clean towel on the draining board for him and the doctor acknowledged his thanks with a nod.

'Shouldn't normally talk about a patient, you know,' he said, 'but we're all friends here. And I can't be reprimanded for it, can I? She thinks it was drawing pins stuck in her. Remembers waking at some time tied to a chair. Luckily she can't or doesn't want to remember much more. There's drugs out there now that can do that, take away all memory of attacks. She's got a fever and she's been drugged but a decent sleep will help her. Luckily she'd already spewed up a lot of the substances. She's been badly assaulted. I've cleaned her up and stitched her but she'll need looking after. There's drugs and creams on the bedside table and I'll call back tomorrow. She's lucky she's a fit young woman. And I don't have to say she's twice as lucky to be alive.'

'You won't say anything?' Vera had her hand on his arm.

He shook his head at her. 'You know you can trust me.'

'Always have,' she replied.

Vera put the polishing rag down and examined her nails. Thank God she hadn't chipped one. She looked about her at the clean room.

'That's better,' she said. 'Can't abide dirt.' Cleanliness was one of the reasons Vera had made a good living on the game and she knew it. Being fastidious in her habits, making sure the blokes always wore johnnies and having regular check-ups herself were things she swore by. Now she made sure her girls were just as clean.

Vera wasn't stupid. Jacky was on the game.

She went and sat by the side of Jacky's bed. She'd closed the windows now the flat smelled sweeter. After staying with Jacky all night, kipping on the lumpy sofa, her back was giving her gyp. But she could spare the time to look after Jacky. After all, what if she herself ever needed looking after? Daisy would do it for her, but Jacky didn't have anyone else and Daisy had work to do. So did Vera, she had a salon to run. But Sam, Margo and Kirsty were good girls. Robin might get a bit lairy and Madam ZaZa have a few too many gins but they could carry on all right without her for a while. She'd phoned and told them she'd be along to Heavenly Bodies later.

What she couldn't understand was why didn't Jacky keep this place clean? Nice little flat it was as well. Not like the caff. That place hadn't been modernised and it had gone from bad to worse now Daisy wasn't the owner any more. When she and Daisy lived there they'd kept the place clean, and Daisy was forever washing them stairs down with Zoflora disinfectant or Jeyes Fluid.

She put her hand to Jacky's face and pushed a strand of blonde hair away from her eyes. Jacky was still a pretty woman. Or was, before this. But Henry had done a good job. When all the swelling went down and her body was healed, she'd be all right. Not sure about her mind, though. Trauma like that could leave nasty scars. Jacky was like an over-ripe peach, she thought. And now she had the finger marks to show where she'd been handled too often. She'd been a right sassy girl once and now she was running to fat, just like her mother.

'Vera?' Jacky was staring at her.

'Shh, you're all right now.'

'Am I?'

''Course you are. You're with me, ain't you?' Jacky gave her a weak smile. 'Want to talk about it? Though by rights you should still be sleeping the pain away. I made some Bovril. An' you ain't sayin' a dicky bird 'til you've 'ad a drop.' Vera bustled along to the kitchen and came back with a mug of the dark beefy liquid.

'It ain't boiling 'ot so you can sip it down easily. Lift yer 'ead. I don't want to touch you in case I hurts you.'

Tears welled in Jacky's eyes.

'Stop that and drink this.' Briskness was Vera's way of dealing with sentimentality and pain. She'd always tried to hide her feelings. Except where Kibbles was concerned, and of course Daisy. She held the mug to Jacky's lips until it was nearly drained of liquid.

'That's a good girl. I'd have made some chicken soup but you got sod all to eat in your cupboards and I didn't want to leave you.'

Vera placed the mug on the bedside table. 'Now, Jacky, I know what you been doin' to make extra money. I wasn't born yesterday.'

'You won't tell Bri, will you?'

Vera stared at her for a long time before answering.

'Bri's a good bloke. Whether you gets hold of him or not he deserves to be told the truth. Daisy knows what you been up to an' all, only because she ain't stupid either. I got where I am today by opening me legs, but I ain't never got beat up like you did. No one should 'ave to go through that. Who did this?'

'You won't say nothin'?'

'No.'

'I got into debt with Sammy. The markets ain't all they're cracked up to be an' a few days' rain can cripple you. Then me van was off the road. I didn't 'ave the cash for another gearbox and Sammy lent me the money. Then he added interest until he was taking a lot of money off me.'

'You one of 'is stable of girls? Or rather, Roy Kemp's girls?'

Jacky shook her head. 'I'm not one of Roy Kemp's whores.'

'Part-timer?'

'Yes.' Jacky's eyes grew huge. 'I 'ad to pay off me debts. Sammy lets me use the place.'

Vera thought for a moment. 'I bet you owes even more money now?'

Jacky sighed. 'It's the interest.'

'The bastard!' Vera said. She smoothed Jacky's hair again.

'I went over to the caff and done me punters but Sammy wouldn't pay me. Everyone's after me for fuckin' cash...' Jacky started crying.

'There, there,' soothed Vera. She'd already looked through the unpaid bills behind the clock on Jacky's mantelpiece, and she'd seen the empty fridge and food cabinet.

'I 'ad a go at him. He knocked me senseless. But that was after he'd given me red wine. Then, I remember waking up in a chair, tied up. He'd hurt me. I could see that. But funny thing was I didn't feel like I was hurting, not then. Then I remember being on the grass outside Holy Trinity Church and tryin' to get home.'

'Do you remember what happened with the blokes?' Vera could see by Jacky's frown she obviously didn't. Thank God for that, thought Vera. At least that's one blessing.

'I remember thinkin' I had gold buttons all over me.'

'Not that. Do you remember what they did to you? You're torn up pretty bad. Any ATM?'

'Arse to mouth? I don't do that, Vera. Golden showers, I don't mind, if the money's good.'

'It looks like they've had a good ol' party at your expense. You was in a right state. Mess all over you. Only good thing, perhaps, is that you never knew.'

Vera smoothed her forehead.

'Vera?' Jacky's voice was a whisper. 'Thank you.'

Vera looked down at her and her heart melted. Poor bitch had had a hard life. She looked away but didn't stop smoothing Jacky's forehead.

'You'd 'ave done the same for me. Now shut up.' Her voice had a strangled quality to it. She cleared her throat. 'You can 'ave another painkiller in a little while. But nothing else until whatever that bastard give you is right out of your system.'

Jackie managed to move her head. 'How come you're here?'

'You left the door open,' Vera said. 'I was on me way round Daisy's about Christmas. Bri's mum has invited me and Daisy round for dinner. You can come an' all now, Queenie won't mind, but only if you promise to go to sleep now. Sleep it all away.' Then she bent down and kissed Jacky on the forehead. 'C'mon, shut your eyes.'

Vera got up and took the mug into the kitchen. She sat on a chair and put her hands over her ears to shut out the sound of Jacky's crying. She knew if she didn't manage to blot it all out, she'd start crying as well.

CHAPTER 14

'Violet? I'm so sorry. You'll be thinking I meant to bloody nick your brooch. Only that's not true at all. I'm just sorting me clothes out properly after moving into the flat above the shop and blow me down if it ain't still pinned to me dress.' Daisy fingered the expensive diamond brooch. It twinkled and winked at her beneath the electric light.

'Keep it, Daisy. Looked better on you than it ever did on me.' Daisy took the telephone away from her ear and looked at it as though she couldn't believe what was coming from it.

'I can't possibly do that, it must 'ave cost fucking thousands. An' it was a birthday present to you from Roy. I'm bringing it back . . . That's right, tomorrow.'

Daisy replaced the phone in its cradle and went in search of Bri. She found him in the kitchen making a sandwich.

'Want one?' he said.

Daisy looked at the doorstep he was cutting and shook her head.

'I'm driving up to London tomorrow.' Just then the phone rang. She sighed and trekked back into the shop. This time it was Roy Kemp.

'All right, Dais?' Bri asked when she returned. He

spoke through a mouthful of bread and cheddar cheese.

'Yes, I'm fine, but correction,' Daisy said. 'Roy Kemp is coming down to collect me tomorrow. His mum 'as decided we're going out.'

'Somewhere nice?'

'Bloody boxing match!'

'Didn't know you liked boxing?'

'Neither did I,' she replied. But her thoughts went back to her last visit to London and Valentine Waite.

'You sure you're all right, you look a bit flushed?'

'Said I was all right, didn't I?' She flounced back into the shop. Saved by the bell, she thought, as the doorbell jangled and a customer entered.

She thought about Valentine Waite and what might have happened if they hadn't been disturbed in the corridor of the club. Would they have made love? Perhaps love was overstated and only reserved for her and Eddie but there was no denying Val had certainly aroused her senses. Daisy wondered how it was possible to have sex with a man if you didn't particularly like him? Or did she like him but didn't know it? And was it possible she didn't know as much about men as she thought she did?

'Eddie, you're a bastard,' she said so quietly she knew no one else would overhear. 'You spoilt me for everyone else. I wish you were here now, I bloody need you.' A tear threatened and she brushed it away. The customer approached.

'Thank you,' Daisy said. The woman was giving her a strange look but Daisy popped the book into a paper bag and put the money in the till, then watched as the woman left the shop.

She wasn't sure how she felt about all this close

contact with Roy and his mother, but she couldn't cut them out of her life at this point because Roy would definitely smell a rat and think she was up to something. Anyway, what had Eddie said? 'Keep your friends close and your enemies closer.' Of course she liked Violet, with her cooking and the lashings of love that she doled out to her chosen ones like a second mother. And Roy? She had to admit he was a fair man – for a gangster. His business was what it was, simply a business that he ran smoothly. She'd never forget the first time she'd met him at his house. He'd taken her breath away with the sexuality that oozed from every pore. No wonder his wife, Daisy's friend Moira, had been possessive of him. And Daisy had to admit, another time, another place and without Eddie, she too might have fallen beneath the bastard's spell. But he was still married. Moira might be a very sick lady and living in Spain but Roy was *her* husband.

'Anything untoward happening in my cafe premises, Daisy?'

Charles, the chauffeur, was driving as usual and Daisy and Roy were sitting in the back of Roy's gleaming silver Humber. Daisy shook her head and wished she hadn't promised Jacky and Vera she'd keep quiet about the assault on Jacky. If there was one person who could sort Sammy out, it was Roy. After all, Sammy worked for Roy, didn't he? Still, Jacky's silence meant that Roy wouldn't be hanging about in Gosport, which was all the better for Daisy and what she needed.

'Violet said something about going to a fight?'

He turned to look at her again and slipped one of his tanned hands over hers. The smells from the leather interior of the car and Roy's cologne were both expensive and subtle. She smiled at him.

'Mum's partial to boxing matches. She used to make Charlie Kray give me boxing lessons with Ronnie and Reggie. He was pretty good, you know, Charlie was. Later on she got a proper trainer for me. Harry Collins only weighed about ten stone an' his face was a terrible mess, broken nose, scars, lost teeth, the lot. But he would spar with any fighter. Us three boys learned a lot from him. The two Violets would be in the front row cheering us on. Ron and Reg once fought each other. They was about sixteen at the time and their old lady went mad about that as you can imagine. But she let them build a gym in the back room at Vallance Road. I used to get round there before six in the mornings to train with them. Mum would have liked me to be a professional boxer until I persuaded her there was more money to be made outside the ring.'

'Is this how come you know Valentine Waite?' Daisy felt the sudden pressure of Roy's hand as she mentioned Valentine's name. Then he took it away. It was like her words had touched him on a nerve end. She turned towards him and his eyes were cold.

'Like him, do you, Daisy?'

'He's an attractive man.'

'He's an unknown quantity, Daisy.'

'What do you mean?'

'Celebrities flock about the twins like flies around shit. It don't mean they like the people that are hanging about. Sometimes they tolerate people because they're useful to them. Valentine Waite's like that.'

'He seemed all right.'

'He owns a club and a couple of breakers' yards. He gets motors for the twins. He's an empty shell.'

'Nothing wrong with owning scrapyards.' What did he mean, an empty shell? She wondered why Roy didn't like him.

'No, there ain't. Scrap made a fortune for the Richardsons. Charlie's proud of his roots and he has every right to be.'

'But you don't like Valentine Waite?'

'He might have gained fame as a boxer but there's something about him I can't quite get to the bottom of. Anyway, all I'm saying is you be careful. 'Course I know I don't need to tell you . . .'

'No, you fucking don't, Roy Kemp. Anyway I only accepted this invite 'cause Violet asked me an' because I realised I still had 'er diamond brooch, and here you go practically telling me I shouldn't make new friends . . .'

He put his fingers over her lips to stem her flow of words.

'New friends, old friends, which brings me to this,' he said. Then fumbling inside his coat breast pocket he brought out a long blue velvet box. He handed it to her. 'Open it.'

Inside was a gold necklace with ruby drops. It was fragile, but Daisy knew it must have cost the earth. 'This a present for your mum?'

'Would I be giving it to you if it was?'

Daisy gasped. 'It's never for me?'

'Don't you like it?' He looked hurt.

''*Course* I like it – but I can't take it.'

'Why?'

Daisy wanted to say because you killed my Eddie an' I'm about to pay you back for it.

'Because I can't.'

'Not even if I say Mum picked it out, my suggestion, of course? I like to buy gifts for friends and I don't have anyone else to buy pretty things for.'

Neither of them spoke but Daisy knew he was thinking about Moira and the gifts they used to buy each other before she became unhinged. Now Daisy was in a quandary. If she didn't take it, he'd remember later when the shit hit the fan that she'd turned away from his friendship. She didn't want to think about the consequences of that. Daisy reached out and with the back of her hand smoothed his cheek. His slate-grey eyes held hers.

'It's very beautiful,' she said. 'Put it on for me.'

'It didn't seem right taking back Mum's brooch an' leaving you with nothing. She likes you, Daisy.'

He fiddled with the clasp at the back of her neck and she ran her fingers over the smooth stones.

'I like her an' all, but because I've accepted this gift it don't mean nothing, understand? I don't want no strings about our relationship. We're just mates, okay?'

He laughed. 'Mates and no strings, Daisy.'

Why, she wondered, did she think he was laughing at her?

Charles the chauffeur dropped them in front of the Hilton Hotel and carried on round the back to park the car. Violet was waiting in the bar and waved to them as they entered. She got up from her seat and came towards them, clasping Daisy to her bosom in a cloud of violet-scented perfume.

'Come and sit down, dear. I've saved you a chair next to me. Sort the drinks, son,' she said to Roy after she'd finished hugging him as well.

'I've no idea what to expect, Violet.' Daisy sipped at her brandy and lime. Violet touched the necklace at Daisy's throat and winked at Roy.

'Suits you, dear. So you never been to a boxing match before, dear?'

Reggie Kray looks very good tonight, thought Daisy. There was a softness about him, especially in the way he was behaving towards the pretty young woman sitting next to him. He could hardly take his eyes off her.

Daisy shook her head at Violet's question. 'No, never,' she said.

'We'll have to get you out and about a bit more. You only got one life, you know. Make the most of it before you're pushing up them daisies, Daisy!' Violet gave one of her full-throated chuckles and nudged the other Violet, the twins' mother. They both laughed.

Roy said, 'You know everyone here, Daisy, except Frances.'

The young woman gave a shy smile then huddled closer to Reggie on the velvet seat.

'Hello,' Daisy said. She thought the woman was nervous. She was younger than Daisy, barely out of her teens, she guessed. Frances was very pretty and wearing a glittery cream sheath dress. Daisy suddenly felt quite old in her tight black dress with its satin bow beneath her bustline and the black stole around her shoulders.

'Reggie and Frances are going to get married,' Roy told her.

'That's really lovely,' said Daisy, turning towards the couple. 'Anyone can see how devoted you are to each other.' The girl blushed and fiddled with her upswept blonde hair do as though it had miraculously escaped from its lacquered style. 'I love your dress,' Daisy added.

Before Frances could speak, Reggie said, 'I bought it for her. I choose all her clothes.'

'Well, you made a good choice, there,' said Daisy. Though she wasn't sure she'd want a man picking out all her clothes, no matter how much she loved him. She remembered Eddie buying her dresses that time in Southampton, telling her to choose whatever she wanted, and that he would pay for them. But he'd left the final decisions to her. A bout of loneliness stole over her. She took another sip at her drink and told herself not to be so silly and to enjoy the evening.

She looked around the crowded bar, seeing many of the same faces remembered from the previous party she'd been invited to. Only this time Ronnie Kray wasn't there; neither was Valentine Waite.

'I expected we'd be going to a big hall somewhere, not a hotel.'

'This is a private function, Daisy, and the hotel caters for boxing matches and anything else a punter can pay for. We'll be taking our seats shortly.' Roy squeezed her hand.

Sandwiched between Violet and Roy, Daisy had a good view of the crowded and noisy cocktail lounge. Most of the men were in dinner jackets and their women in glamorous dresses. There was a scent of expectancy in the air along with the cigarette smoke and heavy perfume.

'That necklace looks a treat on you, dear,' Violet Kray said. 'Don't she look lovely, Vi?' Daisy felt herself blush.

'You shouldn't let Roy spend his money on me. Though it is quite special, thank you,' Daisy agreed.

She smiled into Violet's eyes. An attack of nerves suddenly ran through her body. How could she ever think of being such a bitch to Violet when all the woman had ever done was treat her like a daughter? She looked away. As her eyes scanned the room they were suddenly held by Vinnie Endersby.

He was sitting at a corner table flanked by two men. One was remarkably chubby but around the same age as Vinnie, and the other older, more severe looking, with curly dark hair and bushy eyebrows. He looked like a boxer, she decided. Vinnie raised his glass to her. He had on a dinner jacket and it made him look so handsome. Of all the people to run into in the whole of fucking London, she thought, it has to be a copper from the nick round the corner in Gosport!

'Who you starin' at, Daisy? You must 'ave a thing about boxers. You know who that is over there, don't you?' Daisy shook her head. Did Roy mean Vinnie? No he couldn't, could he? But the dark-haired man with Vinnie did look familiar to her.

'Come on, let's go an' have a chat with Freddie. He's a mate of mine.' The penny dropped. Freddie Mills! Of course, but why was he with Vinnie Endersby? Roy had slipped from his seat and was waiting for Daisy to stand up.

He guided her in front of him towards the table in the corner.

'Hello, Freddie,' he said. 'Like a drink?' Roy was obviously including the other two men. The plump one nodded. Vinnie shook his head and Freddie said, 'Let me buy you one, Roy. And who's this pretty little thing?'

Roy looked proudly at her as though she was more than his guest for the evening. Daisy smiled nervously at Vinnie who had a twinkle in his strange but gorgeous eyes.

'This is Daisy Lane from Gosport, Freddie.' The boxer rose lightly to his feet and shook her hand. His touch was warm. Daisy's heart was thumping so loudly she was sure they would all hear it.

'These are a couple of mates of mine,' he said waving towards the chubby bloke. 'Mickey, and George is the other pretty one, besides me, that is.' He laughed as Vinnie got up and took Daisy's hand.

'Pleased to meet you, Daisy,' he said. 'Gosport's that little town across the ferry from Portsmouth, ain't it?'

So this is the way we're playing the game are we, thought Daisy? You don't know me and I don't know you, Vinnie Endersby. And your name is George.

'Gosport's a nice place. You should visit sometime,' she said. She saw the relief flood into his odd-coloured eyes. Vinnie gripped her fingers just a little tighter than was necessary. If he didn't want these men to know who he really was, it was no business of hers.

'I might do that, one of these days,' he said and let her go.

Just then a buzzer sounded. Daisy felt Roy's hand lightly touch her waist.

'We'll have to take our seats now,' he said. His voice was soft against her ear. To the others he said, 'I'll have a bottle of bubbly sent over to you but I gotta get my old lady settled in her ringside seat. You know what the two Vis are like about their boxing.'

Soon the auditorium was filled with noise and more cigarette smoke. The two boxers came in to be introduced amid cheers and boos. Dark skin was glistening with health and perspiration as the two men

172

air-punched and danced round the ring to the delight of the crowd. Both the Violets were sitting forward on their seats shouting loudly at the two fighters.

When the match began Daisy immediately knew she wouldn't be able to sit through it to the end, no matter how long or how short it would be.

In a flurry of brightly coloured silk shorts and laced boots the two magnificent men seemed intent on killing each other with fists of steel encased in gloves.

'Heavyweights,' said Roy, speaking close to her ear.

Just when Daisy thought she couldn't bear to watch the massacre any more, the bell would sound and they'd retire to their corners to be swabbed and watered and dictated to.

And then it would begin again and Daisy could hear the terminology of the boxing fraternity echoing over the noise of the exhilarated, bloodthirsty crowd. Upper cuts, hooks, swings, straight jabs. She couldn't believe any man would want to take punishment like this. She saw blood spurting from one of the boxer's cut eyebrows. His opponent kept on jabbing at it until the bright red fluid was streaming down his face.

The first three rounds were gruelling enough. In the fourth round one of the fighters swung again and again, jerking the head of his adversary, then threw punches to his body which caused the heavy man to sag to the canvas. Daisy saw the referee count to eight before she finally got up and squeezed through the mad throng of people to run out into the foyer. No more, no more, she was crying inside her head. She found the ladies' lavatory and pushed open the door of the nearest cubicle and was sick in the bowl. After a while she got up from the cold lino and pulled the chain. She sat down on the toilet seat and put her head on to her knees. She was breathing deeply, trying to shut the scenes from her mind, of the blood, the noise, the sickening smell. Then she heard Roy's voice and the sound of the cubicle doors being opened one by one.

'Daisy, where are you?' She scrambled to her feet and opened the door. He pushed a hand through his dark hair and said, 'I've been worried sick about you.'

Daisy fell into his arms.

'It's horrible. I can't go back in there. Don't make me.'

He pushed her away from him. His eyes held hers.

'Daisy, you don't ever have to do anything you don't want to do. Not when I'm around.' She tried a small grin. The memory of the boxing match imprinted in her mind, the fists, the blood, the sounds, the spittle. She wanted to tell him how much it had frightened her, how glad she was to see him, but instead she tried to joke.

'And I'm worried about you. This is the ladies' and you shouldn't be in here.'

'Bugger what anyone thinks,' he said. He pointed to an upholstered sofa in the waiting area where the mirrors and washbasins were. 'Sit down, there.' Then he took tissues from a fancy dispenser and wetted them beneath a tap. Standing in front of her he carefully wiped her forehead and her mouth and she didn't resist. Then he threw the tissues into the wastepaper basket beneath the vanity unit.

Daisy didn't think she could argue with him even if she wanted to. If he'd taken off her clothes and washed her all over, she'd have let him. She felt as weak as a kitten and her head was thumping. She sank back into the depths of the sofa and he sat down beside her. He picked up her hand.

'You really didn't like that, did you?' Normally she would have come back at him with some clever answer but she didn't have any more clever answers left in her.

'No.'

'Want to know why they do it? The fighters?' He didn't wait for her to speak but went on, 'For some men it's the only way out of the poverty trap. Not just our own boys but the American blacks, the Irish, especially them. We learn the art of survival in back alleys, Daisy. Kill or be killed. The last man standing takes the money and eats tomorrow, gets the best women, the best clothes, the biggest motor.'

'But they're killing each other . . .'

'It's a cold-blooded occupation true enough, Daisy. But there's also an art to it. And if the man's ambitious enough, clever enough, there's plenty of money to be made. Chasing a dream, Daisy. We all do it. Even Nipper Read has many, many trophies for boxing.'

'Even Freddie Mills? Is he chasing dreams?'

'Freddie didn't come from a poor family, Daisy. But he wanted to do it. Wanted to fight so badly he wouldn't be discouraged. Come on. Let's get out of here and get a drink. Or would you rather I drove you home?'

'No!' If Daisy allowed herself to be driven home so early it might spoil Violet's evening. She didn't want to do that. 'A drink would be nice.'

'Shall I stay while you put on a bit of paint and powder or shall I wait outside?'

'Stay,' she said, opening her clutch bag and scraping her comb through her hair. A dab of powder and a quick wipe of lipstick and she was ready. She smiled at Roy in the mirror. 'Here am I in a London ladies' toilet with a big-shot gangster waiting while I make me face up,' she said. 'I don't do this every day.'

He laughed. 'Not only that, madam,' and he gave her a broad wink, 'but the gangster has one of his men outside telling the ladies to form an orderly queue while you're doing it.'

CHAPTER 15

Vinnie Endersby saw her before she spotted him. For a few moments he watched her laughing with the man on the fish stall. She was a sight for sore eyes, he thought. Blonde hair swinging about her pretty face, her cheeks russet with the cold wind whipping against them and her eyes sparkling. She took the package wrapped in newspaper and waved a cheery goodbye and set off further into the town. He noted her neat figure enveloped in the tightly belted fawn raincoat and the small, quick steps she took in the black patent high heels, her seamed stockings perfectly straight. At first he thought he'd call out to her but decided, what with the stallholders shouting out their Christmas wares, she wouldn't hear him. The market was a noisy crush of bargain hunters carrying bags and packages and he had to move quickly to catch up with her.

She'd just turned into Bemisters Lane when he managed to reach her.

'Christmas shopping, Daisy?' She turned at the sound of her name but he was disappointed she didn't give him a smile.

'Cat,' she said, showing him the newspaper-wrapped parcel. He must have looked confused. 'Fish for the cat,' she said and laughed. 'Not like you to be so slow on the uptake, is it?'

'And thank God you're not,' he said. 'I appreciate you keeping quiet that night in the London hotel.'

'Did you think I might not?'

'I don't know you well enough to answer that, do I?'

'S'pose not,' she said. He noticed how very white her teeth were. A sudden gust of wind took hold of the stallholder's canvas sheet and tore it away from the metal clip. The sheet flapped dangerously close to Daisy and he pulled her towards him and out of harm's way.

'You don't know me well enough for this either,' she said stepping away from his arms. No, he thought but I wouldn't mind.

'Fancy a cuppa out of this wind?' Vinnie didn't know he was going to say the words until they'd rolled from his tongue and he was even more surprised when she said, 'All right.'

'Where?'

'They do a good strong brew in The Dive. You can buy me a sticky bun with butter in to go with it,' she said. 'Or don't a copper's pay allow for life's little luxuries?'

'What you really mean by that remark is, was I moonlighting and somehow making a bit of money on the side when I was chatting to Freddie Mills in London, don't you?'

'Perhaps you are beginning to know me,' she laughed. And taking his arm she pushed him in the direction of the ferry.

As they neared the end of the High Street the wind was cutting down the alleys and many of the stallholders had concrete blocks and weights roped over their stalls to hold them down. What an awful day for a market trader to try to make a living, Vinnie thought. There was sleet in the wind now, blowing straight in from the Solent. He could smell fish and chips from The Porthole cafe and realised how hungry he was. Across the strip of water separating Portsmouth from Gosport the boats were riding on the waves like bob apples in a barrel at an Autumn Fayre. The water was the colour of grey sludge. He certainly wouldn't fancy being out in a boat on a day like this.

Daisy paused at the entrance to The Dive cafe. Then she descended the flight of stone steps as the cafe was in an underground passage below the old market house. Run for years by the same family, the place was renowned for its tea and buns and good service and was the haunt of the local bus conductors and taxi drivers.

Vinnie did the ordering while Daisy found a couple of seats. His mouth watered at the array of fresh and wholesome food for sale. He decided on the fragant butter-filled currant buns.

'Thank God we're out of the bleeding wind,' Daisy said, stirring her cup of tea. A halo of brightness from the electric light behind her shone around her head. She looked like an angel, Vinnie thought.

He took a bite of the soft currant bun and licked his lips. 'You're right, this is good.'

'Don't your missus make you nice things to eat?' Daisy was fiddling with her coat, pulling the front of it straight across her knees. She looked at him. He could smell her perfume, it was more delicious than the aromatic scent of the bun.

'When I had a wife, she never liked to cook.'

'If I'm supposed to say Oh, I am sorry, forget it. I

had a fella and he didn't cook neither an' you won't find me looking for sympathy!'

'Why are you always so prickly? So on the defensive?'

Daisy stared at him for a moment then burst out laughing before she raised a hand and pushed her fingers through her hair, which did no good at all as it quickly fell back over her forehead.

'S'pose I asked for that,' she said.

He nodded. 'You going to tell me why you were with that lot of London undesirables?'

'Only if you tell me how come you an' the great Freddie Mills is such good mates?' She was looking at him while he took a swig of the tea, which was thick, brown and sweet just the way he liked it. He put the cup down on the saucer and undid his coat. The cafe was warm, dimly lit and intimate, with only one other couple sitting nearer the door and the tea counter.

'As we're on our own here now, I'll be frank,' he said. 'What you tell me and I say to you goes no further, okay?' He saw furrows crease her forehead.

'Your word against mine? 'Cause we're alone?'

'If that's the way you want to see it?'

'Okay,' Daisy said. 'It ain't no secret, Roy Kemp bought the caff off me. I was mates with his wife before she went abroad to recover from a breakdown. His mum likes me so we all see each other now and then. That horrible fucking massacre of a boxing match was the first and last one I'll ever see . . .'

'You involved with Roy Kemp?'

Daisy laughed. 'What? Like involved as in sleeping with 'im?'

He nodded. He knew he had no right to ask her

personal questions. It would serve him right if she leaned over and slapped him one.

'You're having me on,' she said. 'Ain't you?'

'All right,' he said, surprised at the relief he felt. 'What do you know about him?'

Her lips pressed to a thin line before she said, 'You don't need to interrogate me. I ain't a fucking criminal an' I think that's my business.'

'I'm sorry,' he said. 'What if I told you I know he was behind Eddie's death?' He saw the colour leave her face. She picked up her cup but she couldn't stop her hand shaking. He reached across and steadied it, setting the cup down again on the saucer.

'What if I told you you was right? But is that common knowledge down at South Street nick?'

He shook his head. So Daisy knew Eddie had been killed by Roy Kemp, did she? Yet she was out socialising with the killer and his crowd? Well, one step at a time, Daisy was nobody's fool. There must be a reason why she'd taken up with Roy Kemp. He answered her question.

'To them Eddie's simply a local villain who moved away, end of story. He's not on the books for anything.'

'He thought you had that girl found dead in the boatyard down to 'im.'

'I did at the time. But the possibility that it was an accidental death was also suggested. Of course, he wasn't around when the second girl was found so he definitely had nothing to do with that. You don't believe he killed her, do you?'

Daisy shook her head. 'Don't be daft, why would he? Besides, Vera swore he was home at the caff. That's good enough for me. Vera don't tell no lies.

How come you reckon you know so much about my Eddie an' Roy Kemp, anyway?'

'I'm going to trust you.' He waited for some sign from her. Daisy nodded. 'Before I came down here I was doing some work with Nipper Read.' Vinnie paused again, letting Daisy digest the name and when he saw she was on his wavelength and knew who he was talking about, he said, 'He's a bloody clever copper and he's going to put the twins away. No ifs or buts, he's going to do it. Their business interests are like a spider's web with so many people caught up in it.' He paused. 'In London I'd been investigating the disappearances of prostitutes, with the link being the boxing fraternity. Reggie and Ronnie are always surrounded by celebrities, especially fighters. They used to be quite good themselves, you know?' Daisy nodded. He continued. 'Freddie's got a club, the Freddie Mills Nite Spot, used to be a Chinese restaurant only it was losing money, but not now the twins spend time there. I've got to know Freddie, he's a nice guy, got a lovely wife and family, nice home in south London. I'm down here now and theoretically I'm not on that case any more but I can't simply disappear into thin air when it's taken me a while to get myself known as George Boyd and I thought I was finally getting somewhere.'

'And the fat bloke, he's a copper as well?'

Vinnie nodded.

'But if the girls have simply disappeared, how do you know they been with boxers in the first place?' Vinnie tapped the side of his nose.

'They all worked in that same environment. Pretty much like our Vera, well respected and extremely clean, would never be found soliciting outside St

George's Barracks or the Dockyard. The ferry, yes. These girls always hung around the places where the fights are held.'

'But couldn't the girls have simply moved on?'

'No. I don't think so. One had a little boy she idolised. Always left him with her mother. It was the mother reported her missing. Since the girl had been looking forward to taking her mother and the kiddie away on holiday to Bournemouth and had been on about it for weeks there was no way she'd have run off voluntarily.' Vinnie knew he was taking a chance talking to Daisy like this. Strictly speaking it wasn't on. But also strictly speaking, what he'd told her about the missing women was common knowledge in London. In the public domain, he reckoned the right term was.

'So you're down 'ere in Gosport but keeping a hand in up there in London as well? And you reckon Roy Kemp 'as something to do with these prostitutes' disappearances.'

He shook his head. 'Not his style,' he said. 'But someone close to him and the twins knows something. I'd bet my promotion on that.' Vinnie noted Daisy's cup was now empty. 'Want another tea?'

She shook her head and picked up the wrapped fish from the seat beside her.

'You reckon them girls are dead, don't you?'

He nodded. 'I think we got a killer on the loose.'

'You think the girl in the boatyard . . . ?'

'No. Nor the kiddie. We got two killers on the loose.'

Daisy took a deep breath and let it out slowly. 'Then there's a sadistic bastard here an' your psycho up in the Smoke?' He nodded. Daisy gathered her handbag while not letting go of her parcel containing Bertie's tea. 'This little chat between you and me didn't happen, did it?' Vinnie realised what an astute woman she was. Daisy suddenly smiled and as her eyes held his he felt his heart miss a beat. 'I hope we both sort our different problems out. I still maintain none of this is Roy's style but you already knows that. He makes money from prossies, he don't kill 'em. I gotta go. If I don't get this back for Bertie it'll go off in the heat in 'ere.'

'I also know Roy Kemp thinks a lot of you,' he told her.

'Ah,' Daisy smiled. 'But that don't matter at all if I don't care about him, does it?' She went to gather the cups and the plate but Vinnie stopped her.

'Let me do that,' he said. 'If you need me, you know where I am. Or if I can do anything . . .' He was wondering why she was so ready to jump to Roy Kemp's defence when she replied,

'There is one thing.' She was standing close to him. He saw how small she was, barely reaching his shoulder. She looked up at him with eyes fringed by long dark lashes. There was a sadness there that cut straight through him.

'Yes?'

'If you ever find out where Roy Kemp put my Eddie, please promise you'll let me know?'

CHAPTER 16

'How can I keep my hat on while I eats my Christmas dinner?'

Daisy pushed aside the remains of the wrapping paper and put the scissors in the drawer.

'How can you break your mother's 'eart by showing her you've dyed your hair?' said Daisy. 'Why don't you bend the truth a bit by saying you're keeping your 'at on because you've got alopecia and don't want any more hair to fall out?'

Bri sniffed. 'Nothing's serious with you, is it? I don't think I want to lie to my mother at all, thank you very much. I know! I'll tell her I've got a cold.'

'Ain't that a bleeding lie?'

'Might be.'

'You're funny.' Daisy picked up the last remaining present and put it into a brown carrier bag with the others. She was glad she'd sent money to Maria in Greece and to Susie. Susie had written back straight away telling her the long list of toys she intended buying for Meggie. That kiddie is the apple of her eye, Daisy thought. And why not? Susie was going to make sure she gave her daughter the kind of childhood that Susie had had stolen from her.

Daisy had also driven over to Portchester crematorium and in the quiet of the evergreen garden talked to Kenny about their life together. She'd felt close to him there and before she left she'd placed a wreath beneath a holly tree. Roy Kemp had never divulged Eddie's resting place. Daisy believed he'd take that secret to his own grave, so in her heart, as usual, she talked to Eddie and told him the latest news of his son.

'You nearly finished?'

Daisy snapped back to the task in hand.

'That's it,' she said, 'A blue knitted sweater for Jacky. Marabou-trimmed wedge-heeled slippers for Vera and a pair of silver drop earrings for your mum.'

'What about me?'

'What about you?'

'Present?'

'Forgot.' She hadn't really forgotten. She'd a cable-stitched fisherman's jumper for Bri, in navy blue because he looked really great in that colour. 'Took me ages to wrap that lot,' she said. 'Anyway, what you bought for everyone?'

'Was I supposed to buy stuff as well?'

Daisy turned and looked at him. 'You haven't?'

''Course I have.'

He began to laugh. Daisy picked up the nearest thing to hand, a teaspoon, and threw it at him. It hit him on the knuckle of his hands and must have hurt him.

'Ouch! You little . . .' He lunged towards her and Daisy wasn't quick enough to escape as he made a grab at her. She slid to the carpet and he began tickling her.

'Leave me, leave me. I can't stand it . . .'

And then he kissed her.

She pushed him away, pulled back from him and scrambled to her feet. The hurt in his eyes filled her with sadness. He used the sofa to pull himself up and turning his back on her, walked quickly away. She heard the bathroom door close. Then silence.

Oh, God, she'd upset him. Two minutes ago they'd been larking about. And now, this. Over one little kiss, she'd spoiled it all.

Daisy sat down on a chair. She gave a long sigh and stared at the carrier bag full of gifts. She liked being around Bri. In a funny kind of way it was like being married but without the sex and responsibilities of married life. To tell the truth she'd often wondered how he really felt about her, but he'd not made a move on her until today. Bri gave little of himself away. It was impossible to know what he was thinking half the time.

One thing she was sure of, he was one hundred percent reliable, the scam was going well and she needed him. So why had she pushed him away if she liked him so much?

Daisy knew the answer all right. Because today was Christmas Day and she had a child she couldn't be with and it was cutting her up something terrible. That little Eddie didn't really understand much about Christmas didn't matter – she did. And a few days ago she'd had to steel herself from chucking all her plans away and getting the first plane back to Greece to be with him. Another reason she'd pushed Bri away? He might be a nice man that she liked, admired and even cared about. *But he wasn't Eddie*. She thought of Eddie's seductive grin, his dark eyes, the softness of his hair and the way he'd made love to her that had left her begging for more.

This time she allowed the tears to roll down her cheeks. Inside she felt hollow and empty and so lonely she wanted to go out into North Street and scream and scream her pain away. Only it wouldn't go away, would it? It was Eddie she wanted, not a substitute.

After a while she dried her eyes. For fuck's sake, Daisy, she told herself. All Bri had done was kiss her. He was a bloke in a million. Without him she'd be sunk. The secure lock-ups contained stock. The warehouse employees were getting to know him by name, not his own name of course, and so far all the invoices had been paid by cheque, signed by him, on the dot. Daisy had put money into the account for this so the cheques wouldn't bounce, and only yesterday he'd told her he'd arranged a mammoth sale on January the first. Daisy was nervous as hell about it. Other big sales would follow in quick succession, strike while the iron's hot, he'd said. Go further afield with the sales, start getting known on the Kray and Richardson manors. That was the next step, he'd said.

He was playing his part to perfection.

And she'd bloody spoiled it.

Daisy heard the bathroom door open and he came back holding a small silver-paper-wrapped gift. He looked like a naughty little boy as he shyly handed her the present. Was it going to be all right after all?

'I'd rather you open your gift now.'

Daisy took it and without a word ripped at the paper. Inside was a jeweller's box. Warily, she snapped it open to reveal, nestling on the black velvet, a gold heart-shaped locket on a chain.

'It's beautiful,' she said. He looked worried. Carols were coming from the transistor radio. 'In The Bleak Midwinter', her favourite, was playing. It had been her mother's favourite carol as well and every time Daisy heard it she wanted to cry.

'Do you really like it?'

'I love it,' she said, taking it out.

'There's a special place inside for two photographs.' Daisy reached up on tiptoe to give him a thank you kiss. But before her lips reached his cheek she felt his whole body stiffen and he moved away from her.

'I'll wear it now if you'll sort the clip out for me.' She handed him the necklace and turned away and felt the warmth of his fingers as they brushed the back of her neck. 'I've never felt unable to communicate with you before,' she said. 'But I'm tongue tied.'

He turned her round and stared at the locket.

Then he smiled at her. 'It looks good on you.' His eyes darkened. 'I'm sorry for what just happened. Christmas without Eddie must be fuckin' awful for you, all the memories an' that.'

'I'm glad you understand but it's not your fault. I'm sorry,' Daisy said. 'Can we forget it?'

'Yeah. In fact, it's a good job we're off now to collect Jacky and Vera and walk round to me mum's.' Then he kissed her on her forehead. 'Merry Christmas,' he said.

Jacky was waiting outside the entrance to her flat. 'All right?' she asked, linking her arm with Bri. Daisy moved to the other side of her so she'd be in the middle and could use her as a support as well. It was taking Jacky a long time to get over her ordeal and she was nervous when she was out of the confines of her home. Daisy kissed her on the cheek.

'Merry Christmas, Jacky,' she said.

'And to you,' came her reply, then Jacky turned to Bri. He bent his head down so she could reach the side of his face for a kiss there, but instead she kissed him on the lips. And clung on. Daisy could see Bri was embarrassed.

'Come on, you two, break it up,' she said. She laughed to ease the sudden tension and was relieved when Jacky said, 'I'm bloody starvin'. I hope your mum does a good roast tater.'

'You're definitely feeling better, then,' Bri said.

A shadow crossed Jacky's face. 'Getting better every day.' She was wrapped up like an Eskimo in a snowstorm. Daisy took her brown carrier bag of gifts so it would be easier for Jacky to walk. She held up her own brown bag.

'Snap.'

'My mum's a terrific cook,' Bri said. 'As long as Vera and her don't get started on the bloody sherry.'

Daisy opened her mouth to say, 'I remember when Vera and I . . . ' But she realised no one except Vera and herself would remember a drunken Christmas Day together that turned out to be one of the best Christmases she'd ever had.

Vera was waiting outside Heavenly Bodies. Daisy could see the hem of her glittery red dress below her tightly belted shorty raincoat. Red high heels with straps showed to perfection her small feet in their sheer nylons. Totally inappropriate for the freezing cold weather, thought Daisy.

'Wotcha, Dais.' Vera slipped her arm through Daisy's. 'Happy Christmas everyone.' They murmured greetings back at her and the quartet walked down Bemisters Lane's cobbles and across the green by Holy Trinity Church to Barclay House.

'We ought to go to church,' said Jacky.

'No,' said Vera and Daisy in unison. Daisy looked into Vera's face and knew she was remembering that special Christmas when Eddie and Kenny were still alive and they'd gone to Midnight Mass together.

'I think God knows what's in our hearts. Especially at Christmas time.'

'Why, Vera, that's a bit bleedin' philosophical for you, ain't it?' said Jacky.

They'd reached the door of Barclay House and Daisy had her finger on the buzzer, waiting to be let in.

'Well at least I can spell the long word,' Jacky added. And they were still laughing as the door opened and they felt the warmth of the underfloor heating suck them in.

'Ain't you done your place up nice?' Daisy touched the holly, careful not to prick her fingers. 'Where did you get this? I ain't seen none with berries on this year.' Queenie's small flat looked like a Christmas grotto.

'Joe, who works at the cemetery, brought it round for me. And the mistletoe. Plenty of it, there. Per'aps them old bones works as good fertiliser.'

'Ugh!' said Vera. 'Ain't you the 'appy little woman this Christmas time?'

Daisy looked above her. Bri quickly dropped a kiss on her forehead, and broke away laughing.

'That'll teach you,' he said.

'My turn,' said Vera. And as he obliged she put her arms around him, lowering her hands to his firm bum. 'Ooh, I do like all this taut, young male flesh.' She broke away as Jacky elbowed her way towards Bri, who was now looking decidedly uncomfortable. He put his hands on her shoulders and went to kiss her on the forehead but she twisted up so she got him full on the lips again. Daisy saw the knuckles of her hands whiten as she fought to keep him close before he broke away. His face had gone cherry red.

'Come on, Mum,' he mumbled, putting out his hand and grabbing at his mother. Queenie passed her stick to Vera and practically fell into her son's arms.

'Happy Christmas,' he said. She looked like a doll against his brawny frame, Daisy thought.

'Get off with yer,' Queenie said. 'Never thought a bit of green and white berry could cause such a fuss. Get your coats and 'ats off.'

'I'll leave me 'at, Mum, if you don't mind...' Bri willingly slipped off his coat to reveal a grey shirt, slim tie and grey cardigan above grey trousers.

'He said he's bin up all night coughing,' jumped in Daisy, knowing he didn't really want to lie to his mother. But for once she had no such scruples. Daisy didn't like liars, but there were times when a white lie was an absolute necessity and this was one of them. 'I told him he wasn't to come but was to stay in bed.'

Bri's face was a picture. Daisy smothered a grin. He glared at her.

'You look like a Christmas tree bauble, all glittery,' said Daisy to Vera to change the subject.

'Gotta make an effort,' she said.

'That chicken smells delicious,' Jacky said. 'My mouth's watering.'

Queenie said, 'It's a big bugger of a bird. Got it off Kelly's Meats in the market. Bri paid for it. I never thought I was gonna get it in me oven. Let's 'ave some sherry.' She filled glasses before anyone could refuse.

Daisy said, 'To us and to friendship. And an 'appy Christmas. And to absent friends.' She was thinking of Susie, Si and Meggie and the rest of their family. Strangely, she was also thinking about Roy Kemp, wondering if he was with Moira in Spain or if Violet was making a dinner fit for a king. And she hoped Vinnie wasn't on duty today. To all these people Daisy wished a happy Christmas, but her special thoughts she kept for Kenny, for her Eddie and for his son.

They pulled crackers and read the same motto out over and over again because the crackers had come from Mabel's stall and were a bit duff, having the same in each cracker. Then they pigged out on Christmas pudding with custard and opened the presents they'd bought each other and ooh'd and aah'd their thanks. Bri was over the moon with his pullover.

After Vera and Jacky had fallen into a sherry stupor on the sofa, Queenie, with the aid of her stick, hobbled about and got Daisy and Bri's coats.

Bri stared at his mother in amazement.

'What we done? You sending us home?'

'I booked a taxi for five minutes' time. Them two'll be all right asleep on that sofa. You, me and Daisy are off to see your father.'

Daisy could see Bri didn't want to go, yet she knew he wouldn't hurt his mother's feelings, and certainly not on Christmas Day. He didn't say a word, then, after a few moments, he shrugged himself into his coat.

Daisy asked, 'Why do you want me there? I'm not a bleeding relation.'

'Yes you is, an' you're footing the bills, ain't you?' Queenie said. 'Don't fuckin' argue with me. Put your coat on. An' where's me stick gone again?'

Bri insisted on paying for the taxi even though it was double rate. The driver was to pick them up from The Cedars after tea.

'I've only just finished me dinner,' Daisy moaned.

'Yeah, well. Think yourself lucky you didn't get landed with the washing up. I've written a note tellin' Jacky an' Vera to get on with it,' said Queenie.

Daisy took Bri's arm as they walked up the gravel path. His face was a picture of misery. The last place he wanted to be at Christmas was visiting a man who'd banished him and ignored his very existence all his life. Daisy could see that.

The Cedars had a good atmosphere though the decorations weren't expensive. They were told by a cheery helper that many of the hangings had been made by the children of St John's School. A Christmas tree stood in the corner of the family room. Fairy lights twinkled, flashing on and off. Daisy had never seen flashing ones before.

There was no disinfectant masking the smell of incontinence. Just the scent of lavender polish, and the fading aroma of Christmas dinner and the spice of the pudding.

'Look at the food.' Daisy nudged Bri's arm and pointed at the table groaning beneath sandwiches and cake, mince pies and sausage rolls. Carols were playing from somewhere down the hall. The white-coated helper opened a door.

'Mr Lane is in the corner. He's awake but his emphysema's bad today,' she told them.

'I can't do this.' Bri pushed his way past Daisy and back down the hall they'd just walked up. Daisy looked at Queenie. There were tears in her eyes.

'Leave him be. You all right?'

'I think so.' Queenie's face was very white. She took a deep breath and with the aid of her stick moved determinedly towards the corner of the room.

Pappy Lane was a shrivelled replica of Eddie, scrunched up in a wheelchair. Or at least, thought Daisy, how she would have imagined Eddie might have looked in old age, if he'd been allowed to reach it. But Pappy wasn't old. The heavy booze and fags had caught up with him and his laboured breathing proved it.

'Hallo,' said Daisy. Queenie had somehow positioned herself behind Daisy despite Daisy urging her to come forward. If Pappy knew Queenie was there he didn't show it. Daisy took his gnarled hand and said, 'I'm Daisy.' What else could she say? Queenie, clearly mesmerised, her face as white as chalk, hadn't taken her eyes from him.

'I'll leave you to it. I'm going to Bri, all right?' Daisy never gave Queenie a chance to protest.

When Daisy got back to the hall, Bri was staring at a picture in a big gold frame. It showed a fluffy kitten with an impossibly large ball of wool which the animal had somehow managed to get itself tangled up in. From the look on Bri's face Daisy knew he was looking at the picture without seeing it.

'You're doing this for your mother,' Daisy said quietly. 'It's the best Christmas present you could ever give 'er.'

He stood there, staring at the silly cat. After a while he turned and looked at Daisy, his eyes glittering with unshed tears.

Then he went to greet his father.

CHAPTER 17

New Year's Eve 1964 came and almost went for Daisy. She knew for most people it was a magical time, a fresh beginning when the clock struck for the dawning of a new year. Alone in her double bed, she was aware she had to be up at four o'clock in the morning. She had been woken by ships in the harbour sounding their fog horns. North Street was alive with music and drunken wellwishers singing 'Auld Lang Syne'.

She lay listening to the revellers, her eyes cutting through the gloom of her bedroom. On the chair her jeans and warm clothes were laid out ready for her to jump into. The flat was warmer than the cafe had ever been. It seemed funny for Daisy to be living alone. Always there had been people around her, especially at the cafe. In Greece there were different sounds: cocks crowing, birds singing, the wind in the branches of the cypress trees. And, of course, her baby. Earlier, she'd telephoned Maria to wish them a happy new year. Maria had held the telephone towards little Eddie and Daisy heard his baby gurglings. Now she missed him more than ever. She'd pictured little Eddie's sturdy body, his chubby arms around her neck, the milky, talcum powder smell of him. Still, today would be another stepping stone, and if every-thing went according to plan it wouldn't be too long before they were reunited.

Bertie moved in her sleep. Daisy shifted her body so as not to disturb the cat and ran her fingers through the soft fur. The sound of purring filled the room.

'Why don't you sleep in the other bedroom, miss?' But Daisy knew the cat preferred company. Even though the spare bedroom had a double bed over which she had put a brightly coloured patchwork quilt, it was a room no one had yet used.

At five o'clock a bleary-eyed Daisy was sitting in Bri's van. They were on their way to the sale rooms where floor space had been hired to sell some of the stock they'd bought. It was dark and frosty and remnants of the previous night's celebrations were strewn across pavements.

'Don't worry,' said Bri. 'I know my blokes. They're being paid well to sell the stuff. Every one of them is reliable and used to trading.'

Daisy sipped at the sweet tea he'd brought in a thermos to warm her up. He was in his jeans and donkey jacket. This was one part of the operation where he wasn't required to look like Roy Kemp. His mates Jamie and Mikey, and the others who were selling the gear, knew nothing about the scam. To them the series of sales were simply extra days of work, selling for Bri.

'Never knew it could all go so smoothly,' said Daisy. By eight o'clock they'd done the indoor market at Chichester and Jamie and Syd were quids in and almost sold out of kitchen wares. Daisy had gawped at the punters leaving with boxed electrical items and happy smiles on their faces at the bargains they'd picked up cheaply. 'New Year's Day sales are bloody marvellous,' she said.

'Trust market traders to know how to sell,' Bri said, negotiating the roundabout that led towards Little-hampton and the covered market where a triple pitch had been hired. The sky was light now and more vehicles were on the road. It was still bitterly cold and Daisy was glad Bri had the van's heater on.

'Trust you, you said, an' I bloody do,' said Daisy, cuddling into him on the bench seat. 'Bri, you're a bloody marvel.'

'Thanks for the compliment. All it boils down to is the blokes are doing what they always do. Shifting gear quickly and making a profit. I'll collect the takings later and give them their well deserved cash in hand. And thank God I ain't 'ad to dress up in that bloody monkey suit today.' He glanced down at his casual gear.

'Don't you like wearing a suit?'

'I just don't like Roy Kemp's choice of clobber, Daisy. Though I have to admit you did a fine job of choosing the clothes, even down to the leather wallet with his initials in gold.'

'You look the part and that's fair enough,' she said.

'Did you put food out for Bertie?'

''Course,' Daisy said. 'You and that bloody cat. You're worse than Vera!'

All the shops were open in Littlehampton. Daisy remembered the time she'd been there with Eddie in the MG. That was the day he'd kissed her for the very first time. Sometimes now, try as she might, she couldn't remember the exact features and contours of his beloved face.

'We'll need quite a few good sales before the final one.'

Daisy was brought back to the present. She took out her hanky and dabbed at her eyes then blew her nose.

Bri asked, 'What's the matter?'

'Grit in me eye,' she said. Then, 'Yes, we're building up a really good relationship with the wholesalers, ain't we?'

'Sure are,' he said. 'Paying on the dot as soon as the bills come in.'

'An' don't forget we're ordering bigger amounts of stock all the time at these places.'

He nodded and squeezed her knee. 'And afterwards, when this is all over, I get to be myself again. Not a carbon copy of someone else.'

'Yes. I really don't like you as Roy Kemp. It's quite creepy.'

'That's a laugh. I'm doing this for you, Daisy . . .' She laid her fingers on his arm.

'I know.' Daisy paused. 'You're a strange bloke, Bri. You ever let anyone penetrate that thick shell of yours?' She waited for an answer, watching the dead countryside as they rolled along the road towards the sea. The ploughed fields were white and bare.

'Only once.'

'Really? Who was she?' Daisy had never heard him talk about his past before. Even working together all day he seldom let his guard down.

'That's another story for another day. It's a painful one.' He pulled the van into the market car park and turned the engine off. 'I hope Mikey's doing all right,' he said, changing the subject while helping her down from the cab. 'Mind you don't slip, there's some nasty ice patches.'

In the covered market the activity was intense. Everyone was selling something, from antiques to cheese, from bedding to birthday cards, and the place was alive with chatter from the crowds. Mikey and his son were sitting on wooden boxes; empty mugs were on the floor. Mikey was a skinny bloke with hair that puffed out from his head like a grey halo. His teenage son was a clone but with acne. Both of them gave Daisy and Bri huge grins.

'Fuck me,' said Mikey. 'Thought you was never coming.'

'Where's the gear?' asked Bri. The three pitches stood empty apart from bits of rubbish and cardboard swept into a neat pile in one corner.

'Me gear's back in the van 'cause we've sold all the stock, mate.'

'What? All of it?' Bri's face was a picture.

'The whole bloody lot.'

'Bugger me,' said Bri. Daisy saw the pleased look he bestowed on Mikey.

'What do you expect? Everything was priced to sell and we got a bloody good profit margin. People was aching to spend their Christmas dosh. Want to go somewhere quiet and cash up now?' Mikey began to untie the money belt around his waist. Bri stopped him.

'Nah. You sort it. Take your cut and I'll collect the rest tonight. All right, kid?' He playfully punched the lad's shoulder. The boy laughed and Daisy watched as they sparred with each other.

Daisy walked with Mikey's boy out to the car park

and Bri and Mikey followed. She heard them discussing a further sale date. Mikey and his son left the car park first in their van and Daisy and Bri followed along the road until they turned off to take a different route.

'Next stop, Brighton. Wonder how Pete and his brother are getting on.'

Pete was sweeping rubbish into a corner of the near deserted saleroom.

'All gone except for half a dozen glass dolphins I dropped when I took a pile of stuff from me van,' confessed Pete. He hitched up his trousers over his vast waistline and leaned on the practically bristle-free broom. 'But I'll pay you for them.'

'You'll do no such fuckin' thing,' said Bri sharply.

'Actually I fell over that bugger's big feet.' Pete pointed to his brother, who'd discarded his broom and was now chatting up a willowy brunette at a stall a few yards away. He handed Bri an envelope but took a sheet of paper from his pocket and handed that over as well. 'Petrol, wages, I took some off for breakfast . . .'

'Silly bastard,' said Bri. 'You know I don't need you to keep a record.' Without scanning the paper, he opened the envelope and looked inside. Then he took out a couple of large notes.

'Have a good drink on me at the Palais tonight.'

'I been paid, mate . . .'

'Call it a bonus, then. All right for next time?' Pete nodded.

Later, Bri said, 'It's been quite a day, ain't it? Sales on the south coast are always popular after the sitting indoors and stuffing yourself silly days of Christmas. The punters ate up our stocks.'

'We bought in bulk, sold cheap, made a good profit. Now it has to be done all over again,' said Daisy.

Back at the flat she cooked Bri one of his favourite meals, and made him eat every bit of the toad-in-the-hole before he went out collecting the money. Bertie sat on the chair next to him, begrudging him every mouthful, and he fed her bits of sausage. When Bri had gone, Daisy sat on the sofa and with a pad and pencil worked out her finances. The scent of flowers and cooking filled the flat.

Roy and his mum had apparently sent a cheque to the flower shop in Stoke Road and the delivery boy had turned up with a huge bouquet of forced spring blooms as a New Year's gift. The deep yellow of the daffodil trumpets made the flat look very cheery. Daisy had phoned and thanked Violet.

The scent of arum lilies overpowered the daffodils' delicate perfume though. Vera had been with Daisy when the same lad had delivered the second bouquet. Her mouth had dropped open at the sight of the creamy white blooms.

'Fuck me, they're death lilies,' Vera had insisted. 'Who'd do a nasty thing like that?'

'I'll 'ave to look at the bleeding card, won't I?' said Daisy.

With shaking fingers she'd taken the white card from its envelope.

In memory of a stolen kiss in a corridor. There was no name but Daisy knew the flowers had come from Valentine Waite.

Vera had snatched the card away.

'You been 'oldin' out on me, you got a fuckin' fancy man. 'E's that bleedin' boxer, ain't 'e?' Daisy had blushed. 'Good for you, gal. You can't live on bleedin' memories.'

Now Daisy looked down at her notepad. She'd been sending money back to Greece regularly for her son. She wrote down the amount of money needed for Pappy. She didn't resent one penny of that for she wouldn't have a bank balance at all if it hadn't been for inheriting the cafe from Kenny and the property and money Eddie had left her. Christmas hadn't been expensive but the refurbishment of the bookshop had strained her finances. Bri had put in money of his own, and he'd also taken it upon himself to provide the wages for the blokes he'd hired to paint and decorate the place. Tonight when Bri returned with the sales profits, all the proceeds had to be ploughed back into the scam. The only fly in the ointment was the large house in Alverstoke that Eddie had left her. He'd no doubt expected them both to live there, in that posh part of Gosport, but Daisy had no such desire. Perhaps with Eddie by her side it might have been different. The only house she really cared about was the small place in Greece.

The house on Western Way, Alverstoke, was, or had been until just before Christmas, rented out to a naval couple. It was a beamed, thatched place, in need of some minor updating. Did she want to bother with that? Perhaps it might be better if she put it in the hands of an estate agent to sell. She could certainly do with the money. The telephone rang.

It was Vera. 'I want to ask Jacky if she'll maid for me. I needs someone at Heavenly Bodies. Me girls ain't got the time or the inclination.'

'Why you asking me, Vera? I ain't Jacky.' Daisy heard her sigh.

'Do you think she will?'

'Dunno. She's got no money, and she's not strong enough to go back on the stall, them iron bars is too heavy for her to manage now. An' she can't go selling her body . . .'

'I know all that,' broke in Vera. 'You ain't no fuckin' 'elp at all.'

'Is that why you phoned me? To tell me how bleeding useless I am?'

'No.'

'What then?'

'You know that lad as stole the old bloke's purse when we was on the market?'

'Yeah, I remember,' Daisy said.

'He's gone missing.'

'Since when?'

'Christmas Day. Had a barney with 'is stepdad and slung 'is hook. Ain't been seen since.'

'How do you know this?'

'Vinnie Endersby. He's on the case. That's all I knows. Poor little bleeder.'

'Perhaps he's stayin' with a mate until it cools down at 'ome. He looked pretty savvy to me.'

'Per'aps you're right. Tell Bri, maybe the traders'll keep their eyes and ears open.'

'I will.'

'Everything go all right today?'

'You shouldn't ask because I don't want you to be involved any more than you have to be.' Daisy could picture her at the other end of the line. Fluffy high-heeled slippers, make-up immaculate – or maybe she'd scrubbed it all off and was sitting there with her face all clean and shiny. She'd smell of Californian Poppy.

Vera even dabbed a bit on to go to bed in. 'Never know who I'll meet in me dreams,' she'd say.

'Can I ask if everything's all right in Greece, then?'

'No, you can't! Yes it is! So don't ask me nothin' else.'

'Sorry, Dais.'

'Go and have a big gin and tonic. That'll make you feel better. I'll have one an' all. If we drink and think of each other at the same time, we won't be alone.'

'You are lovely, Dais.'

'Silly cow.'

Daisy was just pouring a finger of gin into a glass when she heard banging on the shop door.

'Can't be your dad,' Daisy said to Bertie. 'He's got his key.'

As Daisy approached the door downstairs she could see a shape behind the frosted glass. Too small for Bri. It was a woman. She thought at first it might be Jacky so she opened the door straight away. The woman pushed her way inside.

She was young, perhaps in her very early twenties, with a bandanna tied round her long dark hair. She was wearing a fringed shawl and a mauve fringed skirt that reached her ankles. Over one shoulder hung a huge grubby patchwork bag.

'What d'you want? We're closed.'

'I don't give a flying fuck whether you're closed or not. Who the fuck are you?'

It was then Daisy saw the bundle held close to her breast beneath the shawl. It was a baby in a sort of sling pouch. The shock took away the indignation of being asked who she was in her own home. The baby started to cry, a thin wail.

'You shouldn't 'ave a little one out in this cold so late at night.' It was then Daisy saw the child had no bootees or mittens on. Its tiny feet and hands were red and blue with the cold.

'Don't go tellin' me what I should or shouldn't be doin'. Where's Bri? I suppose you're his fancy bit.'

'Whose?'

'Don't come the innocent with me. Where's my old man?'

Daisy didn't like this young woman. Not one little bit. And a foul smell was coming from her. The child was still grizzling. What was it she'd said, 'Where's my old man?' The woman was surely deranged.

Daisy felt sorry for the child. It looked sickly. But obviously the woman knew Bri. Thank God it wouldn't be long now before he came back.

'You'd better come upstairs, out of the cold. Up them stairs, there.' Daisy walked behind her wondering how she managed to keep herself warm, for she only had thonged leather sandals on her grubby feet.

When they reached the living area the woman took off her shawl and sling and propped the child in the corner of the sofa. Bertie slunk away in disgust. The woman then wandered about, fingering Daisy's ornaments, touching a picture in a frame, taking not one bit of notice of the child who hadn't stopped crying.

'I s'pose you'd like a cup of tea?'

'If you've nothing else on offer.' She'd spotted the gin bottle and the half poured drink.

'I got gin. I was just having a drink meself.'

'That'll do.'

Daisy took a fresh glass and poured her a measure. She was about to ask whether she'd like some tonic or orange juice in it when the woman said, 'Fill it up.'

Daisy gave her a more generous measure and was surprised to see it disappear down her throat in a flash.

'Well, that didn't touch the sides, did it?' Daisy said. 'Who are you?' The warmth of the room must have got to the child for it had stopped moaning and was now trying to play with its toes. But the smell coming from the little one was awful. It badly needed changing. The woman had a ring on her finger, a gold band.

'Who are you?' Daisy repeated. The woman, without asking, poured herself another neat gin.

'Don't suppose he told you about me. Very deep, our Bri is. Very deep.' Daisy looked from her to the child.

The woman laughed.

'Yes,' she said. 'It's his.'

Bri's child? Her heart was banging inside her rib cage. It was then she realised that not once had the woman referred to the child by any name, only 'it'.

'What's the child's name?'

'Summer.'

'That's pretty.' Daisy saw that the woman's hands were shaking. 'Bri never said he was married.'

'Well, he wouldn't.' She'd started pacing the room, drink in hand. 'When's the bugger due back? I take it he's not hiding away somewhere?'

'He shouldn't be long.' Daisy could see a nasty confrontation coming when Bri did appear and she didn't want to be a part of it. Why had he abandoned the kiddie? And why hadn't he told Daisy he was married?

'Me name's Belle. I'm tired and I could do with another drink.'

'I'm Daisy. Help yourself, you did the last time. Where d'you come from?'

'Scotland, an' before you asks, I got a lift down with a lorry driver.'

Daisy thought hard. Bri had sold the trout farm in Scotland, hadn't he? Some place on the west coast it was. Pat, fond of the bottle, had driven himself off the road, leaving Bri to carry on alone.

Daisy trusted Bri. He was Eddie's brother, wasn't he? If he had a life he wanted to keep secret, even though he promised to help her pay back Roy Kemp, it was his own business. After all, she hadn't told Bri everything. She looked at the baby and something tore at her heart.

'Look, I ain't sure exactly when Bri'll be back. But you're welcome to stay the night.'

Belle gave her a funny look. Daisy realised the woman thought she and Bri were living together.

'We don't sleep together,' she added. 'Or even live together, come to that. Who said he might be here?'

'The bloke in the pub at the other end of the road. Said he spends all 'is time 'ere.' Fair enough, it was true, wasn't it?

'I could do with another drink.' The baby whimpered in her sleep.

'Does she want changing?' Daisy asked. It was obvious she did and Daisy had had enough of the stench.

'It'll settle. Usually does if you ignore it.'

Daisy was appalled. She quickly gathered her wits about her. Let Bri sort this out. Where to put Belle? Spare room? Away from Daisy's room where she had deeds, money, cheque books and other information lying around that she didn't want this woman poking her nose into.

'Come with me,' she said, showing her into the bedroom. Daisy needed to get her out of the living room. If Bri came bounding up the stairs with a couple of bags full of cash . . . She didn't want to think what Belle might make of that. And let's hope he's still got his woollen hat on, or else there'll be more explaining to do, she thought. After a quick glance around the room, Daisy left her to it. Belle had grabbed the gin bottle and the baby and taken them both in with her.

Daisy breathed a sigh of relief at being alone in the living room. She wrinkled her nose at the smell left behind. She wasn't alone for long.

Bri came upstairs, taking two steps at a time. The grin on his face stretched from ear to ear. He had a heavy cloth bag in his hands which he slung on the sofa and it landed with a heavy thud of rattling coins and crackling money. It didn't take long to wipe the smile from his face.

'Belle's here.'

'Who?' But already Daisy could see the name had floored him.

'Belle.'

'Fuck.'

'I don't want her knowing our business.'

The colour had drained from his usual healthy complexion. 'Where is she?'

'In my spare room.'

'I don't want her here,' he snapped. 'You had no right to ask her—'

'She said she's your wife and I couldn't let her roam the streets with the baby . . .'

'Baby?' His eyebrows shot up. 'What baby? It's not my baby.'

'Don't matter whose baby it is, she can't cart it round the streets in the cold.'

'Fair enough.' He went to the kettle in the kitchen, shaking it first to make sure there was enough water in it.

'Don't you want to see 'er?' Daisy had followed him.

'I wouldn't have left Scotland if I wanted to see her, would I?'

'Okay,' Daisy said. 'It's your business. I just don't want her still here tomorrow.'

'And I didn't want her here tonight. I'm off back to The Black Bear.'

'Oh no you don't.' Daisy grabbed his arm and pulled him round to face her. 'You ain't leaving me with your fucking unfinished business!'

She could see the anger flood his face from grey to red. A nerve at the corner of his mouth started to twitch.

'What's that bleeding stink, you let that cat shit somewhere?' He flung himself from her.

'That stink, as you call it, is your daughter an' your wife!' Daisy picked up the money, using both hands to scoop the heavy bag, and walked towards her own room, where she spotted Bertie who had fled from the living room at the sound of raised voices. She pulled the door to keep the cat in her room and turned once more to Bri who had his back to her. He was breathing heavily, his hunched shoulders rising and falling with each angry breath. 'You don't leave this flat until you sort all this out.'

He whirled around. 'And where am I supposed to sleep?'

'I don't give a fuck!' shouted Daisy. 'As long as it ain't in *my* bed.' She pushed open the door and then kicked it shut behind her.

Daisy put the money bag in the bottom of the wardrobe then got into bed. After a while Bertie crept in beside her.

'Don't like arguments, do you, lovey? No more do I.' Daisy snuggled into her fur but she couldn't sleep.

She listened to Belle's raised voice.

She listened to Bri's anger.

She listened to the baby crying.

She got out of bed when she heard doors slamming and wrapped her white dressing gown around her. It wasn't so white any more. Countless washings and constant wearing had changed it to a grubby grey. She remembered when Eddie had shyly presented her with it. She wished with all her heart he could be with her now.

Going to the window she looked down into the street. Everything in the flat had at last gone quiet. No crying, no raised voices.

Outside she could see the frost-covered bomb site. A burned-out van had brambles swallowing it up like hungry barbed wire. Now there was no green anywhere and even during the day it seemed to Daisy that the winter had changed everything to black and grey. An unwanted bedstead was propped against the side of the van. Daisy prised the window up a couple of inches. It was so quiet she could hear the jangling of mast tops from the nearby boatyard. A smattering of sleet hurled itself against the window pane.

How many times had she stood across the road

looking down at the bicycle shop? And now she was on the other side of the road, staring at the cafe.

Had Belle and Bri made up? How would she feel if Belle and the baby were now a permanent fixture in Bri's life?

'Jesus, Daisy. You frightened the life out of me.'

'What you doing sleeping on the fucking sofa?'

'Where else am I supposed to sleep? You wouldn't let me go home, remember?' Bri stared at Daisy. Her hair was tousled and half moons of darkness sat beneath her eyes.

'She still here?' Daisy looked towards the spare room. He nodded. 'This place smells like a doss house,' she flung at him, then quietly, 'I thought . . .'

'I know what you thought. She means nothing to me.' He realised as soon as the words were out of his mouth that she'd pounce on him.

'Ain't that what all fucking men say?'

'It happens to be the truth.'

'You can't just ignore the fact that she's 'ere.' What Daisy really meant, Bri knew, was how is this going to affect our *business* relationship? 'What I need to know is am I going to be left in the lurch now? I got a lot of money tied up in this deal. But by the same token you got to do something about that poor little scrap of a baby in there. Even a blind man can see it ain't being looked after properly.'

She flounced off into the kitchen and he hopped after her trying to get his long legs into his jeans without falling over.

'You forget, I got money tied up in it, too!' He jammed his foot into a trouser leg and lost his footing, stumbling against Daisy. It was a reflex action for her to put her arms around him to stop him falling. She began to laugh.

'I didn't know you had such long white legs.'

'Yeah,' he muttered. 'I got one each side.' He disentangled himself and finished the business of putting his jeans on.

'Shall I make some tea?'

'You don't 'ave to.'

'I want a cup. Did you sleep in that bloody hat?' He felt for the woollen cap and pulled it into place.

'Yes.'

'Wasn't it hot?'

'Not half as hot as it was Christmas Day when you told me mum I had a chill.'

Daisy was setting out mugs. A smile lit her face.

'Oh, sit down before I wet meself laughing.' Bri pulled out a stool and sat down. 'Are you going to tell me what all this is about or not?' She plonked a mug down in front of him. The tea slopped on to the table.

He pulled up a stool for her. He listened to the sleet beating against the window. The drizzle of last night had developed into a freezing windy deluge. The slate roof of Murphy's the Ironmongers was shining with water gushing off it. His knees were inches away from Daisy's. She pulled at her dressing gown to cover them and laid her hands in her lap, waiting.

'When I left Gosport with Pat it was with the intention of leaving my past behind. I hated the life of drugs, beatings and extortion I'd got caught up in because of Eddie. There was no need for me to worry about him any more. He was with you an' he was making a new start.' He took a gulp at his tea.

'And I thought we'd kept things secret.'

'Not from me, Daisy. Cal – Eddie's right-hand

man – Pat and me, we knew the score all right. Though anyone with half an eye could see you two were crazy about each other. And don't forget I knew Kenny was Bert's son. So even if Kenny didn't have you waiting for him when he came out of the nick, he'd have a damn good business to come home to. You'd done wonders with the caff. Like I've said before, he'd have got over you and Eddie in time because he loved the pair of you.' Bri could see she was relaxed and listening. She lifted her tea to her lips.

'I wanted to be in a place that was quiet and where I could make an honest living. I knew Pat well enough and when he wasn't in the drink he was a hard worker.'

'So Bonnie Scotland it was,' said Daisy, setting down her tea.

He nodded. 'I had nothing to worry about here. Mum was settled, I'd finished being Eddie's minder. Now it was my turn to do what I wanted. I asked Mum if she'd come with me but she didn't want to leave the place she was used to.'

'So where does Miss Hippy come in?'

'I'm getting to her. You asked me to tell you, so listen.' Daisy made a face at him.

'We was making a go of the trout farm. It was very isolated, I loved it. But the old Black and White drink proved too much of a temptation to Pat. Then we heard that Cal had been killed. I realise now that was down to your gangster mate, and we didn't get that news for quite a while, by the way. He started fretting then, saying we'd be next. The name of Roy Kemp put the fear of God in Pat. He went missing and turned up at the bottom of a ravine. Gone straight off the edge of the road in his jeep, but you already know that part.'

'An' Belle?'

'I picked her up one day. She was on her way to Thurso.'

'Hitching?'

'She made me laugh. One of the first people I'd spoken to since Pat's accident. I dropped her in the main street and that was that. But a few weeks later she turned up at the farm in a bus with some of her pals. They stayed the night. There was drugs and drink but nothing bad, a few spliffs and a couple of snorts of some new expensive stuff they'd smuggled back from Germany. Lots of music and laughter. One of her mates played the fiddle an' we even danced. Her friends went in the morning but she stayed on.'

'And that's how it started?'

'That's how it started. I knew very little about her. Found out later she was into anything that gave her a kick. She's a manic depressive, I think that's the right term. She was in a high period, very happy and excitable, so I didn't know then how bad it could get when she was on a downer.'

Bri put his head in his hands. He hated talking about all this, remembering the depths of despair Belle had taken him to.

'I got used to having her around, though. She smoked a lot of weed and even rigged up some heat lamps so she could grow plants in the greenhouse from some seed she had. Then she starting doin' the disappearing act and I'd go and find her in some squat or other in Inverness. She'd slope away from the farm to find something to put up her nose or stick in her veins. But by that time I cared for her, an' honestly believed I could help her.' Bri shrugged. He didn't want to tell Daisy about some of the places and blokes he'd found her with. 'When she'd been gone for two weeks and I couldn't find her, I knew then I loved her.'

'You didn't think you might have been lonely? Living out there and with Pat gone?'

He shook his head. 'At that time I was sure I loved her. And I thought if only I could get her off the shit, everything would be all right. She came back in the bus with her mates and I was overjoyed to see her again. But she was furious because I'd destroyed all the cannabis and smashed up all the equipment. She said she'd been to Aberdeen to see her mother. I knew she was lying. She looked awful. I found the needles and some gear in that big patchwork bag of hers. The van left without her. To tell the truth I'd begun to think her mates were only using her.'

'You took her back?'

'What else could I do?' He shrugged. 'When she ran out of stuff, that was the worst time. It was awful. I thought she was going to die with all the vomiting and pains. And the sweating. She was out of her mind. But she'd get these little calm moments when it seemed she knew I was trying to care for her. My heart was bleeding and in one of those moments she begged me not to leave her, said I was the only bloke who truly understood her and that she wanted me to marry her. I told her if I married her she'd have to stay off the crap. She was like a bag of bones, not an ounce of meat on her anywhere. At one point I thought she was gonna die on me. I quickly got her into a special unit at Aberdeen that cost me a bomb.

'When she came back to the farm the only medication she was on was for her depression. There was no booze, nothing to harm her. I wouldn't even have a beer in the place. She'd put on weight and for a while it was bloody good between us. I knew she'd tried to commit suicide before, her wrists told me that, and I soon learnt that she didn't know how to tell the truth about anything. But I thought I could make a difference. You know, love conquers all and that crap? For a while she was in a really stable period. We got married in Inverness and I was happy; I thought she was, too.'

'So what happened?'

'Hang on. I'm coming to that. I needed to go to Aberdeen to see the accountant. I was gone two nights and three days. When I drove into the yard the bloody bus was there. Its door was open and I could see a tangle of arms and legs on one of the double bunks. I went into the house and got my shotgun. Told the lot of them to fuck off my land. Belle was as high as a kite and didn't even know who she'd been with. I told her I never wanted to see her again. They went and she went with them. Shortly after, I put the place up for sale. Came back here to the markets and Mum. I haven't seen her since then and that's why I was so angry about her bein' here last night. I would have turned her away, and the kid.'

'No! You'd never see that kiddie out in the cold!'

'I would. It ain't mine and you don't know the hell I've been through.' He wasn't sure whether Daisy understood. Was it really too much to ask to expect the woman you loved to keep off the shit and to stay faithful?

'You must have known you wasn't the first man . . .'

'But I expected to be the fuckin' last!' Bertie jumped down from his lap. 'I can't help the way I'm made,

Daisy. I'm not against women who sleep around, men neither. That's fine if you ain't got a regular partner. Commitment means everything to me, though. I think you're the same. I'm willing to bet the last man you slept with was Eddie.'

'None of your fucking business.'

But he knew he was right.

'You still got the problem of Belle and the kiddie to sort . . .'

'It ain't my kid.'

The door opened and Belle came in. She looked like she'd slept in her clothes. Bri's heart sank. He didn't want another argument with her.

'You can't stay here,' he said firmly.

Daisy cut in with, 'Summer's good. I never heard a peep out of 'er after she'd settled.'

'Well, you wouldn't. Not when her bottle's got gin in it. Usually does the trick. Any tea going?' Belle slouched over to the pot and felt it. 'It's cold.'

'Fuckin' make yourself some more then.' Bri got up and went into the bedroom closely followed by Daisy.

The child lay in the centre of the bed. She was fast asleep. Bri watched as Daisy scooped her up and held her close to her own warm body. He could smell the dried vomit on the baby and the rank stench of the room. Summer was still in last night's nappy.

'She's breathing,' said Daisy.

Bri said, 'She's got red hair.'

'She can't be yours then, can she? Not with hair that bloody colour.' He heard the contempt in Daisy's voice. He stared at the child as Daisy put her down on the bed and started to unravel her clothing. 'Go and get a bowl of lukewarm water and a clean towel. In my bedroom in the top drawer there's a pale blue blouse. A cotton one. Bring that and . . .' He could see Daisy thinking. 'Some zinc and castor oil from the bathroom cabinet. Go on then.'

Half an hour later he was standing in the shower with the jets of water cascading over him. His mind was busily working out dates. The kiddie was small for her age, even he could see that. And Belle giving her gin! What else had she tried to poison the kiddie with?

He towelled his hair dry and dressed for the shop, putting on his hat. He didn't know much about babies. Daisy seemed pretty much in command though.

In the spare room, he stripped the bed. He took out his wallet and was about to put some money in Belle's bag when he realised that wasn't the answer. He might as well hand her the drugs. He finished in the bedroom, leaving the window open to air the room. He went back into the kitchen carrying Belle's bag and the soiled bedding.

Daisy was trying to feed the baby some mashed-up muck.

He faced Belle. 'How old?'

'Four months.' Belle flicked the end of her cigarette into the remains of her tea.

Bri felt an unreasonable surge of anger at the ease with which Daisy seemed to have taken to the child.

'Like babies, do you?' He threw Belle's bag on the floor beside her but his question was directed at Daisy.

'As a matter of fact, I bloody well do.' Daisy's eyes narrowed at him, then she returned her attention to the child.

He stared at the maternal sight. The baby was quite

agreeable looking as babies go, he thought. Daisy had fingered the red hair into some kind of ridiculous top knot. It stood up like a tiny row of fiery marigolds down the centre of the child's head.

'She ain't very big for her age.'

'What do you know about fuckin' kids? It's been sickly,' Belle said.

'Any ideas where you're staying tonight?' Bri looked at his watch. He badly wanted to get out of here and down to open the shop. This was all too much for him. He needed quiet and space to do some thinking.

'It's sorted,' said Daisy. She had the baby up to her shoulder and was patting its back. The child burped loudly and Daisy wiped away a milky gob of spit from its mouth.

'There's a good girl. A very good girl.'

Belle had lit another cigarette. Bri went to open the window.

'Fuck me,' he said as he leaned across the sink. 'Dais, I think you'd better come 'ere.'

'I'm off to the bathroom,' said Belle. 'Thought you was never coming out. I'm dying for a piss.'

Bri pulled Daisy and the child towards the window, and watched her face as she stared down into the street. On the corner stood a man in a black suit, not quite covered by a long dark coat which was slung across his shoulders.

Bri said, 'Don't need to mention names, do I?'

'It's Roy Kemp.' She quickly pulled away from the window as though she was hiding and might get caught.

'Take her.' Daisy thrust the child at Bri. 'Got to get you out of 'ere. Never mind the shop. Don't let Belle down there, neither. I got to slip some bloody clothes on.'

Bri held the baby at arm's length.

'She won't fucking bite, you know.' Daisy ran to her room and emerged seconds later dressed in a pair of jeans and a chunky black sweater. 'Get Belle and take her to my house in Western Way.' She thrust some money at him and the keys to the Alverstoke house and her car. Belle came wandering in from the bathroom.

'Get your bag, missy,' ordered Daisy. She threw one of her cardigans at Bri. 'Use that as a shawl for Summer. Stay with 'em until the house is warmed up, it's been empty for a while. On the way, go into The World's Stores and buy food for them. Baby milk for her.' She nodded at the child, now asleep in Bri's arms. 'Just don't let Roy see you.'

Bri opened his mouth but Daisy waved him away. 'Hurry up! Go *now*!'

Twenty minutes later Daisy was sorting the float money, still amazed that Bri, the baby and Belle had got away without argument under Roy Kemp's nose.

Belle was a fucking walking disaster area, thought Daisy. One night in the flat and she'd left behind stinking sheets, stale cigarette smoke, dog ends everywhere and a burn on the sofa. The only place that was relatively clean was the bath and shower because she'd used neither. Daisy shuddered to think what she would accomplish in the Alverstoke house.

But it was Summer Daisy was really worrying about. Luckily she appeared to have no bad effects from the gin. She wondered if Vera's doctor friend could check the child out sometime soon? And Bri?

God knows what Bri was thinking about to get himself tangled up with Belle, but loneliness brings strange bedfellows. She'd never understand blokes as long as she lived.

A few customers were browsing. Daisy sat on a stool behind the counter. Bertie was asleep next to the till, curled in a ball.

She really liked the shop, she decided. Books had a tranquillising effect. All those words written to communicate to people. All that imagination gone into telling stories. It seemed to Daisy the books were saying ease up, calm down, everything will be all right.

'Nice selection you've got here. I'll take this.'

Daisy popped the murder mystery into a bag and handed it to the man. He returned her smile. She looked about the premises. Yes, she liked this shop. And she liked working alongside Bri. He'd told her more about himself last night than in all the time they'd known each other. He was a strange one all right. But Daisy didn't care what he thought, that child was the spitting image of him.

'Have you any romances?'

'Over there, in alphabetical order.' Perhaps Bri really had loved Belle, once upon a time. But then, in his warped mind, his dad had loved Queenie until things didn't go his way. No one ever knew what went on in a person's heart. Most people had an inner person, Daisy thought, and an outer person they showed the world.

Pappy had insisted Bri wasn't his child. Was history repeating itself, with Bri saying the same about Summer?

'Trade's brisk, Daisy.' The familiar voice broke into her thoughts.

'You haven't come to talk about me business, 'ave you, Roy?' She handed a woman her change. Then she remembered she had to keep on the right side of Roy so she treated him to a dazzling smile. The scent of his citrus cologne wafted over her, a smell she was beginning to get used to and like.

'How's Moira?'

He looked uncomfortable. Daisy knew Roy hated to appear less than perfect and she had touched a nerve with Moira.

'Happy enough. Seemed to enjoy Christmas. You just say the word and I'll fly you over. I'm sure she'd love to meet you again.'

'Maybe, Roy.' Daisy thanked another customer. 'But as you can see I've got me 'ands full at the moment.'

Roy tapped a foot. 'Friendly little town, Gosport. Do you know, I walked across the road out there and some woman said hello to me?' Daisy's heart thudded against her rib cage: no doubt the woman thought Roy was Bri. She thought quickly.

'Well it's a myth, ain't it, about snooty southerners? We're real friendly round here. Why do you think I love it so much?'

'Very true,' he said.

'Anyway, Roy, what can I do for you?'

Before he could answer Daisy had to leave him while she attended to a man who had brought in a box of westerns. She checked them through for torn or missing pages. They were good stock. She knew what Bri would have offered so Daisy gave him her price. He accepted and the deal was struck. Bri's going to be pleased with me, she thought. When she turned back to Roy he took hold of her arm.

'Look, Daisy, is there somewhere we can go and talk without being interrupted?'

'I think you've forgotten this shop is my bread and butter, Roy. I've sunk everything I've got into this, and I have to make it work.' He lifted a hand and began examining spotless fingernails. The gold ring with the black 'R' shone against his tanned skin.

Then he smiled. 'Fair enough, Daisy. Though why a bright girl like you is fart-arsing around with copper and silver coins when I could give you more money than this place will ever make is beyond me.'

Daisy reached across and put her hand on his arm. 'That's just it, Roy. I am bright, so I'm building an honest business. Ain't that why Violet, your dear mum, likes me? Because I am so fucking honest? And didn't we agree on no strings?'

'Daisy, Daisy,' he laughed. 'Always so bloody independent . . .'

Daisy cut him off. 'Go on upstairs, Roy.' She nodded towards the staircase. 'I'll close for five minutes. Not a minute longer, mind!' She pushed him in the direction of the stairs and went over to the door, turning the closed sign to face outwards. Then she followed him. 'Stick the kettle on, Roy,' she called. She breathed a sigh of relief that she'd opened the windows, had a quick tidy up and that the place looked and smelled all right now.

He was sitting astride a stool and she worked around him making the tea.

He didn't speak until she'd placed a cup in front of him and she was stirring her own mug.

'There's a bit of bother going on in the Smoke at present,' he said. 'I want you to know I ain't involved.'

Daisy raised the cup to her lips.

'Bother?'

'The twins have been implicated in a shooting incident. Happened just before the end of the year.'

'Why're you telling me this?'

'Because it matters to me if you think I'm in on it.'

'I didn't know nothing about it, Roy. Ain't seen it reported in a paper an' I ain't got a television set to watch. Are they inside?' He shook his head. 'They got mates in the force so they'll get it all sorted, that's if they did anything, won't they, Roy?'

'Sometimes I think you live in a little world of your own, Daisy. Life ain't so simple. There's this fucking copper, name of Nipper Read. He's like a dog with a bone. He won't rest until he's put Reggie and Ronnie away for good.'

'What's that got to do with you?'

'Nothing, as long as he don't make me his next bone to chew on.'

'What are you trying to say to me?'

He took a deep breath.

'I care about you. I care about me old lady. But that's the point, she is an old lady. I got a few of the boys who'd not see a hair on her head touched, like Charles, but as in most businesses it's the survival of the fittest. If anything goes wrong will you look after the old lady?'

Daisy's hands began to shake and she could hear the blood rushing around her veins.

'You want me to look after Violet if you ain't around to do it?' She said the words slowly, as if she was listening to every word she spoke. He nodded. She stared into his eyes. She saw trust there and something more, something she couldn't quite put her finger on. Daisy didn't speak, she was savouring the moment. It was almost as though a change was taking place inside her and she had no control over it. Yet if someone had asked her what was the matter she couldn't have told them.

'There'll be money for you to do it properly.' He was waiting patiently for her reply. What should she say? 'I'm trying to get rid of you myself, Roy, for killing my Eddie, so why would I look after your mother who is possibly a bigger rogue than you?' But Violet cared about Daisy and Daisy knew it. The words she came out with took her by surprise, but it was the truth.

'For some of the stunts you pulled, you deserve everything you're gonna get. But I'll always be there for Violet if she wants me.' Daisy saw the relief spread over his face.

'Thank you,' he said quietly. Then he shrugged as though to dispel any further show of vulnerability. He'd laid his emotions bare and now wanted to cover them quickly for fear of ridicule. 'I got a bit of a problem over the way.' He nodded towards the cafe. 'I'd value an honest opinion. My boy Sammy ain't exactly a ladies' man.'

'So?'

'I got nothing against those that like their bread cut the other way. My mate Ronnie being a prime example. But Sammy really don't like women. He tends to get a bit heavy handed at times. Keeps 'em in their place, but I can't sell damaged goods.' Daisy nodded. She'd heard tales about the punishments he inflicted on the girls. And look at what had happened to Jacky.

'I got a girl in a bad way in hospital.'

'Oh my God!'

226

'Sammy's had a little taster this morning of what I can be like when I'm crossed. I've told him he'd better replenish my stock as soon as possible. I don't even mind if he gives the bints time to get used to shagging. Some of my best earners had to be led along slowly, like Rosa. She knocked on the door at Forton Road and asked to be taken in. Said she was a virgin and she was scared stiff of blokes. Took nearly three months before she'd let anyone near her. But I look on cases like that as an investment. All these years later, she's a top earner and, after Sammy, keeps the toms in order. I already got a friend up at the cop shop who turns a blind eye to the caff goings-on for a nice bonus.' He laughed. 'After all, you can't get rich on a copper's pay. So I don't suppose anything'll come of Sammy's latest stunt.'

'So Sammy gets away with stuff?'

'I make up my own mind on that score. Daisy, don't be naïve. Keeping a brothel is illegal. The police don't ignore my places, they know where they are and what goes on, but they also know if they closed them down I'd only move 'em a couple of miles up the road. If they keep an eye on things and there's not too much bother, I'm happy and they're happy.'

'What do you want me for then?'

'Sometimes an employee thinks he can get one over on me. Sammy's a good example. Understand me, Daisy?'

'I suppose so. You want me to tell you if I find there's something going on over there, what's out of the norm? Even though you know I'm no informer?'

'Yes.'

She was caught between the devil and the fucking deep blue sea. Daisy was fitting Roy Kemp up and here he was asking her to inform him of anyone who might do just that!

'All right,' she said. He smiled at her and she looked away. He was clever all right. She couldn't help but like the bastard. Roy fucking Kemp, she thought, if I didn't hate you so much for what you did to me and mine, I could really care for you. His next question surprised her.

'When was the last time you went out?'

'That fight, and I ain't planning a return visit.'

'You like clubs, though?'

'I've gone off nightclubs, especially your clubs. I read in the papers once that people can get disembowelled in them.' He narrowed his eyes and made a steeple of his fingers. She knew he was remembering how he'd snuffed out a bloke who'd crossed him.

'You shouldn't believe all you read in the papers. The twins have opened a nice place called The Oxford Rooms on the Kingston bypass. Would you like to come with me? The boys have taken a big liking to you.'

'Sorry?' Was she hearing right? 'They don't know me.' He began to laugh.

'They know enough. Reggie also wants you to come to his wedding. I'll ring you and come down in the car to pick you up. You need money?' He started to dig around in his inside pocket.

'No! I don't need money, Roy. Why d'you want me to come with you anyway?' Daisy was thinking that he surely wouldn't be short of women. She remembered Elaine, the girl his wife Moira had been so jealous of.

'What about that Elaine? She still about?'

Daisy could see she'd shaken him.

'Don't you start.' He shook his head. 'I wouldn't be a bloke if I didn't like the attentions of a pretty girl. But there's women and there's women. My Moira, before her paranoia, was all I ever wanted. Violet'll say the same.' He pursed his lips together making them into a thin line. 'What's this? Analyse Roy Kemp week? You coming to this fuckin' wedding or not!' Daisy started to laugh.

'All right,' she said.

CHAPTER 18

'I can't get in this bloody thing.' Vera's face was about two inches away from Daisy's in the MG, and her head was tilted at an angle.

'Take that bleedin' 'at off then. I can't drive with a feather up me nose.'

'Stop 'aving a go at me. I'm doin' me best.' Daisy could be so unreasonable at times, thought Vera.

'Where's the door 'andle, I can't shut the door.'

'Oh, for fuck's sake.' Daisy climbed out of the driver's side and stomped round to the passenger side of the two-seater. Then she started laughing.

'What's the matter?'

Daisy slammed the door. 'Your hat is touching the top of the car. It's bent in the middle.'

'You know, I thought it felt a bit strange every time I moved me 'ead. I don't want the feather to break. Why don't you get a bigger car?'

'For a small woman you can be a big bloody nightmare. I don't *want* a bigger car, this one reminds me of my Eddie. Wind the window shut and get your 'andbag off the gearstick.' Vera pushed her black plastic handbag down beneath the seat and sighed as Daisy leaned across and wound up the window. She heard Daisy grumble quietly, 'I don't know why I just don't let you fall out the car . . .'

When, at last, Daisy was sitting comfortably in the driver's seat she turned to Vera. 'Right. Shall we go?'

'Why don't you leave that poor girl and her baby alone?' said Vera, watching as Daisy made a left turn past the War Memorial Hospital and into the almost permanent leafy greenness of The Avenue.

'It ain't 'er I'm worried about. Anyone who gives gin to a baby needs watching.'

'They used to do that in the old days. Little nip of whisky or brandy to make a kiddie sleep. Sometimes you can be so bloody 'ard, Dais.'

'Used to make tiny kids here in England haul coal in the mines. Don't mean it's right, does it? Besides, that Belle can't keep her hands off anything that gives her a different perspective on life. Why do you think I let her 'ave me house?'

'To keep an eye on the baby?'

'Right. And to keep her out of me spare room where she might discover what me and Bri is up to. I've planned this too long to have some druggie spoil things. And another thing. I thought a nice place to live might give 'er a bit of confidence. Help 'er clean up 'er act, make her realise how precious her baby is.'

'Exactly, Daisy. *Her* baby. It ain't *your* baby.'

'No. But it don't mean just because I can't be with my little Eddie that I mustn't care about anyone else's kiddie, does it?'

'She knock it about?'

'Not that I could see. Summer seemed okay. Sore bum where the lazy cow hadn't bothered to change it enough. But then sometimes babies get sore bums, don't they?'

'What you askin' me for?' Vera went quiet. She was thinking about her own boy. She shook herself. What was she doing dwelling on a past she couldn't change? Her kid had grown up well and strong with foster parents, and on her back, Vera had paid for him to go to university. She'd given him away to a couple who'd loved him as their own. Vera's one condition had been that the new parents were never to let on who his real mother was.

He'd had a fine education and now he was a high-flying solicitor in London. Vera had made herself a bargain that whatever happened he'd never know his true mother was a prostitute. She blessed the fact that past punters in high places enabled her to keep tabs on him without him ever knowing it.

'I know what you're thinking, you silly old tart.' Daisy patted Vera's knee. 'Stop it at once, it'll only make you sad.' Vera took out a hanky and dabbed at her eyes. Daisy always knew what she was thinking.

Vera sniffed and looked at her friend. Neither spoke. Their eyes, meeting, said it all. She wished with all her heart that Daisy would bring her little lad back to Gosport and settle here. Daisy didn't belong in Greece, no matter how much she said she loved it and the place was helping to heal the wounds of Eddie's death. Daisy was a Gosport girl. She had the dirty, friendly, sleazy little town in her blood. Got to think of something else, Vera thought, else I'll end up wanting to slit me bleeding wrists! She stared through the window at the view.

'Pretty, ain't it? In the morning light these tiny terraced houses look like something out of a film set, don't they?' Vera nodded towards Alverstoke village.

Daisy didn't answer her question but said, 'Sometimes, the real mum ain't necessarily the right mum.'

Vera gave a deep sigh. 'We back on that discussion, are we? Summer ain't your kid. You can't do nothin'.'

'We'll see. If that's Bri's kid, I fucking well can.'

'Ain't you got enough on your plate at present?'

'Kids come first.'

Vera stared at the willow trees in Western Way overhanging the pavement. The houses were much bigger and set back from the road in tree-filled gardens.

'I bet some of these people never speak to their neighbours, Vera.'

'Don't be so sure. You ain't never lived in the house you own here. People are just people. Good and bad, caring and uncaring...'

'Shut up, you're giving me a headache.'

'Ever think about the past, Dais?'

'I should say so. It makes us what we are today.' Vera jumped as Daisy sounded the horn to warn a cyclist who was about to come straight out from Vectis Road without looking. The cyclist wobbled to a stop and then gave the two-fingered V sign. 'How's Jacky?'

'Good, Dais. She's a bloody good maid. Given up the market now. She gets tips an' all, from the women as well as the blokes.'

'Has she given up the other?'

'What she does in her own time is her own business. If you asks me, she's scared stiff to walk by the caff, let alone anything else. But her bookkeeping is spot on. Well, she been used to doing it for her flower stall, see, an' she got my three girls running about like they got prickles up their arses. An' Robin, she stops 'im flouncin' about like he owns the place an' he loves 'er for it. Mind you, 'e's very good with women, is Robin. I think all me staff is a bit frightened of Jacky.'

'What about Bri? She still got a hankering for him?'

'I don't know. I think so but she don't say nothin' to me. She was all over 'im at Christmas, wasn't she? But I think it's a front. That beating she took 'as put her right off blokes. Oh, she's polite an' all that to the punters – well, it's her job an' she does it well. But when we got a bit of slack time an' the girls are larkin' about telling tales about men an' what they gets up to, she don't join in.'

Daisy swung the car into the wide driveway hedged by conifers. Daisy's open gates could do with a lick of paint, thought Vera.

'What the fuck is that?'

'I think you call it a bus, Vera. Even if it is painted in weird colours.' Daisy's face had lost its colour.

'Listen to that racket! That's modern music but it ain't modern music as we know it, like the Rollin' Stones and the Beatles. It's sort of Eastern, ain't it, Daisy?'

'It's fucking loud.' Daisy set the handbrake on the car and got out. She went round and let Vera out.

'I'm stayin' 'ere.'

'No, you ain't. I need your moral support.'

'Oh, Dais,' said Vera.

They walked through the open French doors at the side of the house. The music was coming from an LP record on the turntable, set to replay. Daisy switched it off.

'Where is everyone? It's a wonder the neighbours ain't phoned the police.'

'Fuckin' 'ell, this place is a mess,' Vera said. Bottles and fag ends littered the room and bits of food were trodden into the wall-to-wall carpeting. She picked up some newspaper that had obviously had chips wrapped in it and looked about for somewhere to put it, couldn't find anywhere so put it down on the table again.

'I expected a shithouse but hoped I wouldn't really find it.' Daisy marched into the kitchen and came out again. 'Only empty bottles and all sorts of crap in there. Let's look upstairs.'

'It's bleedin' chaos up 'ere,' said Vera who had gone ahead of her.

Vera found Belle in the bathroom, on the floor with her head in a pool of vomit.

'I s'pose I expected that as well. Get 'er up,' said Daisy. 'Is she breathing?'

There was white residue around Belle's nose and mouth. Vera slapped her face. Belle's head lolled back. Vera saw some of the powder on the floor and dipped a finger in it, raising it to her mouth. She pulled a face.

'It's fuckin' powdered morphine.'

'Where'd she get that from?'

'Lord knows. But I've 'eard that Sammy from the caff does a nice line in whatever you fancy. Mind you, her mates might have got it for 'er.'

'How do you know what it is?'

'Come on, Dais. I ain't so green as I'm cabbage looking.'

'She gonna be all right?'

'Not left 'ere. We'll clean her up and put her on the bed. Let 'er sleep it off.'

Just then a thin wail rose. Vera got up from the bathroom floor.

'Bugger me,' she said. 'I've laddered me new nylons.' She bent to examine the run, which was fast disappearing up her leg. 'I'll go and see if the kiddie's all right. You sort 'er.'

'Shut the fuck up,' called a woman's slurred voice.

In the end bedroom Vera found a skinny girl, probably only about sixteen years old, she reckoned. The girl was dressed in a grubby bra and nothing else and was sprawled across the bed. The needle marks on her arms and groin were festering. 'Shut the fuck . . .' the girl slurred, sounding as though she were a record with the needle stuck.

'Where's the kid?' Vera stood on the makings and gear that were on the floor by the side of the bed and heard the syringe crack beneath her shoe. She was furious and wanted to hit the girl for destroying herself. She could see she'd once been a pretty little thing with long dark hair. 'Where's the kid?' The muffled cry of the child was disturbing.

'Shu' the fu . . .'

Vera got hold of the girl's bony shoulder, digging her fingernails into the skin. 'Where's the fuckin' kid!' Through half opened eyes the girl tried to focus, then her eyes closed again. Vera slapped the side of her head and her eyes opened again. 'Kiddie?' shouted Vera.

'Over there.'

Vera let her fall back on the bed and looked around. She could see no sign of a child. The room had fitted wardrobes along one side, a built-in dressing table and a blanket box beneath the latticed window. Vera pulled open the lid of the box. It was empty. She pulled back the heavy full-length brocade curtains. She could hear the child, why couldn't she find her?

Fear suddenly got hold of Vera. She peered beneath the bed. Then she searched through the drawers, irrationally scrabbling at the few clothes there. She was scared; memories were crowding her brain making her unable to think straight. Still the child was wailing, but the sound was muted like it was shut in somewhere. One by one she opened the wardrobe doors. She was dry-mouthed, remembering that time at the cafe when she'd discovered the body of Moira's dead child in the wardrobe. Only this baby wasn't dead, it was crying, so where the fuck was it?

She came to the last door and flung it open. The child gazed up at her and immediately went quiet, its sticky eyes blinking as the light dazzled. Vera's shoulders collapsed with a sob and she fell on her knees on the carpet.

'You poor little mite.' She swept up the wet bundle and pressed it to her body. 'Daisy,' she yelled. 'I got 'er. Got a fuckin' live one in the wardrobe this time!'

Later, Summer was warmly wrapped up and lying safely in the well at the back of the MG, mumbling and cooing to herself. Vera sniffed at her hands and wrinkled her nose. Her nail polish was well and truly ruined and her skin stank of Jeyes Fluid, but between the two of them, they'd had a bit of a clean up of the house and sorted out the two women. Then they'd destroyed anything that could be swallowed, sniffed or injected.

'I'm not sure we should be doin' this, Dais,' Vera had cautioned. 'Goin' cold turkey ain't no picnic. Though I suppose when them two find their stash has vanished they'll soon get more.'

'Coming to my house and finding it in that state with that poor little mite shut away, who could 'ave died, ain't no picnic either. So fuck 'em.'

They'd left Summer's meagre wardrobe and feeding bottles. Daisy said she'd buy the kiddie new stuff. The little girl had been washed, and fed with a spoon from a tin of baby chocolate pudding which Vera had found in Belle's bag.

'What we gonna do with a kid, Dais?'

'You mean, what's Bri going to do with his daughter? It's his problem.'

'He ain't gonna like it,' said Vera.

'I couldn't leave Summer there, could I?'

'You left them two to sleep it off; 'ow could they look after a little 'un in that state? You did what you thought was best. Ought to be strung up, that Belle.'

'What I can't understand is why the bus was there and no other bugger was.'

'Don't know the answer to that one, Dais, an' I got other things to worry about. I told Jacky I wouldn't be long.' No way did Vera want to get involved in a verbal battle between Daisy and Bri about little Summer. She was getting too old for dramas, she reckoned, even though they did seem to follow her around like stray dogs.

'Oh, no, you don't run away that easy. Bri's in the shop. I can see through you like a pane of glass. You ain't leaving me to confront him on me own.'

Vera groaned and resigned herself to Bri's wrath.

There were no customers in the shop. Bri was bending over an apple box examining and marking prices inside books. He looked up and smiled as they entered.

'Got a good deal here, Dais . . .' His words petered out when he saw Vera holding the child. Vera's heart started beating fast.

'I brought you your daughter,' said Daisy. 'Her

fucking mother is spark out on morphine. There's a circus bus on my gravel drive and another junkie in my bedroom. I won't even tell you where Vera found Summer, 'cause you'll never believe me . . .'

'. . . Tell me.' His face reminded Vera of a lump of grey granite.

'She was shut in a wardrobe. I'm not saying Belle put 'er there, but someone did.' Then she turned and took Summer from Vera's arms. 'Don't give me no crap about she ain't yours. If you don't want to turn out like your old man you'd better face up to your responsibilities.' She handed him the child. 'We can get the authorities involved. Or you can be the parent she needs.'

His mouth crumpled in on itself as he stared at the baby. He glanced at Vera. She couldn't begin to guess what Bri was thinking. His face gave nothing away. Daisy looked at Vera. It was, Vera thought, as though each of them was scared to speak first.

'All right.'

'Fuck me,' said Vera. 'I need a sit down.'

'But I don't know nothin' about kids . . .'

'You can learn,' snapped Daisy.

'A wardrobe?' Bri uttered the words as though he couldn't believe what she'd said.

'Yes. Belle won't even know she's gone for a while yet, and I'm certain when she does, she won't care,' said Vera.

Daisy said, 'Ever wondered if she came looking for Bri to unload the kiddie? Thinking he might . . .'

'I'm here,' Bri said. 'I can speak for myself.' He looked down at the child again. Vera saw his face soften. 'Belle was all right when you left?'

''Course. Else we wouldn't 'ave left her, would we?'

239

'Won't this child need some stuff?'

'Told you it was a waste of time putting the car away, Vera.'

Vera laughed. 'We off again, then?'

'Where you two going?' Vera was pushing Daisy towards the door.

'Shopping,' she said, glancing back at him.

'You can't leave her with me?' Panic flooded his face.

'Oh yes we can. There's towels in the airing cupboard to change 'er bum. We'll be back soon,' said Daisy. 'You're a daddy now.'

'I like buying 'er things,' Daisy said later as they came out of Boots.

'Seems like it,' said Vera. 'You've filled the bleedin' boot. Only you can't keep 'er with you at the flat. You do realise that. You got a lot on your plate, Dais.'

Daisy ignored her. 'I'm not listening.'

Vera tried again. 'She can't stay in the shop all day. It's not fair on 'er or you two. Neither can you leave a baby alone in the flat upstairs while you're working downstairs. And what about when Bri's out an' about ordering and buying stuff? Just when it's all beginnin' to shape up nicely, what you gonna do with a baby? Ain't that why you left your own little love?'

Trouble with Daisy was she was too kindhearted sometimes for her own good.

'I could get a baby minder.'

'Now you're thinking in the right direction. Mrs 'Arris round in South Street looks after a little boy aged two. She's ever so nice. What's more important, she's got permission to look after kiddies.'

'Permission? What you on about?'

'Mick Edmunds is on the council.'

'A friend of yours?'

Vera nodded. 'Ever so nice 'e is . . .'

'Get on with it.'

'He has to vet all the homes and make sure the would-be minders ain't kiddie fiddlers and people on the make. I don't think you wants that for little Summer, else you might as well 'ave left 'er with 'er cow of a mother.'

'Bloody sure I don't. Could this Mick Edmunds find a decent place for Summer?'

'If I ask him, he will. But you couldn't do no better than Mrs 'Arris. I've known her for years and she dotes on the kids that have passed through her hands.'

'If she's only looking after the one kiddie you think she might look after Summer as well, until Bri gets himself sorted out?'

'It's possible,' said Vera. I won't let that little scrap come to any more harm, she promised herself.

The terraced house in South Street had starched white nets up at the sash windows and a polished brass dolphin for a door knocker.

Immediately the door was opened Daisy liked the look of the small round woman standing before her. After introductions and questions had been asked and answered, Elsie Harris brought in a plate of home-made shortbread on a tray along with a teapot and cups and saucers. A guarded fire was burning brightly and a little boy sat in a playpen surrounded by toys but carefully trying to colour in a picture from a book.

Daisy ignored Vera's advice and decided to tell Elsie Harris the truth. After an hour and a good look around her pretty home, Daisy had come to some terms and conditions after Elsie explained herself.

'My Alf got gassed during the war. He can't work but he likes 'is allotment, so everything I cook is 'ome grown. I got the one boy of me own an' he's still at college near London. He's going to be a teacher,' she said. Pride shone from her eyes. 'I would 'ave liked more kiddies but it wasn't to be. Mind you, this little 'un is a real darlin'.' She waved her hand towards the playpen. 'Tell you what, why don't you tell Summer's daddy – ain't that just a lovely name, Summer? – tell him to bring her around tonight to meet me?'

Daisy nodded. The woman was genuine and her love of kiddies shone out. As she and Vera stepped out into the January cold again, Daisy knew she was taking a lot on herself making decisions for Summer. But what else could she do?

'What did I tell you? Woman's a bloody gem, ain't she?'

'An' you're a bloody know-all,' Daisy replied good-naturedly. 'Summer ain't going to live to be a toddler if she stays with Belle. The courts would take 'er away if they knew what was going on. This way we'll know she'll be well looked after until Bri can sort himself out.'

'Queenie'll love findin' out she's a granny,' said Vera.

'Don't you take a bloody poke at me because I ain't told 'er about little Eddie. I will, when the time's right.'

The shop was silent when Daisy got back, the only customer an old man choosing thrillers from some new stock.

'Where is she?' Daisy demanded, dumping her packages and bags on the floor. It was too quiet. Bri put his fingers to his lips and led Daisy to the back of the counter.

In a large drawer on the carpet, on a pillow lay the baby girl. She was wearing another of Daisy's cotton blouses. There was flaky brown stuff around her small mouth. It didn't seem to worry her. One tiny arm was flung above her head and she was fast asleep. Daisy's heart melted at the sight of her.

'What's she been eatin'?'

'Weetabix. I mashed it up with some warm milk and sugar and she chomped it down.' He looked pleased with himself.

'So you changed your mind about her not being your daughter?' He gave her an old-fashioned look and then glanced at Summer.

'Might 'ave.'

Daisy laughed. 'We need to talk.'

The man came over to the till with a pile of books. Bri added up the cost and put them in a large paper bag. He deposited the money in the till's drawer and thanked the customer. Daisy had perched herself on the counter next to Bertie, who didn't move a hair.

'You might need to get the stool and sit down to hear what I've got to say,' she said. Yet after she told him what she'd arranged he wasn't angry at all. He looked relieved.

'I ain't stupid, Daisy. Don't you think I was wondering how we was going to cope? It's not just the shop, it's the scam. We need no ties to do it.'

And Daisy immediately knew, despite her heartache at leaving her own child, she'd done the sensible thing in not bringing him with her to Gosport.

Daisy didn't go with him when he took Summer round to meet Elsie Harris. The woman could speak for herself and Bri would surely see what happy surroundings the family lived in. But when eventually he came back without her he was subdued.

'When this is all over, I'm going to bring her up,' he declared. Daisy smiled at him. She knew that now he'd accepted the little girl he would do right by her. 'I'm also going to visit Summer every day so she gets to know who I am.'

He didn't take off his coat but went to the window and looked down to the street below. Daisy started gathering all Summer's new things together for Elsie Harris. When she'd finished he was still gazing out of the window. Daisy could feel Bri's sadness and it matched her own. But it wasn't the right time to tell him how the little girl had in such a short time wormed her way into her own heart. She put her arm through his.

'Want a cup of tea?'

He surprised her by replying, 'No. After I've taken round Summer's belongings, I'm going out.'

After he'd gone she decided to have a bath and wash her hair. Maybe the scented water and warm bubbles might lift her spirits. It'd certainly help to get rid of the disinfectant smell and the memory of the carnage in the Western Way house.

Later, wrapped in her dressing gown, she curled up on the sofa with Bertie on her lap and dozed off. Bri shook her awake.

'They've gone,' he said.

'Get off me, you're cold.' He seemed to have brought the winter indoors with him. 'You mean Belle?'

He nodded.

'But it wasn't that long ago we left her and her mate

sleeping off the shit. I wouldn't 'ave thought they could go anywhere.'

'Maybe not, but they have.' He took off his coat and hat and threw them across the back of the sofa. 'I had a bit of a tidy-up as well. Burnt some of their rubbish at the bottom of the garden.'

'That's not what you went there for though, is it? Not to clean up a bleeding house?'

He shook his head. 'No. I went to 'ave a go at 'er about the kiddie.'

'Just as well she'd scarpered then.' She searched Bri's face for signs of distress and found none. 'Belle don't care about Summer after all.'

He shook his head. 'She didn't leave the key you gave her neither.'

'No matter. That's the least of me worries. I think I'll put that place on the market. I'd really rather 'ave the money than the worry of it. The house was never me, was it? I'm happier living here.' His face lit up.

'Are you really, Dais?'

'Well, I am when things are going all right.' He gave her a large wink and walked away, the cat following him.

Daisy heard him busying himself in the kitchen and then he came back with two steaming mugs of tea. 'Worried about Roy Kemp?'

'Nah. He don't suspect a thing. And as long as I keep him happy, it'll work out fine. The next thing on the bleedin' agenda is Reggie Kray's wedding on the nineteenth of April. I'll need some new clobber for that.'

'Move your feet,' Bri said, and slid his body on to the sofa, replacing Daisy's feet on his lap. 'Here, have this ticking thing as well.' He passed her Bertie who was hanging like a limp piece of rag. Daisy sniffed and wrinkled her nose.

'Sardines,' said Bri. 'I opened a tin for her.'

Daisy nodded.

'He can't get married from where he is, Daisy.'

'A charge of demanding money with menaces will hardly keep them two boys in gaol forever, will it?'

'No, but no bail means Reggie and Ronnie'll have to stay where they are until it's sorted.'

Daisy nodded. 'Trust Ron to get copped for 'aving a knife an' all.'

'Do you like the twins, Dais?' Bri was looking at her, waiting for her answer.

'I'm not sure. I think they're fair minded, especially where their own folk are concerned.' She paused. 'But like the mafia they're bastards if anyone slights them. I like the way they're protective of each other. That twin thing, I suppose. Anyway, the best thing to do is to keep on the right side of them. Charlie, their brother, ain't nobody's fool, either. Just because he's quieter don't mean he ain't just as dangerous. Violet's a laugh but she's obsessive about her boys. They don't half think a lot of her too.'

Daisy went quiet. She thought about her own mum and how she'd died of cancer believing that Kenny would look after her beloved daughter. All water under the bridge now, thought Daisy. Men could come and go, but you only ever had one mum. Mums were special. Unless you were like Summer and your mum couldn't give a shit about you.

'And Roy Kemp?'

'He did the dirty on me, Bri. I have to pay him back. Funny thing is I admire the bastard, even understand his motives, but I can't let that stand in me way. Does that answer your questions, Mr Nosy Parker?'

Bri was giving her a strange look. Then he seemed to shake himself out of wherever place he'd gone to.

'Got everything sorted for tomorrow? You'll be all right alone in the shop?' He took a good pull on his tea.

'Ain't I always?' Daisy answered. 'And you?'

'Different venues and more of them. Getting into the London outskirts good and proper. Same mates, same wholesalers, so we got a really good deal goin' with them now. Them wholesalers love me for the money I keep spending with them. I'm even getting discounts for prompt payments. And the stuff we got to sell is beyond your wildest dreams . . .'

Daisy laughed. 'Stop that old flannel! I'm your partner not a bleeding punter! And get off home, I'm ready for me bed.'

CHAPTER 19

What to do with the kid's body? The radio was playing 'It's Over'. Well, it certainly was over for the boy. And would be for him, if he couldn't pull himself together.

Sammy paced up and down in his room. The boy was still tied over the stools. Feet, legs and buttocks splayed. Stupid fuckin' kid wasn't supposed to peg it. He'd taken it before like that, hadn't he?

The kid had screamed when old Hagerty had entered him. But Hagerty liked his kids to make a noise. Maximum penetration they got, he said, and they only screamed because they liked it. Sammy had pushed a pillow into the kid's face to muffle his cries. He didn't want anyone hearing the noise outside in the street, did he?

'He all right?' As if you care, thought Sammy as Hagerty wiped his cock and did up his flies. He'd barely glanced at the still figure of the boy as he'd handed Sammy the bank notes.

'He's fainted. Bit of a shock that fuckin' great cock of yours going into that piddling little space. He'll come round in a minute. You better get out without being seen.'

Hagerty had laughed at the compliment. Get the fuck out of here, thought Sammy, I need to think.

He didn't want to lose Hagerty, he was a good customer. Paid well to fuck kids, the younger the better. Boys preferably, though he wasn't fussed.

The boy really was dead. He'd better untie him, quick.

Sammy had seen him take a struggling gasp as the bloated body of Hagerty thrust away. The lad was crying with pain and trying to take air into his lungs at the same time. But it was Sammy who couldn't stand the high pitch of his screams. They seemed to remind him of other times, other screams, and no one had helped him when the bloke, his foster father, had pounded away at him. So Sammy had stuffed the feather cushion in his face and cut off his air supply. Hagerty was too far gone to notice, all he cared about was his own satisfaction.

Now he had another fuckin' body to dispose of. Sammy sighed.

He pulled the torn net curtain aside and stared down into the darkness of the street. Fuckin' cold out there. Would this miserable winter never end? He looked back at the boy, then went and sat on the bed. He looked around the room. What a fuckin' dump.

What he needed was something to roll the body in, then he could carry the bastard. The little swine wouldn't be missed for a while, Sammy was sure of that. He was hardly ever at home anyway, and Sammy had been feeding him for favours since Christmas. He'd had a big row with his stepfather, so the lad said. His stepdad had beaten him, then slung him out. The kid had spent some time with his mates before coming to Sammy. Always knew where the grass was greenest, did kids, Sammy chuckled to himself. Only this one would be pushing up the daisies, beneath the green grass. Since coming to the cafe the kid had hardly left the place because he didn't want to be seen by anyone and taken home again. That was going to work in Sammy's favour. Mind you, he thought, the brat had gotten friendly with Rosa. If the cunt dared to ask him where the lad was, he'd tell her he'd moved on. Or else give her something to shut her up.

With a bit of luck, he might get away with dumping the kid in the creek. No, not the creek. The other little bastard had ended up there. Didn't want the coppers thinking there was some kind of pattern, did he? Need to strip and wash the corpse first though. Didn't want them new police forensic buggers making two and two add up to five. But it was too early to get rid of him yet.

The pubs hadn't long turned out. His girls, bringing punters back, might think it a bit odd meeting him in the street, especially him carrying a carpet. Besides, they didn't have keys and relied on him to let them in. And that fuckin' bookshop opposite was lit up like Blackpool Illuminations.

Sammy had been to Blackpool. Lived in a caravan on a site just off The Golden Mile. It was fine until he got badly done over in a cottage one night. Never liked public toilets much after that. Now, when he stuck up his cards in the urinals he was in and out like a rabbit fucking. He'd always remember those four blokes built like brick shithouses and with cocks to match. Some queers dream about a gang bang. Their idea of heaven. In reality it had been a fuckin' nightmare.

He came down south after that. Anything was better than going back to his mother. The one place he never went was home after he'd managed to escape her clutches. In a funny kind of way he'd preferred living in the foster homes than going back to his own flesh and blood.

London first. That's where he'd met Roy Kemp. Not that Roy liked blokes, fuckin' 'ell, no. But Roy let him run a few errands, make himself useful, that kind of shit, and paid him well for it. From Roy he met Ronnie Kray. He liked Ronnie.

Ronnie showed him a life he never thought it was possible to have. Clubs, the boxing scene, celebrities. Ronnie dressed him in clothes from Savile Row, said he didn't want him showing him or his brothers up. Of course, Sammy was younger then. That was the trouble. He got older, and was replaced by a lad still in his teens who Ronnie met in The Magnolia Club. So Sammy started working full time for Roy Kemp. And renting himself out.

The buzzer sounded downstairs. Sammy poked his head out of the window. Must be a slow night tonight, the cunts were on their own. He ran lightly down the stairs and let four girls enter in a haze of cheap perfume, fags and stale sex. He took their money off them.

'Better make it up tomorrow,' he growled, counting coins and notes. To Big Sal he gave back a note. She preened before the other three and they climbed the stairs ahead of Sammy. He watched their fat legs and wobbling arses and his stomach heaved, but all the whores were accounted for now. Two hotel over-nighters and that dozy cow, the new girl who was fuckin' slow on the uptake, already in her room. But wasn't it just like Roy Kemp to let a new girl learn the ropes slowly? Left up to Sammy he'd have made sure she was earning her fuckin' keep long ago. Rosa was visiting her mother in Southsea. He could begin thinking again about the lad upstairs.

Sammy liked his men a bit older, they were more kind and appreciative, but lately they only wanted to fuck, not take him out for meals or give him presents. He didn't think he'd ever fall in love again. Not after Ronnie. And Ronnie couldn't care less about him now. And why should he when there was always someone else who'd slip into Ronnie Kray's bed.

A bit of procuring, a bit of flaying and whipping, that was okay. Better give the kids a wide berth from now onwards, though. It had gotten way too risky.

What if Roy found out? Sometimes it seemed Roy Kemp had eyes up his bleedin' arse. Well, he wouldn't think about that. If Roy Kemp got a whiff of kids bein' involved on his premises ... No, he wouldn't think about that.

Roy kept him on the payroll because he kept the girls in order, well mostly. And he collected their money promptly. So Roy frequently overlooked the little perks that Sammy had going for himself.

Back in his room he looked out the window again. No lights on over the road. He'd take a chance.

When he'd washed him the kid didn't look too bad – apart from the bruises. Skinny little runt, though. He'd already hidden the clothes the lad had previously discarded under the sofa. He'd dispose of them later. Now he cleared a space on the floor and rolled the kid in the blue rag rug. Thank God this boy was small.

When he'd rolled the rug as tightly as possible he tied it in three places with rope and hoisted it to his shoulder. It wasn't that heavy, just a bit bulky.

He remembered to put his Stanley knife in his pocket; after all, he couldn't leave the rug with the body, could he? Someone might recognise it. He'd need to cut the rope away.

He took a last look out of both windows before picking up the body and making for the door.

'Sorry, kid,' he said. 'Never did ask your fuckin' name.'

Daisy had been crying and she couldn't sleep. She kept going over her earlier conversations with Bri. Her head was a mess of jumbled thoughts.

'I'm going to do my best for Summer,' Bri had said. 'You know that.' He had put his arm around her shoulders. Daisy was beginning to feel like one of those large dead cods on the fishmonger's market stall, all glossy and fresh but dead inside. Even her eyes had lost their sparkle, she reckoned, just like the dead fishes' eyes.

She thought about Susie, she had sparkly eyes. Susie had had a childhood to end all childhoods. Fingered by her mother's boyfriends until she'd run away to escape the drugs and the men and ended up in Gosport. She'd slept on the ferry boats until Eddie found her and reckoned he could get good money for her body. Daisy had rescued her. For a long time Susie had stayed in a mental shell, terrified of blokes, especially Eddie. Then she had met Si and fallen truly in love. Susie had found contentment. And after all this was over, would Daisy find it too?

Why didn't she have any feelings for Bri? He'd make a lovely husband and a good father. He wasn't a child-man like Kenny had been, a man she'd almost had to nurse into adulthood. True, she liked Bri, felt close and natural with him, but whatever thoughts he might have of them getting together, she just wasn't interested.

Trouble was, she liked the bad boys.

Like Eddie.

But Eddie was gone, and all the crying for him and the thinking about him wasn't going to bring him back. The realisation of that had hit her hard. Once upon a time, not so long ago, Daisy had thought she'd be able to say she never wanted another man. No one could match up to Eddie. She'd had the best, what did she want with the rest? But that wasn't natural, was it?

It wasn't in the big scheme of things that she could resist the pain of loneliness, resist wanting to feel a man's arms about her. Or that special feeling that comes in the aftermath of the deliciousness of sex with the right person. She wanted to bury her face in a man's warm chest and inhale the sleepy smell of him. She wanted to shut her eyes and let their tongues taste each other with him holding her close, knowing what she liked, what was irresistible to her. She wanted him inside her, listening to his murmurs of pleasure.

And Eddie was gone.

Was that why she'd almost fallen for Valentine Waite's silver tongue and hands that knew exactly the right spots to touch? Val had kissed her, sucked at her, running his tongue under her lower lip until she'd thought he might swallow her. His fingers had probed, sending shock waves through her body, and she had wanted it to go on – until something had stopped her, pulled her back from the brink. He'd sent her flowers, but nothing more. Not a phone call, nor a letter. She'd found that strange until Violet had let out the information he had gone to America for a fight at some place called Caesar's Palace in Las Vegas. Magic names that Daisy had only ever read in the film magazines like *Picture Show* and *Picturegoer*.

And Bri had chattered on about Summer, the little girl who'd stolen his heart.

'She's such a little girl, Daisy. How could anyone not love her?' What he'd really meant was why hadn't Belle been in touch? 'She ain't 'alf packing on the pounds now Elsie is feeding her.'

Daisy had to admit the child was growing prettier every day.

Bri continued, 'And she loves it when I tell her stories . . .'

'She don't know what you're on about. She's too bleeding young,' Daisy said. But she smiled at the thought of the tiny mite lying there in her cot or in Bri's arms while he told her about princesses dressed in pretty pink dresses with tiaras on their flowing auburn hair, who just happened to have the name Summer.

'Maybe not. But I like reading to her from a picture book every night. And I swear she knows who I am. C'mon, Daisy, what else is bothering you?'

Bertie had decided she didn't like being left out and had jumped up on Bri's lap. 'What do you want, girl?' He'd tickled the cat. Daisy had sighed and shaken her head. What could she say about how she felt?

'You make a fine pair, you an' that soddin' cat. Both dopey. An' if you must know I'm worried about tomorrow as well.' Of course she was worried. Didn't she always get into a right strop in case anything went wrong?

'It's just another sale, Dais. All the others have gone like clockwork. Why should this one be any different?'

'There's a lot of money involved.'

'We knew when we started that the day would come when we'd be getting goods on credit. What's to worry about?'

Bri squeezed her shoulder. She could feel the heat coming from his body. His chest was bare and so were his feet. He was wearing a pair of old clean jeans, as he'd just used her shower. The Black Bear only had a bathroom with a bath and everyone used that. He'd tried to pull her towards him but she'd moved away.

'You worry too much.' He'd unravelled himself and got up from the sofa, finished dressing and left.

Daisy had gone to bed. She'd tossed and turned until finally she'd got up, hoping a drink would settle her.

'I won't put the kitchen light on, that street lamp does the job well enough,' Daisy told Bertie as she leaned across the sink to fill the kettle.

She sighed, and gazed into the street below. She lifted her hand to move the net curtain aside but something stopped her.

'What's he got there, cat? Looks like a roll of lino. Funny hour to be putting down lino.' She watched Sammy struggle with his burden in the doorway of the cafe and realised it was coming out, not going in.

Daisy thought of what Sammy had done to Jacky and it made her sick to her stomach. She set down the kettle. 'I'm going down to find out what that bastard's up to,' she muttered.

Within moments she was pulling on jeans and a jumper and tying her coat around her. Another look through the window and she saw Sammy going across the spare bit of ground. She ran downstairs and let herself, heart beating wildly, out of the shop and into the darkness.

She slipped the key into the lock of the side door of The Black Bear. There was a light beneath Bri's door. He answered her light knock immediately. He was still dressed.

'Nice surprise . . .' he started, but stopped immediately she entered his sparse room and pulled the door closed, the words tumbling from her. 'Well, you ain't going on your own,' he said.

'Better hurry, then. We got to catch him up.' Bri pulled on a jacket as he went and followed her down the darkened stairs.

'He's bloody gone,' whispered Bri. 'An' it's fuckin' cold.'

'Well, he didn't seem as though he was in a hurry. It was more like he didn't want to draw attention to himself. Shush! I just saw a movement across the bomb site.'

'Could have been a fox.'

'Bloody big one then.'

'See that derelict lorry?' Daisy said. 'If we can get behind it without 'im noticing we can see which direction he's going. Quick. Hold my hand.'

'Why?'

'We got to look like we're together.'

They made it to the back of the lorry. Bri pushed Daisy against the open door of the burned-out vehicle and covered Daisy's mouth with his. She tried to struggle in the shadows but he was stronger. Then Bri broke away and hissed. 'He's watching.' And once more his lips were on hers, a kiss that seemed to go on and on, until the pit of her stomach began sending out waves of heat to her nerve endings. Bri broke away.

'Sorry about that. He looked back and saw us. I had to do something. Let him think we're a courting couple with nowhere to go.'

Daisy pushed back the hair from her face and glared. 'He might 'ave already dumped whatever it was he was carrying.' Her eyes scoured the line of the creek. The tide was out. Rocks and the skeletons of rotting wooden ships looked as though they were climbing from the mud. The stony beach was deserted and where the sea lapped far out it was almost like glass. Lights from moored craft shimmered crazily on the tiny ripples of the water.

She said, 'Weevil Lane?'

He nodded.

Daisy hated Weevil Lane. It led to the red brick buildings in Royal Clarence Yard where Gosport had supplied the Navy with gunpowder and shells since the beginning of the eighteenth century and still did. Daisy knew all about it because she'd read up on all the local history from books in the library. On a triangular setting with Portsmouth to two sides and Gosport's ramparts holding the deserted piece of land safe, it was a difficult place for invaders to find. But it was an eerie spot and gave Daisy the creeps. Deserted now, in the morning it would be a hive of activity as people arrived in their hundreds on bikes, down the narrow lane to start work.

Daisy shivered. 'He needn't have come back this way. He could 'ave gone down the railway line and come out on Mumby Road.' She stopped. 'Fuck!'

'What's the matter?'

'Brambles.' She rubbed her ankle. She could just make out the iron gates ahead leading to the dark buildings. She thought of the stories she'd heard, of how the women workers ended up with orange hair due to the gunpowder and how the ghost of a murdered woman was supposed to walk near the creek water's edge.

'Jesus Christ!'

Daisy saw Bri run towards the grass where the trees overhung the narrow gauge railway line. She followed.

The boy was lying naked, sprawled face up on the icy ground. Immediately Daisy bent down to him. He looked asleep, but his skinny white limbs were twisted unnaturally, as though he'd been thrown to the ground like a bit of unwanted rubbish. Her eyes left the boy and scanned the grass. Sammy must have taken that covering away with him.

'You know who this is?'

''Course I do,' Bri said.

Daisy remembered the boy's cheeky grin, his bravado in the market that day when he'd stolen the old man's purse. Now he looked like a very young child indeed. She put out her hand. Bri pulled her away.

'Look but don't touch.'

'He might be . . .'

'He's dead, Dais. Let's go. We can't do nothing.'

Bri grabbed her hand.

'We can't just leave 'im.'

'We have to,' Bri said. Daisy couldn't escape Bri's strong grip as he half dragged, half pulled her back to the main road, but instead of heading towards the town he strode in the opposite direction towards the closed pub on the corner of Spring Garden Lane. He stopped in the shadow of the Railway Tavern's doorway.

'We go down here and along by Walpole Park, take

259

that way back towards the town,' he said. Daisy was breathing fast, her wrist hurt where he'd grabbed her and she rubbed at it now he'd set her free. 'Sorry about bein' a bit rough, Dais, but I really thought you was going to get a bit funny back there. You looked as though you wanted to pick up the lad and carry him to a place of safety. But now we know what Sammy dumped we got to keep our mouths shut. Act as if we think nothing has happened. Okay?'

She was trying not to cry, not to think about the boy in the grass. Bri slipped his arm through hers. For once she was happy to let him tell her what to do. All she could see in her mind was the boy running off down the market and the sarky grin he'd had when Bri had made him apologise to the old fella.

What had happened to the boy? Where had he been since Christmas when he'd been reported missing? That bastard Sammy had a hand in this and Daisy wanted a few answers. Surely Roy Kemp wasn't involved?

When they reached the shop, Bri produced the key and opened the door, switching on the light as he pulled her inside.

'If Sammy's looking, he'll think we've just got home after a night out. We don't want him thinking we followed him.'

In the comfort of the kitchen upstairs, Daisy sat on a stool and wept.

She wiped her face with the back of her hand. 'We should call the police.'

'And what would happen then?' Bri led her to the bathroom and turned on the shower. 'Get in, get washed and warmed, get dried and into bed.'

Daisy did as she was told. As the hot water ran over

her body and her senses gradually returned to near normal she realised how foolish it would be to call the police. Once they knew of Sammy's involvement, it would also mean, as the legal owner of the cafe, Roy Kemp's involvement. All her months of scheming would be wasted while the police swarmed over the cafe.

But what about the boy? Lying there in the cold.

'Get out and get into bed,' said Bri. He hung a clean fluffy towel over the shower rail. As Daisy rubbed herself dry she could hear Bri clattering cups in the kitchen. When she climbed into her bed Bri had already set two mugs of tea on the bedside table.

'It's almost dawn,' he said. 'As soon as it's light his body will be found by the first arrivals at the factory yard. The police will be called. Sammy meant the lad to be found else he'd have hidden the body.'

'You think Sammy did it?'

Bri shrugged. 'Used the kid for sex, no doubt. Probably got some kind of alibi lined up and felt it was safe to dump him. We leave this to the coppers, Dais. Let them sort out it out.'

Bertie was curled in a doughnut shape on her pillow, too sleepy even to move when Daisy reached for her tea. She took a mouthful and made a face.

'There's plenty of sugar in that. Good for shock.'

'But it's the lad who stole the purse, Bri.'

'I know, but listen to me. We mustn't get involved. They might even think we had a hand in the lad's death. I clouted him round the ear in the market. People'll remember that.'

Daisy knew he was right.

'Okay. But if the coppers ain't got anyone for it by

the time I've finished with Roy Kemp, I'm going to see some kind of fucking justice is sorted out . . .'

'Fair enough. And I'll be with you every step of the way. Now drink some more of that tea and move over.'

'What you mean, move over?

Bri smiled at her. 'Don't worry, I ain't going to ravish you. I just want to settle you down before I go back to the pub. You think I don't know you're going to lay there and fret all night? Now shove over and drink that bleedin' tea.'

Daisy drank. But the tea's sweetness seemed to make the tears flow afresh. Bri climbed on to the counterpane. Bertie took exception to all the moving about and walked away with her tail stuck straight up in the air. At the bottom of the bed she made herself comfortable again.

Taking the mug, Bri put it back on the bedside table and pulled her into his arms. Daisy rested her head on his chest. It was comforting, breathing his warmth and listening to the steady beat of his heart.

Daisy's eyes closed.

CHAPTER 20

'Daisy, Daisy. Whatever shall I fuckin' do?'

'Calm down, Vera. What's the matter? Just found your invitation to Ringo's weddin' a day late?'

'It's not funny, Daisy Lane!'

'No, it's not. His new wife Maureen'll be right pissed off you never turned up. They'll 'ave all that food you never ate left over.'

Daisy could imagine Vera at the other end of the telephone, trying to compose herself, taking deep breaths, her gold earrings bobbing about. She'd have her eyes closed, waiting for Daisy to stop messing about.

'My son wants to visit!'

'Fuckin' hell!'

'Now I 'ave to tell *you* to calm down, don' I?'

'Do you want me to come round?'

'No. But I need to talk for a minute then ask a favour.'

'Anything,' Daisy said.

Good Lord! What a turn-up for the books. Vera must be over the moon yet trying so hard to be calm about it. Daisy was alone in the shop. Bri had gone out hiring venues in London and the suburbs. Bertie was asleep on the counter and the shop was busy.

'Let me call you back in a few minutes when this

crowd has thinned. I can close up for a while, then we can talk in peace.'

Daisy hung up. Her hands were shaking. Vera had had a child when she was hardly more than a child herself and she'd never expected her boy to seek her out. It had been her wish that he'd never know his birth mother and certainly not that she was a prostitute, even though it had been Vera's earnings that had kept him and put him through university.

Ten minutes later Daisy phoned Vera back.

'You must 'ave been sitting next to the bleeding phone to answer as quick as that,' said Daisy. 'Why don't you want me to come round? One of the biggest moments of your life and you want to talk over the fucking phone . . .'

'Don't be cross, Dais. If I see you, I'll start cryin'. This way I can pour me heart out and you can't see me emotions.'

'All right. Talk away,' Daisy said.

'I've got a letter. He wants to see me and thank me. Imagine that, Dais?'

'Oh, my love,' Daisy said. She was near to tears herself.

'Goin' through his parents' stuff he came across letters. His mum an' dad promised me he'd never find out about me, Dais. You knows it was one of my conditions. But they went and got themselves killed in a car smash.'

'He must have been distraught to find out that his mum and dad wasn't his mum and dad.'

'They shouldn't have kept no letters, Dais.'

'They couldn't know what was going to happen.'

'I didn't want him to find out!'

'Well, he has! Even if he hadn't come across the

264

information, times are changing. There's talk of making things easier for adopted children to find their real parents . . .'

'But I don't want to be found. Look at me!'

'I'm going to come round there in a minute and smack you one! Stop putting yourself down. If he knows where you are he's done some digging, so he knows quite a bit about you, you daft ol' bat! He's a fucking solicitor for Christ's sake. They got access to all kinds of information . . .'

'But this is a glorified knockin' shop. You said so yourself.'

'If you're not going to be sensible . . .'

'I can't see 'im 'ere an' I wants you with me.'

'This is a very private moment between mother and son.'

'Please?'

There was such pleading in her voice that tears sprang to Daisy's eyes. She wiped her face with the back of her hand.

'I do want to see him, Dais. Just once more in me lifetime. I remember that day when we 'ad nowhere to go. I cuddled 'im to me, feelin' 'is little warm body an' lookin' at 'is tiny 'ands with 'is fingernails just like mine, and we slept in a cornfield. An' if it 'adn't been for the travellin' folk who found me we'd both be dead now.'

Daisy remembered her story: the gold earrings given her by the gypsy woman who'd looked after her and Vera promising she would wear them until her dying day.

'There's so many gaps in 'is life and he needs to know about the gypsies, about 'is father, so he can understand 'is roots. He might even want to find 'is real dad, who knows? He should be told these things. But I need you close to me, Dais. I can't do it without you.'

'You are a fucking lovely woman, you know that? How could anyone, let alone your own flesh and blood, fail to realise what a remarkable person you are, you silly cow!'

'I ain't said I won't see 'im but not 'ere. Not when I got Jacky ushering in clients to me girls. He's a *solicitor*. An' my *son*.'

'So take 'im out for lunch.'

'What, up the chip shop? I won't feel comfortable.' Vera was making excuses and Daisy wondered why. Then the penny dropped. 'You want to invite 'im here? You reckon a second-hand bookshop is better than your place?'

'Better than Heavenly Bodies, an' I feel at 'ome round your place. 'Sides, you'll be there.'

'Oh, my love,' said Daisy. 'When?'

'Couple of days?'

'Fine.'

'Really?'

'Really.'

'You're a good friend.'

'An' you really are a daft old bat. An' I wouldn't want to be without you, ever.'

Vera hung up.

'Jacky, why can't you print clearer? I can't decide whether this bloke 'as paid or we fuckin' owe 'im!'

'Keep your hair on. It's 'ardly likely we got to pay 'im, is it?' Jacky was fed up with Vera. She'd been picking on her all morning. Peck, peck, peck, like an

266

old black crow. Hopping about and finding fault where there really wasn't any to be found.

Jacky breathed in the smell of lavender, at least that was soothing. So was the music coming softly from the radio. It wasn't pop music but something classy like Bri listened to and often had playing in the bookshop. Jacky left Vera to look for fault in something else she'd done and walked carefully through to the back to make tea. At least the girls would be grateful for a cuppa. Moments later she was piling cups on a tray. Impulsively she tipped extra bourbon biscuits onto a plate. She counted the cups. Then relented and took a cup down for Vera. Her heart softened towards Vera. It seemed as though she had something on her mind, eating away at her, but hadn't Vera been there for her when she needed her? And Daisy, too. She shuddered to think what might have happened if Vera hadn't found her that night when she was attacked.

Jacky still had little memory of what had occurred, beyond the men pulling at her and the pain. The scars on the outside of her body had started to fade, until . . .

And now it was all starting again.

'What's the matter with you? You know I like plain digestive, me bum's getting too big with all this sugary stuff.'

Jacky looked into Vera's blazing eyes. 'Make your own soddin' tea then!' She pushed the tray into Vera's hands and hobbled down the centre of the shop towards the cubicles. Number three was empty so she slipped in and slammed the door. She lowered herself down on the hard couch and cried. She heard Vera's clacking high heels, searching for her.

Vera pushed open the door and came in trailing clouds of Californian Poppy.

'If you don't want to be found you should put the bleedin' engaged sign on, like the others.'

Jacky lifted her head and saw genuine concern on Vera's face.

'Whatever's the matter, ducky? You ain't in the puddin' club are you? I couldn't bear to lose you now.'

With that Jacky shrunk further into the white-sheeted couch. 'I wish it was that simple,' she wept. Then she remembered Vera knew she couldn't have a kiddie and was just trying to make her talk.

Vera produced a handkerchief. Jacky sat up, took it and blew her nose loudly. Would things ever come right for her, she wondered? Vera plonked herself on the bed.

'Well, girl, you goin' to tell me or am I going to shake it out of you?' Vera held her hands out menacingly and advanced on Jacky.

'Don't hit me, Vera!'

Jacky saw Vera's face change and take on a horrified look.

'Hit you? Hit you? Why would I hit you?'

Jacky stared into Vera's eyes, with their familiar heavy lashes, then unbuttoned her white Heavenly Bodies overall and pulled up her pink angora sweater. She wasn't wearing a bra and Vera gasped. A huge bruise was in that last purple to green stage before it would begin to fade. The centre where the skin had broken beneath her left breast showed where Jacky had obviously been kicked with great force. Vera got off the couch and hauled Jacky upright so she could see the full extent of the injuries.

'Is there more on the rest of your body?'

Jacky hung her head. 'Yes.' Vera got hold of Jacky's chin and forced her to look her in the eyes.

'Whoever did that to you?' Vera's face was ashen. 'An' I don't want no fuckin' lies.'

'Sammy,' said Jacky quietly. 'He was waiting for me the other night, hidin' in the shadows near the tobacconist. He jumped me so quick I didn't 'ave time to do nothin'. He wants 'is money.'

'Get yourself covered up.' Vera was brisk now. 'No wonder you ain't wearin' a bra with that kind of bruising. I can see the studmarks from his shoes, the fuckin' bastard.'

'I don't want you to say nothing.'

Vera sat down again on the edge of the bed.

'I don't understand why you kept this to yourself, especially after last time.'

'You ain't been exactly approachable this last couple of days.'

'I got things on me mind,' said Vera quickly. 'But it ain't nothin' like this, an' shouldn't 'ave stopped you confidin' in me. I thought we was mates?'

Jacky was so comforted by Vera's familiar heavy perfume and sympathetic words that tears began to swim in her eyes.

'We are mates.'

'Come on then, girl. You lay your 'ead down there a minute while I sort out that dozy lot out there, then I'll be back, all right?' Jacky nodded. Vera went out, closing the door behind her. Jacky still had Vera's hanky in her hand and when she looked at it she thought of Vera's kindness and it made her want to cry all the more. She could hear the clatter of Vera's high heels again and a few swear words and knew she was bustling about giving orders.

After a while Vera returned carrying a bottle of sherry and two tumblers. She moved the stuff on the side table to make room, and then fiddled with the door.

'We won't be disturbed now. Get this down you.' She poured two generous measures and passed one to Jacky. 'I thought after the last time he'd leave you alone.'

Jacky gulped back the sherry. It was the same sweet brand as the one they'd got pissed on at Christmas round Queenie's. She looked at Vera's earnest face and tried to smile.

'Not where money's concerned, Vera.'

'How much d'you owe the bastard?'

'Six hundred pounds.' Vera whistled.

'You borrowed all that?'

'No. I borrowed enough to put me van back on the road. I started out by paying him without fail, even though the interest was terrible. Then the weather was bad and I couldn't work on the stall. When I missed a payment the interest trebled. He took most of me money I earned on me back but it still ain't enough. Couldn't pay 'im a fuckin' penny after that night he drugged me. So the interest gets piled on, an' piled on again on the new interest. That's how he works, Vera. The girls get so far in debt one way or another they can't get out of it. He's always ready to lend money because he knows he can't lose.'

'But you sold your van?'

'It wasn't enough. I only got half of what it was worth. I sold the stall to Eric Lumbley, the fancy goods bloke, but now I ain't got nothing left to sell.

Even meself ain't worth a fuckin' light, now me confidence is gone. But that's what he wants. Me, full time, over there. He'll get me cranked up on drugs and 'ave me laid out all day . . . An' he won't declare any of that money to 'is boss, just like he don't tell Roy Kemp about the part-timers, or the queers, or the very young kids. I don't want no more of it, Vera. I don't want . . .' Jacky tried very hard not to cry but the tears just seemed to pour from her. Vera pulled her closer and made her bury her face in the powerful scent of Californian Poppy from her new blouse.

She patted Jacky on her back like she was a baby. 'You ain't going back there. Leave it to me.'

'No, you mustn't do nothin', that's not what I want . . .'

'I don't give a flyin' fuck what you want. It's what I fuckin' wants.' Vera pushed her away and took the hanky from her hand and dabbed at Jacky's face with it.

'You been 'andling me money in 'ere. Much more money than that huge amount you owes and you ain't dipped your fingers in me till once. That's loyalty in my book.'

'I wouldn't take a penny from you!' Jacky was horrified Vera would even consider it.

'I ain't givin' you a penny, but I am goin' to give you a raise. An' I'm goin' to sort out Sammy once and for all. I listened well to what you was tellin' me.' Her eyes grew thoughtful.

Jacky looked at the small dark figure then, over-come with emotion, threw her arms around Vera. But this time Vera thrust her away.

'Get off me!' Jacky could see she was trying to appear cross because she couldn't bear to be thanked for anything. 'You're gettin' even more tear stains on me silk blouse.' Vera turned to the sherry and poured two more very generous measures. 'Lovely drop of stuff, this, gal. Remember Christmas?'

Jacky sat back, and smiled and took the glass.

'Best Christmas I ever 'ad.'

They toasted each other and emptied the glasses. Then Vera put her head on one side, listening like a wary blackbird, before getting up and unlocking the door. Along with the sounds of the girls' voices from the shop, a cat meowed and Vera waited.

Kibbles slid into the cubicle and wound himself round Vera's feet. She picked the cat up and buried her face in his mackerel-coloured fur.

'Do you know, Jacky, all cats smell different. Just like us humans. I love the smell of my Kibbles.' Vera looked at the cat. 'We'll soon work something out, won't we, Kibbles?'

CHAPTER 21

'What do you think then, Daisy?'

'He's a bit of all right, isn't he?'

'If you say so.' Though Bri had to admit Vera's son cut an imposing figure in his real leather jacket, well-cut slacks and shoes that obviously hadn't come off a market stall. James' black Mercedes was parked over on the bomb site and the bunch of flowers he'd taken up to Vera, who was waiting in the flat above the bookshop, had more blooms than he'd ever seen on Jacky's stall.

'I expected him to be dark like Vera,' he said.

He knew Daisy was blown away by the whole experience. Later, her and Vera would be chatting until the early hours about all this.

'Vera's only dark because it comes out of a bleeding bottle. Many years ago she was told she looked like that film star, Hedy Lamarr, so she's been playing on it ever since. Trouble is, it's only the old blokes today who remembers who Hedy Lamarr was.'

'He's got her eyes and that determined chin. Only on him it's stronger, more manly.'

'I should bloody hope so.'

'You'll be telling me next that you ain't a natural blonde, Daisy,' he said. 'Pass them cowboy books over 'ere.' Daisy slid the half dozen or so books along the counter. When Bri looked up at her he couldn't understand why she had put her hand to her mouth and was trying not to laugh. Then it dawned on him.

'Ain't your hair natural?' Daisy shook her head. 'What colour are you, then?'

'A sort of mousy blonde. I been bleaching it since I was fifteen. I don't know what me real colour is now.'

He got down again on the carpet where he'd been kneeling, sorting books. 'I never knew that,' he said. 'Though I guessed you sort of played around with the colour sometimes. And you was pretty canny about doing mine, touching up the roots an' all.' He absentmindedly tucked a few dark strands beneath his woollen cap then he looked over at her and studied her carefully. 'Actually you're a very pretty woman.'

'Don't be daft,' she answered. 'I'm under no illusions about meself. Looks don't bleeding worry me none.'

'Straight up, Daisy. You was attractive before, but you was like a young colt. Now you've grown into an Arab.'

'Horse, I presume? And as long as it's female an' not an Arab stallion!'

'You always poke fun at me, don't you?'

He saw Daisy was staring hard at him. She'd pierced his armour and she knew it. He went back to his book sorting. 'Vera looked smart today,' he said, 'in that red suit with the flared bit at the waist.' Daisy had told him she'd checked Vera over, and had stopped her continually changing her outfits. She'd even sorted out her false eyelashes for her. They were glued on so well she said Vera might never get them off again! Daisy had also banned her from drinking any more cups of tea, otherwise she'd be sitting on the bleedin' lavatory all the time.

'Wonder how long they'll be nattering?'

'Dunno. They seemed quite at ease with each other while I was up there. I did feel her son deserved some time alone with his real mother. Even though Vera looked daggers at me when I said I was coming down 'ere.'

Bri came round to where Daisy was sitting on the stool and searched along the shelf beneath the till.

'I got provisions for us. Only a pork pie each.' He showed her the fresh pies inside the brown paper bag. 'Got 'em from The World's Stores.'

'Fucking yummy,' said Daisy. She took one of the golden crusted treasures from the bag and munched a big bite. Just then a large lady brought an armful of books to the counter.

'Carry on eating,' said Bri. 'I'll serve.'

'Me and my hubby are going on holiday to Cornwall,' the woman said. 'Why pay full price for books when you got such a good selection here?'

'Thank you,' mumbled Daisy with her mouth full. Bri started adding up the prices and putting the books in bags. Then he put her money in the till and said goodbye.

'If they're up there at dinner time, I'll pop down to The Porthole and get us some fish and chips.'

'Do solicitors from London eat fish and chips?'

'They do when they've been bought from The Porthole if they've got any sense.'

She dabbed at her mouth with her fingers and ran her tongue around her lips.

'It's been all over the *Evening News* about that

kiddie found down Weevil Lane,' she said. 'The lad had had terrible things done to 'im.'

'We both guessed that, Daisy. I hope it don't take long for the police to work out who did it.'

'They need to find the lad's clothes. What if another boy is killed? That lad wasn't the first, you know, there was another kiddie around the same time as I came back to Gosport. An' that woman who was found in the boatyard.'

'Don't even think about them things. We got to keep our minds on Roy Kemp. Not much longer and we'll be finished with him. We're into the final stages now. Then we can sit back and wait for the shit to fly. Sammy will get his comeuppance for his part in whatever he's been up to – that's if your mate Vinnie don't get to him first.' He saw Daisy open her mouth to speak, then think better of it. 'Mark my words, Dais. What is it you always say? What goes around, comes around?'

It was nearly four in the afternoon when Vera and her son came down from the flat. Bri searched Vera's face. He'd never seen her look so radiant.

James spoke first.

'Thank you for letting us use your flat.' Bri noted his voice was clipped. Public school geezer, obviously. But his eyes were twinkling and his smile was as broad as Vera's and just as genuine. 'We haven't really talked, have we?' he said to Daisy and Bri.

'You weren't here to see us.' Bri felt his hand being shaken firmly in a warm grip.

'Where do you practise?' Daisy asked.

'Heart of London.'

'I expect you've represented some interesting cases?'

'Daisy, you can't ask the man about his work. Leave 'im alone, you're bein' like a mother who's trying to find out her future son-in-law's prospects.' Vera was quite agitated.

James laughed. 'It's okay, I like my work and I don't mind talking about it. But obviously I can't specify cases and individuals.'

'Gangsters?'

He looked surprised. 'I'd rather call them clients.'

'The Krays?'

'Daisy, be quiet, or I'll smack you one.' This from Vera who immediately realised what she'd said and went as red as a beetroot. Daisy threw her arms around Vera's neck and started laughing.

'You been tryin' to impress 'im, ain't you?' Bri heard Daisy whisper. 'Vera, he can see through you like a bloody looking glass. He knows how lovely you are.'

And now James was laughing as well.

'Hush, Ma. It's okay.' Vera pushed Daisy away and practically swelled with joy at the title of 'Ma'. Then her son continued. 'Everyone assumes that because the firm – our firm – handles some of their business, I'm in the know. No one really knows them.'

'It's only that I've read in the papers ...'

'Ah, Daisy, don't believe what you read in the papers.' He looked at his watch. 'Today's news, tomorrow's fish and chip wrapping. I'd really like to thank you by taking you all out for a meal.'

'No,' Vera broke in hastily before either Daisy or Bri had a chance to answer.

'As you wish, Ma.' He looked thoughtful and nodded at her as though they shared a secret. 'Will you walk me to the car?' Vera blushed like a girl and together, after warm goodbyes, mother and son crossed the road to the bomb site and his Merc.

'Nice,' said Daisy. 'Whoever gets 'im will get a bargain and a half. He might not have been brought up by 'er but he's Vera to a fucking tee.'

Vera cradled the hot mug of tea.

'Well,' asked Daisy. 'You gonna tell me, or do I drag it out of you?'

'He's a fine man, ain't he?'

'Sure is. Seems well set up, well educated. Smashing looking.' Vera preened. 'And it's all down to you, Vera.'

'Not just me. I only provided the cash. His parents did a pretty good job on 'im. He's got an 'ouse in St John's Wood.'

Daisy whistled. 'Married?' Vera shook her head.

'When you seeing 'im again?' Vera's face darkened. 'I'm not.'

'What? Why not? Didn't he want to? I'll swing for that bugger if . . . '

'It wasn't 'im. It was me. I told 'im this was the first and only time we would meet.'

'But why? He's gone to such trouble to find you.'

'I know what I'm doing.'

'For fuck's sake explain it to me, then, 'cause I haven't got a bleedin' clue.'

'It's no good you gettin' angry, Dais, it's over and done with now. An' in case you wondered, that was the reason I didn't want us all to go out for a meal. I didn't want us gettin' all pally-pally then not seein' each other any more. It's better to 'ave a clean break.'

'But why? After all you've done for 'im over the

years. He's the only person you've ever truly loved . . .'

'Besides you, Dais . . . And my Kibbles.'

'All right.' Daisy softened. 'But your son has been the reason for your life. He wouldn't be where he is today if it wasn't for you.'

'Exactly.'

'Look at me, Dais.' Vera put down the mug and twisted round on the cushions. She took hold of Daisy's hands. 'I'm a worn-out old whore who owns a massage parlour.'

'There's many a woman would like to be in your enviable position, madam!' Daisy snapped. 'Own business, own flat. Money . . .'

'Stop it, Daisy. And 'ow would it look for 'im, a well set up, educated man with friends in 'igh places and a promising career, if his mother's past all came out? How could he 'old his 'ead high?'

'He said this? I'll bloody have 'im if he did . . .'

'No, Dais. I said it. He says it shows how courageous I was and am. He says he's proud of me an' wants to buy me a flat near 'im. Put the past behind us.'

Daisy thought for a moment. 'That's more like it.'

'What would I do in London? My mates are all 'ere. You're 'ere – well, most of the bleedin' time.'

Daisy threw her arms around Vera's small frame and hugged her body to her.

'Oh, Vera. He's your son!'

'And I don't want 'im to ruin his life. I don't 'ave the faith he does that his friends would accept me. I don't even want to try.' Vera's voice was muffled, but even so Daisy knew she had started to cry. And it wasn't often Vera shed tears. 'It was a bonus seeing 'im. A bigger bonus knowing 'e liked me. I know I did the right thing all those years ago.' Vera composed herself and disentangled herself from Daisy's clasp. 'Daisy, James 'as a life. I 'ave a life. I told 'im I would be 'ere if he ever needed me. I know in my 'eart it was the right thing to do.'

Daisy sat looking at Vera's small white face, her dyed hair, the ridiculous eyelashes.

'Vera, you're a woman in a fucking million,' she said.

'No,' Vera replied. 'Just a mother who'd like to think she knows best for 'er only son.'

CHAPTER 22

'Do you realise, Daisy Lane, if it wasn't for this market, I'd never see you?'

Daisy replaced the black suede high-heeled shoe in the box with its twin, and turned to him. She looked tired, Vinnie thought. He adjusted his coat collar against the sharp wind.

'Would that be a bad or good thing?' Then to the stallholder she said, 'If you got them in a size four I'll 'ave 'em.' She turned back to Vinnie while the trader foraged around beneath the tables.

'I was in your shop . . .'

'Doing the house to house for that lad?' He nodded. 'Bri told me.' She opened her clutch bag and took a note from her purse which she handed to the stallholder. 'I'm bringing these back if they pinch, Al.' The man handed her the change.

'How can they pinch when they already been pinched, Daisy?' He laughed at his own joke and Vinnie laughed as well.

'Al don't know you're a copper, Vinnie. He's used to wooden-tops, not plain-clothes dicks.' Al coloured and Daisy laughed. 'It's a joke, Vinnie, a joke about stolen goods. Everything's straight up, 'ere. No knocked-off stuff.' She winked at the stallholder and moved away, only to hesitate before the buckets of flowers and potted plants belonging to the flower seller who'd replaced Jacky. 'Don't they smell lovely? Soon be summer at this rate.' She picked up a bunch of daffodils. 'I'll take these, Mac.' But before she could open her bag, Vinnie's hand snaked out and the stallholder took his money. 'You didn't 'ave to do that,' she said, treating Vinnie to a big smile.

'No, but I wanted to.'

'Thank you,' she said and thrust the yellow blooms towards him. He sniffed at their yellow majesty and grinned back at her. 'Next stop is a dress shop. I'm shopping for the bleeding wedding of the year. You can come with me if you like and afterwards I'll buy you a cuppa and a sticky bun. That's if you've nothing better to do?'

'Looking on the bright side, aren't you? The Kray trial has only started today.'

'Reggie and Ronnie ain't goin' to let a little mishap like that spoil Reggie's wedding to Frances. So I'm getting myself prepared.'

'I'm off duty, so of course I want to see what Daisy Lane'll be wearing to dazzle the London lads. It's been a while since I went shopping with a lovely lady.'

She jabbed him in the arm with her elbow. 'Oy! None of your cheek!'

In Chantelle's, the small gown shop near the ferry, Vinnie sat, thoroughly ill at ease, on a hard wooden chair near the room set aside for ladies to change in. He wished he had a book to read because he seemed to have been there for ages. Every so often the dour-faced woman owner would go into the room with a dress over her arm, stay a few moments then retreat with a different dress. Vinnie reckoned Daisy must be trying everything on in the shop. Just when he thought he could stand no more waiting, Daisy opened the door and stepped out. She had on the shoes she'd just bought in the market and a black dress of some chiffon stuff that was fitted to her body like a second skin. When he got past admiring her neat figure and tiny waist he saw it had a kind of swathed bit at the front, clipped by a diamante brooch thing at her waist, then the swathe fell to the hem. He couldn't help himself, he whistled. Daisy immediately coloured up.

'Is it all right?'

'All right? You look lovely.' Then he said, 'Why black?'

'I'm still in mourning, aren't I?'

'Oh, Daisy,' he said, 'I never meant . . .'

She turned and faced him. 'Trouble with you is you never can tell when I'm teasing you or not, you daft bloody copper. This dress is for the evening an' anyway I like wearing black. I feel I can melt into the woodwork.'

'Daisy you'll never melt into anything. You'll always stand out. It's a great fit and you look good.' She gave him a back view, grinning over her shoulder, and then she turned to the attendant.

'I'll take this one.' Daisy disappeared back into the room and the door closed again.

They left the shop and were swallowed into the noisy market.

'How you getting to London?' Vinnie asked.

'Why? You offering to give me a lift?' He frowned. 'Just another joke. Roy Kemp's taking me.'

Once inside The Dive cafe, Daisy went on ahead and managed to find an empty couple of seats. Vinnie appeared down the centre aisle balancing two cups of tea and the sticky buns. Daisy took the plates and cups off him. He threw his hat on to the bench and sat down opposite her.

'Got anyone for the kiddie yet?'

He stirred his tea. 'I can't talk about it, enquiries are pending.'

'That means, no, and you're stuck. What about that other woman in the boatyard?'

Vinnie shook his head. 'It means I might have a couple of ideas. Bri told me you and him was out for a walk that night before we were called to the lad, but you never saw anything. Do you often go out walking late at night?' He bit into the currant bun and chewed, relishing every delicious mouthful.

'Only when being in the bleedin' shop all day has got on me tits.'

Vinnie laughed. 'Shop going well?'

'Must be, Mr Detective. You saw how much that dress cost me. Stop asking me questions and tell me how your little boy is.'

Vinnie was pleased Daisy remembered he had a son. 'He's growing faster than a runner bean, Daisy. I spent the weekend up at my in-laws' place in the country and the little lad ran me ragged.' He felt she really did want to know about him and the boy and so he went on telling her about the walks they'd taken together, the games they'd played and the new pony his father-in-law had purchased for the kiddie for when he was old enough to get on it. Apparently him and Snowflake were already firm friends. Then Vinnie realised he'd chattered on far too long.

'I . . . I'm sorry. I didn't mean to bore you.'

'I ain't bored. It's lovely to hear a bloke talk about 'is son like this.'

284

'Well, I'm not saying another word. I liked going shopping with you.' She was staring into his eyes.

'No, you didn't! No sensible man likes shopping, they only ever goes because their women wants 'em to. I'll let you into a secret. The only other man I been shopping with was Eddie.'

'Really?' Vinnie didn't know what to say.

'I wish I hadn't said that.' She drank the last of her tea and replaced the cup on the saucer then put them both on a plate.

'I know how much you cared about him,' he said.

'I miss him so much.'

Her words moved him, yet her voice was quite flat and devoid of emotion. Rather like she was trying not to remember the past and all that went with it.

'What if you meet someone else?'

'Ah,' she said. And there was so much sadness in her eyes that he wished he'd never asked the question. 'That's something I couldn't begin to answer. Not with all the fucking baggage I'm carrying around.'

Sammy, standing at his window, saw the small figure coming across the road. He smiled to himself. Fuckin' worn-out old tart. If she wanted a tip or two on how to make a bit more money he could soon tell her – get rid of that bleedin' hat for a start. He smoothed his hair back. Not that it needed to be smoothed. He'd just spent the best part of ten minutes in front of the mirror with his steel comb getting his hair just right. That new hair gel stuff was good. Kept his hair neat and smelled really nice as well, like sandalwood. He fingered the neck of his new, white roll-necked sweater. Let her buzz the buzzer. And wait. He was in no hurry to talk to her, even though it had started to drizzle and was getting dark. It was her wanted to chat to him, wasn't it? Let her cool her heels in the rain.

The buzzer sounded loud and strident and after four rings he casually switched off the radio, giving a grim smile as the lyrics faded from The Supremes asking where their love had gone, sauntered from his room and began the descent of the stairs.

Must get one of the cows to clean this shit up, he thought, looking at the trash and filth on the stairs.

He thought about Vera. She must have been quite a looker once, still okay now, in a frayed sort of way. Must admit she did all right for herself. But he was going to do better.

He wasn't prepared for the red-suited virago who lunged at him the moment the door was unlocked, hurtling herself inside and slamming the door shut behind her.

'Here's yer fuckin' money that Jacky owes. I wants you to count it, you bastard, 'ere in front of me. Then I expect you to leave 'er alone.' She thrust an envelope at him. He took the packet and stared at her. There was grim determination written all over her small fierce face. He half expected any minute to see steam coming from her ears. The smell of her cheap perfume was making him want to chuck up. God, how he hated fucking women, and this loudmouthed one in particular.

'Count it!'

'Who the fuck . . .' He didn't say anything more. If he wanted to get rid of her, short of knocking her to kingdom come and bundling her back out into the rain, the only way was to do what she wanted. He began counting.

'It's all there,' he said finally.

She took a fountain pen from her red plastic bag and a sheet of paper with some writing on it. She thrust it beneath his chin.

'Sign this.' He looked at it, it was some kind of receipt.

'You don't think . . .'

'But I do think. Sign this fucker or I'll go to DS Vinnie Endersby. I'm sure he'll be interested to know how you drugged Jacky and had her gang-raped.'

'She won't tell the police . . .'

'No! But I might tell 'em about you – and your other dealings. 'Specially young lads.' She poked him in the chest with the pen. Sammy hated being poked. Especially by a woman. He looked down at his new sweater. He moved her hand away as casually as he could, even though inside he was fuming that she'd got the upper hand with him.

'You don't seriously think an ol' bag like you can threaten me?'

'I just fuckin' 'ave,' she said.

He snatched the paper and read it. It was a receipt for the amount she'd given him. It said Jacky's debt was paid in full.

'There's no need for this. Let's discuss . . .'

'Sign it!'

He scrawled his name. 'Now get off these fuckin' premises,' he snarled.

Sammy knew she had enough friends in high places to make it awkward for him and the last thing he needed was for the coppers to start taking an interest. Or for the dozy cow to talk to Roy Kemp. After all, wasn't his boss and that Daisy getting it together? And hadn't Roy Kemp put his hand in his pocket for the widows and orphans of the Gosport nick? Or at least that's the way Roy put it. What he meant was he gave a backhander to someone in authority to turn a blind eye to what went on in the cafe. But there might have to be an investigation if Mouthy Vera started talking to some of her posh bloke friends.

He pushed her towards the door and practically threw her out into the rain. As he slammed the door he patted the wad in his trouser pocket. He pulled back the net curtain and watched Vera stomping across the road in her black ankle-strapped high heels.

Sammy said softly, 'I'll see you get yours, madam.'

'Want a sandwich?

Bri was sprawled along the sofa, his head on a soft cushion and Bertie stretched full length along his body.

'Wouldn't mind, Dais,' he said. 'What you got?' He put down the book he was reading and turned his head to watch her in the kitchen as she worked. She looked over at him and grinned. She'd just had a bath and her hair was still damp and she was wearing her comfortable, tatty dressing gown.

'Cheese and ham, cheese and pickle, cheese and onion, cheese and marmite. What do you fancy?'

'S'pose you haven't got cheese on its own?'

Daisy, already on her way over to him with a mug in one hand, stopped by an armchair, picked up a cushion and threw it at him.

He ducked. 'Ow! What's that for?'

''Cause you're a bloody bloke,' she replied.

He'd had to steady Bertie who thought the missile had been aimed at her.

'Don't be frightened of that nasty Daisy, my Bertie girl,' he whispered into her fur. The cat eyed Daisy

288

warily as she set the mug of tea on the table near Bri. Daisy glared at Bri and swept back to the kitchen area. She returned with a plate piled high with crusty bread, cheese and pickled onions.

'All set for the weekend. Last of the special sales.' He popped a pickled onion in his mouth and crunched it. Daisy sat down on the space vacated by Bertie and Bri moved to make more room for her, steadying the plate of remaining food which now rested on his stomach.

'The amount of money Roy's gonna owe is gonna stun 'im, but I'm working on the assumption that his gangster mates in London ain't goin' to like 'im taking over their territories one little bit.'

'No, they won't. But my lads like the cash in hand, extra dosh is always an incentive for anyone to work that bit harder.'

He could see she was digesting his words.

'I told you in the beginning that all monies 'ad to be ploughed back into the scam. But this weekend, Bri, we take the fucking lot, except for paying your mates and the immediate expenses.'

'And it's gonna work?'

'Foolproof. Listen to me again.' She picked up another pickled onion and said, 'Open wide.' Daisy popped the onion into his mouth and he crunched. 'You was the front man. Not Bri Deveraux, but as Roy Kemp. You're the one with the money, which we put in to start the running costs, an' you're the bloke who set up the bank account. You, as Roy Kemp, yes?' He nodded, so far so good. 'Then you goes out and selects wholesalers. Big ones who usually got insurances to cover losses. Little firms would probably go under and I never meant to harm anyone else. Then

289

you buys stock from them to sell on at markets, halls, sale rooms, whatever. But you pays in cash at first, then you issues cheques at the same time you selects goods, so's they get to know you're a good payer. And always you buy stuff you know goes like a bomb – electrical gear, toys, women's clothing, household stuff an' fancy goods. Every week you buys. Don't matter if it ain't sold on every week, the gear was stored in the yards until we was able to hold really big sales. But you got yourself in with the wholesalers, bein' chatty, tellin' about yourself as Roy Kemp, of course. Right?' He nodded again.

'Then we started the sales rolling in force. All the venues was booked in Roy's name, and all the people got to know this dark-haired, good-looking, well-dressed bloke who paid his bills and had plenty of money to flash about. All the money from the sales went into your account which only you, as Roy Kemp, could use – not a problem 'cause you could sign his name backwards. Then you started paying by cheque when they issued an invoice. Not a problem. 'Cause everyone knows you got the money. Besides most people pays that way, only not in such enormous amounts of course. The bank manager is happy, the account's healthy. The wholesalers are happy, 'cause you always pays up immediately.

'Next step was growing even bigger. Bigger sales venues across the south and into London, in areas where already big names is doing this same scam. All the goods is sold at rock bottom prices, the more you sell the bigger the profit now, an' your own mates are working for you, Bri, so it's smiles all round an' they ain't never heard of no Roy Kemp, have they? They only sees you in your ordinary clothes as Bri

Deveraux.' Bri shook his head. 'Now you're paying your wholesalers' accounts at the end of the month like everyone else does. And big dollops of money is going in and out the bank account and still everyone's happy, an' more time goes by. Remember this is called long-firming because it takes a long while to set up. An' we been doing this now since last November, nearly six months. So at last it's time for the final sale, ain't it? It's crunch time. You worried, Bri?'

'Trying not to be, Dais.' He reached for her hand. Her skin was warm and he could smell the warmth from her body coming tantalisingly from the folds of her dressing gown.

'We got the goods, fucking loads and loads of saleable gear. We got the venues all paid up ahead, mostly in the heart an' around London where the big boys can't fail to notice that Roy Kemp is pulling a flanker. You got your blokes itching to make some extra money. The bank account is in the red but that don't matter because they know you, Roy Kemp. You now got an agreement with the manager an' you overdraws and puts the money back in, and your bank is on the corner near the caff you bought. So everyone knows your address, Mr Kemp. After all, ain't everyone been sending letters and bills to you there? And ain't you been replying promptly because I been sneaking in with me key and getting the post?' Daisy put her hands over her mouth and giggled. 'Remember that time I told you about when I opened the door an' found one of Roy's girl's drugged and asleep on the stairs? She gave me a fright, I can tell you. I thought I'd been rumbled but she never even woke.'

'You was bloody lucky, Dais.'

'This weekend we'll be luckier still 'cause after the

goods 'ave been sold we pockets the cash. The whole fucking lot of it. And we don't put the money back in the bank to cover the huge overdraft, an' we don't pay the wholesalers when they send Roy the bills. We pockets the money. And we go about our bookshop business. And you can go back to being a coppernob, an' we don't know nothing at all.'

'It's the last stage that worries me, Daisy.'

'Don't see why. We won't know much about it, until eventually – when everyone is after Roy for their money an' the police is finally called in to investigate him for fraud. The insurance will cough up for the losses. And it might take a couple of months, maybe more, but they'll find Roy in the end – not you, 'cause you're not Roy Kemp 'an there's nothin' to tie him to you at all. Not even all the clobber you been wearing, that's long gone. But I'm betting the coppers will be the last to get hold of Mr Kemp, 'cause he's been a naughty boy and Reggie an' Ronnie – and maybe a few more of his so called pals – will take exception to his muscling in on their territories. Mr Roy Kemp may have to buy air tickets to go abroad on a long holiday that he never expected to have. And I will clap me 'ands and say good bloody riddance! I'll say, "I owed you, Roy, and now we're fucking even."'

Daisy's face was animated, her eyes glowing.

'You won't get him killed?'

'It won't be me, will it? If the London mob do the same to 'im as he done to my Eddie, that's only justice. I want him to know that messing around with Daisy Lane don't pay.'

Daisy was looking into the distance, into some far-off place that only she could see. Bri saw the tears in her eyes but she blinked them away. She'd considered all the angles while she'd been away in Greece, but one thing bugged him.

'I think you like Roy Kemp a little too much for your own good.'

Daisy got up and faced him. Anger showed in her eyes.

'Why're you saying that?'

'He killed Eddie. What you got planned for him ain't exactly an eye for an eye, is it?'

'That's because I'm no killer.'

'Fair enough. But you don't mind leaving his fate in the hands of others?'

Daisy didn't answer, and it seemed to Bri that all the stuffing had been knocked out of her.

'Let's change the subject. I didn't mean to upset you.' Then, 'I really admire Vera for giving her son a good life, don't you?'

'Ain't that exactly what you're doing for Summer? She's bonny now, putting on weight. She'll be trying to walk soon, mark my words.'

Bri felt his chest expand with pride. The little girl had wormed her way into his life and his heart and he couldn't imagine being without her now.

He said, 'I wonder where Belle is.'

'Do you really want to know? She fucked you about. You can't help a person like her. Belle's got to want to help herself first.'

'I know.' Then he remembered how kind Daisy had been to Belle, how she'd helped him with Summer. He thought of the kiss he'd given her the night they'd followed Sammy. A kiss that held so much promise he'd been sorry that he was the one to break it.

'And how about you, Daisy? What else do you want?'

'Me? I want to get this over with and go back to Greece.'

'Is that all, Dais?'

She looked at him. She knew exactly what he meant. Then she started to laugh, a full-throated chuckle.

'You know I can't abide blokes what dyes their hair!'

Vinnie Endersby looked up at the lighted windows above the bookshop. He thought he heard laughter but it might have come from the cafe. Lights shone from several upstairs rooms there. It seemed everyone was in, out of the rain, except him.

Much earlier he'd seen Bri Deveraux disappearing into a house the other side of South Street. He'd had a kiddie's book in his hand. Got to give it to the bloke, thought Vinnie, he went practically every night to see his little girl. This weekend, Vinnie was off to Liss so he'd be able to spend time with his own lad. He couldn't wait. What he wasn't looking forward to was seeing Clare, his wife. It was her father's birthday so it was a family gathering. He'd have refused the invitation if it hadn't been for seeing his boy. A nasty little wind blew his hat and he grabbed at it, jamming it more tightly on to his head. He pulled the collar of his long coat up and walked on.

She was a funny little body, was Daisy Lane. Sharp, intelligent, heart of gold and what you saw, you got. He smiled, thinking of her in the dress shop, looking over her shoulder at him in her new frock. She'd be wearing it soon: the case against the Krays had fallen apart today. After a retrial at the Old Bailey, they'd been cleared of demanding money with menaces, and no doubt at this very moment they were partying it up and celebrating.

Nipper Read had his work cut out there, decided Vinnie. But Nipper wouldn't let go, he'd get those boys behind bars if it was the last thing he did. Vinnie turned the corner towards the ferry.

A ferry boat was just leaving the pontoon. It reminded him of a shiny slug crawling across the dark waters. The April rain was cold, the north wind still chilling the air. He took out a packet of chewing gum and unwrapped a stick, putting it in his mouth. The minty flavour was soothing. He threw the wrapper down and watched it swirl away in the rain-streamed gutter until it disappeared down the grid of a drain. There were very few people about tonight. He wondered if The Dive was open. He could do with a good strong cuppa.

A girl was standing near the taxi rank. She was dressed in rainsoaked clothes that stuck to her body. As he passed she murmured, 'Want some company?' Vinnie shook his head and walked quickly on. Poor little bleeder, he thought, what a way to make a living. And he was turning a blind eye. Seeing her reminded him of the London girls who'd disappeared. Those cases were going cold, so he'd been told. He reckoned there was more to it than the girls going off on their own, and he hadn't ruled out abductions, especially as the prostitutes all seemed to be working in the same twenty-mile radius. Sooner or later, if there was a killer at large, he'd make a mistake, they always did. It would be great if they could get the bastard before another girl went missing, wouldn't it just? But not much chance of that when already the London coppers were stumped. Yes, they had a problem up in the Smoke with that one.

And didn't he have a problem here? Two lads and a prossie from Forton Road murdered on his own patch? Vinnie knew there was more going on in that fucking cafe back in North Street than met the eye. He didn't like that smooth git Sammy. But his hands were tied while his superiors were telling him Roy Kemp kept a tight ship. And the funny thing was that Vinnie knew Roy Kemp wasn't into messing about with kids so it ruled him out of the equation on that one. And he'd have to have a bloody good reason to get rid of a moneymaking young whore. None of it added up. But Vinnie had an idea that might just work, an idea he'd been working on and had put into operation a while back.

His eyes lit up and his heart lifted as he saw the lights and the open door of The Dive cafe.

'Cuppa and a sticky bun, here I come.'

Daisy ran the cold tap and filled a glass, drinking slowly. Bri had just closed the shop for the day and she was looking forward to a long scented soak in the bath and an early night. She was tired, and it didn't help that she felt the weight of her guilt heavy in her heart at not telling Bri about little Eddie, when it was clear he cared so much about her.

Bri had been quiet all day. Several times she'd felt his eyes on her, yet when she'd turned, he had looked away. Sooner or later she knew he was going to ask her about the future, their future. And what could she tell him?

A footfall told her Bri was behind her. Daisy could feel the tension oozing from him.

'I've been thinking about things,' he said.

'What?' She refilled the glass and offered it to him. He took it and drank noisily.

'You, mostly. Wanting to leave Gosport again, when all your mates are here.'

She took the glass off him, rinsed it under the tap and left it upside down on the draining board.

'I 'ave to get away. Everyone I care about living 'ere gets taken from me sooner or later. Mum, Kenny, Eddie. This is your shop, your home as soon as I leave. All this,' she waved her arm to encompass the flat, 'this ain't real to me, Bri. I needs to go back.'

'Why? What's so fucking special about Kos?' She could hear the anger building in his voice. She stalled. She couldn't tell him the whole truth. Rain was hitting the windows. She could hear the steady stream of water running down the outside gulleys and along the pipes into the gutters. Daisy knew it would be icy rain. Almost as cold as the chill in her heart. She took hold of his hands and looked into his face.

'Listen to that deluge out there? It's different where my house is. The air smells of sage. And in the spring, earlier than the spring 'ere, the countryside is blazing with wild flowers. Gardenias scent the garden an' you can't tell which is the strongest, them or the jasmine. The village is high up in the hills, and it takes about fifteen minutes to walk the track to the sand and the sea. You can hear goat bells and cocks crowing. My house ain't large but it has blue shutters and white walls. In nineteen thirty-three an earthquake flattened the village to the ground but people 'ave moved back and are rebuilding homes. There's a buzz in the air, like stuff is all new. I have to go back.'

'You sure you're not going back just because it's a

way of holding on to Eddie 'cause he bought the place for you?'

She shook her head. She felt his grip tighten on her hands; his eyes held hers. 'Eddie's gone.' There, she'd finally said out loud what she knew was true in her heart.

'Oh Daisy, Daisy, at last you realise you have to move on?' She nodded. Yes, she thought, it was time. 'But I don't see why you have to leave, Dais,' Bri persisted. 'This town is in your blood. The ferry, the market, the pubs, the dirt, the people. Me.'

'Bri, I *have* to go back. And I don't want to get entangled with any man, not even you.' She paused and her voice almost faltered. 'Not until I know the time is right. And you seem to 'ave forgotten something very important.'

'What?'

'You already got a wife, Bri Deveraux!'

'Ain't you ever heard of divorce? Don't I stand a chance, Daisy?' She could see she'd hurt him. But she knew too that deep in his heart he understood that if they were going to get it together it would probably have happened before now.

She sighed. 'We're all broken bodies, Bri. We have to pick up the pieces the best way we know how. There's nothing to stop you and Summer coming to visit.' She could see him mulling over the thought. She wanted to tell him about little Eddie, and Vera had been right – the longer she kept the secret about her child from the people she'd come to care about, the harder it was to speak of it. What would he think when he realised how closely they'd worked together, and she'd still not been able to share the fact her son existed? Would he be hurt? Of course he would be hurt. She and Bri had gone through a lot together. Would he eventually understand she'd kept little Eddie's birth a secret from *everyone* except Vera because she wanted to keep her child safe? Probably, because he was a good man. He would understand that one little slip of the tongue in the wrong ear could endanger her son's life. She was playing for heavy stakes mixing with the London mob and doing the dirty on Roy Kemp. You only had to look at the men employed by some of them. Sammy, for instance. He had no qualms about who he hurt. What if he or someone hired by the mob hurt little Eddie? No, it was better she told her friends about her son when the time was exactly right. And if they couldn't understand her reasons for the secret then it was up to them, wasn't it?

'Summer needs a passport for that, or I could put her on my passport. But I don't have her birth certificate.'

'No?' Daisy frowned. 'You'll need that. Belle must have it.'

'Yes,' he said thoughtfully. 'But Belle could be anywhere.'

CHAPTER 23

'Oh, Vera. I've done something really awful.'

'Can't be that bad, ducky. There ain't a malicious bone in your body.' Vera adjusted the button at the top of her frilled red blouse so that just the right amount of cleavage was showing.

Daisy could see an elderly woman sifting through the romance section but with one ear open to Vera's raised voice. She nodded her head towards the woman.

'What you done?' Vera whispered.

'I'll tell you when she's gone. It's time to close up, and I could do with a cuppa, don't know about you?'

Then to the customer, 'Thank you very much.' She took the coins and put the two books in a bag, following the woman to the door where she turned the sign around so that it read CLOSED and put the bolts on. She went back to the till and slid out the drawer. 'Let's go,' she said to Vera and together they climbed the stairs.

After she'd made the tea and set a mug in front of Vera, Daisy said, 'I told Bri I didn't want our partnership to go any further.'

'Fucking 'ell, is that all? 'Bout time if you asks me.'

'Is that all you can say?'

'He does care about you, Dais, but he ain't for you.

If he could only see it, Jacky would make 'im a smashin' wife. She'd dote on that kiddie. An' she's 'ad her fill of blokes what 'urts 'er so she'd worship the ground 'e walks on. She do now.'

'I know that. One day he'll wake up an' realise that himself, dozy bloke. But . . . But I don't know what to do.'

'About what?'

Daisy looked shamefaced. 'I keep thinking about the bloke that sent me the lilies.'

'Not them death lilies?'

'Shut up, Vera, or I won't tell you. And they're arum lilies and just like any other beautiful flower. You don't call carnations death flowers, do you? And excuse me, but ain't they used in bleeding wreaths?' Vera dutifully sat holding her tea mug and waiting, her legs crossed at the knees. 'Him and me, in the heat of the moment, had a little thing going,' Daisy went on, 'and it was nice while it lasted. But afterwards I hated myself.'

'But why?'

'Because of Eddie.'

'But Eddie's gone! How many times do I 'ave to try to get it into that thick skull of yours?'

Daisy froze Vera with a look.

'Sorry,' Vera said. 'I would think Bri knows the score, Dais.'

'We're a good team. An' he's such a nice bloke. Only the other day he told an old woman off because she wanted to buy a book she'd already bought the previous week. He told her not to waste her money.'

'That was nice of him.' Vera seemed thoughtful. 'But 'e don't make your legs go to jelly like this other bloke, do 'e?'

Daisy shook her head.

'Where's Bri now?'

'Buying books.'

Vera nodded. 'You finished with the sales?'

'Yes. It's all over. Now we sit back an' wait for things to happen. I'm probably feeling some kind of anti-climax thing about that an' all. Anyway, here's me selfishly gabbling on an' not giving you a breath to talk. What you been up to?'

'Don't matter about me. What you been up to is more important.'

'Bri thinks Roy Kemp's after me.'

'What do you think?'

'I know what I done to Roy ain't nice. In fact it's fucking diabolical, but if he screws his loaf he could get over it an' he ain't a bad bloke. He's a bit like Eddie only more so. I'm off to Reggie Kray's wedding with 'im soon.'

'He's the one for you, Dais.'

Daisy sighed. Trust Vera to say something like that. She stared at Vera who raised her eyes heavenwards, then said with a twinkle in her eye, 'An' I knows you been 'avin' cups of tea in The Dive with Vinnie Endersby, so where does 'e fit in?'

'How d'you know about that?'

'I know he bought you flowers.'

'I can't do nothing without you finding out, can I?'

'Malkie Evans saw you in The Dive an' ... '

'An' Malkie Evans being an old friend of yours, a good payer ... '

'You can be 'urtful when you wants, Daisy Lane. But 'e did tell me, and Big Sonia saw Vinnie fork out for them daffs down the market ... '

'Jesus Christ, I'm going to stay indoors from now on . . .'

'An' if you do, madam, there'll be all kinds of rumours flyin' about as to who you're stayin' indoors with!'

Daisy grinned at her. 'Vinnie's nice. He's comfortable to be around.'

'Comfortable's good, Dais. You can do a lot worse than comfortable.'

'If you ain't got nothing else to say, I'm goin' down The Porthole to get us some fish an' chips.'

'But I 'ave. Stay still a bit, Dais.' She put out her hand and stopped Daisy who had already started to rise from her seat. 'I 'ad a bit of a run-in with Sammy. Nothin' to worry about but 'e was startin' on Jacky again an', well, I paid the arsehole off.'

'I thought you wasn't all that keen on 'er?'

Vera looked uncomfortable. 'That was ages ago. She's all right, is Jacky.'

'But Sammy ain't all right, Vera. Roy told me, he holds grudges. You look after yourself, promise me?' Vera nodded. 'How much?'

Vera told her the amount of money she'd paid Sammy and Daisy couldn't believe her ears. 'You made of money?'

'That's what Jacky said when I told 'er I'd pay.'

'I hope she realises what a bleeding good friend she's got in you, Vera. You need any money?' Daisy thought of the carrier bags full of notes and coins locked in her wardrobe.

Vera shook her head. 'Nah, Dais. I'm all right. Heavenly Bodies is doing fine. What I could do with right now is a nice bit of cod in batter, though.' Daisy watched as she got up and searched for her jacket and hat and got dressed in front of the oval wall mirror. Daisy slung on her coat and gathered her purse and together they went downstairs. She was glad she'd told Vera what was on her mind. A problem shared is a problem halved, she thought. And Vera was right. Vera was always right.

Daisy unlocked the door and nearly fell over the smelly bundle in the doorway. Beneath the light of the streetlamp she recognised the fringed mauve skirt.

'Fuckin' 'ell,' said Vera.

Belle moaned.

'What's up?' Daisy asked, but as soon as she looked at Belle's vomit-stained clothes and grey face she knew she'd get no sense out of her, she was too far out of it. 'Out the way, Vera.' Daisy dragged Belle into the shop and kicked the door shut.

'Fuck, fuck, fuck,' Vera said, then bent down to her. 'At least she's still breathin'. She's overdosed 'erself. Like a fuckin' bad penny, this one. I'll phone for an ambulance. My old mate, the Doc, can't be used this time, she might peg out on us. We daren't let 'er sleep this one off. Do you know what she's taken?'

'How should I know? I just opened the door and there she was.' Daisy ran to the phone.

After she'd made the call she saw Vera was still on the floor beside Belle. Vera looked in Belle's half open eyes then peered at her nose and touched the residue there.

'By the state of 'er it's a wonder she ain't killed 'erself the way she messes about with stuff. Still might.'

Daisy sat on the floor holding Belle's cold hand and it seemed less than a few minutes had gone by before they heard the noise of the ambulance siren.

'You two girls can travel in the back with her if you like.' Daisy had never seen men move so swiftly and with such kindness.

Daisy asked the young ambulance bloke, 'She going to be all right?'

'Let's get her to hospital, then we'll soon find out.' His voice was soft and he smiled at her, even though he looked dead tired.

Daisy and Vera sat on a hard ledge watching the medic attending to Belle, while the ambulance travelled round to Clayhall.

'Try not to worry. It's a very good hospital,' he said. They drew up and he opened the doors to let them out and to unload Belle, who hadn't moved and already looked like a corpse. Don't let her die, begged Daisy. It ain't right that little Summer should grow up without her mummy.

'Wait there,' said a very efficient nurse inside Haslar Hospital's Casualty Department. 'I'm afraid it might be a very long wait. If you'd prefer to go home ... '

'We'll wait,' said Vera. But after sitting on the bench for a while she got up and went wandering off.

Daisy sat thumbing through dog-eared magazines. She found an article in a local magazine with information about Haslar which had originally been built in 1746 and was then supposed to have been the largest brick building in Europe. Daisy could believe this, as it was a maze of corridors and small garden areas. Later, it said, the hospital had become the best medical research centre in the country.

Even without reading the article Daisy knew Belle was in safe hands at the Haslar.

Eventually a different nurse came in and said to Vera, 'You can see your daughter, now.' Daisy frowned at Vera. 'Come along this way,' she said, and hurried off. They ran to catch up with the trim little figure travelling as though on wheels down the old, scrubbed corridors.

'You ain't her mother, you daft old trout,' Daisy murmured.

'No, an' I ain't yours neither, but I 'ad to say something or they wouldn't let us see 'er at all. Don't forget we ain't relatives or nothin', an' it ain't visitin' time.' Vera nudged her arm. 'I used to have a nurse's uniform, Dais. My girls wear 'em when ... '

'Shut up,' Daisy hissed, as they were led along white-tiled passageways that smelled strongly of disinfectant. 'This ain't the place.'

'Here she is.'

Belle was in a corner bed, her face as white as the counterpane covering her. At first Daisy thought she was asleep. Until she heard Belle speak.

'You ain't done me no favours.'

'Gave us a fucking shock, you did,' said Vera. 'Ungrateful little bitch. What they done to you in 'ere?'

'Dunno. But I wish ... '

'Stop that,' said Daisy, pulling up a chair. 'We been told not to stay more'n a couple of minutes. You're going to be all right. An' it's no good you saying you don't care because it weren't no accident you collapsed on my doorstep.' Daisy took hold of Belle's hand. It was like ice. 'I can't promise we can change things for you, but if we can help, you only got to say.' Belle was clothed in one of the hospital gowns. Its short sleeves showed the festering track marks and scabby skin on her stick-like arms.

'Where's Bri?' Belle had tears in her eyes. For a moment Daisy had forgotten she was still his wife.

'He's out on business. We'll let 'im know as soon as we can. What did you take?'

'Dunno. I was drunk. I remember bein' in the van with the others. Then I picked up some fat bloke down where the ferry is. Afterwards he gave me some money. An' I think we went and scored some gear from some caff near you. We went back to the bus. I don't know ... The next moment I was on your doorstep and you were draggin' me in the shop.'

'Nice lot of pals you got,' sniffed Vera.

Daisy thought about Summer. If she'd been with Belle tonight ... Daisy shuddered. Vera sat and held Belle's other hand and then she pushed Belle's stringy hair out of her eyes and tried to tuck it behind her ears. Nobody spoke, until the nurse popped her head round the door.

'You'll have to leave now.' Her voice was no more than a whisper. 'Come back in the morning if you like.'

'She'll do it again,' Vera said. Daisy was holding on to her so she wouldn't slip on the polished stone floors. Her shoes were making a right racket. 'She won't be able to stop herself.'

'Is that what the doctor said?'

'I 'ad quite a chat with that young Asian doctor. He said she needs to go into a drug rehabilitation place.' Vera pronounced the words very carefully. 'If she agrees, and I doubt that, she'll be fine. I reckons she'll get fixed up again the minute she gets out the 'ospital.'

'Happy little soul, ain't you? Can't we help, for goodness' sake?'

'If you ask me, Daisy, she don't want to be 'elped.

Don't be so fuckin' naive. Do you reckon Bri knows where 'er real mum is?'

Daisy shook her head, 'From what I remember, she ain't got anyone else, only 'er kiddie.'

Vera made a tutting noise. 'An' the cow never even asked about 'er, did she?' she said.

Eventually they navigated the stairs and corridors and emerged into the fresh air. Daisy breathed a sigh of relief.

'God knows what times the bus goes from 'ere. We could be waiting all night an' all day. I don't fancy walking.'

'We'll get a taxi then.'

'You'll have to pay. I come out with nothing except the shop door key.'

Vera said, 'You're bloody kidding!'

'Why would I do that?'

'Because I left me fuckin' 'andbag underneath your counter, didn't I?'

'We'll 'ave to walk, then.'

Bri was in the shop when Daisy got back and she told him everything.

'I'm not going to the hospital and I bet she never mentioned Summer, did she?'

'She's ill,' Daisy said. Belle hadn't asked about her daughter at all but she wasn't going to tell Bri that.

'What good will it do? If I visit, it'll only confuse things.'

'She might let you have Summer's birth certificate.' He brightened.

He left for the hospital during normal visiting hours and with a scowl on his face. Daisy waited for his return. She'd made him promise to come to her first, and knew he wouldn't stay long at Belle's bedside. She'd sent him off with a bag of fruit from the market and a bunch of flowers.

'She says all her personal bits and pieces were in her bag,' Bri told her when he came back. 'Only the bag ain't with her at the hospital. It was in the bus, and the bus was on its way to Winchester where some pop groups were playing in a field. There's something else, Dais,' he said, 'apart from her being in a right state.'

'What's that?'

'She can't be let out of hospital until she's got somewhere to go. An' she says she'll sell me the birth certificate.'

'Fucking 'ell,' exploded Daisy. 'Your missus is really something else, ain't she?' He looked shame-faced and Daisy immediately felt sorry for him. 'So?'

'I told her she could go back to the house – your house.'

'But it's on the market.'

'I only said she could stay there because if she disappears again I'll never get Summer's birth certificate. I have to know my name's on it. What if I can't prove the child belongs to me? I ain't going to lose her now.'

'I believe you can apply to some place in London about birth certificates. We could find out. If I get an offer on my place she has to move on.' He nodded. Daisy glared at him then took a deep breath and puffed out her cheeks before letting the air out.

'But, Daisy, if she's got the information already in her possession I don't 'ave to do that, do I?'

'Stop thinking about yourself and that bloody bit of paper. I ain't happy after the mess she made last time but I guess you did what you thought was best. An' I did say in the hospital that I'd help in any way I could. She's a conniving little bitch, ain't she?'

'Most people are that're on drugs. They do anything to get the money for a fix. Sell their fucking souls,' he said. 'An' I don't suppose for one minute she's been taking her proper medication to help with her depression.' Bri put his arms around Daisy and gave her a squeeze. 'Thanks, Dais. You're an angel.'

In due course Bri collected Belle from Haslar Hospital and took her to the house in Western Way. Since Daisy had been there earlier and filled the fridge with food and made sure the house was warm for her return, she felt she'd done enough. She left some money on the kitchen table for Belle's immediate needs. Whatever Bri was going to do, it wasn't her business.

When he got back to the shop, Daisy was surprised he said nothing more than, 'It's sorted.' Then he shut up like a bloody clam.

Three days later Belle was back in the shop. She wanted money.

Bri was furious. 'By the state of you I don't need to ask what you want it for and the answer is no!' God knows where she'd spent the night but she stank to high heaven again and there was a big tear in her skirt.

Belle's face had a grey tinge. Daisy wondered if she'd eaten. It didn't look like it, she was now thinner than ever and her cheekbones were almost showing through her skin.

'If you want Summer's birth certificate, I need money to get to Winchester,' Belle wheedled.

'You 'ad money but I can drive you there,' Daisy offered. Belle shook her head. Then she started crying. Daisy had never seen Bri really angry before, but he shouted at her to shut it. Belle kept on crying. It was more a high-pitched wail and Daisy guessed she'd done this before to gain sympathy. Bri opened the till and took out some money, notes and silver.

'Take the fucking money,' he said and threw it at her. She stopped crying and immediately scrabbled on the carpet. Bri didn't even look at her but simply walked away and up the stairs, his shoulders hunched up like he was an old man. Daisy stayed in the shop until she'd gone. How could any person be brought so low as this, she thought, poor Belle. But Daisy knew if she tried to restrain her, get her upstairs, force food into her, call a doctor, it wouldn't do any good.

She slipped the CLOSED card around on the door and went to find Bri. He was sitting on the sofa, staring into space.

'She's gone,' said Daisy. He must have gone through proper hell with her, she thought. Bri had once loved the girl and it would have cut him to the quick to see what she'd become. She went back down to the shop.

Bri was still sitting in the same spot on the sofa when Daisy closed the shop and cashed up. She tried to speak to him but he couldn't drag himself back from the black place he'd fallen into to answer her.

Finally she said softly, 'I'm going to bed. Stay here if you want.' She went into the spare room and brought back a quilt and put it around his shoulders. 'Come in if you need me.'

She couldn't sleep and got up twice to tiptoe in and see his dark outline in the shadows. The third time she went into the living room, the sofa was empty.

Daisy went back to her own room and slept.

CHAPTER 24

'This is fucking woman's stuff!'

Bri was staring at the brightly coloured packet with the smiling girl on the front. Red water ran down his neck, his shoulders and arms then on to the packet in his hands. Daisy snatched the packet away from him and threw it in the bath. The radio in the living room was on and The Beatles were calling out about a hard day's night and Daisy had been humming along with the music.

'It's done now, so shut up, will you? At least you won't 'ave to wear the bleeding knitted 'at any more that you've never let up about. And I done your eyebrows. Turn round and let me towel your hair dry.' God give me strength, she thought, why were men such babies!

She pulled him round and he leaned into her so she could vigorously rub his head.

'Why didn't you get some stuff from the hair-dresser's like before?' came the muffled sound of his voice. Daisy pursed her lips and purposefully rubbed even harder. 'Ow! Go steady!'

'I couldn't very well go back to Mr Hill and say my friend wants to dye 'er hair back red again, from black, could I? When things start leaking out about Roy

Kemp, the hairdresser might remember about the hair dye.'

'S'pose so,' came the grudging reply. 'I s'pose women do this all the time.' Daisy heard but chose to ignore him. 'What if it ain't me own colour?'

'Shut up and trust me,' Daisy said.

'I can't believe it's all over, Dais.'

'What? Your hair colour back to normal or the long firm fraud?' She didn't get an answer from him.

'Thirty days and the firms call in the credit,' he went on. 'And what debts those're gonna be!'

'It's not going to happen overnight, Bri. We did it nice and easy. But my mum always said you catch more flies with honey than with vinegar.'

'It's a lot of money we've made.'

'It was never about the money for me.' She finished towelling his hair and allowed him to stand and stretch after bending so long over the washbasin. His naked upper body was firmly muscled. God, he's tasty, Daisy thought – what a pity there's no spark there for me. She thought instead about the money stacked so high in the wardrobe she could hardly shut the door. So much money it frightened her and she didn't know how to begin sorting it. Bri stared at himself in the mirror, turning his head this way and that.

'You've made a good job of this, Dais.' He slicked a comb through his damp hair and it sprang back into the familiar auburn waves. She saw his reflection and his eyes were cold. 'No, it wasn't about the money for you, was it? It was Eddie, always Eddie. But we all use each other in this life, Dais, so I'm not complaining.' Then he threw the comb down into the sink and walked out of the bathroom.

She stood looking at his retreating form, then after a few minutes followed him into the living room.

'It's not just about Eddie.'

He sat down heavily on the sofa and turned his face away from her. She couldn't see his eyes, couldn't tell what he was thinking. She scrambled on to the sofa and sat close to him, half expecting him to push her away. He was hurting and she couldn't do a thing about it. It was time to tell him the truth, spell it out.

'You and I would never 'ave made a go of it together. And in your heart you know that.'

She waited for an answer but none came. Daisy took hold of one of his hands. He didn't pull away but there was no reassuring squeeze.

'You know I loved Eddie.' This time there was a response: he made to withdraw his hand but she held on firmly. 'In fact I was so bloody besotted I couldn't see he wasn't a very nice person. When I knew he was being a cruel bastard to other people I ignored it. 'Cause he loved me. And you know well enough, if he liked you he'd give you the world. If you crossed 'im, he'd kill you.' Bri turned his head and stared into her eyes. He opened his mouth to speak but she shook her head. 'Please, let me finish,' she said.

'He was giving up everything for me. Eventually Roy Kemp wised up and had to sort him out. And the worst of it is, I've only just realised it myself.'

'Daisy, this is history,' Bri interrupted. 'All you're doing is hurting yourself by dragging it all up again. And why didn't you go to the police when you knew Roy Kemp had killed Eddie?'

'I'm no grass. If I'd done that, it's possible I wouldn't be here now.' It was time for her secret to come out. The main reason she had needed to get even with Roy Kemp.

'Roy Kemp didn't only kill Eddie. He took away my unborn child's father.'

Daisy could hear the clock ticking in the silence that followed.

'You were *pregnant*? Eddie's baby? Is that why Eddie wanted to make a new start?'

'Eddie didn't know. I was going to tell him that night but it wasn't to be. Roy Kemp saw to that.'

'But where's the baby now?'

'Asfendiou, in Kos. A wonderful Greek couple are looking after him.' Daisy saw him sigh. As though he'd been carrying a heavy load up a very steep hill and was finally allowed to put it down. 'How could I let some gangster kill my child's father and let him get away with it? Whatever would my boy think of me if I accept that his father can be killed on a whim, yet I do fucking nothing?'

'But you haven't killed Roy Kemp.'

'Bri? Could you honestly see me kill any living thing? But I've made sure Roy Kemp has to worry that Reggie and Ronnie may well want to teach him a lesson for moving in on their patch, just as he taught Eddie a lesson. An' it's very possible the Richardsons might not take too kindly to Roy either, seeing as they're into the art of the long firm in a very big way. And you know when those boys give out punishment it's not just a tap on the hand with a bleeding ruler! Roy can deny everything, but there's his bank account, his signature on all the cheques, the invoices. He personally chose the goods to sell on. He's been seen by a thousand people willing to say what a nice bloke he was, and who'd 'ave thought it? No, I haven't personally killed Roy Kemp but what I've done is revenge enough for me and mine.'

'But you've forgotten something, Daisy. Roy isn't stupid. He'll find out eventually who did this to him.'

'I hope he does. No one will believe the great Roy Kemp allowed a woman to get the better of him. It will make 'im a fucking laughing stock.'

Daisy saw Bri was watching her intently. He lowered his gaze, then put his elbows on his knees and leaned his head in his hands. After a while he looked up and Daisy saw his eyes were damp.

'So, you got a little boy. Eddie's boy?'

'You'll be wondering why he's not here with me?'

Bri nodded.

'He has to grow up away from all this seedy filth and violence.'

'What's his name?'

'Edward, same as his dad.' Daisy got up and went into her own room, and after rifling through a drawer, went back into the living room with a large brown envelope. 'Open it. I want you to.'

He slipped his finger beneath the flap and lifted it, tipping the envelope as he did so. Photographs poured on to the sofa. Bri picked them up and one by one began studying them.

'He's Eddie's child, all right.'

Daisy smiled at him. Then she handed him a photograph of herself and Eddie, with the sea in the background.

'This is all I got left of your brother. It was taken at Bere. Of course, I had another one done and gave it to your mum. And I'll tell her about little Eddie as soon as the time's right.'

He smiled back at her, gathered up the photographs and put them back into the envelope.

'Now I know why you've been sending money to Greece.'

'Aristo and Maria look after my child and my house. I wouldn't come back to Gosport until I was sure it was safe enough to leave him for a while. And I can't wait to get back to him. I'd do anything for him. You do see that, don't you?'

'Even sort out his father's killer. Now I can understand how you were with Summer, the softness about you. I guess it's called motherhood.' He leaned towards her and kissed her gently on the forehead. 'That's a friendship kiss, Daisy. We're good mates, eh?'

'Mates,' she laughed. '*And* your bleeding hair looks a treat!'

'I still don't understand why I 'ave to come with you?'

'Because, Vera, I asked you to. And for God's sake get in the car.'

'This bloody little thing. Why don't you get a proper car?'

'Don't you dare start on that, again.' Vera snorted and pulled the door shut. 'I suppose if that psychedelic bus 'as come back you'll need me to protect you?' She positioned her legs in the front and breathed a sigh of relief that she was finally tucked in the confined space.

'Yeah, sure,' said Daisy. 'You're gonna protect me against a busload of hippies all high as kites? What you gonna do? Tickle 'em to death with your false eyelashes?'

'I don't like it when you gets in a mood like this. I

can easily hate you,' said Vera, but she couldn't really, she just wanted to have the last word.

'Did you really 'ave to ask the estate agent to call that couple back and beg 'em to visit the house again next week?'

'Would I lie? They took one look and walked straight out again, apparently.' Which was why Daisy was going over there now to sort it out. Belle had to go.

'At least that dear little Summer's safe. 'As Belle ever asked about 'er kiddie?'

'Has she, fuck!'

'Ain't natural. Ain't natural at all. And 'ow's little Eddie?'

'Blooming.' Vera saw a shadow cross Daisy's face and wished she hadn't asked about the kiddie. She knew how much Daisy missed him.

'You sorted out the money yet?' she said, to change the subject.

'You don't want to be asking questions with answers that might incriminate you.'

Vera glared at her. 'Think the bank's insured?' she asked.

'Should be. That's why Bonnie and Clyde robbed banks.'

'Is it, Dais?'

'How should I know? The wholesalers'll be insured. If they ain't, they ain't gonna be pleased.'

'Where did you learn about such things, Daisy?'

'Eddie told me all about it. But I first got to learn of it when I was in London, that New Year at the club, with Ronnie and Reggie Kray. I'm beginning to hope Roy Kemp's smart enough to get 'imself out of the way when the shit hits the fan. Perhaps someone else'll take over his rackets. Because if he tries to run things from abroad, he'll get into difficulties. Ronnie and Reggie don't forget things easily, see?'

'You're ever so clever, Daisy.'

'No. I just had plenty of time to work things out. But Roy won't be allowed to forget me in a hurry.'

'But supposing he 'as alibis?'

'Vera, you been watching too many of them B gangster movies they been showing at the Criterion Picture House. It's only Humphrey Bogart and James Cagney that gets away with things, not Roy Kemp.'

'But what about 'is mum? I thought you liked 'er?'

'That's the sad part. I do. But Violet is a clever old stick. She spends a good lot of time in Spain with Moira, so it won't be no hardship to go there for while. Or else she'll stay where she bleeding well is an' run his business. She's well respected and a tough old bird. I admire her.'

Vera sighed. 'Roy might think Sammy 'ad something to do with his downfall. All the correspondence went to the caff, didn't it?'

Daisy shrugged.

'I hated going over every morning to sort out the post. Remember when I first came back to Gosport and I wouldn't set foot in the place for the memories of Eddie there?' Vera nodded. 'Well, I soon had to get over that feeling while making sure Sammy didn't catch me. That bastard's still got it coming for that kiddy's death.'

'Too right, Dais. It was all over the *Evening News* and then nothing.'

The car drew up outside Daisy's house and on the gravel driveway she cut the engine.

'No bus.'

'No music either,' said Daisy, helping Vera from the confines of the car. 'I really hope it means she's gone for good and we can get on and clear the place up.'

She unlocked the oak door and Vera went in ahead of her.

'What's that smell? Mind 'ow you tread.' She shoved Daisy aside. 'Someone's been sick near the door.' She bent at the knees and peered at the mess. 'Ugh!'

'For fuck's sake come away from it then.' Daisy went ahead to the kitchen.

'Jesus Christ!'

'Not more sick?' Vera called out. She followed Daisy and saw her friend's eyes were filled with tears.

'Don't worry, ducky, we can soon clear it up.'

Mouldy food was encrusted on plates. A few fat flies buzzing and crawling lazily in the mess added to the mad scene. Vomit was everywhere, in the sink, on the table. Where the back door had been left open to the elements, the floor was wet with the recent rain they'd had. Vera saw Daisy was near to breaking point.

Vera repeated, 'Don't worry.' She was trying to be positive. 'We'll get 'em out once and for all this time.'

Daisy looked at her. 'I don't think I can take much more of this. I don't even want to look at the downstairs toilet. No wonder me prospective buyers bailed out quick.' She walked into the dining room.

'It's not so bad in here,' she called. 'Evidence of a party. Beer bottles and cans.'

'Wonder what we'll find upstairs?' Vera had joined Daisy, and kept close to her, her eyes on the carpet in case she trod in something she'd rather not have done.

'It's ever so quiet. I fuckin' hope they've gone,' Vera said.

Daisy had now reached the top of the stairs and gone into the master bedroom. Vera walked into the nearest bedroom.

'This room's not so bad, only needs a tidy.' She pulled back the curtains letting the sun stream into the dishevelled room. 'You should get the bleedin' locks changed, Dais. We'll sort this out between us, and once it's clean it'll sell.'

'Get up, you lazy bitch!' she heard Daisy shout. 'Vera? Get in 'ere!'

Vera hurried into the main bedroom. What a stench, she thought. Then she remembered the smell. From long ago, from Moira's bedroom at the caff. From the wardrobe.

The stench of death.

Daisy was holding up the edge of the counterpane. Belle's face was like wax.

'Don't touch 'er.' Vera took the edge of the material from Daisy's clenched hand. She stared at Belle's face. Oddly, she looked serene. 'She's gone, Dais. Don't look at 'er no more. It ain't gonna make 'er come back.' She gently replaced the counterpane. 'We got to get the police out 'ere.'

'I can't think, Vera. When I saw 'er lyin' in the bed . . . She was all cold . . .'

'It don't matter, pet. Go down and use the phone.' Vera patiently turned Daisy in the direction of the door.

'Phone's cut off. Whoever buys the place got to have it connected again.'

'Then get next door and ask to use theirs. Don't touch nothing, mind. Fingerprints.'

Vera touched the side of her nose, she knew all about the police and their methods. 'That's 'ow they caught Steve Cochran in that film at the Forum cinema last week. One fingerprint . . .'

'Vera, you're doing my head in.'

Half an hour later police were swarming over the house. DS Vinnie Endersby was asking what happened. Vera and Daisy told him.

'It's the drugs, ain't it?' Vera insisted.

'I can't say for sure. There'll be an autopsy.' But she didn't need a copper to tell her what she already knew.

'It's the drugs. Check at the Haslar Hospital. We had to take 'er there . . . If it wasn't for Daisy helping her over bad patches, she'd 'ave come to this end before now.'

'We'll investigate. You two sure you're all right? It's a big shock finding a dead person, you know?' He gave Daisy a worried look. Vera saw her colour up. She likes him, she thought. And that feeling goes both ways.

'We'll be all right,' Vera said, firmly.

When they were allowed to leave and Daisy was driving towards the village, Vera said, 'He's a nice man, that Vinnie. He fancies you.'

'You say that about every bloke who talks to me, and you always 'ave done. I'm worried about how Bri's gonna take this.'

'That's anybody's guess. He keeps a lot inside 'im, that one.'

'It'll take Bri ages to go through all the channels to prove he's Summer's dad. You don't think they'll take Summer away and foster 'er in some state-run home, do you? That would break his heart.'

'Shouldn't think so,' said Vera. She fiddled in her

handbag and brought out a scrap of cream-coloured paper. 'Not when I give Bri this.'

'What you got there?'

Vera gave a big grin. 'The birth certificate. And he's named as the father. It was with the rest of 'er bits and pieces in 'er bag . . .'

'You never rifled through a dead woman's belongings?'

'Only a little bit. 'Ad to do something while we was waiting for the cop shop to show up.'

Daisy sighed. 'There'll probably be an inquest before the body is released for burial. I wonder who'll bury her?'

'Bri?'

'I suppose so. I'll do my bit as well,' said Daisy.

''Course you will. When the coppers 'ave finished with the 'ouse we'll go back and give it a good clean. Of course, now a dead body 'as been discovered there, you'll 'ave to drop the price even more before you find a buyer for it. No one's gonna want the place now, Dais.'

'Thank you, Vera. You just made my day, telling me that.'

CHAPTER 25

Daisy didn't think she'd ever seen a man look at a woman the way Reggie Kray looked at his brand new wife, Frances. His eyes followed her whenever she stepped away from him, not that she'd moved far from his side since the ring had been placed on her finger.

Roy handed Daisy a glass of champagne, 'Were you married in a church?'

'Fareham Registry Office,' Daisy replied. All the little lines at the corners of his eyes fanned out when he smiled. She thought he looked very handsome in his expensively tailored black suit and shiny shoes and a white carnation in his buttonhole. She'd already spotted several women in the church and now, at the reception in the spacious hotel ballroom, giving him the once-over. This man had killed her Eddie and she was in the process of paying him back for it. Yet she was ashamed because she could feel herself being drawn to him like a needle to a magnet. She knew he didn't belong to her but she was proud to be seen with him and kept taking shy glances at him. A couple of times he caught her and she'd coloured up. But he just laughed at her, like they were in some conspiracy together. Daisy was disgusted with herself because she fancied the pants off him.

Daisy looked about her and said, 'I can't get over the amount of well-wishers who've turned up. Never realised the twins was so bleeding popular.'

'You'd be surprised, they ain't as bad as they're painted and both boys do a great deal for the local charities. It's the jumped-up villains who think they can muscle in on the boys' territories or who don't give them the respect they deserve who get it in the neck. Anyway, Reggie's popular enough for that David Bailey to have taken all today's photos.'

Daisy wondered if and when Roy would 'get it in the neck' when the twins found out he'd pulled a flanker on them.

'David Bailey won't have chopped any heads off or left someone's auntie out the picture then, will he?' Roy laughed. Daisy sipped at her champagne and looked across the room to where Violet, Roy's mum, was enjoying a good laugh with Violet, Reggie's mum.

Then she caught sight of someone she thought she knew, until she realised she only recognised them from the cinema. 'Is that, her – what's 'er name – over there? You know, the one with the big boobies in them really funny films?'

'Our Barbara. 'Course it is. And if you look a bit closer you'll see all sorts of people: politicians, singers, actors and actresses, boxers, all friends of Reg and Ron. Celebrities who was invited but couldn't make it sent telegrams. Judy sent a telegram.'

'Judy?'

'Garland, Judy Garland,'

'Fucking hell,' said Daisy. 'Fancy that!' She gulped at her champagne, but she'd heard the word boxer and her heart fluttered alarmingly. Supposing *he* was here? It was more than possible, wasn't it? What would she say to Valentine Waite? He might find it rude that she'd never thanked him for the lilies at Christmas, but she hadn't wanted to ask Roy for his address and she had no telephone number for him. Daisy felt her colour rise, so she pushed all thoughts of the man away.

'They going on honeymoon?' she asked.

'They're off to Greece,' said Roy. He put his arm around her shoulder and pulled her towards him. 'One of your favourite places, eh, Daisy?' She began to panic, her heart suddenly doing a frantic war dance inside her chest. She remembered another time when he'd mentioned she'd come back from abroad. Did he know more than he was letting on? No, there was no way Roy could know about her child. Or was there?

For fuck's sake, Daisy Lane, stop getting paranoid, she told herself. So she took a deep breath and replied, 'I love the sun, Roy. But I guess you do as well, your tan has to be kept up, don't it? But your special place is Spain, ain't it?' He grinned down at her. Daisy could smell his familiar citrus cologne.

'I've asked you before to visit my place over there. You'd really love it, Daisy. I can see you shopping in the town in a pretty sun dress, basket over your arm all full of Spanish lacy things. Coming back to lie by the pool and getting a nice healthy glow to your skin. A glass of something cold on the table next to you. I'll even set it all up for you. Moira would love to see you and I could take some time off from business myself, fly out with you and show you some of the glorious countryside. You'd love it.'

'Who knows?' Daisy said. It had been a long day and her smile was beginning to flag. She looked at his mouth, firm lips, teeth strong and white, that tiny front chip adding to his ruggedness. She suddenly wondered what it would be like to kiss him ... For God's sake, woman, she thought, you've just spent months setting the bloke up and now you're wondering what he'd kiss like! Time to think of other things, Daisy.

'He's older than her, ain't he?' She waved across the floor at the happy couple standing near the bar.

'Reggie?'

Daisy nodded.

'About ten or eleven years, Dais. But that's how it should be, don't you think?' Daisy wondered if he was thinking about the difference in their ages; she suspected he was. All this hinting about her and him getting together was nerve-racking. It reminded her of Eddie and the way he'd gone about things. Trouble was, Roy was a very tasty bloke, and she couldn't deny it. But he wouldn't be so anxious to get involved with her when he found out what she'd done to get even with him, would he? And Roy wasn't stupid, eventually he might find out. She was almost relieved when two men clapped Roy on the shoulders. They both had heavy foreign-sounding accents with American undertones and Daisy was fascinated by their voices.

She wasn't so delighted ten minutes later when, after the initial introductions, the two men spoke solely to Roy of the merits of various boxing matches between Cassius Clay and others. Daisy tried not to appear bored but her first visit to the fights had been her last as far as she was concerned, and boxing held no interest. She gazed around the glass chandelier and gilt-filled room, happy to spot the two Violets so she could disappear politely.

Both ladies were over by the packed bar, arms about each other's waists, giggling and laughing to a crowd of onlookers and making a fair job of the steps to the Palais Glide. Daisy lightly touched Roy's arm.

'Just going over to see your mum.' He gave her a wink and an understanding look as he took her glass from her and set it down on a nearby table along with his own.

She breathed a sigh of relief at escaping from the bores. Couples were dancing and she, not wanting to charge across the floor, began threading her way around the room.

She felt a soft touch on her shoulder and turned to look up into the long-lashed eyes of Valentine Waite.

Her body froze. People were all around her, the band was playing and yet everything seemed suddenly to be suspended in time.

'We can't talk or be seen together here. Meet me near the cigarette kiosk on the corner. I'm leaving now.' And then he was gone, leaving Daisy to continue her way around the room, wondering if she'd dreamed what had just happened and why he hadn't even asked her for a dance. There had been no greeting, no idle chit-chat from him, just the command to meet him. The bloody cheek of him! Who did he think he was, ordering her around? But she knew she'd do as he'd asked.

Daisy bypassed the two Violets and disappeared out of the smoke-filled room through a door which led into a small garden area. She saw the half open gate and made her way towards it. There was a chill in the air and a damp mist. She breathed deeply and pushed the gate wider and two suited men appeared as if from nowhere.

'Evenin', miss,' said the taller of the two. 'Shall I call a taxi?' Daisy had to think quickly.

'No thanks. Just popping out for some ciggies. All they got in here are those bloody Turkish things an' posh jobs.'

The man grinned at her. 'Can't beat a good ol' Woodbine, can you?'

Daisy treated him to one of her special smiles and sailed past. They were probably a couple of the twins' men making sure undesirables didn't get in.

She saw the lights from the kiosk at the end of the road and her high heels clicked on the pavement as she walked swiftly towards it, disappointed he wasn't already there waiting for her.

'Daisy?' She halted her steps. He was standing in the shadows just inside a cobbled alleyway. He pulled her towards him and the darkness swallowed them up.

'I've missed you,' he said. 'Don't you think we ought to make up for lost time?' Lightly he ran his hands over her black dress, up beyond her waist to her breasts then down again lingering on her slim hips. 'I love the dress but you'd be better without it. Expose yourself to me.' His voice was husky. Daisy felt a fluttering in her loins. 'Show me what you think I might need, Daisy.'

Daisy felt the flutter change to heat which rushed over her body. Nobody had ever said things like that to her. She had the strangest feeling she wanted to obey him. Wanted to feel what it would be like to give herself to a good-looking man, one she felt nothing for. Wasn't it blokes who fucked and walked away? It was the Swinging Sixties, for Christ's sake, why couldn't she do what she wanted for once? Give in to her body's yearnings. Without a word and powerless to refuse his command she eased her dress up over her hips and waist and pulled it over her head. It was in her hand for only seconds before it fluttered to the cobbles. She looked directly at him and then smoothed her hands, fingers splayed, down over her body, over her black lacy bra, lingering on her breasts, across the taut skin of her stomach and her black suspender belt worn beneath lacy black knickers. Her fingers traced down the lines of the elastic straps holding up her sheer black stockings, then rested briefly on the tops of her thighs before her hands began making circular movements towards her crotch. Was she really doing this, she asked herself? This was her body, and she was using it to tempt a man she hardly knew, but who seemed able to draw her into some kind of sexual trance. She knew it was sluttish but her body was purring with pleasure. What the fuck was happening to her?

He stood back leaning against the red brick wall watching her. She could see his moist lips and insolent eyes and it was as if he was almost mocking her because he knew she wanted him.

'This is what's on offer,' she said, her heart fluttering inside her breast like a caged bird. Then she leaned forward so her body brushed against his. She drew her fingers across his mouth and up the line of his nose then down again, slowly tracing them back over his mouth to his neck, lingering a while on his hard chest and further down stroking his taut stomach through the material of his suit. She stopped, made him wait before she unzipped his trousers and slipped her small hand inside the opening.

Daisy closed her eyes as her fingers found the tangle of warmth that was his pubic hair and rising from it, his prick. She waited, heard his sharp intake of breath then he moved slightly so her hand could close around the heaviness, the fullness of him. His breath on her cheek had made her nipples hard. She felt the throbbing in her breasts and that delightful tingling heat between her legs. She released him from his trousers and slid her hand along the pulsing, satin-ridged swell of his erection.

She heard him gasp as her fingers first circled then lightly played across the engorged head of his thick shaft. His lips found hers, his mouth opened and his tongue claimed her.

'Daisy! Daisy!'

The moment was gone. The heady anticipation was replaced by sudden, heart-pounding fear.

'Fuck! It's Roy.' Daisy crouched to the cobbles, her hands scrabbling in the darkness for her dress. No sooner had her fingers encountered the material than it was over her head and she was tugging at the side zip and smoothing away the creases. Valentine was zipping up his trousers over his fast-flagging erection.

'Daisy?' She could hear heavy footsteps now. Her heart was pounding.

'We can't be seen together,' he breathed.

She looked into the darkness of the alleyway; it seemed unending.

She stepped out into the shadowed light from the street lamps.

'Daisy! Where have you been?' She saw the worry etched on Roy's face.

'Hello, Roy,' she said brightly. 'Why're you looking for me?'

Take a leaf from Vera's book, she thought, answer a question with a question.

'Two of the lads said you'd gone to get fags. You don't smoke.'

Daisy thought quickly. 'If I'd told 'em the truth, that I was fucking fed up with being treated like an empty-headed bitch an' needed a bit of space from them two wankers in there that was talking to you and ignoring me, like I was some piece of shit, I don't think that would have gone down too well. But that was the truth. Who the fuck did those two poncey blokes think they was?'

She saw him frown. He was staring into her eyes and she felt guilty for deceiving him. Then he took off his jacket and drew it across her shoulders.

'Let me put this around you, you'll catch a chill. Why didn't you put your coat on?' His voice was soft, tender, and he gazed at her with such kindness.

'I came out without thinking, just wanted to get away.' And then Daisy became aware of the lies that were dripping from her mouth. She, Daisy Lane, who hated lies, wasn't telling the truth. She felt disgusted with herself. 'Who were those blokes?'

He sighed. 'The twins are hoping for a Mafia hookup.'

That accounted for the poncey accents, thought Daisy. 'Well, Sicilian gangsters ain't as polite as London ones!'

It was then he laughed, full and throaty, but he wasn't relaxed and the crinkles at the corners of his eyes stayed fixed on his handsome face.

'Now don't get upset,' he said. He pulled the lapels of his coat together and towards him so that she was imprisoned in its warmth. He looked down at her. 'I'm sure it's nothing that can't be sorted but Vera's been calling the switchboard of the hotel . . .'

'What for?' Daisy had given her the number knowing she'd only contact her in a case of dire emergency. Little Eddie, it had to be, something's happened to him, oh, my God ... Daisy gripped Roy's arm.

'Someone called Suze,' he said. 'Vera says you must come back ...' Daisy was about to breathe a sigh of relief that it was nothing to do with her child, but fresh anxiety immediately took over. *Must* come back. *Must*? Suze? What had happened to her friend?

'What?' He shook his head.

'She wouldn't say over the phone. C'mon, I've already made apologies for us, Mum collected your bag and coat and I've got the car waiting.'

'You'll take me to Gosport?'

'How else are you going to get there, walk?' He grabbed her and started hurrying her up the street. 'Anything could have 'appened to you, Dais. You shouldn't go wandering around London in the dark, there's all kinds of nasty people about.'

'No, there ain't,' she said, relieved he was taking control. 'They're all back in that fucking hotel there.'

No sooner had the car drawn up outside Heavenly Bodies when Daisy was pounding on the door. She saw the lights go on and Vera padding through from the back in her mules.

'Oh, thank God you're here.' Daisy swept inside followed by Roy.

She'd never seen Vera in such a state. Her face was completely without make-up and puffy with tears. Vera hardly ever cried and a knot of fear curled tightly in Daisy's stomach.

Roy pushed the door closed.

'Let's sit down,' he said, leading Vera towards one of her blue leather sofas. 'Why don't you tell us what's happened?'

Just then there was a movement at the back of the shop and Daisy saw a stooped figure slowly come forward. Si's face was grey. He looked as though all the colour and life had been squeezed out of him. Daisy went to him and put her arms around him. She felt his body curve in towards her almost as if he was trying to withdraw some of her vibrant energy. For a while they clung and the silence was like no other silence Daisy had ever experienced. It was as though any moment all her darkest fears would be realised. Then Si pulled away.

'I need your help,' he said.

Roy moved up to make room for Daisy, who sat down between him and Vera. Vera clenched Daisy's hand.

'No need to fanny about,' Si began. Daisy thought he seemed to have become middle-aged, his speech halting, and every so often he smoothed the hair at the side of his head even though it hadn't moved. 'Yesterday morning, I was working in the garden. Round the back, mending the hen house where a fox had got in. Meggie was playing in the dirt, well wrapped up and making her usual little girl noises that she does to her dollies.' Daisy could visualise the scene. 'Suze was indoors, upstairs, making the bed. From the top windows there's a pretty good view of the gardens, road and meadows surrounding us. Every so often, I'd look up and Suze would wave.' Si's voice began to falter.

'Come and sit down, mate,' said Roy. He got up so that Si could have his seat but Si shook his head.

'I prefer to stand,' he said. He was leaning against one of Vera's shelves containing herbal remedies.

'I was banging away with the hammer and when I looked up again at the window there was no sign of Suze. Neither was Meggie around me. Only her dolly in the dirt. My heart stopped then, almost like it was a premonition. I rushed round to the front of the house and there in the road, I could see it above the high privet hedge, was this bread lorry, all swerved at an angle. Then the noise hit me. Its engine was still running, someone was shouting, there was feet pounding on the tarmac and our gate was open. The fuckin' gate I was going to fix after I'd sorted the bleedin' hen house.' Si put his hands to his face and began crying into them, his shoulders shaking. Daisy made a move to rise but he put a hand out, palm upwards, and again shook his head. He wiped his tears away with that hand. Daisy saw his other hand was now gripping the edge of a shelf and his knuckles were white. She sat back again. 'When I got out onto the road, Meggie was lying partly beneath the front of the lorry. Somehow the impact had torn her arm and leg from her body. Her little face was unmarked. That was what I saw first. The second thing will live with me to my dying day. Suze was on her hands and knees, she was covered in Meggie's blood because somehow she'd managed to retrieve my baby's limbs. She was screaming and trying to fit Meggie's arm back to her little body.'

Si broke. Vera rose and put her arms around him. Roy got up and together, he and Vera took Si upstairs.

Daisy watched without seeing any of them. She put her elbows on her knees and held her head in her hands. With her eyes closed she watched the scenes replay in her head. She thought of little Eddie and her heart bled for Susie and Si.

After a while, Daisy had no idea how long, Vera and Roy came back. Roy handed her a mug of tea.

'Drink this,' he said.

'Where's Suze?' Daisy asked, sipping at the tea. Vera gave a long drawn out sigh.

'She got it into her head that Si was to blame. She won't let 'im near 'er. She don't know the time of day, even. Only that 'er Meggie's dead. She wouldn't let them take the child away at first. All she said was she 'ad to find you, Dais. That you'd know what to do. That you sorted everything out for her before and would do again. Si's been worried sick, Meggie was his baby too. But she wouldn't talk to 'im or be anywhere near 'im, then she ran off. It was like she was out of her mind, he said.' Vera was fingering one of her long, gold gypsy earrings. Daisy put her mug on the floor, got up, and made her sit down again next to her. She held both her hands.

Daisy felt so numb inside it took her all her strength to ask, 'Then what?'

'Bri, who didn't know anything about this then, well, none of us did, spotted Susie sitting in the doorway of the caff. Bloody good job he did, an' all. Don't bear thinkin' about if that animal Sammy 'ad got 'old of Suze first. She didn't 'ave any money on 'er so she must 'ave got a lift down 'ere. At least she 'ad sense enough to know where she was goin'. Bri coaxed her into the shop an' 'e phones me. I goes round sharpish. "Where's Daisy?" That's all you can get out of 'er. Over an' over again, Where's Daisy?' I got these pills, knocked her out, they 'ave. She's in your spare room, fast asleep. Bri's kippin' on your sofa to make sure she don't go wandering. Not that she will with what I've dosed 'er with.' Daisy looked into Vera's tear-stained face. Her eyes without their false lashes had almost disappeared into the folds of puffy skin. She knew whatever Vera had given Suze to make her sleep wouldn't harm her.

'Anyway, I got 'old of Si. He was bloody glad to find she was safe. He come down on the train an' the rest you knows.'

'Is she going back with Si?' Vera shook her head. 'She only wants you. From the little 'e's said I feel sure 'e'd be bleedin' grateful if you'd look after her a while. He shouldn't be 'ere, 'e should be sorting out his dead baby.'

Daisy put her arms around Vera, breathing in the smell of the ever present Californian Poppy.

'We'll get through this, Vera. You mark my words. You and me, we'll make Suze whole again.'

Nobody spoke for a long while, then Roy said, 'I expect that poor bugger upstairs is torn between the devil and the bloody deep blue sea. He won't want to leave his missus but he knows he's got to get back. If I can help, I will. What if I run him back to Devon?' Daisy saw Vera stare at him. He shrugged. 'It's a sensible option until whatever thoughts running around Susie's head have untangled themselves. The woman wants Daisy. Daisy's here. He knows she'll be in good hands.'

'Fuckin' clever clogs you are,' said Vera. But she gave him a weak smile then turned to Daisy. 'You know, Suze made me promise I wouldn't let Si stay in your flat?' Daisy shook her head. 'I didn't know which of them two needed me most,' Vera said.

'Suze wasn't going far after you dosed her up, was she?'

'No. But Si brought down the medication her doctor prescribed for 'er.'

Daisy nodded. 'What you've said makes sense, Roy.' After all, he'd had enough experience of women who went to pieces. Moira had never fully recovered from her breakdown and had tried to kill herself. That didn't mean, God willing, that Suze wouldn't get better, given time. And Daisy had all the time in the world for Suze.

'Better get ourselves sorted out, then.' Roy went upstairs to return moments later with Si, his coat and shoes on and a brown carrier bag in his hands. Si hugged Daisy and pressed the bag at her.

'A change of underwear an' stuff for Suze, you know, toothbrush and things. Mum said she'd need these if she wouldn't come home.' He suddenly changed his tone. 'I don't want to leave her.' Daisy heard the sob in his throat.

'I know,' she said. 'And I'll make sure she knows how much you love 'er.'

'We can drop you off at the bookshop, Dais. But we'd best get going to Devon else we'll get caught in all the early morning traffic.'

'Fine, Roy. Little treasure, you are.' She saw him blush and the crinkles at the corners of his eyes deepen.

'You be all right, Vera? Want to come round mine, with me?'

Vera shook her head. 'I needs to be by meself for a bit to get all this sorted out in me mind. But I won't be lonely, Kibbles is upstairs waiting on the bed for me.'

Daisy kissed her and opened the door out on to the

High Street. It was then she realised Vera must have given her girls the night off, or else they'd finished business early for once. Madam ZaZa always left around five o'clock.

Si sat in the back of the car, merging into the blackness, and Daisy got in next to Roy. Charles, Roy's chauffeur, had been left behind in London to make sure Violet got home all right. Roy drew up opposite the cafe in North Street, got out and opened the passenger door for her.

'You'll be all right?'

Daisy nodded. 'Thank you.' She leaned up to kiss him on the cheek. He let her lips touch his skin, staring at her, his eyes unwavering. Then he bent down and returned her kiss. She felt his lips on her hair, smelled his cologne, and then he was gone.

Daisy climbed the stairs without putting on the light. Bri didn't deserve to be woken from his sleep on the sofa. As she tiptoed past the still forms of him and Bertie draped across his chest, Bri put out a hand and grabbed her.

'Oh, you gave me a fright,' she said. He sat up, careful not to wake the cat.

'I'd make a useless bodyguard if I didn't notice every sound, wouldn't I?' Daisy smiled at him. Her eyes became accustomed to the dimness of the room, helped by the slowly brightening sky outside showing through the undrawn curtains. 'She's still dead to the world.' He nodded towards the bedrooms. 'You want me to stay? Or shall I go back to The Black Bear? You cold? Want a cup of tea?'

Daisy shook her head.

'No to everything and you're all right where you are. Unless you want to use my bed?' His eyes lit up.

'I only meant I'm going in with Suze an' I thought you'd be more comfortable.'

'Thought the offer was too good to be true,' he said. Then more seriously, 'This is a fucking awful business, Daisy. That kid in there don't know what's 'it 'er. If I can do anything . . .' Daisy bent down and kissed his forehead. He smelled of bed and warmth and Bertie growled as though to say, leave us alone.

'You've done more than enough,' Daisy said and left the room.

In her spare bedroom, the lump in the bed that was Susie looked very small. Daisy undressed, leaving her clothes in a pile on the floor, and climbed into the bed wearing just her slip. Susie was facing the middle and as Daisy pulled aside the sheet she saw the blonde curls were spread across the pillow. With the minimum of movement, Daisy slid close to Susie, studying her face. In sleep she looked like an angel. A child angel. A lump rose in Daisy's throat.

'You shouldn't have to go through this, lovey. You've had enough to contend with in your short life.' Her voice was barely a whisper as she stroked Susie's hair.

Susie opened her eyes, slowly focusing on Daisy.

'Meggie's dead,' she said.

'I know, love.'

'I been waiting for you, knew you wouldn't let me down, Dais. Am I going mad like Moira?'

Daisy shook her head. 'No. But you are mad with grief.'

Susie's big blue eyes widened. 'Will I come to terms with this?'

Daisy stared at her. 'Only if you go back to sleep, love,' she said, 'and let me look after you.'

CHAPTER 26

Valentine Waite pushed aside a veil of branches and pulled her into the clearing. He knew the beech leaves were young on the trees and brimming with bright greenery, but now everything was saturated with the night's darkness As his eyes grew accustomed to the shadows, he saw at his feet a bed of soft decay, springy and scented with the new growth of primroses. Her cheap perfume almost eclipsed the smells of the forest coming to life after the winter.

His hand strayed to his suit pocket and he took out the knife, pressing on the handle. The blade sprang forward with a sharp click. A new desire rippled through him, adding another layer on top of the anger he had so far held in check.

She was small and blonde and wearing a red satin dress with bootlace shoulder straps that made the material cling to her body like a second skin. He could see she wore neither bra nor panties. With a lightning flick of his sharp knife he cut through one of the straps, watching as the satin slipped, exposing one small, round breast. She had flinched, thinking most probably the blade was meant for her. A birdlike sound of concern escaped her lips. He could almost smell her fear.

'Aren't you going to ask me what I want?' He

skimmed a kiss across her shoulder. Her skin was bitter with her perfume. It had that strange musky smell that reminded him of the scent his mother used to wear as she kissed him before she left the house each night. Before her cheap scent was overlaid with the smell of men and sex that he smelled on her when she'd come into his room to check on him before she'd fall, laughing, into bed with her final customer of the evening. The overnighter.

It wasn't that he really minded her going with the men. After all, she had to put food on the table. Rent had to be paid and schoolclothes bought. And all out of her earnings. But when she was with them, she wasn't with him.

'Go into the other room for a while, Val,' she'd say. He'd climb into the green velvet chair in the living room and put his hands over his ears as he'd hear the footsteps running up the thinly carpeted stars. He'd listen to the laughter, the voices, the grunting, then the silence before the footsteps rang out again on the stairs. It never took long during the day, usually. Then his mother would call him back into the warm kitchen and she'd carry on helping him with his Johnnie Appleseed jigsaw puzzle. Or they'd finish the game of snakes and ladders. Her face would be flushed and he'd watch to see how far the little yellow teapot on the windowsill had moved. That was where his mother put the money she got from the men. He never saw any of the men. The stairs led up from the kitchen and that was why he had to go into the cold living room. Even the overnighters had left before he woke in the mornings. But why was it always him who had to wait? 'I won't be long,' she'd call. And it didn't matter if they were eating dinner or listening to

342

the wireless, if a knock came at the door, he would have to go into the living room.

But not now he was grown up. He called the shots now.

'I think you'll do whatever you want,' the girl before him said. He knew she was expecting him to cut the other strap, so he tucked the sharp blade beneath the corded satin and pulled the knife towards him. Now both her breasts were waiting for his attention and the dress fell to her waist. He replaced the knife in his inside pocket and smiled at her. Women never could refuse his smile. They all wilted beneath his boyish grin and now he made sure he used that smile to his best advantage, putting her at her ease. Calmly she wriggled out of her dress and stood before him clad only in her red satin shoes.

He began caressing her breasts, her arms, her shoulders, and she hardly moved except to put an arm around his neck to steady herself. He realised her high heels were sinking in the soft earth, making her unsteady on her feet. Her mouth tasted of the gin and tonics he had bought her, sweet and sour at the same time. His mother had drunk brandy. One tiny smell of it and the memories came flooding back of brandy-flavoured kisses. 'Amuse yourself, Val. I won't be long. You'll hardly miss me.' Lies had dripped from his mother's lips. He *had* missed her – especially when he was left in the dark, in the cold, in the green velvet chair, taking from it all the comfort he could until his mother's return.

And now, one of his hands was kneading the girl's breast, then pulling and twisting at the hardened nipple. His other hand searched his fly and released his hardened cock. Next came his belt buckle, the noise of the clasp sharp in the night. When he was free of his trousers he felt the rush of desire so great and out of control that with little more than one quick motion he threw her on to her back on the bed of leaves and pinned her wrists behind her head, pushing into her with his groin until she was gasping for air and his erection led him easily into her warm wetness.

He was thrusting again and again, groaning and weak from suppressed desire. Wet, so very warm and wet, and she was sucking him in, making him lose control, making everything disappear into the very blackness around them that held no beginning, no end, only the delicious hard fuck, fuck, fuck, until he came in one magnificent flowing gush that seemed unending in its intensity.

He lay quite still, breathing hard. Then he became aware of her gasping great gulps of air into her small frame still pinned beneath his body. He was wrung out and rolled off her on to his side. He felt her move against him. A light wind ruffled his hair and he knew his anger was still there, the demon in his head still not appeased, sleeping beneath the surface like an iceberg, its magnitude unexposed.

He rose, then bent down and found his trousers, pulling them on. She was whimpering, scrabbling about for her dress. He kicked it towards her.

'Cover yourself,' he said. 'Skinny cow. You make me sick.'

He could see she was frightened, clutching the dress, puckering the material in one clenched fist to keep it from falling down as she waited for him to take her back to the Mercedes, back to the part of town he'd picked her up from. He stared at her. Had he thought her attractive? He supposed so, but with him it wasn't about the sex. It was the power. To do what he wanted when he wanted. Just like his mother. His mother had despised the men. She'd told him that. 'They're dirty bastards. Not fit to walk the earth.'

Once he'd asked her where his daddy was but she'd shrugged. When he was eleven he realised she didn't know who his father was.

It was at that moment he began hating her. He was thirteen when she told him for the last time to go into the other room.

He could see it now, the warm kitchen, the rain on the window pane; remember the scent of her perfume as she'd bent over him helping him look in the atlas. For Kenya and Mombasa. So that tomorrow in school he would be able to put up his hand and say, 'Please, miss, Africa. Mombasa is in Kenya and Kenya is in Africa.' And then the knock at the door.

'Go in the other room, Val,' she'd said. And he'd left the warmth and gone to sit in his chair. For now it had become his chair. And then the anger grew. Sitting in the dark, for there was no bulb in the central swinging light socket. He had never, ever told his mother he didn't like the dark. He began to cry. How could she really love him if she was always willing to leave him whenever that knock sounded on the door?

And it was then that higher power in his head sent the demon to calm him. To explain if he did whatever the demon wanted, his mother would never, ever leave him. So he stopped crying and listened. And when his mother called him back into the kitchen and he saw the yellow teapot was nearly next to the brass candlestick, he opened the map book.

'Athens? Where is Athens?' he asked.

But that night the demon proved how clever he was

by allowing no overnighter to spoil the plan. Val, when he was sure his mother was asleep, got up and went into her bedroom. Picking up the peach-coloured frilled pillow he put it over her face and kept it there until she stopped struggling. He was amazed at how easy it had been. But then at thirteen he was already strong and well built. He lifted her head and put the pillow beneath it and went back to bed.

Before he slept, the demon told him he was satisfied and, although the earthly body of his mother would leave, her spirit would always remain in his heart.

And all he had to do was say he was already in bed when the man knocked on the door and that he never saw any of his mother's customers. Which of course was the truth. He never saw the men, did he? He could feel his mother already in his heart, but just to make sure the demon wasn't trying to trick him, he went back into her bedroom and shook his head at the woman lying in his mother's bed. He didn't know her.

He went back to his room and slept.

In the morning he could still feel his mother in his heart. The demon told Val, as he was getting ready for school, that he must always do his bidding. Anything he wanted he could have – as long as he satisfied the demon in his head. He could hear the demon laughing now. Not that it mattered. The game was always played straight. He did what the demon wanted and the demon let him win his fights, one after another.

And all the women who were like his mother had to be punished.

Of course, when he got to school that day, he had to pretend it was exactly like any other day. He even got the highest test mark in Geography. But when he got home he had to go to a neighbour and tell her his mother was still in bed and that wasn't like her at all, was it?

Everyone was worried about him. What a dreadful thing to have happened to such a nice, polite boy. An overnighter must have done it. No other explanation, they reckoned. Valentine was sent to a home; after all he was too young to fend for himself and there were no other relatives to look after him. But once more the demon stepped in to help.

The boys in the home told him he had a sissy name. So he had to fight them. And win. One of the house fathers got him enrolled in a gym and Val started boxing. But that was a long time ago. And now he knew when he put the women out of their misery they were never truly gone. Someone, somewhere, would always hold them close, in their hearts. After all, wasn't his mother still in his heart?

Val finished making himself presentable, even combed his hair. An owl hooted. The girl jumped.

'Cold?' he asked. She nodded. 'You'll be all right in a minute,' he said. 'Come here, I've got something for that.' She was standing at his side, leaning into him for warmth.

He slipped his hand into his breast pocket and her sudden cry was cut short as he plunged the knife high into her skin, gripping her shoulder as he did so. Then he threw her forwards, mindful of the spurting blood from her neck. She fell to her knees, her eyes big and questioning. Bending down he removed his knife, wiped it on the leaves and depressed the blade. He stood up and watched dispassionately as the blood flowed from her neck.

Now he was calm. And the demon was happy.

Before her body had stopped convulsing he was digging at the soft earth.

When he considered the shallow grave was of a sufficient depth he used his feet to move her into it and then he began covering her with the bloody leaves and peaty soil. A fall of rain was dripping through the branches as he worked. He was glad. It would wash away any traces of him, her blood, and his tyre tracks.

With twigs and branches snapping beneath his feet he walked back to the car. An animal shrieked. His steps faltered and he wondered if it was a rabbit being killed by a bigger animal. Survival of the fittest, that old power game again. First, his mother and the power she'd held over him as a child, and then the power he had over the young blonde prostitutes as he finally put them out of their misery, away from the sordid lives they led and the children they perhaps lied to, just as he'd been lied to. As the woods fell away to reveal the shape of his car in the layby, the rain was coming straight down fast and furious, drenching him and making his shoes slip on the soaking grass. He unlocked the car and climbed inside, frowning at the sight of the prostitute's handbag left on the seat. He started the ignition and switched on the lights and windscreen wipers. Within minutes he was on the outskirts of town. He pulled over near a closed fish and chip shop and got out of the car, throwing the handbag into the first of a row of three metal dustbins, having first used the car's chamois leather to dispel fingerprints. Then he got back in his car and replaced the chamois in the glove compartment along with his usual keepsake from the crime.

Before driving off he pulled the rear view mirror towards him so he could see himself. His hair was wet and he snaked a hand through it, tidying it. He looked at his hands; he would clean his fingernails when he reached home, remove the earth ingrained around his nails. He narrowed his eyes and smiled at himself before replacing the mirror. He thought about Daisy Lane. Now there was a prick teaser who deserved to be taught a lesson. But something different for her, he thought, after all she wasn't a prostitute. Then flicking the tiny leather boxing gloves to set them swinging, he drove home.

CHAPTER 27

Susie was in bed again. She spent a great deal of time asleep, which Daisy reckoned could only do her good – after all, cats slept most of the time and they never seemed unhappy. Susie was grieving in her own way. When she was awake her constant tears ate into Daisy's heart. But this morning they'd walked through the market together and Susie had stopped to admire some blooms on the flower stall, which showed Daisy she was now capable of letting something else into her mind.

Bri had been late in the shop. He'd sat down on the sofa for five minutes and fallen asleep. Daisy shook her head and started buttering crackers and slicing cheddar cheese. She was making an evening snack for the four of them. Nothing like a nice bit of strong cheddar, she thought, not being able to resist popping the broken bits of biscuits with slivers of cheese into her mouth. Why did crackers always break, she wondered? Don't even have to press hard with the knife and butter before they split.

She was expecting Vera to join them. Her friend was popping round to pick up her favourite black handbag, left under the counter at the shop.

Forty minutes later Daisy stared at the clock.

'Where is she? It don't take this long to walk from

her place?' Her voice echoed in the quiet of the flat. Bri's eyes opened and he stretched. His hair was all sticking up.

'Sorry, Dais,' he said.

'Don't worry about it. It's hard being on your feet all day, ain't it?' He nodded and got up. After a while the lavatory flushed and he came out. Daisy hoped he'd aimed straight.

'I'm off,' he said and grabbed his jacket.

'Vera ain't got here yet,' Daisy said.

'Phone 'er. Must be some delay.' She could see he was eager to get off to The Black Bear.

'It ain't like Vera to say she'll do something and then not do it.' Daisy suddenly felt scared. 'You go down an' phone 'er,' she said.

A frown crossed his face but he went, only to shout back a few moments later, 'She ain't answering.' When he came back he was more alert. 'Look, she's probably on her way round here. But if you're that worried, we'll go and meet her.'

'The Black Bear's on the way. I'll wake Suze up and make her come with us. She's been in bed nearly all day apart from her stroll this morning. A bit of fresh evening air will do her good.'

'She knows she's got to go back for the funeral?'

Daisy nodded. 'Me an' her have come to an understanding. She knows now that poor Si was no more to blame than she was herself for what happened. She wants to be with 'im again but she don't want to live away from Gosport no more. I told her if Si agrees they can live in my house in Western Way until they gets themselves sorted out.'

'Ain't she worried about Belle dying there?'

'Someone's died in almost every bleeding house at some time or other!'

'S'pose so.'

Daisy went into the spare room and sorted out Susie, who emerged ten minutes later bleary eyed, in jeans and a jumper.

Five minutes later they were opening the bookshop door and stepping into the blackness. It had just started raining.

'Someone's in a hurry,' said Daisy, as a running figure disappeared around the corner. The street door of the cafe slammed, the sound loud in the softly falling rain.

'One of Sammy's girls,' Daisy said.

'How do you know it was the caff?'

'Lived there long enough, Bri, didn't I? I know every bleeding sound that old place makes.'

It's all about chances, thought Sammy, you have to take one once in a while. No good thinking, I'll let it slip by, the chance doesn't present itself twice. He moved the torn net and rubbed at the dirty window so he could see more clearly.

That cunning cow Eve had shut up her row now. Choosy bitch said she'd only do telephone bookings. She wouldn't fuck out in the street, she said. Who the fuck did she think she was, dictating to him? Roy said she'd be an asset to the place when she found her feet and, for the moment, phone bookings were fine, they brought the money in, didn't they? Even Sammy had to admit she was a pretty girl. He laughed to himself. Well, she had been before tonight.

The lights across the water in Portsmouth were twinkling like stars. The sky was black as pitch.

Sammy knew it was going to rain soon. He'd felt it in the air as he'd walked back earlier today from the pontoon where he'd met a new client. Nice bloke who'd picked up Sammy's tart card from the toilets at the ferry, said he lived across the water in the old town near the Cathedral.

That nosy Eve was waiting outside his door when he got back with the bloke. She'd brought up the letters the postman had left. Not that Sammy ever worried about collecting letters. No one wrote to him, so why should he? Sometimes the post lay scattered in the hall for days, getting trodden on until someone picked it all up. One to Roy Kemp had been tampered with. That's another thing, Sammy thought, Roy was getting a lot of mail just lately. Much more than usual.

But that Eve? There was something sneaky about her and though he couldn't swear to it, he had the feeling she'd been in his room. Which meant she'd got hold of a key or had managed to pick the lock – not difficult with these big old keyholes.

He couldn't do much with the new bloke at his heels but he gave his room the quick once-over and had come to the conclusion stuff had been sifted through. His wardrobe door wasn't shut tightly. He always slammed it shut because the old walls in the cafe were uneven and furniture tended to tilt.

It wasn't the first time he'd wondered about the woman. She was lippy enough to ask him questions, which the other girls didn't dare. And once last week, when he'd been counting money, he swore there was someone breathing outside the room. He'd ignored it until he'd moved and his chair had scraped on the lino, when he'd heard soft scrabbling footsteps in the hall.

And now he'd been right, hadn't he? Nosy bitch.

The new client was a shy boy. They'd shaken hands very formally when they'd met at the ferry.

'Thought you'd be older,' Sammy said. He liked the look of him, tall, masculine, and obviously well set up. Sammy could tell that by his clothes. He was also very clean cut.

'Do I have to be older?'

'No, not at all.'

The man was hesitant. Walking back to the cafe they hardly spoke. Sammy, who had always preferred older men, suddenly found himself warming to the young bloke and his comfortable silence. Sammy wanted to please him. That in itself was unusual and quite a turn-on.

After Sammy had unlocked the street door of the cafe and pushed the man in the direction of the stairs, he was aware of his surroundings as though for the first time.

'Sorry about the state of the place but there's some real mucky women live here.' The man turned his head towards Sammy as he climbed the stairs and he could see the bloke was breathing shallowly. He didn't blame him. The place reeked.

Once Sammy was in his room, he felt ashamed of the state he'd let it get in.

'My cleaner only comes in once a year,' he joked. 'Take your coat off and sit down.'

Sammy wondered at his age. Around thirty or so, perhaps? Lovely hair, he had. He wanted to touch the dark curls to see if they were springy or soft. The man took off his long mac and went to put it on the chair, but it was piled high with dirty washing. Sammy sprang forward.

'Sorry about that.' He swept the stuff to the floor and kicked it under the chair.

'Look, perhaps another time.' The bloke seemed anxious.

'Your first time?' The man nodded then sat down. 'Can we chat a bit first? I don't mind paying extra,' he said.

''Course we can.' Maybe, Sammy thought, it was time he became the older man. A nice clean young fella like this could be an added bonus. Sammy smiled at him. 'What do you want to talk about?'

They'd chatted about all sorts. Mostly the young fella had asked him questions and Sammy had answered and tried to put him at his ease, but try as he might he couldn't get near him. Apart from learning of his interest in renovating British sports cars and liking to race them when he could afford to, he didn't give much away. He knew this bloke could possibly be something more than a casual fuck, and he liked the feeling that for once in his life he was being given the chance of something special happening.

If he was going to be the man's first proper fuck after his few childhood fumblings, he might possibly be the last. So he had to woo him. And why not? It wasn't as though Sammy couldn't afford it. He'd take it slow and easy. After all, the bloke had got in touch with him, so he was up for it, and he hadn't run away yet so it was obvious he liked Sammy. It was the shitty fucking surroundings that was putting him off.

'I don't know that I'm ready . . .'

'I'm not forcing you.' Sammy laughed. 'Tell you what, how do you fancy a meal in Southsea one night, a bottle of champers? Maybe a hotel?' The man looked suddenly happier.

'I'd like that,' he said. 'Can I phone you?' He got up and took his coat from the back of the chair and slipped it on.

'I don't even know your name,' said Sammy.

'Paul,' came the reply.

He wondered if Paul was manipulating him, had perhaps seen a chance to make himself some money? Sammy wished he hadn't made it so obvious he liked the bloke. Still, nothing ventured, nothing gained, and even if Paul was out to play with his feelings, he could take it. Somehow though he didn't think Paul was that kind of guy. No, more your straight man who wanted to try something different, something he'd been suppressing for a long time. Sammy would soon show Paul who the manipulator could be. And Paul would love it.

He opened the door and heard another door in the building slam shut. As he walked Paul down to the street door and opened it, Paul inched past him and Sammy breathed in his pine cologne.

'Bye then, Paul.' And Paul treated Sammy to a beguiling smile that was a real come-on.

Sammy took the stairs two at a time. What a knockout of a bloke, he thought. And those eyes. Odd brown and amber colours that only made him more of a stunner.

When he got back to his room, his first thought was to have a tidy-up. But why should he? He'd make sure Paul never came back again to this shithole. Maybe it was time to think of getting out of all this. Move into a place of his own, somewhere nice. Alverstoke? Nah. Roy wouldn't be best pleased with him when he scarpered, but he'd have to find him first. So perhaps some village further up the coast. Bosham? That was a pretty place. Brighton was even better. Yes, Brighton. He'd fit in there like a glove on a hand.

He picked up his comb and ran it through his hair. The steel comb with the long thin knife-like handle was excellent for his wiry hair. Them bloody plastic things was rubbish, always breaking. He left the tail comb on the chest of drawers, pulled up a chair and opened the table's drawer. He took out the red-covered book he kept for the whores' accounts and then pulled out the notes and coins that were in a blue bank bag. Might as well get this lot sorted now while he was in a good mood as it was one of the jobs he hated. Roy was very particular about his money and the accounts. More so since that toe-rag Eddie Lane had messed him about.

Five minutes into sorting out the notes and Sammy thought he heard someone outside. He went on counting, then he put the money down and opened the drawer, making a show of looking for something. He closed the drawer and rose from the chair. He went over to the chest of drawers which he knew was out of sight of the keyhole and picked up his steel comb. Then he crept around, still out of sight from the door, and bent down. He was as silent as he could be as he positioned the implement over the keyhole.

Then he slipped the end into the large opening and rammed it as hard as he could. A great scream came from the other side of the door, followed by the sound of running feet and doors opening, and all the while the screaming continued.

Sammy withdrew the pointed metal handle of his comb and wiped it on the arm of the chair, where it left a slimy trail of blood. He didn't bother to open the door. Instead he shouted, 'The next cunt to spy on me gets both eyes done. No fuckin' hospital this time, Rosa. Sort the bitch out, and be fuckin' quick about it. The rest of you cunts get back to work.' Rosa would look after her.

And then he went back to his bookkeeping.

But he couldn't concentrate. The anger was growing inside him about that cunt, Eve. What the fuck was she up to and why had she been keeping an eye on him? He laughed. 'Keeping an eye on me. Well, she's got one less to do it with now!'

Was he going soft or something? Everyone trying to take advantage of him? Even that bitch, Vera, flinging that money at him and giving him orders.

Through the window he stared at the lights of Portsmouth. Their brightness seemed to fuse into one large orange glow in the sky. And then he saw her, Vera, trotting down from the corner. He turned away from the window and took a small, weighty object out of the drawer. He opened the door and began running down the now deserted stairs.

He didn't even bother to think twice about it.

Vera was annoyed with herself. If there was one thing she hated it was having to rush. Her high heels clattered on the pavement. God knows what time it was now and she still had to have a bath and sort her nails out for tomorrow. A nice deep blood red would go well with her black suit, black shoes and bag. She'd still be able to wear her favourite red hat then, the one she had on now.

Fancy her mate Ellie having a heart attack. Mind you, she liked her food, had got very large over the years. Them doctors did say getting fat was bad for you. Ellie had it rough when she was a young slip of a thing. Skinny she was then. There wasn't the food about and Ellie had younger brothers and sisters to feed since her mum and dad got caught in the bad bombing of Portsmouth. It was after that Ellie started on the game. The Americans was over here then. Those was the days, thought Vera. Her and Ellie and all them Yanks! What a fuckin' laugh. That's when Ellie started eating proper again. The money made such a difference. Ellie never cared about jewellery or clothes. But she fed them kids and stuffed herself silly saying she wasn't going to go hungry again. Trouble was she never stopped eatin'. An' now she was dead.

Ellie was popular so there'd be a good turn-out, plenty of old mates to chat to. Vera started humming 'Wheel of Fortune' then realised she'd better not keep that up. It had been Eddie's favourite song and Daisy still got upset when she heard it.

And now it had started to rain, poxy weather, didn't it bleedin' know it was supposed to be summer coming?

Vera thought she heard footsteps behind her. She turned but saw no one, must have imagined it. Up ahead she could see the lights from the flat above the shop shining down into the street. I could do with a cuppa, she thought, Daisy'll have put the kettle on by now. The hairs on the back of her neck stood to attention. Vera stopped and looked about her.

'No one there, you daft ol' bat,' she said aloud, more to bolster her confidence than because she really believed it. But however hard she peered into the gathering darkness she couldn't see anyone. She continued walking.

The man chucked himself at her, holding the side of her head and scraping something sharp down her skin.

Vera didn't have time to scream before he threw her down. She saw the Stanley knife slide across the pavement. Then she was face up, he was astride her and the punch hit her cheekbone and a second punch slammed into her nose. She heard it crack before the pain hit her. Now he had his hands about her throat and somehow her clothes had ridden up and everything was so tight round her neck, so tight, she could barely breathe.

'Cunt, you don't get one over on me!'

'Sammy,' she could hardly get the words out, 'please . . .'

'Please, is it? Wasn't no please when you made me sign off Jacky, was it?' Then he lifted her by the bunched up clothing at her neck and thumped her on the pavement. The pain shot through her skull to collide with the stinging, searing heat from her face. Vera heard a second crack and felt the hard rain on her face before her limbs and brain went to jelly and blackness swamped her.

Daisy saw the shape on the pavement and nudged Bri. 'A drunk?'

As they drew nearer Susie let out a scream. 'It's Vera.'

Daisy ran the last few steps, throwing herself down across the still body. 'She's been cut, Bri!'

In the light from the street lamp Daisy could see there was blood in Vera's hair and down her clothes. But it was her face, her poor face and nose that seemed to Daisy to have taken the brunt of the beating.

'Vera, what they done to you? Oh, my darling Vera. Whoever done this?'

'Don't touch her. Get out of the way, Daisy, let me

look,' Bri commanded. Daisy reluctantly moved, allowing him access. Suze was crying. Blood had run down Vera's neck on to her new green silk blouse. All Daisy could think was how cross Vera would be when she realised her blouse was ruined.

From the corner of Vera's left eye, past her ear to her neck, a long gash oozed blood.

'She's not dead, there's a pulse, but it looks like she's taken a hell of a bashing. I'll get an ambulance.' Bri rose and began running back towards the shop and the telephone.

For the first time in her life Daisy didn't know what to do. She wept. Vera was so still. Her Vera. Daisy wanted to change places with her, take her pain away. She felt for Vera's hand, found it and held it, hoping her warmth would help her. Vera might die! No! Please God, no. How could she ever live without her lovely friend? She looked at Susie.

'Don't let her fuckin' die. Whatever will I do if she dies? Vera, you can't leave me, Vera . . .' Vera's eyes fluttered. Daisy could see her trying to focus. When it came her voice was a hoarse, nasal whisper.

'I ain't fuckin' dead yet. You keep on blubbin' an' I'll do it to spite you. Get a fuckin' grip, girl!' Then her head fell sideways and she was out of it again.

'Oh, Vera,' Daisy said, and a momentary flash of joy overtook her: Vera would be all right if only she could be got to the hospital soon. 'No!' she shouted down the street to Bri. 'Get the fucking van. Make him get the van, Suze.'

Suze left her and started running down North Street. Bri stopped, turned and waved to show he understood, then carried on running.

Daisy looked down at Vera, whose eyes had opened again.

'Daisy?' A tear had escaped from one of Vera's eyes and mingled with the blood. Her grip tightened on Daisy's fingers. The long wound was still oozing.

'I'm here. I'll always be 'ere.' There was dried blood around Vera's mouth and her lips were cracked. The rain was belting down now and Daisy bent over Vera to shelter her as best she could. She heard her say in a tiny voice, 'Kibbles . . .'

'You silly tart! Don't you worry. He'll be all right with me, love.' Vera and that bloody cat, she thought. But she knew Vera would have given anything just to run her fingers through his fur at that moment. Daisy felt the tears rise again. But Vera had told her to get a grip, hadn't she?

'Who did this?'

Vera disconnected her hand from Daisy's and tried to raise it to her face. Daisy blocked it. 'Don't touch nothin'. That's you all over, got to bloody touch.'

'Will I die?'

'No. But I might kill you if you don't tell me who did this?'

Daisy was telling herself, I mustn't cry, I mustn't cry, I must try to be strong for her sake.

'Sammy,' Vera whispered. 'The bastard 'ad a Stanley knife.'

'Hush now. Don't talk any more.' She thanked God when she saw the familiar Thames van trundling down the street.

'How we gonna get her in?' Daisy asked, as Bri jumped down. 'She can't even stand up.'

'You get in, I'll lift her in to you,' said Suze. 'We should call and wait for the ambulance.'

Daisy glared at her. 'I ain't leaving 'er in this fucking rain. You be careful with 'er.' She climbed in the van and slid along the bench seat, waiting. Bri and Suze lifted Vera and gently passed the small woman along the seat to Daisy.

Then Suze got in and Bri closed the door and started for the driver's side. Vera was trying to say something. Daisy bent in close to listen.

'What is it, love? What you tryin' to say?' Then, 'For fuck's sake!'

Bri was climbing in the driver's door.

'She wants 'er hat. Go and pick up her fucking hat with the feather in it. It's on the pavement.'

At Haslar Hospital Bri carried Vera into Casualty where she was whisked away on a trolley. Daisy answered questions as best she could about the attack and when she and Susie were sitting down, waiting, she realised she couldn't even remember what she'd been asked.

'We could be here a long time, Dais,' Bri said.

'I'm sitting in exactly the same place in this waiting room as I was when we was here with Belle. I didn't leave then, an' I ain't leaving now until I know she's going to get better.' Bri and Suze exchanged looks.

Suze put her arm around her shoulder. Daisy saw her pyjama collar poking up from the neck of her jumper. She bent down and lifted the leg of her jeans to reveal her pyjama bottoms.

'I got dressed in a hurry, didn't I, when I thought you was goin' to traipse round the streets on yer own?' Daisy smiled weakly at her.

'You're a lazy cow,' she said and leaned her head against Susie's shoulder and closed her eyes.

'You can see her now,' said a nurse. Daisy opened

her eyes. How on earth could she have dozed off at a time like this? 'She's asking for her daughters.'

Daisy got up and looked at Bri, daring him to say a word. Susie followed.

'Is she going to be all right?' Bri asked.

'As well as can be expected,' came the kindly reply. 'Come this way.'

'Won't be long,' mouthed Daisy, knowing they wouldn't let Vera see anyone for long, not even her daughters! She practically had to run to keep up with the small dark nurse whose shoes squeaked on the polished floor. She knew Vera had said she was their mother in case they would only let relatives in to visit.

After what seemed miles and miles of corridors and stairs Daisy and Susie were led into a long ward where the light was very dim. Most patients were asleep and only snoring noises and whimpers broke the silence. The nurse removed part of a screen to a corner unit so they could go in and sit down by Vera's bed.

'Please be as quiet as possible for the other patients' sake,' whispered the nurse. 'Five minutes only,' she warned.

Vera's face and head was swathed in bandages; even her nose was covered up. She had on an unbecoming hospital gown. How she'd hate that, thought Daisy. She was propped up. Her eyes were very bright.

Daisy sat down and picked up one of Vera's hands, trying very hard not to let her fear for her friend show. Two of Vera's long fingernails had been broken straight across, and Daisy laid that hand against her own cheek. Vera tried to speak but the sounds were fuzzy, like she was speaking underwater. Daisy guessed they'd given her something for the pain and it was making her brain woozy.

'You look like the fucking invisible man, with all them bandages. Try not to talk.'

Vera was very small beneath the white bedspread. 'Thank you,' she whispered.

'I told you not to bloody talk!'

A tear escaped and rolled from one eye and made a channel down part of Vera's face until it was soaked up by a bandage.

'I 'urt, Dais.'

'I know you do,' was all Daisy could say. Vera closed her eyes and Daisy, after a few minutes, released her hand. Vera was asleep.

Daisy held herself together until she was out of the ward. Then she turned to Susie and the both of them wept together.

'When's it all gonna end?' asked Susie. And Daisy realised this must have brought Meggie's death back sharply in focus for Susie, just when the girl was doing so well. 'Dais, stop a moment,' she said.

Daisy turned and looked at her.

'I'm sorry for everything I've put you through. I think I'm all right now, well sort of. An' seeing Vera lying there but knowing she'll still be with us 'as made me realise how precious life is. And 'ow we mustn't waste a minute of it blaming people for things they got no control over.' Daisy looked into her face, at her eyes brimming with tears. She rubbed her hand across her own nose and eyes to ward off the fresh tears that had suddenly welled up. Then she pulled Susie close, feeling her curls across her cheek, the warm smell of her, mingled with the 4711 cologne she liked so much.

'We'll always have each other. Been through too much together, we have.' She coughed as though embarrassed and glared at Susie. 'Silly cow,' she said.

When they reached the reception area Daisy asked to see the duty doctor.

He was young and kind and looked tired. 'Obviously we're keeping her in. She was lucky not to have suffered more damage being brought in the way she was. That's what ambulances are for.' Daisy knew she was being ticked off and had to take it. 'She's had many facial stitches as well as stitches to the back of her head. We've had to set her nose. I'm sure you're aware this was a violent assault so . . .' Daisy listened as he told her the medical terms for the injured parts of Vera's body, which seemed so many that she lost count, but he finally ended with, 'But your mother's a gutsy lady, so try not to worry. She was delirious for a while, calling for you and someone called Kibbles? Is that the gentleman waiting outside with your sister?' Daisy looked into his weary face and a smile began at the corner of her mouth.

'No,' she said. 'But I've told her not to worry about him. Thank you ever so much.'

Bri helped her into the van and as soon as he got in he put his arms around her.

'Mr Kibbles,' she said, looking at him. A frown creased his forehead.

'What you on about? Is she really going to be all right?' asked Bri.

Daisy let out a huge sigh that seemed to fill the van. 'I bloody hope so. Let's go home, Mr Kibbles,' she said.

As they drove round by the cafe Daisy could see the lights on in the top room that used to be hers. It was nearly two in the morning and the rain had stopped. The street lamps shone their feeble light barely illuminating the blackness. She wondered if Sammy was in that room.

'Bastard, bastard.' Daisy had nothing to lose now. Anger, hatred – feelings she thought she had mastered – rose to the surface once more. Lovingly she fingered Vera's red felt hat with the tall feather. 'Bastard, bastard,' she mouthed at the cafe.

Bri drove round to the yard with Susie. Daisy carried the hat into the shop and laid it carefully on the counter. It would take Bri only a short while to sort out the van, the gates and the back door, and lock up. She had to move fast. She didn't want him or Susie stopping her.

She dialled Roy's number.

Violet answered the phone, and so quickly that Daisy guessed they had been out to a show or a club.

'Can I speak to Roy?'

''Course, dear, how lovely to hear from you. I'll just get him. He's having a wee brandy to round off the evening.' She liked to have her finger on the button, did Violet. She dotes on that man, thought Daisy. Almost instantly Roy picked up the receiver.

'What can I do for you, Daisy? Not a social call at this time of the morning, surely. How's Suze?'

'She's fine and I wouldn't phone if I didn't need to,' she said.

'Can this wait until tomorrow, I'm a bit tired?'

'No, it bloody can't, and may I remind you you was quick enough to get down here when you sorted out my Eddie.' She heard him draw breath. Heard a clicking sound. Realised he probably had a pen in his hand and was tapping the brandy glass with it. She'd seen him do this before.

'You mean you want me there now?'

'There's a possibility he'll fucking go if you leave it any longer.'

'Give me a break, Daisy.'

'You asked me to keep an eye on things. Either you sort it, or I go to Vinnie Endersby. I'm pretty sure it ain't him on your fuckin' payroll over in the nick.'

'Sammy?'

Did Roy know something? 'Women and a kid. He's been messin' about with a kid and he's dead. A woman as well.'

'You *have* been looking after my interests, but how do you know it's Sammy?'

'I followed him.'

She knew he would believe her. He trusted her, didn't he?

'An hour and a half?'

'Not my place, nor the caff. I'll be waiting by St George's Barracks.' Daisy put the phone down.

The lights in the top room above the caff had been switched off. If Sammy had gone, so be it. He wouldn't get far. Roy Kemp would see to that. And if Sammy was watching the bookshop from behind those dirty net curtains, well that was all right, too, thought Daisy.

By the time Bri and Susie came upstairs, the kettle was on the boil. They didn't talk about what had happened to Vera and Daisy was glad. Bri said he was going home to The Black Bear. He stood before her, held her chin in his hand and whispered, 'She'll be all right, you know.' Daisy looked up into his eyes.

'Do you honestly think so?'

'Yes.'

Daisy stood on tiptoe and kissed his cheek.

He stared at her. 'The next man you love will be a

very lucky bloke if you love him as much as you care about Vera.'

'No,' Daisy said. 'I'll never care about anyone like that. There's always different men, but there's only one Vera.' Then she looked across as Susie draped herself along the sofa. 'And only one Suze.'

Later, after Daisy and Susie had drunk numerous cups of strong tea, she said, 'You know I ain't coming to Devon with you for Meggie's funeral, don't you?' She saw the sudden panic in Susie's eyes. Then, just as it had appeared, it left.

Susie nodded. 'You got to sort out Vera and I got to learn to stand on me own two feet. Don't mean you won't be there with me in your thoughts, does it?'

Daisy shook her head. 'Si's goin' to look after you. But I reckon after tonight, you're the strong one and Si might need to rely on you.' Daisy knew it was time to slip into her coat and leave the flat. 'Go to bed, Suze. I got a bit of business to attend to. You needn't ask if I know what I'm doing. I do and nothin's going to happen to me, so you can sleep easy.' She went over and kissed Susie on the cheek. 'Anyway, you're already dressed for bed, ain't you?' She gave a tug on Susie's pyjama sleeve poking from her jumper.

It smelled fresh in the street after the rain. The tide was out and Daisy could almost taste the silt from the creek. The cobbles were shiny and hard to walk on in her high heels. There was an old pram sticking up out of the mud, she could see its outline in the lamplight. She wondered about the kiddie or kiddies who'd been ferried around in it before it became surplus to requirements, and thought of little Eddie. She would phone Maria tomorrow. Ahead was St George's

Barracks. She wondered why the locals called the soldiers there Pongos? She eyed the clock on the tall white gate tower. Not much longer to wait now, she thought.

Daisy heard the purring of the big motor seconds before it came into view. As she stepped out of the dark arch of the barracks and into the light, the car pulled up. As usual, Charles the chauffeur was driving.

A rear door opened.

'Get in,' said Roy. Daisy's heart was jumping wildly as she slid inside the car to the warmth and the remembered smell of the leather. She could also smell Roy's tangy cologne and peppermint mixed with cigarettes. Oddly the scents made her feel stronger.

There was another man sitting in the front seat next to Charles.

'Don't mind Mick,' Roy said. 'He's a big help at times like this.'

'Need a minder, do you?' Daisy managed a smile.

'Not me, someone else might need to mind him. Want a brandy?' Daisy nodded. They always seemed to have a brandy together in the back of his car when they had their little chats. It was a comforting ritual. 'You like a drop of lime with yours, don't you, Daisy?' He produced the drinks from the built-in cocktail cabinet. Drinks for only him and her, she noted. And that's the way it always was. She downed hers in one go, hoping the heat from the spirit would give her the courage to say what needed to be said. He anticipated this.

'Tell me, Daisy.'

'You told me to keep an eye on things . . .'

'Requested, Daisy. Requested you keep an eye on my property.'

'You got a big problem with Sammy.'

'Do you think I don't know this? He's been fucking me over.'

'You ain't the only one he's been fucking with.'

The car was parked off the road, on a piece of waste ground. A place where at weekends lorries parked up. Daisy could see Roy was agitated.

'Don't piss me about. What's he been up to?' He took her glass and refilled it.

'You draw the line at mutilating women and sodomy with kids. Violet would have a fit if . . .'

'Leave Mum out of this.'

'He slashed my friend, Vera, with a Stanley knife. She's in Haslar Hospital now. He beat 'er up so bad I thought she was goin' to die.'

'Not that old tart?' He passed the glass back to Daisy. Daisy wasn't angry that he called Vera a tart. Hadn't she witnessed his kindness to her, Si and herself at Heavenly Bodies a short while ago?

'Yes, that old tart.'

'What made Sammy do that?'

'Because she had the guts to stand up to him for something you should have seen coming. He drugged one of your casual girls, let some blokes loose on 'er. All 'cause the casual owed 'im money.' He frowned. Daisy downed her drink. 'Vera paid the girl's debt. Spoilt his fun. So he slashed 'er.' She handed him back the glass and shook her head as he raised his eyebrows asking if she wanted another refill. He held his own glass to his lips, swallowing before he spoke.

Daisy knew Roy well enough to know that he hated anyone having one over on him. In his empire his employees did what he said. Sammy had stepped out of line.

371

'This is the first I've heard I have casual girls. I've got a girl, Eve, who's taking her time but she ain't a casual. You taking over where Eddie left off, Daisy? Getting all protective of your loved ones?'

Daisy ignored his sarcasm. 'What if it had happened to Violet?'

'I'd fucking kill him and string him up by his balls.'

Daisy shrugged. 'Get out the car.'

'Now?' His grey eyes crinkled at the corners, but he replaced his glass in the cabinet and made to move.

'I want to show you something.'

Charles let her out. Mick also left the car. He was huge. About seven foot tall and bald as a billiard ball. For a moment Daisy was terrified. What if Roy'd brought him along to get rid of her? What if Roy suspected about the long firms? Impossible, Daisy thought. It was too soon for any of that to become common knowledge. Daisy told herself to keep calm. Then another thought struck her.

She was here in the early hours of the morning, grassing on one of Roy's men because her friend had been cut. And she expected Roy to sort the bloke out, and without a doubt, he'd do it.

For her.

She remembered Reg Kray's wedding and the way Roy had taken care of her, worried about her when she'd slipped out of the hotel. How he'd taken off his coat and wrapped it around her. How he'd willingly driven her home to Gosport when Vera had phoned with the sad news of Meggie's death and Susie's grief. She looked into his dark features, and realised this man would do almost anything for her.

And what had she done in return? Kicked him in the bollocks with the long-firming.

Did he really deserve that?

Did he? Doubts began to crowd themselves in her mind. All this time she was thinking she was paying him back for Eddie's death. But Eddie had been wrong in screwing Roy Kemp. There, she'd dared to think the truth at last.

Eddie had been *WRONG* to muscle in on Roy's territory! She'd loved Eddie with all her heart but he was every bit as bad as Roy.

So Roy Kemp had paid him back. The gangland way. The underworld's accepted way. The very same way she was expecting Roy Kemp to pay back Sammy for what he'd done to the kiddie she'd seen him take from the caff. And the other kiddie found in the mud and the women, including Jacky, he'd mutilated and possibly killed. But most of all she expected Roy to pay back Sammy for putting Vera in hospital.

Daisy, she wondered, what kind of a woman are you?

Had she really brought herself down to gangster level? Fucking hell, she thought. It was like someone had suddenly switched the light on in her head!

The trio walked to where the woodland started. She showed Roy the scene of crime tape. Or what was left of it now the local kids had finished messing about there.

'This is where your fucking Sammy dumped a nude, dead kiddie.'

He was quiet as he looked about. Daisy saw him narrow his eyes. His features were hard and practically set in stone.

'Sure it was him?'

'I followed him, didn't I? The kiddie was wrapped in an old rug. Vera and me spent a long time sorting out that young woman, Sammy's part-timer, who he drugged and had gang-fucked. She ain't got over it yet, nor never might. Gosport's got another similar unsolved murder and a prostitute . . .'

'All right.'

Daisy ignored him.

'The other kid was found in the creek. The prostitute was dumped near the boatyard. She had holes in 'er body like she'd been tortured. Like my mate had been hurt. You ain't half gonna lose your street cred with a paedophile running your business, not to mention find it difficult to explain you knew nothing about any of this. After all, you own the bleeding caff.'

It had started to rain again. 'No need for you to get wet, Daisy. I don't want you catching a chill. Go back and sit in the car with Charles.'

Daisy knew he wanted to think about what she'd told him, so she left the two men and walked back to his new silver Humber.

When Roy returned to the car, he said, 'You've done good in coming to me.' Then he gave her a funny little grin. 'By the way, how's your empire going? Read any good books lately?' Daisy thought if anyone else but Roy Kemp had said that to her she'd have told them to take a flying fuck.

'Only crime novels,' she answered. He laughed again, showing his remarkably white teeth. Good-looking bastard.

Roy told Charles to drive into town.

'Ever wondered why I never put a lick of paint on the caff, Daisy?' He didn't wait for her to answer but put his hand on her knee like it was the most natural thing in the world to do and carried on speaking. 'To tell you the truth I always felt a bit guilty about buying it off you.'

Daisy turned on the seat and stared at him. She didn't remove his hand, in fact she felt safer with it there.

'Oh, I gave you more than a fair price for it. And quick like you wanted.' Daisy wondered what he was going to come out with. 'But if only you'd screwed your loaf you could have looked at Gosport Council's plans for that corner of town and found they wanted to pull it down.'

Daisy thought about it. 'So?'

'You never saw that one coming, did you, Dais? The council's being screwed by me. They want to clear the town and rebuild. Get rid of eyesores and bomb sites left from the war. The caff's coming down to make way for a car park. That whole area around it will be developed, flats mostly. Only the pub, The Fox, will be left standing. Not on your side of the street, Dais. That's to be left as it is.'

He squeezed her knee and she felt the heat of his hand through her jeans. She let his words sink in. Regeneration after the war. It had to start sometime.

'That don't matter to me, Roy. You came through with the money when I asked.'

'Glad you see it like that.'

And the funny thing was, she did. 'That place never mattered to me after the Lane boys was gone.'

'Think of the money you could have made though? Just when you needed it most, selling books for coppers and silver.'

'So, you made a good business deal, Roy. You'd have really disappointed me if you didn't always keep an ace up your sleeve.' Now why did she feel guilty about the vast amount of money she'd made at his expense that was locked in her wardrobe?

The car had halted outside The Seahorse pub where it couldn't be seen by anyone in the cafe or the flat above the bookshop. Roy was going in to sort out Sammy.

'In your own funny way, you're quite a moral man, ain't you?' She put her hand over his and squeezed it. Then she bent towards him and kissed him lightly on the lips. His dark grey eyes held hers and she felt him holding himself back.

'Thank you,' she said.

She knew then she couldn't leave things as they were between them. Time and circumstances had changed her.

CHAPTER 28

'I got the money from the girls right here.' Sammy handed Roy a large brown envelope and gave him a big grin.

'Don't you ever clean this place?' Roy rubbed his hands along the top of the chest of drawers and grimaced at the muck on his fingers. He wrinkled his nose. 'And it stinks in here. You got something to tell me?'

Mick was searching in the wardrobe. Sammy watched warily.

'Here you are, boss.' Mick produced the Stanley knife and handed it to Roy, who stared at it for a second then slipped it in his pocket.

'Go in for much lino or carpet laying, do you, Sammy?'

Charles was searching down the backs of furniture now. Then he turned over the mattress and ripped at its interior. A brown paper package fell on to the floor. Mick picked it up and gave that to Roy who opened the package then whistled.

'Must be moonlighting, Sammy. I never paid you all that.' He flicked through the notes and glanced at Mick, who grinned at him before feeling behind the filthy sink and the curtain covering the space beneath it.

'Look what I found.'

Into view came a small pair of grubby jeans. Two tee shirts. A pair of sandals and a pair of black wellington boots.

'Two different sizes, two boys?' said Mick, looking at the difference in the footwear's sizes.

'Bingo,' said Roy Kemp. 'Where are the owners of these pathetic belongings?'

'Some kids left 'em behind.' Sammy was sitting on the bed. His face was chalk white.

'And they both went home to their mothers without their clothes? C'mon, Sammy, you can do better than that. Know anything about a little spot in Weevil Lane?' Sammy looked scared. Sweat had appeared on his forehead and chin and his body started to shake.

'No.'

'I think you're telling me porkies. And if there's one thing I can't stand it's liars. My old mum says, "You can believe a thief but you can't believe a liar." But worse than liars I hate blokes what mess with kids. And you know this, don't you, Sammy? I always feel I have to teach a nonce a lesson.'

Sammy's face was beaded with sweat now.

'No, no, Mr Kemp. I didn't do nothing to them kids. I never touched 'em. I only found 'em for clients.'

'Well that's all right then, ain't it, boys?' He looked at Charles and Mick who nodded back at him. 'Or it would be, except the only procuring I expected you to do was girls for clients. Not little kids. Not what I was paying you for, is it, Sammy? You been doing little jobs for yourself.'

Sammy didn't speak. When he did his words tumbled over themselves.

'You knows you can trust me to keep the toms in line ... Ain't I always ...

'Got in a few part-timers? Done a bit of cutting? Damaged my goods? I don't remember that being in my job description, Sammy.'

'We can work this out, Mr Kemp, we ...'

'Sure we can, Sammy. Mick, go down to the yard below and see what you can find.' Mick smiled at Sammy, opened the door and stepped out.

'Boss,' he said, 'there's some dried blood on the floor here.' The bare boards of the stairs creaked as he descended.

'What's that about?' Roy went over and peered at the blood. 'Place is so dark and filthy I never noticed that on the way into this glorious bedroom. Another little accident happen to one of my girls? Find Rosa, Charles, she'll fill me in.' Charles left the room and began knocking on the doors waking the girls. Roy heard him talking in muffled tones and raised his eyebrows at Sammy.

'What?' Sammy asked.

'Then there's a little matter of you forging my signature.'

Sammy looked confused.

'I never ...'

'You been getting me into trouble at the bank.'

'I don't know what you're talking about, Mr Kemp.' Roy produced a letter from an envelope. 'I got hold of this on my last visit. Then lo and behold when I open it, I find I got a bank account with a shitload of money in it and I been doing business down south. Strange really, because I know fuck all about it.'

379

'I don't know what you're talking about.'

'Didn't think you would, Sammy. Didn't think you would at all.' Sammy tried to rise from the bed but Roy pinned him down again. Charles, now he was back in the room, came and stood over Sammy, daring him to move. 'You stay there, 'til we need to move you,' said Roy, biting back the stink coming from Sammy now his fear had released fresh perspiration on top of stale sweat.

Sammy let his bladder go.

'Is that what you are, Sammy? Piss scared?' The strong stench added to the stink of the room.

'Need to 'ave a few words, boss.' Charles took Roy to the doorway and spoke softly to him. Roy narrowed his eyes and set his mouth into a thin line.

'Don't worry, Sammy,' he said. 'Everything gets sorted out in the end. Charles is going to stay with you while I pay a little visit to my shy Evie. The one I had high hopes of making a good profit from but who now appears to have a sight problem. Mutilated by you, apparently. I'd better make sure she gets some medical attention, something you omitted to let her have. Or did you figure Rosa was a bleeding eye doctor, now?' He stared at Sammy then sighed. 'Oh, yes, the money in the bank? Seems there was a nice sum there for me. Of course it ain't there now. The manager said all funds had been withdrawn and he'd be very pleased if I could see my way to clearing a fucking massive overdraft that again I know nothing about. I think you've shafted me.' He pointed to the wad of notes. 'This some of mine, eh, Sammy?'

Sammy shook his head. 'No! I don't know nothin' about the bank. But I can tell you about the boys. And why I did it.'

'Go on then. Tell me your hard luck life story.'

Amidst snot and tears Sammy's words fell from his mouth.

'I was in a home and abused when I was a kid. I told the matron but she was getting a payback so she didn't care. She just laughed at me. There were other boys as well. I ran away as soon as I could. Met a man who said it would be all right if I went to stay with him. By this time I'd been living rough and I was cold and hungry, but when he took me back to his place he locked me in a room. But I wasn't allowed out of that room and there were men, a steady stream of 'em, who fucked me and fucked me.'

'I'm not enjoying your pathetic little tale,' Roy interrupted. He winked at Charles and left the room. When he returned, his face was grey and his eyes hard.

'You've done a good job on Evie, now tell me about the kiddies.' Roy stared at Sammy.

'I got 'em for clients, same as I was got. Been luring 'em with blow and stuff . . .'

'But they're dead.'

'Wasn't my fault. One of the blokes was real big. I didn't know he was going to do damage, did I? I can hardly say, "show me your cock before I'll let you get your jollies", can I? The kid stopped breathing.'

'So it was the bloke's fault, and not yours, eh, Sammy?'

'That's right, Mr Kemp. All I did was put a pillow to the kid's face so his screams wouldn't carry out to the road. They always scream at first, anyway. But that's how he died. The younger one was beaten to death by a client . . .'

'You know,' said Roy, 'I believe every word you've told me.'

Sammy wiped his face and looked relieved. Mick entered the room. He was carrying a heavy, rusty, wooden-handled sledge hammer and a couple of bricks.

'Good boy,' said Roy. 'Well, as our Sammy likes his bed so much I think we'll let him stay there. Mind you, Sammy, you don't have to worry. We won't leave you in bed. Got a nice little spot reserved down Weevil Lane for you. Should be familiar. It's where you dumped one of the boys. Go for it, Mick,' he said. 'And get it over quick, I got to get some help for Evie.'

Sammy watched horrified as Mick placed a brick beneath one of his ankles. He tried to squirm away but Roy said, 'Naughty, naughty. Lay back and let it happen.' Then Charles held his leg at the knee in a vice-like grip and Mick swung the hammer.

The sound of cracking bones must have hit Sammy first, then the metallic smell of fresh blood. The pain was obviously the last to register as Sammy stared mesmerised at his smashed ankle with the splintered bone showing through before his screams filled the room.

'No. Please . . .' Sammy's face was a grotesque mask as his second ankle dissolved into fragments of blood and bone, staining the filthy sheet crimson.

'Now you can't run anywhere, Sammy. But I need to make sure you'll never touch another kiddie again. Try not to get blood on my new coat. Real wool, this is, cost a bomb.' Roy pulled his collar up.

Charles held Sammy's arm across the second brick and the hammer came down. This time his hand was almost severed with one blow. The sharp crack not only split the bones but mingled with Sammy's screams. Sammy's index finger flew into the air to land on the chest of drawers. He vomited.

'Nearly over,' said Roy. And motioned for Charles to place the other hand on the brick.

'Do it now before the bastard passes out,' Mick growled. The glint of the Stanley knife flashed.

The sharp blade approached his genitals.

Sammy passed out.

CHAPTER 29

Daisy woke late. She should be down in the shop. The door opened and Bri came in with a fragrant cup of tea which he put on the dressing table by the side of the bed.

'I've opened up. Stay here and relax.' When he'd gone Daisy marvelled again at his kindness.

She gulped down her tea and headed towards the bathroom. She'd promised to go down to Heavenly Bodies. The girls needed to be told Vera was in hospital before any rumours got started in the town.

'Daisy, phone.' She hastily threw back on her old white dressing gown and went downstairs.

'You don't want to know what happened,' Roy told her. 'But Sammy's already been found where he dumped the kiddie, down that lane. Some of the kids' clothes was still in his room, so we left them underneath his body. I think the woodentops'll get the message. You were right Daisy, that dirty little kiddie fiddler was into anything as long as he could skim off my profits. Can't be having that, can I?'

'The coppers'll be everywhere today.'

'What'll you tell them, Daisy?'

'What do I know, Roy? I know nothing.'

'Good girl. How's Vera?' Daisy was astounded at the man's coolness.

'I'll see her later after I've put Suze on the train.' She took a deep breath. 'Can I come and see you soon?'

'Any time, Daisy. Want me to come down there? I can always find an excuse to see you . . .'

'No! Your house will be fine. Say hello to Violet for me.'

'Will do,' he said, and hung up.

So, thought Daisy, Gosport is free of Sammy and good riddance. She didn't want to think about how it had come about, only that it had.

Within half an hour Daisy was pushing open the brass-handled glass door of Heavenly Bodies.

'Thank God you're here.' Jacky looked haggard with worry. 'I've been banging on Vera's door an' she ain't answering. An' I can 'ear Kibbles . . .'

'That's 'cause she ain't there.' Daisy made all the girls, Madam ZaZa and Robin gather round, then she told them Vera had had an accident and had been taken to Haslar. They all started chattering like a flock of sparrows until Daisy said, 'I'm taking it upon myself to put Jacky in charge an' that means all of you will go on as usual.' She told them the ward number. 'Write a note or send 'er a cheery card, but don't try to visit as she's really not up to seein' anyone at present.' Then to put their minds at ease she told them how Vera had insisted she and Suze were her daughters so they could go up to the ward. It relieved the tension. Daisy knew how much they all cared about Vera. But she also knew Vera needed time to get used to the way her face had been rearranged.

'Jacky, will you come upstairs to the flat?'

Daisy used her spare key to get in and went in search of Kibbles' wicker cat basket. Kibbles watched her every move from his vantage point on the sink top and as soon as he saw the basket, jumped down and slunk out of the room.

'Put the kettle on, Jacky. He's a bugger, ain't he? He knows he's going in that bleeding basket. I'm taking him home with me. You know how Vera worries about the bleeder.' She went over to the fridge and took out a dish which held a salmon steak. 'That cat eats better than I do. I'll cook that for him when I get him home to my place.'

Jacky set the teapot on the table then went back for cups and saucers. She took the salmon with her and slipped it in a plastic bag then put it next to the cat basket so Daisy wouldn't forget it.

'Sammy's dead,' said Daisy, when they were sat at the table together drinking tea. 'And what I'm telling you don't go any further.' She told Jacky about the cutting and the beating of Vera. Jacky's face was like chalk and her eyes filled with tears. Daisy didn't mention Roy's part in Sammy's death.

'So you reckon someone with a grudge must have sorted him, after he cut Vera?'

'Looks like it. It'll be all round Gosport today and most likely in the *Evening News*.' Daisy drained her cup and picked up a Nice biscuit. 'I got a favour to ask you. How d'you fancy taking over this place for a while? Extra money of course and I'd like it if you'd sleep here sometimes? Don't like to think of the place being empty.'

'What about Vera?'

'She won't be in any fit state to handle living on her own when she gets out of Haslar. When them stitches comes out she'll need a bit of peace and quiet. I'm going to take 'er to Greece with me.'

Jacky nodded her head. 'She loves your little boy.'

Daisy turned on her. 'How the fuck do you know about 'im?'

Jacky looked startled. 'I won't say anything. I think I guessed from the beginning. You 'ad that mumsy look about you when you come back to Gosport. Then one day I was in 'ere, and Vera 'ad left some photos on the table. She tried to sweep 'em away but I was too quick an' I saw you and this kiddie, the spittin' image of Eddie. I never said nothin' 'cause I didn't want 'er to 'ave to lie to me.'

Daisy put her hand across the table and stroked Jacky's arm.

'I don't know what to say,' she said.

'There ain't nothin' to say. You an' Vera been true friends to me. I'd do anything for you.' Daisy smiled at her. She looked into her face and saw the honesty shining through. Why couldn't Bri see him and Jacky was like a pair of trousers cut from the same cloth?

Jacky took a hanky from her sleeve and blew her nose. When she'd finished her eyes were still bright with tears.

'I ain't stupid, you know, Daisy. Sammy went for Vera because she paid him off what I owed. If it wasn't for me, she'd be here now. Not in hospital with her face all spoilt. This is all my fault.'

Daisy stared at her 'If Vera heard you say that ... all them self-pitying words, she'd kick your arse so hard you'd end up in the fucking ferry and the crabs'd eat you. What's done is done. An' I don't want to hear no more shit like that. Understood?'

Jacky sniffed, blew her nose again and nodded.

'There's one thing you could help me with, Jacky?'
'Anything. What?'
'Help me catch that bleeding moggie. I bet he's

gone under Vera's bed and that bed's a bugger to move.'

'Got fed up with books and decided to open a cattery?' Vinnie Endersby was standing by the shoe stall.

'Ha, bloody, ha! Where you off to? Want a cuppa and a sticky bun?' Without waiting for an answer, Daisy passed Vinnie the basket containing Kibbles, who growled and spat as soon as he realised someone new was holding him.

'Don't mind if I do. Your turn to pay this time. This animal's a handful. Bloody heavy, too.' Daisy waved at a stallholder who'd called her name. She took Vinnie's arm.

'I'm seeing a friend off on the Portsmouth Harbour train station later but I'm always gasping for a tea. And don't you let Vera know you've cast aspersions on the only man in her life, or she'll have your bloody guts for garters. Let's get a move on to The Dive then. Don't want Kibbles peein' in his box.'

The sun was shining and there wasn't a cloud in the sky. The day was warm and as Vinnie laughed down at her, Daisy felt she ought to feel happy and relaxed. But she couldn't, not with poor Vera in hospital, and Susie going home to her daughter's funeral.

'Bad do last night,' Vinnie said. Daisy stopped to finger some cotton swimsuits. Would Vera like one? She could get a good tan in one of these halter-neck bikinis. The stallholder hovered, looking anxious.

'Can I help you?' Daisy shook her head. She hated shop assistants and stallholders who pounced on her when she'd only just started to look at the goods. She dropped the garment and walked away, on principle.

'What bad do?' It wouldn't do to let Vinnie know she knew more than he thought she did.

'That bloke from the brothel coming to grief.'

'No! Really? Which one?'

They'd reached The Dive and Vinnie gave her an old-fashioned look.

'You don't really expect me to believe you know nothing about it?'

'Believe what you like,' she said.

He narrowed his eyes at her and made to pass the cat box to her. 'Let me go down the steps first while you hold this big bugger then I'll take him off you again.' Kibbles gave a low growl and hooked a tabby paw with dangerous-looking claws on the wire mesh front. Daisy took the box and watched Vinnie descend. When he reached the bottom step he looked back at her then glared at Kibbles.

'Don't even think about it,' he said to the cat. Daisy had to stop herself from laughing at the way he held the imprisoned feline well away from him.

Daisy ordered the teas and buns. She stacked the cups and plates to make for easier carrying and they found a seat near the back.

'We'll have to stop meeting like this,' he said. 'What if I take you somewhere more up-market next time?'

'Where? Over to The Porthole? At least that place is above ground.'

Vinnie threw his coat on the seat and then moved Kibbles along so he could stretch his long legs beneath the table. He looked at her, and Daisy decided she liked the way his lovely odd eyes twinkled when he smiled.

'So, tell me about Sammy, Daisy?'

She wrinkled her forehead and busied herself setting

cups on saucers and buns on plates. 'Sammy? You interrogatin' me, DS Endersby?'

'If I was, I'd have another copper with me, wouldn't I? No, you and I are just chatting about what goes on in Gosport.'

'Well, I'm fed up now. I don't want to talk about stuff I don't know about.'

He bit into a currant bun. 'This is bloody lovely,' he said. 'Eat yours.'

Daisy stirred her tea. 'I will in a minute. I'm savouring it.'

He made a playful grab at the bun on her plate.

'Here, bugger off,' she said and slapped his hand away.

He laughed. 'What if I was to tell you that I'd had my eye on Sammy for some time? Even pretended to be a punter so I could get in there to find out what was going on.'

'You went with one of the girls?' Daisy was shocked.

'Don't be stupid! I didn't do anything, just wanted to find out what was going on. And it was Sammy I pretended to be interested in. Told him my name was Paul.'

'You sure you was only pretending?' Daisy paused with her bun bitten but not chewed, so her voice was muffled.

''Course,' he said. 'Prostitution is victimisation to those who sell and demeaning to those who buy.'

'Fucking hell,' said Daisy. 'Where did that come from? Some police manual? What did you discover about Sammy?'

'Not as much as the person or persons who killed

him. When we got to Weevil Lane after the tip-off, he'd been left in a right state . . .'

'Don't you dare tell me. I don't want to know!'

'I wonder why that makes you squeamish? You sure you don't know anything? We found the dead kiddies' clothes with him.'

'You think someone was trying to tell you something?'

'Almost certainly that the two boys and Sammy were linked.'

'Ain't that a good thing, confirmed your suspicions he was up to no good?' Daisy saw she'd hit a nerve with him.

'If Sammy had died earlier in the day, one of my PCs, Emily Waters, wouldn't be in the Haslar now. That bastard stuck a sharp instrument in her eye. She's lost the sight in it.'

Daisy put down her cup and stared at him. 'The bastard. Was she on duty?'

'Yes, undercover at the cafe. I don't know why I'm telling you this. I never even discussed work with Clare, my wife.'

Daisy put her hand across the table and laid it on top of his and was pleasantly surprised when he twisted his wrist and held her hand. His touch was firm and warm.

'I'm not into mouthing stuff about,' she said. 'I sincerely hope they can sort her eye out, poor cow. Your policewoman didn't have to sleep with none of the weirdos that go in the caff, did she?'

'No. I'll say one thing for your mate, Roy, he tries to look after the girls. Pity the bloke he put in charge wasn't a bit more like him. Emily, or Eve as she was known, was allowed to settle into her new life, slowly. I really don't know why I'm telling you all this.'

'Because you need to talk and I'm a Scorpio, the most secretive sign of the Zodiac. I won't say nothing.'

He gave her a half smile then asked, 'How's Vera?'

Daisy took her hand away. 'How the bloody hell do I know? We're not joined at the hip.'

Vinnie sighed. 'It's my job to know when someone takes a beating like that. I also know you took her to hospital, and that the assault was probably down to that bugger Sammy as well. He'd been saying what a bitch she was for a while now.' Daisy raised her eyes at him. 'Don't forget I had a plant in the cafe,' he added. 'Emily, or Eve, was pretending to be a prossie, one that wouldn't work outside but took phone bookings. The punters just happened to be coppers who paid her to play draughts. The only good words Emily had were for a street girl called Rosa, and your mate Roy Kemp, who got her into a private room as soon as he saw the damage Sammy had inflicted on her.'

Daisy realised she had to be extra careful of what she said or all kinds of secrets might rise to the surface. 'Really?'

'You know more than you're letting on, Daisy Lane. I suspect Sammy also killed the girl that was found near the boatyard. It was his style. She'd been given drugs and violated repeatedly before nails were driven through her breasts.' He stared at her but she kept her gaze level. 'Roy Kemp owns the brothel but I can't take this case any further 'cause I'm blocked every which way. As far as the cop sheet goes, enquiries are probably done with.'

'Roy wouldn't hurt kids . . .'

'Perhaps not. But Sammy must have done. And you should be careful, Daisy. The big boys play rough.' He was looking into her eyes and something stirred deep inside her. She turned away and began piling the plates.

'So what you're saying is, you're sure no case is to be brought against Roy Kemp 'cause his paid police mates are laying the blame for the dead mutilated prossie and the little boys on Sammy?'

'Yes.'

'What about Sammy's death?'

'One of Sammy's punters got their own back on him. Took him down Weevil Lane and killed him. That's what happened, my superiors will probably reckon. Money talks, Daisy.' He winked at her. Daisy knew she'd coloured up. 'End of case, or rather no one on the force will be looking very hard for Sammy's killer. The bastard deserved all he got. Even I can't find anything wrong with that conclusion.'

'So that's it? Money talks, end of case.'

He nodded. 'Ended. But all coppers ain't bent, Daisy. Gosport's a pretty good example of policing at its best, usually. But there's a couple of big boys with clout and Roy Kemp has even more clout and the money to use it.'

Daisy sighed. She thought briefly about Roy and his 'clout'. Did he have enough to look after himself when Ronnie and Reggie found out he'd been long-firming on their patches? She looked at Vinnie, raised her eyebrows and pursed her lips before saying, 'I got to go. After seeing off my mate, I'm visiting Vera.'

Vinnie got up, reluctantly, she thought.

'I'll carry this lump back for you,' he said. 'We'll

stop in the market and I'll buy some flowers for Vera.'
He made to slip on his coat, pulling it from beneath
the cat basket.

'Thanks, Vinnie,' Daisy said. 'You're lovely.'

'More'n I can say for this blasted cat,' Vinnie said.
'It's pissed all over my coat.'

Vera sat up in bed staring at the flowers. All kinds of
blooms that she knew cost the earth but didn't even
know the names of. They made her corner of the ward
smell lovely. She'd asked the nurse if she could have a
look at her face when they changed the dressings but
she said best not and too early for that. She was fed
up, and her body was sore all over.

But it didn't hurt so much to speak now. And the
little nurse said that the doctors had re-set her nose.
Told her that she wouldn't have that bumpy bit in the
middle that she'd been born with. That was something
to look forward to.

The woman in the next bed was on her last legs,
Vera reckoned. She just lay there breathing funny.

Vera wished Kibbles could be with her. He was
magic, that cat, always seemed to know what she was
thinking. Daisy would have taken him back to her
place. Kibbles'd be all right with her Daisy.

She wondered what was happening down at Heavenly Bodies. Jacky would be keeping the girls in order.
Good as fucking gold, was Jacky. When Daisy did
come she'd make sure she phoned Kath and apolo-
gised for her not being at Ellie's funeral. It would be
awful if they thought she just hadn't bothered to go.
But then she couldn't go to little Meggie's funeral,
either, could she? Poor little bugger. Poor Susie and Si.

The doctor said the scar would fade in time. He said

she should go somewhere warm where she could get a bit of sun, it'd help it heal. Would Daisy let her go to her place in Kos? She could be with little Eddie then, couldn't she?

Wonder who sent them flowers?

Wonder where Sammy was now?

She hoped Daisy would bring in one of her nighties. This was a silly nightdress – if you had it on one way it showed all your front bits and if you put it on the other way it showed all your back bits! And her bottle of Californian Poppy, perhaps Daisy would remember that and all.

Fancy getting done over at my time of life, she thought. Been on the game for years yet never got so much as a few slaps. Gives up the life out on the streets to go legit and gets slashed. Don't hardly seem fair to me, she thought. He's a bastard that Sammy.

She heard footsteps, voices. Daisy had come in alone, carrying a bag and an armful of flowers. She had a few more words with the little dark nurse and gave her the flowers. Daisy looked worried sick, thought Vera. Poor little cow. She'd had Susie to contend with and all.

'I want to come home.'

'You can't,' said Daisy.

'I don't like it in here, they wakes you up so early in the morning it can't be good for you.'

Daisy bent and kissed her on her bandages. 'Shut up moaning. You should be happy to be in bed with someone waiting on you hand and foot.'

'I miss my Kibbles.'

'I took him home with me. You know he likes Bertie. He's been sitting in the bookshop.'

''E don't know nothing about books.'

'He'll learn to fucking read, then, won't he!' Vera knew Daisy was trying to cheer her up but all she could do was moan. 'I got you some clean nighties, Californian Poppy, your own toothbrush and stuff. It's in that bag down there.' Daisy moved her foot and the bag crackled.

'Did you get me some orange squash?'

Daisy raised her eyes heavenwards. 'In the bag.'

'Who sent them flowers?'

Daisy looked surprised. 'Vinnie bought 'em in the market this morning for you. He hopes you gets better soon.'

'Not them flowers. Them flowers.'

Daisy looked at Vera and frowned. Then she saw the huge bouquet on a stand near the wall.

'They're beauties, ain't they? Ain't there a card with 'em?'

'No one gave me the card. Go an' look.'

Daisy got up and searched through the sweet-smelling blooms. She found the envelope and opened it. 'Roy sent 'em to you.'

'Roy Kemp?'

'The very man.'

'Oh,' said Vera. 'I've never 'ad a gangster send me flowers before.'

They sat in companionable silence for a while then Daisy told her she'd sorted out Heavenly Bodies. Vera liked being with Daisy even when they didn't talk. She saw Daisy shift about a bit as though she wanted to say something but didn't know how to go about it.

'Spit it out, girl. What's on your mind?'

Daisy took a deep breath. 'Sammy's dead.'

Vera let the words sink in slowly.

'You got Roy Kemp to sort 'im out, didn't you?'

Daisy nodded. 'Don't you go thinking it was anything to do with you. He had it coming. He was responsible for them kids...'

'You're only saying that because you don't want me to 'ave his death on me conscience. Well, Dais, you might think I'm an out and out bitch but I don't care. Not after what he did to Jacky.'

'Well, that's all right then, ain't it?'

Then Vera remembered she wanted to ask Daisy a big favour.

'You had another word with the doctor, Dais?'

Daisy nodded. 'I asked him if he thought it might be a good idea for you to come with me to Greece for a while. He said it would do you the world of good, the sunshine, the beach and...'

Vera couldn't believe her ears. 'I was goin' to ask you that, honest I was.'

'Then it's settled.'

Vera gave a sigh of relief. 'I'm really 'appy about that. I could chase little Eddie into the waves, I bet he'll be walking soon. But could you do something else for me?'

Daisy bent forward to listen carefully. 'What?'

'Will you buy me a new 'at?'

She saw Daisy frown. 'What's wrong with your red hat?'

'I do love it, Daisy, an' I couldn't bear it if it 'adn't got picked up off the street. But this scar is goin' to be a long one. The doctor said it's near me hairline. But I don't want nobody to see me for a while so I thought if you bought me a big black 'at like Joan Crawford wears in *A Woman's Face*, I could pull it down, like she does, to cover me scar. Will you buy me one, Daisy? I'll give you back the money when I get out of 'ere.'

CHAPTER 30

Her MG drew to a stop outside Roy's terraced home. There were no meetings today in Violet's upstairs room and the street was nearly empty.

All the way up on the drive from Gosport to London, she wondered if she would be driving home again. Or would she be shortly joining Eddie in the great hereafter?

She glanced in the rear view mirror and smoothed back her hair. She looked tired and she rubbed at a smear of mascara that had dared to dry on her cheek beneath her lower lashes. Daisy sighed. She'd dressed carefully, in a black suit with a short-sleeved blouse beneath it and black shoes and handbag. She hadn't slept well last night worrying about today and its outcome. Terrible things consciences, she thought. You can't run away from them no matter how hard you try. What goes around, comes around.

'Fucking get on with it,' she mouthed to herself and slid the mirror back to its correct position. She sighed once more, got out of the car and knocked on Roy Kemp's door.

'Hello, dear. Roy's expecting you.' Daisy had phoned earlier to check that he would be there, alone except for Violet. Violet ushered her inside and through to the kitchen. This time she could smell meat cooking. 'Steak and kidney, dear.' Violet pulled out a kitchen chair and Daisy sat down. 'Cup of tea?'

'Please,' said Daisy. She looked about her at the homely kitchen with its lovely smell coming from the oven and Violet setting out three cups and saucers on the draining board, just like anyone's plump, happy mum. And so she was, thought Daisy. An adoring and adored mum, but to one of London's most feared and violent gangsters.

'You're very quiet. You're worried about something, aren't you, Daisy love?' Violet now stood in front of her and Daisy could smell her violet-scented perfume wafting around her. Her blue and pink flowered wraparound pinny was freshly ironed. Daisy could see the creases.

'Yes.'

Violet rested her hand briefly on Daisy's shoulder and looked into her eyes.

'I'll get Roy, he's out in the garden. My clematis fell down in that 'igh wind we had yesterday and Roy's sorting it.'

A great feeling of loneliness rolled over Daisy, which wasn't helped by the song on the radio. Roy Orbison was crooning 'It's Over'. And Daisy felt it really was.

'I'd like to talk to you first, Violet. If you could spare a few moments?'

Worry crept over Violet's face. 'I'll just do this tea for us then we'll sit down together.' Violet bustled about with the kettle and a small teapot with violets on it. Then she opened a round tin and produced a couple of scones. Daisy smiled to herself. She knew exactly what was going to happen. Violet sliced them open and spread on homemade jam and a huge spoonful of cream.

'Made these early this morning,' she said. The tops were golden brown. She slid the plate towards Daisy then, without bothering to put anything away, sat down next to her and began pouring the tea, brown and strong.

'Start when you wants, dear. You got my full attention.'

Daisy blinked back the tears that threatened and said, 'You know when you really love someone you can't think straight, can you? It's like that person is your whole bleeding universe, your reason to get up in the morning, your other half?'

Violet put her head on one side and looked at her, then she stirred Daisy's tea and passed it along.

'Drink that,' she said. After a moment she put her hands in her lap and linked her fingers. 'I only ever had that once in me life. Roy's dad. He set my toes tapping, my heart fluttering and I couldn't wait to be with him. And when I was with him I 'ad to be touching him. Close, like. Holding hands, linking arms, sitting with him. Him putting his foot against mine just to let me know we was within reach of each other.' She looked at Daisy. 'But I don't have to tell you about that, do I?'

A huge sigh shook Daisy's body. Squeezing her lips together in an effort to hold back the emotion that was welling up, she said, 'It was like that with me an' Eddie. When he died, I died with him. Getting up in the mornings, eating, but not being able to taste what I was eating. Walking about but not caring where I went and certainly not being able to tell you where I'd been, 'cause none of it registered with me. I couldn't read. I'd look at a page but it would take me ages 'cause I'd forget which line I was on. Until it dawned on me I was reading the same thing over an' over again . . .'

'That's exactly it, Daisy. When I lost Roy's dad, I didn't care if I lived or died. And if it wasn't for little Roy I'd have gone round the bend. That little boy pulled me through. Yes, and out the other side, love.'

Daisy took a sip of her tea. 'Violet, you really do know, don't you?'

'I might be an old girl, love, but I wasn't always old. The feelings never leave, you know. But I'll tell you something. It's possible to truly love again.'

'You believe that?' Daisy put her cup down on the saucer.

''Course. And sometimes the next love is the sweetest. You're a young woman. Whatever you might think, you needs a man, Daisy. You all right, dear?'

Daisy smiled at her. 'I am now,' she said. 'Thank you, Violet. You've been a big help. You really have. But can I ask you another question?'

Violet smiled and began clearing the table. 'Anything.'

Daisy took a deep breath. 'Would you say you had to be true to yourself? Even if it meant that your life could change forever, and perhaps not for the good?'

Violet tilted her head then reached forward and took Daisy's chin in her hands, bringing her face closer.

'Your conscience tells you what to do, Daisy. You can fool people but you can't fool yourself.'

Impulsively, Daisy kissed Violet on the cheek.

She knew exactly what Violet meant.

Violet looked at the clock on the side. 'How d'you feel now, love?'

'Good, Violet. Very good indeed.'

'Right. Then if you're sure, I'll make Roy a cup of tea. He's been working hard out there in the garden.' She got up and smiled. 'You haven't even touched your scone. Get it down you before you waste away.' Violet went through to the scullery and called Roy's name and Daisy heard him answer. The thought of Roy tying up a climbing plant made Daisy smile. It was a bit out of character. When he came into the kitchen Daisy's eyes opened wide. He was wearing jeans with earth stains around the knees and an old frayed grey cotton shirt with the sleeves rolled up. He looked like a fairground worker with his dark wavy hair falling over his forehead and on to his suntanned skin. In his dirty hands he held sticks of plump rhubarb, pink and white with goodness. He put the rhubarb on the draining board and said, 'I'll be with you in five ticks. Daisy, lovely to see you.' And he turned on the tap and began washing his hands at the sink. Violet picked up the kettle. It didn't take but a few seconds to boil again and soon the tea was made and waiting to be poured.

'I can't imagine you working in the bleeding garden,' Daisy said.

'There's a lot you don't know about me, ain't that right, Mum?' He came and sat down beside Daisy.

Violet giggled like a girl as she handed him a cup of strong tea.

'Want a biscuit? A scone? Dinner's not long.'

'Nah, don't want to spoil it. But Daisy'll have one, she's much too thin these days.' Daisy found herself refusing the biscuits but taking a large bite of her scone. As usual it melted in her mouth. She sighed. Right now she wished she was a million miles away.

She took a deep breath, swallowed and laid down her scone. 'I've done an awful thing to you, Roy.' Violet pulled out a chair and frowning, sat at the freshly scrubbed table.

'What?' Roy's face was like chiselled granite.

'I told you I'd pay you back for Eddie's death. So all the time I was away I was planning how to get even with you.' Daisy took a bigger breath. There was no going back now. 'I've set up long firms in your name. Bank accounts, the lot. It won't be long before your name's going to be shit with everyone.'

'But dear . . .'

'Let me get this off me sodding chest, Violet.' Daisy waved her to be quiet and looked at Roy but there was still no expression on his face.

'But now I can't bear the thought of you getting hurt for something you didn't do. The creditors'll be closing in soon, not to mention your mates, Reggie and Ronnie, who may not like what you – I've – done in workin' their patches . . .' Daisy's voice tailed off.

Roy was staring at her as though he couldn't believe what he was seeing or hearing and even Violet was struck dumb for once.

It seemed to Daisy that the seconds were ticking very slowly, yet her heart was beating faster and faster. She felt she would explode if someone didn't break the silence soon.

Roy ran his fingers through his hair. 'So you've come here to confess, in case I get hurt?'

Daisy nodded.

'Why?'

Daisy wasn't expecting that. Why? Again realisation

hit her like a ton of wet bricks off a lorry. She didn't want him to get hurt because the daft fucking sod had wormed his way into her heart and *she loved him!*

'I . . . er . . .'

Luckily she didn't have to say any more because he was now asking,

'And you planned all this alone?'

Daisy nodded. 'I had people to help me but I'll die sooner than tell you their names.'

'Wouldn't expect you to do that, dear.' Violet picked up her tea and sipped it thoughtfully.

Daisy knew she had nothing to lose now so she said, 'I never expected you to become like a family to me.'

Violet slammed down her cup so forcefully that Daisy thought it was a wonder it didn't break.

'You know what you've got to do, Roy!' His mother stood up and walked over to him.

Daisy began to shake. 'Okay,' she said. 'I'm fucking scared but I know I did the right thing in telling you. I had to give you a chance to leave this place, Roy . . . I don't want either of you to get hurt . . . you mean a great deal to . . .'

'You mustn't let her get away . . . '

'I know, Mum. But what can I do?' Roy's eyes held not anger but deep pain as he searched his mother's face.

'Roy! Do it. You know how long you've wanted to . . .'

Daisy gripped hold of Roy's cold hand.

'Let me have my say before you hurts me. You knew I loved Eddie. You knew how much he meant to me. I hated you for destroying him. That hate went on growing until I did something about it. But now

405

and only now I've realised you did what you had to do, because he wronged you.'

'And you've come into my house to confess sooner than let someone hurt me? Even though you didn't know how I'd react?' He took hold of her shoulders. Daisy's stomach was churning. 'Answer me!'

'Yes! Fucking yes!'

'You are a violent, dangerous woman.'

'For fuck's sake, Roy. *Marry* this woman, before someone else snaps her up!' Violet shouted.

Daisy felt as though someone had given her a punch in the stomach. Was she hearing right? And did Violet really swear?

'I'm going out in the garden to give you two a bit of peace and quiet.'

And Daisy watched as Violet went out, slamming the back door.

Roy knelt down on his haunches in front of Daisy.

'Mum's right. I've been mooning about over you for a long time, but I'm still married to Moira. Let me court you until I can work things out?'

Daisy looked into his steel-coloured eyes and couldn't resist running her fingers through his silky hair. 'Are you mad or am I? I've just got you into the most fucking awful trouble and you come out with "let me *court* you"? I don't want "courting", Roy Kemp!'

'What *do* you want, Daisy?'

Daisy couldn't help herself. 'I want loving!' There, she'd said it. 'I had to tell you what I'd done because I love you!' The look on his face was something Daisy knew she'd remember forever.

'Oh, Daisy. I don't care what you've done. I'll sort it, somehow.'

'Let me go out to the car and get the money I've made on the scams. It's not all there but at least you'll be able to pay some . . .'

'Never mind the money. Keep it. Put it in trust for little Eddie . . .'

'Who told you about him?' She was going mad, she really was. How did he know about her child?

'Daisy, there isn't much I don't know about you. Though I must admit you got me beat with the long-firming. But if you wanted, I could love little Eddie like he was my own. I've always wanted a kiddie.'

'This has got to stop!' Daisy pushed him aside and rose to her feet. He rose with her. 'I've done a really bad thing to you and you want to marry me? Am I bloody daft or are you?'

'A woman who can pull a stunt on me like that deserves my admiration. I always knew you were clever.'

'But . . . ?'

'Nipper Read has vowed to clean up London. A few months abroad in Spain, or your place in Greece to be near your kiddie, I'd like that, or a nice long cruise'll take the heat off. We could all go, Daisy. Take who you want, Vera, little Eddie . . . I bet you've stitched me up to the eyeballs. An eye for an eye, a tooth for a tooth, eh, Daisy?'

He was so close Daisy could feel his warm breath on her cheek. All the tension was leaving her body, making her feel at ease with herself. He took both her arms and draped one over each of his shoulders before bending his head and kissing her.

Roy's mouth was warm and moist and Daisy was surprised how excited the kiss made her feel and how easy it was to kiss him back. She broke away as Violet came back into the kitchen. She looked at them both and a big smile lit her face.

'I just remembered I 'ave an important doctor's appointment. I'll leave right away.' With a swift movement she turned the oven off. 'That'll do for later,' she said.

'If you say so, Mum,' said Roy. 'But you better take your pinny off first.' Daisy realised he was making no attempt to disguise the fact he was holding on to her as though she might melt away like an ice cream on a hot day. And she knew Violet was making excuses to leave the house so she and Roy could be together.

'You don't have to go . . .'

'Oh, I think I do, dear.' Violet treated her to a wide smile. 'But just you remember our little talk.' Daisy nodded. A very short while later the front door slammed.

Roy grinned at Daisy, his eyes crinkling at the corners. He pulled her close. 'I'll never hurt you,' he said.

Then the smile that always hovered at the corner of his mouth broke through and Daisy thought what a beautiful man he was. She stretched up on tiptoe to kiss him again and his tongue pushed her lips open and slipped inside. Then he withdrew, teasing her with little bites and kisses.

Daisy grasped the back of his head and held him to her while he pushed her back towards the table. She was unbuttoning his shirt and kissing his chest and he was pulling at her skirt and she was wriggling to help as he found her panties, stroking her on the outside. Daisy felt the fire between her legs as his fingers moved inside and found the tangle of damp warm hair. He pulled the silk away from her body. Roy's kisses now were deeper, full of sighs and sweetness. Her breasts swelled and her nipples tingled against the thin material of her blouse. The melting began and she laid back across the table and he looked down at her.

'What are you thinking?' she asked.

'That I've never seen anything so desirable as you in all my life.'

She held herself still, taking pleasure from his words, savouring the moment when he would step closer to the table, enter her and take her. And then he did. And she felt his whole length slide deliciously inside her and her body began of its own accord to rise to him. She wrapped her legs tightly round him to draw him in deeper, and she felt that she had finally come home to the right man. Her eyes were closed and her arms held him close, never wanting him to stop.

He raised her gently and then held her shoulders as he thrust into her receptive body. She was crying with pleasure as she came, then moaning for more until Roy's body went rigid and with a last thrust he was calling her name, 'Daisy, Daisy', over and over again until he became still. He lay above her and braced himself with his hands on the table and looked down into her eyes. Then he kissed her eyes, her nose and finally her lips.

'Fucking hell, I love you,' he said. 'You said you wanted loving, was that all right?'

Daisy nodded furiously. Somehow they'd rolled all over the table and she thanked God there wasn't any of Violet's best china on it.

Roy slipped out of her. He was smiling from ear to ear. Daisy began to laugh.

'What's so funny?' he asked.

'I'll never be able to sit at this table to eat a scone without remembering how great this was,' Daisy said.

Roy laughed. 'Me neither. I wanted you so much. I'm sorry I rushed you, I just couldn't help it.'

'We got all the time in the world to take things slower next time, haven't we?' His kiss gave her the answer.

CHAPTER 31

'She's good with my little Eddie, ain't she, Bri? Vera should 'ave 'ad more kiddies than just her James.' Over in the corner of the hall Vera was pulling funny faces and jiggling Daisy's precious son up and down on her knee and he was laughing right back at her, mouth wide open.

A spell in the Greek sun had bronzed Daisy, and Vera had never looked more relaxed. Vera had been worried about the scar on her face, even though Daisy told her it hardly showed at all now.

Daisy had decided to surprise Vera with a party to end all parties when one day on the beach at Tingaki Vera had confessed she'd never had a party of her own.

The music from the group onstage in the Thorngate Hall was loud and Daisy had made them promise to play a mixture of rock'n'roll and old-time tunes so there'd be something for everyone to entice them onto the dance floor. She'd hired the largest hall she could find. An air of joyful festivity filled the ballroom on Bury Road, which had been decorated with paper chains and fairy lights and was packed with their many friends. The hall rang with sounds of laughter and couples danced to Sandy Shaw's hit, 'Always Something There to Remind Me'.

Bri was wearing a suit and Daisy thought he looked very distinguished. Summer was sitting on his shoulders and she was growing into a flame-haired, dainty-featured little stunner with a mind of her own.

'Per'aps Vera thought her lifestyle wasn't right.' Daisy realised Bri had been thinking about Vera.

'S'pose so. Anyway she concentrated her life and money on making sure James was taken care of an' she did a bloody good job. So good I made Vera promise if anything happened to me she'll be little Eddie's guardian until he reaches eighteen. I didn't need to do much about making her, she was over the bleeding moon about that.' Daisy looked up at Bri. 'Don't forget, you're his uncle, so you'll get a say as well.'

'Jesus Christ, you're morbid, Daisy. Why're you thinking about things like that?'

'Eddie thought ahead for me and I'm thinking ahead for my boy.'

'I wish you wouldn't make plans like that when everything is going so well.'

'Best time to make 'em!'

'Don't you get prickly with me!'

'Sorry.' Daisy smiled at him.

'You happy with Roy, then?' He glanced across the hall to where Daisy could see Roy chatting to Si. Every so often Si laughed, like Roy was telling him a joke or something. A warmth stole over Daisy. She pulled Bri round so he was facing her.

'I think he's the right man for me,' she said. 'Are you happy for me?'

Bri raised his hand to her cheek and gently brushed it. 'If he's your man, then I'm happy,' he said. Daisy smiled at him, took his hand and kissed it.

'Thanks,' she said. He looked embarrassed, coughed

and said, 'Vera looks like a young girl in an old wartime film, in that cream dress with the black shoes an' that bloody black felt hat you bought her. Don't she ever take it off?'

'She took it off on the beach. She thinks she's Joan Crawford now, so expect to see all them old forties clothes and that black hat for ever more.'

Bri laughed. 'I heard you bought Jacky's flat?'

'Yeah, it's going through the solicitors' hands now. She wanted the money but didn't say what for. Though I got a sneaking suspicion it's to help you out. Is it?' Daisy was surprised to see Bri was actually blushing.

'Well, er, I've put most of my share of the scam money in trust for Summer. When she's twenty-one she can do what she likes with it. An' I'll tell you straight, your Roy's a good bloke. He may not want to know the ins and outs of the long-firming, but to tell you to do what you want with the money we made shows how much he cares about you. Jacky, er, me and, er, Jacky . . .'

Daisy knew what he was trying to tell her so she helped him out. 'Well, it's about time you two got it together.' He nodded but wouldn't look her straight in the eyes.

'It's early days yet but she's good with Summer.'

'Don't make bleeding excuses. Me an' Vera thought you'd make a good couple ages ago. You, Bri, are too fucking slow to catch a cold. It's a wonder she'll still have you, the way you've kept her on ice.' Daisy looked across the crowded dance floor. 'Good turn-out. I invited everyone to this knees-up. Fancy Vera never having a party of her own? Not even when she was young?'

'That's sad, Daisy. Get your hands off my eyes, Summer.'

He bent down so the little girl could clamber off his shoulders and stand unsteadily but supported by his hand. He waved to Jacky and Daisy saw the besotted smile on her face. She came over, put her glass of gin and tonic on the table and scooped up Summer.

'I've got her now. Why don't you two take a turn on the floor?'

''Bout time you danced with me,' he said. Daisy stepped into his arms.

Bri sighed. 'You staying here now, in Gosport?'

'Yes. My heart's with the silt from the ferry and the dog shit in Gosport's alleys. Don't look at me like that, as though I'm daft.'

'You ain't daft, Dais. I like this town too. I'm thinking of putting in an offer for the place next to the bookshop. Knock it all into one shop. Maybe sell toys as well as second-hand books.'

'And why not? I've invested cash for Eddie's future. Don't want him growing up on the streets, like we did, eh?'

'It didn't do us any harm, Dais.'

'Thanks for looking after Bertie and Kibbles while we was away.'

'Summer pulled them both about a bit. But cats know when children don't mean any harm.'

The music had stopped and people were trooping back to their tables. The smell of perfume mingled with cigarette smoke in the big hall and Vera weaved her way towards them.

'Little Eddie's with Roy,' she said. 'He's taken quite a shine to that man of yours.'

'Perhaps that's just as well,' laughed Daisy, looking

over towards the bar where Roy was still engaged in conversation with Si. Little Eddie was between them, playing Peep Bo between their knees. Susie waved to Daisy, then pointed at Si and Roy and opened and closed her raised hand to show they were still gabbing.

'Dais,' Vera said seriously. 'I feel very special. Look at all these posh Gosport people 'ere.'

'So you should feel special. All these bigwigs haven't forgotten they're friends of yours an' they're here with their wives because it's your party.'

'And me a trollop.'

'Past tense. You are now a very respectable business lady.'

'You know, Dais,' she struck a pose, 'I met a lot of these men before but never their wives. Oh, look, there's Alan.' She pointed to a tall man wearing an expensive suit. He noticed her and waved. Vera waved back and Daisy saw him bend towards a neat dumpy figure who clung to him like ivy on a shithouse wall. 'Bet he's not telling her he was a regular for more years than I like to remember. Do you know he likes to . . .'

'I don't think that's quite appropriate tonight, Vera.'

'All I'm sayin', Dais, is by the look of some of the sour faces on these females, no wonder I made so much money.' Daisy laughed. 'Let's sit down outside,' Vera said. 'I could do with a bit of air and my feet are killing me.'

Daisy and Vera wandered out on the balcony and sat on a wrought-iron bench facing the open door of the hall. Daisy leaned towards Vera and gently pulled back her hair.

'That scar's healed nicely, practically invisible.'

'Yeah, bit of sun on it did it the world of good.' Vera's voice grew serious. 'That attack frightened me, Dais. I don't want to go through that again.' Daisy knew the nightmares were still lingering. She pulled Vera close and they were silent for a while until Vera said, 'Mind you, the rest of me outside packaging is still pretty good.' She gripped Daisy's hand. 'I can't believe all these people came here tonight because of me. An' it's all down to you, Dais. You look pretty good tonight as well, girly, nice bit of costume jewellery you got on there.'

Daisy looked down at her black sheath dress and black suede stiletto heeled shoes. High on the shoulder of her dress was the large diamond brooch.

'This ain't a bit of tat, you silly cow! This is real. It was Violet's and she lent it to me once. Now she's given it to me. It's worth more'n this fucking hall! Certainly more'n that poxy house in Western Way I never could get rid of.'

'Don't need to now Suze and Si are living in it, do you? Is that brooch really the real thing?' Vera's eyes were opened so wide her finely painted brows had almost disappeared beneath her hat.

'Yes.'

'Cor bugger me, Dais!'

'The evening's young yet, Vera and you never know your luck.' Vera looked at her for a few moments then dug her elbow in Daisy's side.

'You cheeky bitch,' she said, then, 'I'm glad you an' Roy finally got it together.'

'It ain't all plain sailing yet. He's still married to Moira and I don't want him to even think about divorce. She's too fragile in the head for that. She's getting worse, not better. She tried to kill herself again.

A few months ago she slit her wrists with a rusty razor blade she picked up on the lane outside their place in Spain. Her nurse found her in time but she needs constant watching now. I know Roy loves me but Moira is still my mate. I'm going to see her in a few weeks.'

'You ain't gonna say anything . . .'

Daisy shook her head. 'I ain't carrying on with Roy like it don't matter, though.' She sighed. 'There's no rush and I can make him happy.'

'You got the fuckin' nerve of the devil, you 'ave, Dais, to do what you did and get away with it. You'd fall into a cesspit an' come up with a rose between your teeth. I'm ever so proud of you.'

'You shouldn't be. There's still every possibility the Krays will come after him. But Roy reckons if he can't sort it somehow then he's in the wrong fucking business.'

''Spose, so, Dais. 'Ere, look out, 'ere comes heart-throb number two.'

'Vera, will you behave!' Daisy watched Vinnie walk across from the car park. 'Hello, Vinnie, glad you could make it.' She stood up to greet him. 'Go an' get us some drinks, Vera?' Daisy shook Vera's shoulder as she sat there, staring up at DS Endersby. 'Please, Vera?'

Vera got up, glared and tottered off in the direction of the bar. 'Does she always gaze at men like that?' Vinnie asked.

'No, only the ones she likes.'

He laughed. 'I'm not stopping, Daisy. I'm on duty.' He stared at her. 'So, you'll have heard by now the inquest on Bri's wife was misadventure?'

Daisy nodded. 'Silly girl, Belle was. She couldn't

help herself with the drugs and wouldn't let anyone else help her.'

'Daisy, I came to tell you I'm moving back to London.' Daisy didn't know whether she felt sad or happy for him.

'No more cups of tea and sticky buns in The Dive, then?' She tried hard to sound as though she didn't care.

He shook his head. 'Bad news is taking me back. Freddie Mills, the boxer, was found dead in his car very early today at the back of his London club. He was taken to Middlesex hospital but was dead on arrival. He'd been shot.'

'Bloody hell, no,' said Daisy. 'You going up to work on that case?' Strings tugged at her heart. She might never see Vinnie again.

He nodded. 'And since I never could get the missing prostitutes to leave my sleep untouched, I'm back on that case as well. They've picked up a suspect for the latest girl who was found in a shallow grave in woodland by a woman walking her dog. The bloke was trying to sell the dead girl's handbag in a pub, said he found it in a dustbin. Pity he never emptied out the contents, there was a photo of her in the wallet. Open and shut case they reckon. I'm not convinced. So, unofficially I'm still on the case. There's nothing to keep me here now.' He gave her a searching look. 'All the murder crimes in Gosport have been successfully put to bed.'

On impulse Daisy reached up and kissed him on the cheek. Vinnie put his arms around her and she felt he held her just a little too long and a little too tightly before releasing her and striding away across the grass. She watched but he didn't look back.

Vera returned with a brandy and lime and a very large sherry.

''Ere you are, Dais.'

Daisy took her glass and sat back down on the seat. 'Where's Vinnie's drink?'

'You got rid of me so's you could talk to 'im. I ain't stupid. He can't drink when he's on duty.'

'Don't be so silly. I'm getting cold, let's go back in.' She rose and sipped at the brandy.

Vera shrugged, but got up and made for the ballroom. 'Don't know how you reckons you're cold. It's bleedin' warm out 'ere.' She paused at the doorway. 'Look at Si and Suze dancing all cuddly. I 'opes they 'ave another baby soon.'

'I'm sure it'll 'appen,' Daisy said. 'All in good time.'

Queenie was sitting near the band, next to the wheelchair with Pappy in it. She was spooning trifle into his mouth and chatting away as though he understood every word. Daisy and Bri had clubbed together with the money so that Queenie could move into a small annex at The Cedars where married couples could stay together. Daisy remembered Queenie's face lighting up with joy when she and Bri had suggested it. 'I'll 'ave the upper 'and now, won't I?' she'd said. 'I'll always love 'im, you knows, Daisy.' She'd even forgiven Daisy for not telling her about little Eddie's birth sooner.

'You know what, Daisy?' said Vera. 'This room is every inch Gosport, an' I love it. I reckon you do too.'

Daisy squeezed Vera's hand and thought about her town, the place where she was born. Gosport was growing. Unsafe buildings were being torn down and concrete tower blocks of flats rising in their places. Bomb-damaged houses and shops were being replaced

419

with new constructions. She thought of the smoke-filled pubs, the dark alleys, the God-awful weekend fights, the loving, the tales Vera and she had listened to from beat-up wives. Daisy thought about Walpole Park and the fairs and circuses that stopped for a while and then moved on again. She thought of the market, the creek, the ferry and the dirt, the shipyard, the navy, the army, the air force and the smell of fish and chips, onions and beer. She remembered the colourful characters who made the town warm and welcoming so that it throbbed with life. She thought, too, of her dead mum, and of Eddie and Kenny who would always be a part of Gosport.

'Trust me, you was born 'ere and I think you'll die 'ere,' said Vera.

'What are you? A fucking fortune teller?'

Vera grinned at her. 'Look, your man wants you. I'm off to the lavatory.'

Roy was beckoning to her from across the room. Little Eddie was in his arms. Daisy started to walk towards them along the edge of the crowded dance floor.

She felt a hand on her shoulder and she was swung round.

'You can't get away from me so easily, Daisy Lane.' Valentine Waite wrapped an arm around her and pulled her close.

'Let me go.' Daisy tried to free herself from his vice-like grip. His breath was on her cheek as he murmured, 'We're cut from the same cloth, Daisy.'

Daisy grabbed at his other hand which had slithered down to her arse and managed to shake him off her. Who had invited him? Had Roy? She certainly hadn't.

Valentine Waite was an incident in her life she wanted to forget.

'I've missed you,' he said.

She looked up into his hypnotic eyes. I have to tell him whatever he thinks is between us is a figment of his imagination, she thought.

'We have to talk,' she said.

'Oh, not of anything bad, I hope?'

Daisy laughed nervously to dispel her fear. 'Not bad, just necessary.' She saw his eyes narrow.

'You shouldn't be with Roy Kemp. You belong to me.'

'You've no bleeding right to say that.' Despite the heat in the room, she was suddenly chilled to the marrow and the wonderful evening was tainted by his presence.

'You remind me of my mother.' As he spoke a tiny muscle at the side of his top lip flickered. 'She made promises she never kept.' He lifted his hand to the centre of his chest, his fingers splayed. 'But she's here in my heart. Where you belong, Daisy. I want to be the last person you love.'

He's creepy, thought Daisy. Why had she never realised it before?

Valentine Waite made another grab for her but she pushed him away and turned quickly, her high heels sliding on the parquet floor. As she regained her balance she could see the welcome figure of Roy, her child in his arms, his face etched with worry.

'You all right, Daisy?' he asked, when he reached her. Automatically she took little Eddie from him and held him close, breathing in the wholesome child's smell. His plump hands slid around her neck and his mouth made loud wet kisses against her cheek. This was what mattered, she thought, her child, the true love of her life. 'What was that all about?'

Daisy's heart was beating fast. As little Eddie squirmed against her she realised she was holding him far too tightly. Roy was looking into the crowd and Daisy followed his gaze. With a huge sigh of relief she saw that Valentine Waite seemed to have disappeared. Roy looked down at her.

'You can talk to me, you know,' he said.

Daisy shifted her child to her hip then reached up to touch Roy's concerned face. Deep in his eyes she could see nothing but love. She shook her head.

'Don't worry,' she said calmly. She was aware that one word from her could ruin this evening she'd prepared so lovingly for Vera. 'It was nothing. He got a bit heated, talking about his dead mother.' At least that wasn't a lie, she thought. Daisy forced herself to laugh lightly. 'The bloke might be a famous boxer but like you once said,' she made a circling motion against the side of her temple with her index finger, 'he's got a screw loose.'

Roy covered Daisy's hand with his own and brought it to his mouth, kissing her fingertips. His other arm encircled both her and her boy. Daisy could feel the strong beat of his heart, almost taste the comfort his body gave her. His mouth was in her hair as he said, 'No one will harm you while I'm around. You'll always be safe with me.'

And Daisy believed him.

JUNE HAMPSON

Daisy Lane lives in a hard, brutal world of poverty, crime and violence. It is a life that **June Hampson** knows only too well. She, through sheer determination and hard graft, escaped grinding poverty, abusive marriages and constant debt to get to where she is today. So, to June, Daisy is far more than just a character. She's a reflection of a world which, even now, feels all too real.

DAISY IS FAR MORE THAN JUST A CHARACTER

June's mother came from travelling people and had run away to be with her father, a sailor seventeen years older than her. They lived in a two-up, two-down house with a lavatory at the end of the garden. The family had no hot water, no bath and only a kitchen range to heat the whole house. When it was cold, her dad's overcoat became an extra blanket for June.

BEING IN AND OUT OF PRISON
WAS A WAY OF LIFE

As a teenager in Gosport, June was surrounded by people who lived on the wrong side of the law. 'People used to say we didn't live on the wrong side of the railway track, it was the end of it,' she remembers.

At sixteen, despite her parents' reluctance, she married into a family 'where being in and out of prison was a way of life'. Only seventeen, alone and pregnant, she had to fend for herself when her husband was put away for breaking and entering. 'I sometimes think that life is worse for those on the outside,' she says. 'At least inside they're getting three meals a day.' Life was tough – constantly buying things 'on tick' she struggled to get out of debt. 'I'm not ashamed to admit that I've sneaked into an allotment at night to steal a cabbage for the kids' tea. Put it this way, I've seen the dark side of life.'

The characters in *Trust Nobody* and *Broken Bodies* are the kind of people June was surrounded by: sailors, prostitutes and criminals.

When her husband was out of prison he was violent. 'I could never write a Barbara Cartland sort of story, with those heroes going down on their knees, because the men I know aren't like that. In my life, they're more likely to give you a backhander. I don't think I've ever been with a man who hasn't hit me.'

I'VE SEEN THE DARK SIDE OF LIFE

June's second marriage was to a close friend of her first husband – and was no easier. He was jealous of his vivacious wife – he went through her photos and cut up any picture that showed a man. As a result, June now has no pictures of her father.

What finally gave June the courage to leave him was the fact that he was unfaithful. 'I'm not a sharer,' she explains. 'It was either kill him, kill myself or go round the bend. So, I put my kids in the car and left.'

After her second divorce June became extremely reclusive but gradually, now she was in control of her own destiny, her life began to look up. Her daughter Rachael, who she is very close to, persuaded her mum to join a singing group, which proved to be a lifeline. She began teaching a creative-writing course and eventually found success with *Trust Nobody*. But just as life was looking rosy, disaster struck: June was diagnosed with breast cancer. 'It felt like such a slap in the face, especially when things had been going so well,' she recalls. 'But when I came out of the operating room to find my son, Danyel, waiting for me I knew then whatever happened I was truly blessed.' Happily, she beat the cancer and is now working on her fourth novel.

JUST AS LIFE WAS LOOKING ROSY, DISASTER STRUCK

June also recently discovered that, despite believing all her life that she was an only child, she actually has older siblings. Her parents were so chronically poor at the start of their marriage that they were forced to give up their children. June's sister tracked her down and they are now in touch regularly, 'which is lovely,' she smiles.

Q & A

What were your early years like?

I was blessed that my early years were very happy. I was brought up as an only child and although we were very poor there were always books in the house. There weren't really any treats – a treat to me was curling up with my dad reading the *Beano* after a walk on Sunday. My parents were madly in love. My dad, when he was young, had travelled the world and would sit at the kitchen table telling me about Africa, America and other wonderful countries.

Have you ever worked in a café like Bert's café?

Yes, when I was seventeen and pregnant with swollen ankles. I lived in a top flat above the café and did all the things Daisy does in *Trust Nobody*, like mopping the floors and stairs and rising early and making fry-ups.

The violence in *Trust Nobody* is powerful and realistic. Have you ever been affected by violence yourself?

Yes. I've been abused by men and it's made me cynical. I once read that some women gravitate towards violent men. I suppose the bad boys were always the exciting ones although I found fear a real turn off.

I've also witnessed many deeds of violence towards others. My first husband's brother was knifed and the caff I worked in had villains coming in with their knuckledusters and knives for a cuppa.

The pub near by was one of the most colourful of all. Rough wasn't the word for it. I once saw a man have his face cut up with a glass in there.

Daisy works incredibly hard. Do you have an ethos of hard work?

Often I've done three jobs at once to provide for my children. I've worked in a shop during the day, a bar at nights, cleaned houses and picked fruit. Up until eighteen months ago, I was getting up at four in the morning, running a market stall and working in a bar a couple of nights a week. I've also been a Creative Writing tutor for about twenty years, teaching at several colleges a week, all at the same time as working in the other jobs!

Broken Bodies introduces Daisy's son. How has motherhood changed her?

Motherhood has bestowed Daisy Lane with a more balanced yet cynical view of life. She's a woman alone with a child. In the Sixties, although times were changing, women still had to prove themselves mentally and physically, to succeed in a man's world. Not only will she have to fight for herself, she has to fight for her child, the son of a gangster. Her child is her life. Motherhood had a similar effect on me. I was fiercely protective of my children – and my grandchildren. I still am!

What have been the highs and lows of your life?

The lowest was giving birth, full term, to a little girl who died. The highlight of my life, not counting the births of my children and grandchildren, was getting *Trust Nobody* accepted by a major publisher. I am still walking on air.

In *Broken Bodies* Daisy opens herself up to the possibility of loving again. Are you an optimist when it comes to love?

Daisy will always be open to love but Eddie Lane is a man most men will never measure up to. Daisy will always love with her heart first and her head second. I'm very much an optimistic person. My glass is always half full, never half empty. Though I do envy my friends who have been happily married for years, I can't see me getting on that merry-go-round again. I am blessed to have loved passionately, not once, like Daisy with Eddie, but many times.

Your depiction of Daisy's life on the borders of the criminal world rings really true. What experiences of crime have you had?

I guess my first marriage made me grow up very quickly. I discovered that violence, thieving, deceit, drugs and gambling aren't a very good recipe for a happy life. On a much lighter side, I suppose I was lucky in that I managed to see quite a bit of England's green countryside 'visiting' Her Majesty's establishments!

Daisy relies on Vera for support. How important is friendship to you?

It's extremely important to me. After my second divorce I joined a group of singers who have propped me up when times get rough. We do many shows a year for charity. Together, we have seen our children grow to be parents themselves, holidayed, laughed and cried. I can't ask for more.

Where did you get the idea of Daisy using long firms to frame Roy?

I did a great deal of research on long firms. Charlie and Eddie Richardson, had, I believe, long firming down to a fine art. Daisy wouldn't physically harm anyone as it just isn't in her nature. But she's a clever lady; to involve Roy in a scam where someone else would sort him out seemed like a good idea and it worked. Even so, Daisy had to tell him the truth because that's the kind of woman she is.

Who inspires you?

Catherine Cookson. Her writing was her life. Hemingway, for his dialogue and ability to tell a tender story. John Steinbeck for his honest grittiness. Alan Sillitoe for his working-class heroes and Nell Dunn for *Poor Cow*, one of my favourite books.

What is the best holiday you've had?

The best holiday I ever had was a two week break in Kenya. I took ten exercise books bought from Asda at 64 pence for five and lots of 2B pencils with rubbers on the end. I sat in the sun and wrote, making myself finish one complete exercise book a day (turning it over and writing on both sides of the paper).

By the end of the holiday I'd finished the exercise books and was writing on hotel notepaper. When the minibus came to take me to the airport I'd completed the first draft of *Trust Nobody*.

Can you tell us anything about what happens to Daisy in the next book?

The third book is called *Damaged Goods* and although I don't want to spoil the plotline, I can tell you that Valentine Waite's obsession with Daisy left a very nasty taste in my mouth. Number four, *Inside Out*, moves up to the Seventies. Daisy's life is an eventful one – she knows how lucky she is to have good friends like Vera and Susie – but she can't escape her heartache or her gangster connections.